J. Butler

S0-EKM-853

100

A DANGEROUS, DARING INNOCENCE . . .

Brianna knew it was scandalous to be alone with Andrew in his coach. She didn't care. All that mattered was that he was going away. . . .

Suddenly the carriage hit a bad bump and Brianna began to fall. Andrew reached for her and she held on tight as he pulled her up from the floor. Her arms went around his neck, and she ended up sitting on his lap.

For one long moment after the danger had passed Andrew held her close. "Brianna—"

Her lips were pressing against his, her tongue against his lips. Remembering the sensations he had invoked in her she tried to make him feel the same things.

Andrew held back, telling himself to push her away, telling himself maybe it was best to kiss her and end her curiosity, calling himself a fool and then reaching for her, deepening the kiss. Every sensation was new to her. She let him draw her tongue into his mouth as little shocks of something wild and deep raced through her blood. She wanted to kiss him forever. . . .

Praise for Sheila O'Hallion's
American Princess

"A charming, light romp, utterly delightful and very funny."

—*Romantic Times*

"I enjoyed every moment of their relationship. . . ."

—*Rendezvous*

Books by Sheila O'Hallion

American Princess
The Captured Heart
Fire and Innocence
Kathleen
Masquerade of Hearts

Published by POCKET BOOKS

Most Pocket Books are available at special quantity discounts for bulk purchases for sales promotions, premiums or fund raising. Special books or book excerpts can also be created to fit specific needs.

For details write the office of the Vice President of Special Markets, Pocket Books, 1230 Avenue of the Americas, New York, New York 10020.

THE CAPTURED HEART

SHEILA O'HALLION

POCKET BOOKS

New York   London   Toronto   Sydney   Tokyo   Singapore

This book is a work of fiction. Names, characters, places and incidents are either the product of the author's imagination or are used fictitiously. Any resemblance to actual events or locales or persons, living or dead, is entirely coincidental.

An *Original* Publication of POCKET BOOKS

POCKET BOOKS, a division of Simon & Schuster
1230 Avenue of the Americas, New York, NY 10020

Copyright © 1991 by Sheila R. Allen

All rights reserved, including the right to reproduce
this book or portions thereof in any form whatsoever.
For information address Pocket Books, 1230 Avenue
of the Americas, New York, NY 10020

ISBN: 0-671-70384-6

First Pocket Books printing May 1991

10 9 8 7 6 5 4 3 2 1

POCKET and colophon are registered trademarks of
Simon & Schuster.

Printed in the U.S.A.

THE
CAPTURED
HEART

Printed in the U.S.A.

Prologue

A chill early-morning mist haunted the river's edge, threading through the branches of Richmond Forest. Along the side of a narrow lane that led back to the London road, a sporting phaeton and two closed carriages sat waiting in the dawn. All were empty but the largest closed coach with the Prince of Wales' crest on its open door. Inside, the prince regent sat fretting.

"We cannot but be uneasy," the regent said, leaning forward to get a better view. "We simply should not have countenanced Ashford's going through with this." The corpulent prince did not take his eyes from the happenings outside.

His two companions held differing views. The regent's brother, the dark-visaged Duke of Cumberland, was bored. "Then leave."

"We can hardly do that, Prince Ernest," Lord Rossmore snapped. To the regent he spoke more respectfully. "Your highness made a most sensible decision, considering the alternatives."

Cumberland's face settled into its habitual scowl. "If you think you're offending me, you're quite out," the duke said nastily.

George August Frederick Hanover, Prince of Wales, ignored their squabbling. Prince Regent of England since his father's final descent from sanity, he was known as Prinny to his friends, of whom he had many. He loved his country, his people, and his honor, but he loved his comfort above all, and at this moment he was morally uncomfortable. He was also sleepy and cold, and fast becoming hungry.

"What is taking them so long?" Prinny peered at the forest clearing that led up the side of a gently rising hill. At the top an ancient tree stood by itself, engulfed in swirling dawn mists. Beneath the tree two men faced each other, three others nearby. The unmoving tableau seemed more ghost than real in the uncertain gray-tinged dawn.

And then they moved. The two men, left arms resting on their hips, heels together, feet at right angles, saluted each other and attacked. The taller of the two parried his opponent's thrust, his thick chestnut hair gleaming tawny as the sun broke through the morning clouds.

Dressed in black, Andrew Henry Arthur Ormsby, sixth Duke of Ashford, barely moved as his opulently dressed opponent lunged and feinted, attempting to get past the duke's seemingly languid parries.

"What the devil is Ashford doing?" the doctor asked the duke's second. They stood just beyond the duelists on the damp grassy ridge.

Lord Effingham favored the rotund doctor with a languid smile. "It would appear he might be napping."

Effingham glanced down the hill toward the royal carriage. He could see Prinny's cheeky face turned up toward the duel. He was saying something Effingham could not hear.

"That young Standish is jumping about like a bloody frog," the regent informed his two coach companions.

"He's no match for Ashford, that's plain," Rossmore agreed.

"Ashford should end it," Cumberland said irritably.

"End it? Or Standish?" Rossmore asked the sour-faced duke.

"Either," Cumberland said.

The regent was not pleased. "Ernest, keep your tongue in your mouth. If not for you, we would not have to suffer through this. Ashford is fighting your duel."

"I didn't ask it," Ernest replied unrepentantly.

"Well, we did," Prinny said sharply.

Silence reigned inside the royal coach, not even Ernest foolish enough to egg Prinny on.

On top of the hill young Standish was lunging and thrusting indiscriminately, the Duke of Ashford deftly parrying the younger man's attempted blows. Standish was breathing heavily, his brow sweaty with effort as the mists began to give way to the risen sun.

"The prince . . ." Lord Effingham said loudly enough for the duke to hear.

Ashford heard the two words and glowered, thinking of Prinny's infamous brother Ernest sitting safely tucked up in the royal coach. His next thought was of poor Prinny, probably most discomforted from the chilly ride out from London in the black hours before dawn. And now waiting for a quick resolution.

His opponent and the onlookers saw Lord Ashford suddenly come alive, knocking Standish's blade away and attacking.

"*Coupé*," the duke said as he cut over. By the time Standish attempted to respond the duke was attacking to the opposite side, his sword passing under Standish's.

"*Dégagé*," Ashford informed his opponent. He moved easily, his blade flashing so fast Standish was sawing the air, trying to do more than parry and fall back. "*Remise*," the duke said, repeating his attack. The young man was in retreat and sweating. The duke advanced calmly, ripping the top edge of the young man's emerald velvet waistcoat, just above the heart.

It should have been over. The duke relaxed his stance. In the same instant he realized the young man was no gentleman. Standish was lunging forward in a mad attempt to kill the contemptuous duke.

Ashford was caught aback, Standish's steel catching the duke's at the hilt, a wild gleam in the younger man's eye, his breath coming in heavy spurts. The duke staggered back and then threw Standish off with main force, going for his reckless opponent's sword arm and cutting through to the thickest part.

"Aye-ee." The younger man's blade dropped, his left hand going to support his dangling right arm. "He's run me through!"

Andrew Ormsby gave his opponent a swift bow. "Your servant, sir." The duke was plainly displeased as he turned his back on the upstart and started down the hill.

The doctor and Standish's second were helping him, a tourniquet at the ready, as Lord Effingham fell into step beside the duke.

"If you must give free fencing lessons, could you in future please do so at a more decentish hour, Andrew?"

"This was not my idea," the duke replied grimly.

"Yes, it was. You switched masks with Cumberland at Raneleigh and allowed that young lady to drag her brother over to slap you with his glove. And that is going to excessive lengths, even for friendship."

The doctor called out to Effingham, who, with an exaggerated sigh, turned back toward the downed young man. The medical man knelt beside the complaining Standish, the second hovering over them both.

"Egad," Prinny said when Ashford arrived at the royal coach. "Andrew, did you stick him through?"

"A mere scratch, Your Highness."

"The man has not honor, and less artistry with the blade, but you, Andrew, perfect form! Reminds us of ourself."

"Your Highness is much too kind."

The regent's brother glowered in Ashford's general direction. "No need to hang about waiting for my thanks. I could have fought my own duel."

"You'd have killed the young fool," Prinny told his brother. "Even we couldn't have saved you from Parliament then. They'd have done more than cut you off, they'd have confiscated your estates, and nothing to be done for it. I tell you, you can't afford another scandal, and you should be demned grateful that Ashford is such a loyal friend to us."

"The truth is, *you* can't afford another scandal, dear brother, or they'll chop your allowance and you'll not be able to continue playing architect with your Chinese Pavilion."

"By God, we thought Kent a problem, but you put him to the pale. What brothers we have!" The regent turned from

4

Cumberland to Ashford. "We must thank you ourself."

"There is no need, Your Highness."

"Yes, well, there is a rather sore point we must discuss. I'm afraid we shall have to ask you to absent yourself from the capital for the rest of the season, dear boy, since word is bound to spread."

"None here will speak," Rossmore put in.

"That boy's sister will never be shut about it. A woman having a duel fought over her is never silent."

"Your Highness," Ashford interjected. "My estates need my presence."

Prinny knew Andrew well enough to hear the anger beneath his circumspect words. "Yes, your duties call, and we shall tell that to one and all," he placated. "We are chilled through from this morning's business. It took too long," he complained.

"I'm sorry, sir," Andrew told his monarch. He bowed and closed the carriage door as the royal driver urged his four grays forward.

James Tolliver waited at the reins of the duke's shiny black phaeton. "Are we ready, your grace?"

"I cannot speak for you, James, but I am more than ready to be quit of this stupidity. Effingham!" the duke called out as he reached for the reins.

"I believe Lord Effingham has agreed to drive the doctor's carriage."

"By Jupiter! Is that man-child still mewling about that scratch?"

"If you don't mind my saying so, your grace, it is your own fault for taking on such a preposterous enterprise."

"I thank you, James," the duke said dryly. "And if I am ever in danger of reaching above myself, I am positive you will be the first to enlighten me as to my folly."

"Rest assured, your grace, I shall do my best."

"No doubt."

Ashford's chestnuts raced toward London and Ashford House, the duke wanting nothing more than to be a league away from Richmond. Fencing was a sport at the very least, an art at its finest. It was not meant to be made into an idiotic spectacle for the delight of dilettantes and dunder-heads.

James took great pride in his master's deft handling of the reins. "I must say, your grace is a dab hand at the ribbons."

"Thank you."

"A nonesuch," the valet said firmly. "The master of every sport."

"You're pitching it far too rum, James. You might as well come out with it."

James studied his master as the duke effortlessly negotiated the twists and turns of the Thames-side road. He had been a tall, blue-eyed youth with long legs, restless energy, a wicked temper, and an even more wicked sense of humor. Now, at thirty-four, his face was manly and square-jawed, matching his square-shouldered body. He was still lean and long-legged, still taller than most. Altogether a fine figure of a man.

"What is it you're after?" the duke demanded.

"Nary a thing, your grace. I'm the one as can list your faults as well as your virtues, if you'd rather I dish up your sins."

"Thank you, no."

Andrew overtook the royal coach, bringing his pair alongside and then past the coach and four. The shrill neigh of one of the regent's horses came back on the wind as the phaeton took off ahead down the Thames-side road.

"I take it we'll be leaving London," James said once the royal party was far behind.

"Yes, and good riddance to it and all its fops and sycophants," Andrew said vehemently.

"Still, it's a pity you'll not be there for Lord Wellington's victory celebrations."

"With the peninsular victory, he's proved the worth of his strategy past any need of my help. There'll be a dukedom in his future, mark my words."

They neared the outskirts of London, the great Rotunda at Raneleigh Gardens visible in the distance beyond the trees. James frowned, his open honest face mirroring his thoughts.

"He wasn't worth it."

Ashford glanced at his valet, seeing the direction of his gaze. The duke returned his attention to the reins, negotiating as smooth a course as possible over the pockmarked high road.

"I had no choice once he challenged me."

"I don't mean that young jackanapes Standish, and well you know it. I mean that cursed fool, Cumberland."

"Enough," the duke told his servant. "The subject is beyond bounds."

"It may be beyond bounds, but it won't be closed until Prince Ernest is safe in his grave, and I'd not say much better for his brother Kent." James was past all politeness, his righteous anger rising with every word. "All the royal brothers together aren't worth a thimbleful of your blood and you taking on their challenges!"

"James, you're dancing close to treason and I won't hear it, and I won't have you repeating whatever it is you think you know. I did nothing amiss at Raneleigh—"

"And well all know it, who know you!"

"A young lady misunderstood my intentions, and her brother felt her virtue was sullied and insisted on demanding redress."

"I'd have to be dicked in the nob to believe such a taradiddle as that."

"James . . ." the duke warned.

James Tolliver's chin jutted out stubbornly. "I shall say no more, but you shan't stop my thoughts in my head, and I'll be blasted if I like any thinking such a bouncer to be true."

Andrew Ormsby, the sixth Duke of Ashford, grimaced.

"I have had my fill of 'polite' society. They may think as they wish."

"And they shall have had their fill of you once this is whispered about town," the valet said baldly. "Mark my words, you'll have none but light-skirts for female companionship, and I'll never live to see a seventh duke."

Andrew groaned. "If you are going to prose to me on that head, I shall shut my ears. You are worse than my mother."

"If your lady-mother were here, she'd say the same as I.

7

No God-fearing mother will let any young female of the first consequence within shouting distance of your grace after this gets 'round. And get 'round it will, with his highness involved. All told wrong, and you the culprit, taking a girl's virtue and then nearly killing her brother, that's what will be said of your grace."

"Is that all?"

"I'm full aware you've naught ambition to marry, but you have an obligation to your rank and title."

"Botheration to my rank and title," Andrew fairly shouted. "I'll do as I please, and all your constant asides on the subject do nothing but convince me I am best alone. If you nag me thus, and you only my servant, I shudder to think what life with a female would be."

"You'll end the bachelor duke, your lands going to cousins you despise."

"I have no cousins," the duke pointed out, "despised or otherwise."

"That's not the point," James told his master primly.

"Well, damn and blast your soul, what *is* the point?"

"The point is you've no right to be so selfish. You've more people than yourself depending upon you, and you should be thinking of them and not your own pleasures. Where would this world be, I ask you, if none thought of any but their own selfish pleasures? What will happen to your people when you're gone and no son to take your place? Although I'll be long since in my grave, so I am sure it's none of my business." Having delivered himself of this message, James lapsed into righteous silence.

"You are absolutely right," he was told.

"Still and all, it is the most serious subject a peer of the realm must consider."

"Right again."

"I am?"

"Yes. This entire subject is most definitely none of your business."

"I'm sure I shan't say another word if such is your lordship's pleasure."

"It is," James was told.

"I shan't speak where my advice is not wanted."

"Good."

The climate in the phaeton was decidedly cool for the next few miles. The duke tried to ignore his valet's hurt sniffs and silence, concentrating on the ribbons and weaving his way through the thickening London traffic toward London Bridge. Not only the traffic, but the air itself seemed to thicken, a smoky haze hanging over the city. The red brick city of Tudor and Stuart times was slowly yielding to the gray-brown Georgian bricks of newer public buildings. The duke's comments on the subject were met with still more silence.

Finally the duke ended the silence.

"Well, James." He spoke bracingly, as if totally unaware of his valet's long-suffering hurt silence. "We shall pack up today and repair at first light to much more congenial circumstances in Sussex, where there's peace and quiet and nary a female that isn't above fifty on the entire estate."

"Thanks to your mother," James said meaningfully.

Andrew groaned. "There is no dealing with you, James. You insist on going against my express wishes at every turn. I don't know why I put up with you."

"I'm sure I don't know what you mean, your grace."

"Peace," the duke said meaningfully. "That is my meaning and my byword. I have had my fill of society and politics and dissension and the endless nattering small talk of bored dandies and those of the female persuasion. And of servants who overstep their bounds because of their long years of service."

"I can't imagine who you could mean," James said righteously.

"Peace and *quiet* is all I ask."

"You'll have nothing else in Sussex," James replied.

In later years, Andrew never let his man forget those last words.

...his two long feet or whatever was crawling, the stench being trapped cold behind something else. The other was a stranger dressed into rumpled

Chapter One

Scudder-on-Thames was a tiny Kentish village of white-washed cottages covered with rambler roses and honey-suckle. It sat in the midst of a peaceful green river valley close enough to London for visits to and from by the squire, but far enough from the capital to seem exotic to villagers who had never ventured the twenty miles upriver.

The village square was filled at one end by a small stone chapel and at the other by a duck pond, the delight of the village boys.

Lieutenant Samuel Morris, arriving home from long campaigns with Lord Wellington, was reminded of his own youthful days by the sight of two village youths racing around the grass at the edge of the pond. He slowed his faithful bay, patting the horse's neck as he drank in the sights and sounds and smells of home.

The last of the roses filled the air with sweetness that mixed with the coastal winds and the shouts of the raucous boys who were now pummeling each other. As they milled about, trying to darken each other's daylights, Samuel came to a stop by the hedgerow that skirted the village square.

A small crowd had gathered across the greensward, watching as the boys lost their balance and landed in the duck pond. The ducks squawked their disapproval, flapping their wings in distaste and threatening to take off.

The boys clambered out of the water, coming up muddy and still fighting. The younger of the two was on top, looking to kill off the boy beneath him.

"Stubble it," the boy on top shouted. "Dub your mummer or I'll send you to Kingdom Come!"

Samuel Morris stared at the crowd of women who were shaking their heads and talking amongst themselves across the pond. A field hand, the cobbler, and two other boys stood nearby, an old man walked toward the square from the lane beyond, but none was going to the aid of the downed boy.

"That's enough," Samuel said. He jumped off his mount, tethering it and striding forward, his uniform causing a bit of a stir in the small crowd.

He grabbed the younger boy, hauling him by his britches up and off his victim. The bigger boy rolled over to his knees, nursing a bloody nose.

"What's the meaning of— Stop it," Samuel told the struggling boy who was trying to get away from the soldier's grip and go after his quarry. Samuel shook the boy so hard his field cap came off. A tumble of dirty red curls fell to the child's shoulders.

"I would have got you," the bigger boy said. "'Cept I'm a gent and I don't hit *girls.*"

"Brianna!" Samuel stared at his little sister in shock.

"Master Samuel? It's me, Old John." An elderly man came near, doffing his cap.

"John, what is the meaning of this?" Samuel demanded.

"None can do a thing with the gel since you've been gone, Master Samuel."

Brianna was still trying to get at the boy, her arms windmilling. "Let go of me, Samuel!"

"I've not been home for over a year, and you've nary a hello, how are you, brother? What did he *do* to you?"

"He called me a pasty-faced *girl!*"

"You *are* a girl!" Samuel told her sharply.

"She's a troublemaker," a woman said behind him.

Samuel turned toward the woman who stood with two others from the village. "I beg your pardon?"

"You'd best take her in hand and teach her some proper manners." The woman glared at them both as she reached for the muddied boy. "She's run wild while you've been gone."

"I've done no such thing," Brianna shouted.

"I—I'm terribly sorry," Samuel told the woman. "It won't happen again, I promise you," he said, hauling Brianna away from the onlookers.

"Where are you taking me?" she demanded shrilly.

"I'm taking you home, and if you're not careful, I shall give you a proper melting, for I think you're long overdue."

"You wouldn't dare," Brianna said, but she knew her brother was a blooded soldier, and said no more until he hauled her back off the horse and deposited her in the center of the Morris front parlor.

Mrs. Hobson came down the small hall from the kitchen, wiping her hands on her apron. "Have you—" she started, but seeing Samuel, she lost the words. "Ohhhh . . ." Tears sprang to her eyes. "You're home safe and sound . . . the Lord be praised . . ." The housekeeper grabbed at her apron, wiping the edge against her teary blue eyes.

"Yes, safe, and thank you," Samuel replied, giving short shrift to the servant's welcome. "Is she always like this?" he demanded. He held his sister at arm's length, mud drying in her hair and plastered to her face and the boy's shirt and trousers she wore. Bits of wet mud fell to the worn carpet.

Brianna stamped on his toe. The fact that his boot was in between saved her from a spanking then and there. "Don't speak as if I weren't here!"

"You're aching for that melting," Samuel said.

"Like this and worse," Mrs. Hobson told him.

"She dresses like a boy!"

"She won't wear proper clothes."

"What has happened? She was always an outspoken child," Samuel temporized. "And headstrong, but this is beyond the pale."

"She's not a child any longer, Master Samuel, more's the pity. She's turned fifteen, and not to mince words, she's an outspoken, undisciplined hoyden, and we no longer know what to do with her."

"I thought she'd grow out of it. Become a young lady."

Mrs. Hobson was a plain-featured, plain-spoken widow of

nearly fifty. "I'll not take blame for Brianna, Master Samuel. She was let to run wild while your parents were alive, and God rest their souls, she never was made to mind. The only one she'd listen to after the Good Lord took them was yourself, and well you know it. Well, you've been gone, and she's grown bigger but no better. Making a proper young lady out of a hoydenish child requires *training,* just as soldiers must be trained. It's past time you were home to take her in hand and see to her future."

"But I'm not," Samuel said, still battling to keep his obstinate sister in his grasp.

Brianna stopped her struggles. "What do you mean, you're not?" she cried. "You've only just arrived, you can't turn 'round and just *leave.*"

"Can I not?" he demanded. "After such a homecoming as this? My own sister looking like a filthy street urchin, parading around in boy's clothing and engaging in fisticuffs, the whole village laughing up their sleeves. I'd rather face the French in battle than face the county in shame for my sister's reputation."

"Oh, Sammy." Brianna's eyes filled with tears. "I don't give two shakes for what people say, but please don't leave. I've missed you so dreadfully. I'll be good as golden guineas, I'll do all you say, if only you will please, please, please, stay . . ."

Mrs. Hobson looked, if anything, more upset than Brianna. "Master Samuel, you cannot leave," she told him flatly.

Lieutenant Morris looked from the housekeeper to his sister as sounds came from the kitchen. Old John called out to Mrs. Hobson, his words carrying down the hall from the kitchen.

"Mrs. H, young Samuel's home from the wars! Mrs. H?" The elderly servant limped into the parlor. "Missus—he's come home at last!" Old John's smile was wide, all the gaps in his teeth showing as he rounded the corner and saw the young master across the room holding his struggling sister in his arms. "And it's that good to see him, it is," Old John said placidly.

Samuel looked toward Mrs. Hobson. "Surely you were expecting me. Your letter said—"

"Brianna." Mrs. Hobson interrupted the lieutenant's words, startling him when she pulled Brianna from his grasp and nattered on as fast as her tongue would go. "You're a sight as should not be seen, and your brother just home and wanting a little peace and quiet." The housekeeper gently pushed the dirty child toward the kitchen. "I must heat water for your tub, and you must go with Old John and clean off the worst of this in the horse trough before you put one foot back inside the house."

"Samuel?" Brianna pleaded with her eyes.

Samuel gave his sister a beastly frown. "If you do not mind, I swear I shall not be here when you come back."

"Mind," Mrs. Hobson scoffed. "She doesn't know the meaning of the word. Why, she even tried to run off to become a soldier last month."

Brianna made a face. "And I'd have fooled them all too, and been the best soldier they ever saw. Excepting Sammy."

"No, you would not," her brother told her in as stern a voice as he could muster.

Brianna stamped her muddy-booted foot. "I would too!"

"Good soldiers must take orders," Samuel informed his willful sister.

The young girl thought about it. Then, with as good a military stance as she could muster, she turned toward Mrs. Hobson. Her back ramrod straight, she stiff-marched past her brother and past Old John.

The old man winked at Samuel and followed the girl outside.

"You'd best give up your fighting, Miss Bree," he told her. "You're getting too big for it, my gel. You'd best have a care or you're liable to hurt one of those village lads."

Mrs. Hobson waited for the door to close before she claimed Samuel's hand and pulled him farther into the parlor. "We must talk," the housekeeper said. "Alone," she added.

Samuel girded himself for bad news. "What now?"

"She doesn't know."

"I beg your pardon?"

Mrs. Hobson released Samuel's hand and began to wring her own. "She doesn't know about my letter to you."

"Mrs. Hobson, you said it was most urgent I return, and return I have. But I cannot stay. Lord Wellington gave me leave to ride here, but we will be leaving for the Continent immediately after he reports to the regent."

Brianna was outside, following Old John around the house and toward the stables. As she passed the open parlor window she heard Mrs. Hobson.

"No!" the housekeeper shrieked.

Brianna stopped in her tracks. Old John continued toward the stables, waxing eloquent on the efficacy of a bit of feminine wile over any amount of masculine muscle. If only Miss Bree would learn the lessons of her gender, she would have no need of milling about with town boys.

"You must not, you *cannot* leave," Mrs. Hobson implored the young soldier inside the parlor.

Brianna moved behind the thick rose bushes that lined the side of the house. The last of the full-blown crimson cabbage roses hid her as she crouched beneath the open window, her breath caught in her throat at the horrendous urgency of Mrs. Hobson's words.

"I've not had the heart to tell young Brianna until you were home to take care of her, but Mr. Stout, as is the cousin of Jasper Stout, the village smithy, as you may remember . . .?" Mrs. Hobson asked, and then pushed on, determined to explain herself. "Mr. Stout—Jed, that is, not Jasper, who is married—well, Mr. Jed Stout has visited his cousin here in Scudder this spring and now is back as of these past weeks and has asked for my hand in marriage and I have agreed." Mrs. Hobson drew in a lungful of air, saw the young master's consternation, and plunged on, speaking as fast as she could form the words. "I've been a widow all these years, and him a widower only just this past winter and with seven children, one a tiny babe in arms, and him with his entire farm to run. He's not a rich man, but he's a good one, and he's asked for my hand and I've accepted, only waiting for your return, as I told him I would inform

16

you we must be off to his lands before the harvest." Mrs. Hobson took another great long breath and waited. "Master Samuel?" she asked when the young master said nothing.

He shook his head. "I am entirely taken aback. I don't know what to say."

"I've given good service all these years, and done all I could for you and your sister, but I won't be able to be responsible for her now. For her sake, as well as mine, she should be where she may learn manners and all that a young lady of her station is required to know."

"Unfortunately, our station is above our means," Samuel said bluntly. "Our parents, may they rest in peace, were the most loving, but not the most practical of progenitors. I have a small competence, perhaps sufficient to engage a tutor for Brianna, but I misdoubt a tutor would take over the household duties."

Mrs. Hobson shook her head. "It won't fadge, Master Samuel. There's nothing for it, you must take the bit between your teeth and keep Brianna with you."

Outside the open window, hunkered down between the autumnal rose bushes and the stone walls of her family home, Brianna held her breath, her eyes alight with anticipation.

"Impossible," her brother said from inside the parlor. "As one of Lord Wellington's attachés, I am quartered in his household, and my single room is in the staff wing, entirely unsuitable for female occupancy, even if he would allow it, which I know he will not. Brianna is wild and willful enough without becoming a cheapened camp follower!"

Mrs. Hobson drew herself up to her entire five-foot-nothing height and glared upward at the much taller soldier. She spoke stiffly. "I hope you are not saying you expect me to give up my expectations for my own future and family because you do not choose to accept your fraternal obligations."

Brianna waited with bated breath for her brother to vehemently deny Mrs. Hobson's charges, to assure the woman that he would henceforth ensure his sister would be kept by his side. Instead she heard words that first raised her hopes and then dashed them to pieces, her heart breaking as her brother spoke.

"I cannot *choose*. I am a soldier and must obey."

"And I am a woman and must obey my future lord and master," Mrs. Hobson countered. "I was not meant to be a saint, Master Samuel. I have been alone a great many years."

Brianna's brother took his time answering. "I cannot ask you to give up your future happiness. You have been a faithful friend and servant since we were born, and well I know it. I am simply saying I do not know what's to be done. Brianna cannot stay on here with only Old John as her chaperone and caretaker."

"Master Samuel!" Mrs. Hobson was shocked. "A young girl living alone with an unmarried, unrelated man? How could you even allow such a thought to enter your mind?"

With great effort Samuel held back the expletives he would have delivered if he had been amongst his military companions. "Although I agree it is entirely improper, I hardly think Old John at his advanced age is a danger to *anyone's* morality."

Mrs. Hobson corrected the young man sharply. "To Brianna's morality, I agree. To her already tattered reputation, I must most vehemently disagree. In later years you may issue all the assurances you wish, but try explaining on some distant day, to a properly brought-up young suitor, why you allowed your sister to be at the mercy of any male, of any age, for any reason. If you have more than passing luck, perhaps Old John will still be alive to add credence to your demurral. But if he is not, or if vicious village tongues wag—and wag they will, since your sister has made a positive art form of alienating all and sundry—how will you prove that the doddering old man is the one of whom they tattle? Would *you* marry a girl under such a cloud?"

". . . No, I would not," Samuel admitted. "But what's to be done at this impasse, I have not the first clue."

Mrs. Hobson spoke firmly. "You must do as your parents wished."

"I beg your pardon?"

"Your sister was nine and you only nineteen and new to

18

the army when they were stricken with the influenza. They made provision for your sister's care. You should have abided by their wishes."

"I could not force Brianna away from the only home she had ever known, to go all alone to a stranger."

"Not a stranger, but your mother's cousin."

"The heir of our grandmother's cousin," he corrected.

"Be that as it may, you must be strong and do as is best for your sister." Mrs. Hobson underscored her words with her firm tone of voice. "She cannot be allowed to run as wild as she pleases, and there's none here whom she will obey."

"There's no guarantee she will obey any other."

"She's a burden to you, it's true, but you are the head of the family and must shoulder your responsibilities."

Leftenant Morris stiffened. "I have no intention of shirking them."

"Good," Mrs. Hobson replied.

"Miss Bree?" Old John came back from the stables, squinting into the autumn sunshine.

Brianna bolted out from behind the rose bushes, hurtling toward the old family retainer. "Shush, I'm here," she told him breathlessly.

"We mustn't keep your brother waiting," Old John said. He turned back toward the water trough around the far side of the stables, still talking. "It's a blessing Master Samuel's back to take charge of things, and that's a fact. He's been gone too long, I'll warrant, fighting those Frenchies, when he should have been safe taking care of . . ."

Old John disappeared around the corner. Brianna was following, her sad-faced expression growing longer and sadder with each step she took. Just before she turned the corner she caught sight of a short, wide, full-chested man walking up the drive.

Brianna ran toward the newcomer, arriving in front of him disheveled, mud-caked, and breathless. "Mr. Stout?"

The placid-faced man blinked. Before him was a sight such as he had never before in all his fifty-seven years encountered. A short gremlin accosted him. Dirty-faced, muddy arms waving, it raced up to block his passage.

"Mr. Stout?" the apparition repeated his name.

"Bless me, yes?"

"Bless you, *no,*" the vision replied. "She'll never marry you, as in good conscience, she cannot!"

Jed Stout was not at ease courting. He had gathered all his courage only once before, and if Mrs. Stout had not died of childbed, he would never have had to bestir himself further. But the father of a motherless brood needed a woman's helping hand, and when he met the wise and practical widow Hobson the previous spring, he found the answer to his prayers and almost offered for her on the spot.

Millie Hobson had been married and left a childless widow; she knew the value of a good man and had always longed for a large family. He felt at ease with the soft-voiced and round-bodied Millie, but his fear of quick decisions made him leave Scudder-on-Thames without asking for her hand. Once back at his farm he was soon convinced his needs and his wants were in total agreement. Absence, together with his contentious children's quarrels, further convinced the practical farmer that Millie Hobson was the woman of his dreams.

He had written, or rather he had paid the village scribe to write her, and he had come this past week to pursue his suit in earnest.

"She . . . *cannot?*" Jed Stout repeated as if the vision was speaking in a foreign tongue.

"Never!" he was told in ringing tones.

"Jed?" Mrs. Hobson called out as she arrived with Samuel to interrupt Brianna's discourse with the confused gentleman whose path she blocked.

Brianna stood her ground until the last. "She cannot marry you, for our Hobby is already married!"

Mrs. Hobson was scandalized. "How can you say such a thing?"

"It's true!" Brianna insisted as her brother's arms went round her middle, pulling her back from her belligerent position in front of the stranger.

"It is *not* true." Mrs. Hobson's voice was hot with indignation.

"She's a widow and you're a widower," Brianna hollered as her brother lifted her from her feet. "All know you may only marry once!"

"You're making a cake of yourself," Samuel told her as he wrestled her away from the startled Mr. Stout.

"Let me be," Brianna cried, her heels kicking at her brother's shins. She struggled to be let free. "He only wants an unpaid nursemaid to take care of his motherless brats."

"How *dare* you!" Mrs. Hobson exclaimed, nettled past all endurance.

"It's true! Besides, you can't want to be called Mrs. *Stout* for the rest of your life!"

Once the words were out of her mouth, Brianna knew she had passed beyond the bounds. Her brother Samuel stared at her, horror-struck. Mrs. Hobson was blushing scarlet to the roots of her hair.

"Miss Bree?" Old John called out, limping as he came near. "Where did you get to?"

"Miss Bree?" Jed Stout repeated, his stolid face mirroring his confusion. "Miss Brianna Morris?" He stared at the short, muddied figure before him. "It's a *girl?*"

Brianna burst into tears and wrenched away from her brother. "Go on, go away and leave me, see if I care!"

"Bree!" Samuel shouted, but she was running for the house. He gave chase, leaving Mrs. Hobson to face Jed Stout as Old John stopped a few paces behind.

"Is something amiss?" the deaf Old John asked when he saw Millie's expression.

"She's selfish beyond permission and should be thoroughly spanked," Mrs. Hobson snapped.

Inside the small stone house that had been home to generations of Morrises, Brianna raced up the short stairway, plummeted into her room and fell across her bed, muffling her sobs in her pillow. Her brother slowed on the threshold as he heard her fierce grief.

"Bree?" Samuel came near his sister cautiously, trying to make himself heard over her loud sobs.

His young sister's words were gulped through racking

sobs. "Go away, you don't want me, nobody wants me. I'll never bother you again, I'll—" she hiccuped. "I'll run away to the Gypsies!" Brianna's words would have been more effective if hiccups had not interrupted her dramatic declaration.

"You don't want Hobby to be unhappy, Bree."

"Oh, Sammy." Brianna sprang up, reaching her thin muddied arms toward her brother. "You can't leave me here alone!"

Lieutenant Morris was a brave young man, his bravery proved in battle against the French and rewarded by his being promoted to a position on Lord Wellington's staff. Samuel Morris had faced death with equanimity, but facing his teary-faced sister nearly undid him.

"Do you imagine I want to?" he replied, his own hazel eyes far from dry.

"I swear I'll do all you say, I'll never be a problem, I'll fight alongside you!" she promised between sobs.

Samuel reached to hold his little sister close. "It's just not possible," he told her.

"But you could make it possible, I know you could. You can do anything," she told her big brother through her tears.

"I don't know how long I shall be in London," he temporized.

"I shall do anything, everything, you say, I swear it."

"We'll see," he told his sobbing sister, wanting nothing so much as to end her tears.

"Do you mean you will take me with you?" she asked, her tear-filled green eyes gleaming like dark emeralds. "Dear Samuel, *dearest* brother who ever lived, please say you mean I can come with you . . ."

Lieutenant Morris was caught in his sister's tearful pleas. "I suppose you must, you cannot very well stay on here without Hobby."

"Oh, *Sammy!*" Brianna flung her arms around her brother's neck. "I shall do everything you say, I shall be the most docile sister man ever knew, you shall never be sorry, I'll keep house for you, I'll fight alongside you, I'll—"

22

"Brianna!" Samuel nearly shouted, bringing her words to a sudden stop.

"Yes, brother dear?" she replied meekly.

Lieutenant Morris tried to look grim, but his sister's meltingly sweet expression softened his eyes and his words.

"If you are to come with me, you must be entirely unexceptional."

"Yes, Samuel," Brianna agreed meekly.

The lieutenant was more worried than he would admit. He would have to contrive to inform their distant relative of her plight and ask his help. His misgivings, he tried to tell himself, were unfounded, Brianna would do as she was told, she had no choice. But he refrained from telling her of his decision just yet. He kissed her dirt-spattered forehead and stood up.

"Now you must clean yourself up."

Brianna's eyes were meekly lowered. "Whatever you say, dear brother."

"And I don't want you saying one more word to Mr. Stout."

"Yes, Samuel," she said obediently.

He stood up, feeling much more in charge. Brianna was willful, but she was not a bad child. Mrs. Hobson was a loyal employee and the best of housekeepers, but she did not use a strong enough hand dealing with the headstrong girl.

"Compose yourself before you come down to join us," Samuel ordered.

"Yes, brother dear."

Very satisfied with himself, Samuel Morris left his sister to her own devices and traveled back down the steep oak stairs to the front parlor and the waiting Mrs. Hobson.

Chapter Two

*T*he London high road was alive with soldiers marching in columns and loitering in tavern yards and inns. Snatches of martial music traveled on the winds, the entire country rejoicing in Viscount Wellington's victories against the French. Napoleon was on the run along with his entire family of upstarts, uneasy on the thrones the self-styled emperor stole in his attempts to legitimatize and protect his precarious position.

Brianna rode a roan pony beside her scarlet-uniformed brother, riding as tall as if she herself were part of the glorious army that was marching across Europe, freeing the world of Napoleon's yoke. Her eyes shone emerald in the sunlight, excitement spotting her cheeks with rising crimson as they rode westward through the throngs of carts and carriages.

Her first view of the capital was through the smoky haze that hung over the city, turning East London into a palette all gray and brown. The people scuttling about the wide boulevards and narrow lanes were dressed in drab clothes, but they seemed exotic to the country-bred youngster.

Bright colors beckoned from inside shop windows, delicious aromas of fresh buns and tarts carrying on the city breezes. Brianna leaned wide in her saddle, drinking in the sights and smells, exclaiming in excited syllables about each strange vision that befell her entranced gaze.

"Brianna," Samuel said dampeningly as they rode ever closer to their destination, "I want no histrionics, no *scenes* once we reach Lord Wellington's establishment."

"Never!" Brianna pledged with all the fierceness of a fifteen-year-old's entire heart and soul.

His sister's vehement agreement caused Lieutenant Morris grave unease. "None must even know you are in the household until I can talk to his lordship and apprise him of my—of *our*—predicament. Females are not allowed in the soldiers' quarters."

"No mouse shall have ever been more quiet," Brianna promised. "The spiders in the walls will not know I am there."

"I care not about the spiders, but I most assuredly do care about my mates and about my general. He is a—"

"A *hero*," Brianna interrupted.

"*But*," Samuel overrode his sister's interruption, "the general is a stickler for propriety."

"Of course," Brianna agreed.

"He must report to Parliament on his campaigns, where, mind you, all have not agreed with his decisions." Samuel sounded as shocked as any right-thinking person should be at such perfidy in the halls of government. "We must not add to his problems."

He led his sister's pony through the thickening London traffic, worrying over how to explain Brianna to the general and how he would manage to deliver her to their relative. "If he knows you are there before I can explain our situation," Samuel said aloud, "he will chuck us both out."

Brianna considered her brother's dire warning. "Would that mean you won't have to leave for Europe and the coming campaign?"

"No," Samuel corrected his sister sharply. "It would mean my career would be in tatters, my life at an end, and yours consigned to the poorhouse forever and ever. And all your fault," he added for effect.

"I would never harm my very own and only brother," Brianna informed Samuel with loud conviction.

"Not on purpose, but mind how many misdemeanors you have committed in error. What might seem small to you could be the death knell to my career and both our future fortunes."

"I shan't do anything to cause trouble, I promise."

The traffic lessened a bit, the air cleared, as brother and

sister neared the temporary Mayfair residence of the nation's greatest hero. Brianna caught glimpses of a whole new world of rich establishments and curried horseflesh and a seemingly endless parade of servants bent on polishing and scrubbing everything in sight. Her eyes round with wonder, she beheld manicured green squares surrounded by opulent town houses that rose toward the murky blue sky.

Samuel slowed his chestnut's pace, reining in his sister's pony. Brianna was awestruck by the size of the gates they were passing through, but she kept her thoughts to herself. Inside the mews that abutted the rear of the large town house, officers of His Majesty's army loitered and lounged against the thick stone walls of the stables. Coachmen polished carriages while young apprentice-devils scurried about seeing to the horses that panted in the warm afternoon air and pawed at the cobblestones.

"Morris?" A deep voice carried toward Samuel and Brianna as they stopped near the kitchen door. "I say, Morris!"

Samuel unwillingly acknowledged the bluff-mannered officer who flagged him down. "Fieldston," Samuel acknowledged.

Lieutenant Fieldston cast a cursory glance toward Morris's companion. "What have you got there, a bat boy?"

"Hardly. I—I've taken on a duty for a relative."

Brianna, concealed in her usual attire of boys' clothing and sporting a large leather cap, kept her eyes on the saddle pommel, avoiding the exchange between her brother and his friend.

"How tedious," Fieldston said.

"You have no idea," Samuel agreed feelingly. He led his chestnut to a dismounting stone and handed the reins to a waiting servant. "Get down." He barked the words, Brianna jumping off the roan as he reached for her valise.

"This way," Samuel said abruptly. Sensing her lagging gait, he reached for her coarse-jacketed arm and hauled her forward by main force. She heard laughter behind them, her ears burning.

"Climb," he hissed when they neared the narrow servants' stairway. Samuel shoved his sister forward and upward, ahead of him, as he negotiated the steps as fast as he could. His room was at the top rear of the three-story establishment.

"Lieutenant?" a voice called out from below. "Lieutenant *Morris?*" the voice questioned in a tone that stopped Samuel in his tracks.

He thrust Brianna and her valise around the stair corner as he looked downward. "Yes? Are you speaking to me?"

"Yes, sir," the young officer said. He put his foot on the lowest tread of the second-floor steps, ready to start upward.

"Stay where you are!" Samuel thundered, surprising the junior officer. "What is it? Speak up, Sergeant!"

"General Wellington sent me to find you. He's in the south parlor."

"I shall be there directly."

The sergeant turned away, and Samuel shoved his sister up the last flight of stairs with one hand whilst unbuttoning his tunic with the other.

"In here." Samuel opened a door and pushed his sister into a tiny bedchamber. Brianna landed upon her brother's narrow bed, her backside sliding across the quilted coverlet. "Now," he said as he divested himself of his travel-stained tunic and reached for a clean uniform, "you will not stir from this room until I return! Brianna?"

"Whatever you say, Sammy."

"Turn 'round."

"I beg your pardon?"

"Turn *around,* I must change my unmentionables."

Brianna turned, her auburn curls falling forward to hide her meekly bowed head. With perfect propriety she kept her eyes averted as her brother changed his breeches.

"You must keep to yourself in this room until I come back. No matter how long I am delayed," he warned.

Brianna agreed with vehement certitude. "If you are gone for days, I shall waste away *dead,* I swear it!"

He was not sure why his sister's agreement made him uneasy, but make him uneasy it did. He tried to impress upon her the importance of doing exactly as he said, but the more he spoke, the more doubts he had. Lord Wellington was awaiting him, so he had to leave, but his admonitions continued as he quitted the doorway.

"None must know," were his parting words, and his young sister assured him none would be the wiser.

Brianna sat on the edge of her brother's Spartan cot, looking around the small bedroom. It was at most eight feet by ten feet, the only furniture his narrow bed, a tall chest of drawers, a wider chest upon which sat a large porcelain pitcher and washing basin, and a chair beside a plain pine wardrobe.

Five minutes stretched into ten and then to twenty, Brianna's booted foot tapping an impatient tattoo upon the wood floor. The boots she wore were ancient relics Old John had discarded when Samuel had made him a present of new ones last Christmas. Inside, covered by three pairs of men's stockings, her feet still swam in the oversized boots, chafing her heels and toes.

In the well-scrubbed pristine room she could smell the sweat of horseflesh and the odors of the long London road reeking from her shirt and breeches. She pulled off the boots, rid herself of the stockings, and rubbed her sore feet. All was silent on the uppermost story of the huge Mayfair house. Brianna fidgeted for a few moments and then tiptoed to the window and peeked out. Far below, soldiers came and went along the mews, stablemen curried their horses, drivers waited for their employers. Brianna reached to open the small dormer window but hesitated, her hand on the frame. Her brother's words of caution ringing in her ears, she left it closed and went to the pitcher of water and washing basin across the room.

The water she poured into the basin was cold. She rummaged in the top drawer of the chest and found towels and washing cloths, then unbuttoned the shirt and breeches, sending them in a heap to the floor as she reached for the basin.

Brianna shivered as she washed with the chilly water, her teeth chattering when she finished. She rubbed her body warmer with the rough towel and then sent it to the floor beside the discarded clothing. She reached for the shirt and held it between two fingers, her nose wrinkling. With a resigned sigh she went to retrieve the dress that lay folded within the leather valise Samuel had made her pack.

Footsteps came near outside. Brianna's heart beat furiously, her breath stopped. Her head whipped around, looking for shelter. The wardrobe was nearest. She wrenched it open and jumped inside as the bedchamber door opened.

A young footman entered the small room, whistling to himself. He carried a pile of starched uniform shirts. He opened the middle drawer of the tall chest, stuffed the folded shirts neatly inside and slammed it shut. When he turned, he tripped over the heap of dirty clothing. Reaching down, he scooped it up and deposited it in a half-filled wash basket just outside the door. Brianna held her breath, waiting for the sound of the closing door.

The footman came back and walked to the wardrobe, shaking out the red military cape. The heavy material flared wide as he opened the door and reached to place it upon a wooden peg.

A naked urchin sat crouched on the floor, knobby knees to chin, arms wound around legs. Strands of long wild hair the color of the devil's own red escaped its cap, its eyes wide and wild and surrounded by unholy purple skin.

"Gor, blimy, it's a devil I'm seeing!" The young footman crossed himself in fright as he backed away from the vision. He turned on his heel and went clattering down the hall and the servants' stairs beyond, calling out to someone named Jim.

Brianna jumped out of the wardrobe, reaching for the valise. She pulled out the tangled skirts and wrestled with them, her heart stuttering inside her narrow chest. Giving up on the complicated clothing, she looked for the dirty clothes and saw they were gone.

Samuel's travel-stained uniform still lay on the wardrobe floor. Brianna shoved the jacket aside and reached for the stained shirt and breeches. She donned them quickly, waiting to hear thundering steps outside. She shoved her

unruly hair up under the brown leather cap and reached for
the boots as excited voices rose up the stairwell ahead of the
feet that accompanied them.

"I tell you, it's a devil I've seen!" The young footman's
voice was loud with fear.

Brianna grabbed the boots and made for the hall, still
trying to button the oversized shirt. She bolted through the
door across the hall, and closing her eyes tightly, prayed
none other was inside with her. She waited for a startled cry
but heard nothing but the words outside.

"And I'm sure you've been having a wee taste of his
lordship's rum," an older man replied firmly.

"Never!"

Brianna ventured to open one eye. Seeing she was alone,
she opened the other. The voices were just outside and then
inside her brother's room.

"You'll see, right here—what the devil?"

"Now, lad—"

"But it was!"

Brianna cautiously prized open the door that hid her.
Through the tiny crack she could see into her brother's
room. She stepped out into the hall and sneaked toward the
stairs. She went fast, reaching the next floor before she heard
the voices behind her coming nearer. Brianna whipped
around the landing, out of sight. A door ahead led to a wide
front hall, and Brianna raced through it.

Family bedchambers could be seen through two open
doors, dark oil portraits lining the wide corridor in between
and beyond. Serious men and women stared silently down
at the young girl as she ran past the paintings toward the
stairs at the far end.

This stairway was wide and highly polished and made of
rich, dark red mahogany. Brianna stumbled, her bare feet
sliding on the slippery wood. She grabbed for the banister,
stopping her fall and gulping in a great lungful of air.

Halfway down she realized her mistake. The stairs led not
to a front hall but to a wide entryway, devoid of cover. The
sounds of movement above cut off her only avenue of
escape. Black boots in hand, she ran forward down the

stairs, her eyes on the large front door. The murmur of male voices came from the parlor beyond, a woman speaking to someone about linen storage on the floor above.

Brianna came to a screeching halt at the oak door, stubbing her toes in the process. She fumbled with its heavy wrought-iron handle and wrenched it open, careening out onto the wide porticoed porch of the Mayfair mansion.

A carriage was pulled up at the steps, no one in sight. Brianna climbed into the coachman's box, out of breath as she shoved her bare feet into the huge boots.

"You, there!" a voice called out. "Boy—hand me down that box."

Brianna froze.

The coachman climbed up beside her. He eyed her critically. "Did ye not hear me? If you're to work here, lad, you'd best move smart-like when you're told."

Brianna ducked her head and lifted the wooden box. "Yes, sir." She spoke in as deep a voice as she could muster.

The man took the box from her and stepped back down. "His lordship gives short shrift to those who don't give their best efforts. Or those as are sloppy. Straighten your shirt and your back, lad, you're so hunkered over, none can see your face."

Brianna mumbled a reply, moving toward the opposite side of the bench as the coachman turned away. She touched her boot to the side step as a group of officers came out onto the covered porch. She pulled back and turned her head.

"Thank you, your lordship," her brother was saying as he accompanied his commanding officer into the coach.

"Levington, see to the gunpowder stores, I want an accurate account of what's been shipped," General Lord Wellington said to one of the men on the porch.

"Yes, sir."

Brianna scrambled toward the far side of the coachman's box, but she was too late. The coachman climbed up, blocking her escape to the road. Samuel's fellow officers blocked her escape to the house. Ducking her head, her chin was almost against her chest as the driver unwound the reins from the brake and urged the horses forward.

Chapter Three

Lord Wellington's coach clattered over the West London cobblestones, the horses clip-clopping at a steady pace through the city crowded with wagons and street hawkers. It was a long drive to Windsor, the low murmur of his lordship's words now and again reaching Brianna's ears once the city was left behind. Her thoughts all went to her brother and what he would do when she was found out, each vision of that horrible fate more worrisome than the last.

She would bolt at first opportunity, fleeing as fast as her legs would carry her and without a backward glance. Convinced of the rightness of her purpose, she fell to musing upon poor Samuel's shock when he returned to his room and found her gone.

He would assume she had been found out, he would question the household, recklessly disregarding his own position, and still find none with answers for his queries. At some juncture he would realize his dear sister had sacrificed herself upon the altar of his career. He would be chastened, chagrined, perhaps even beholden. He would wear her colors into battle as knights of old did for their ladies fair, and conquer entire continents to make worthwhile her loving sacrifice.

What were her colors? Brianna wondered suddenly. How would he know which were hers? It would be a profound shame if he could not proclaim his debt to his selfless sister so all would know the sacrifice she had made.

"Boy . . . boy!" The coachman's gravelly voice intruded upon her thoughts. "Take the reins, I say, and have a care about them." He thrust the leather ribbons into her hands and brought out a flask from his disreputable greatcoat. He betook himself of a long swig, wiping the back of his hand across his mouth and sighing contentedly.

"Aye, and the first swig of the day is a rare treat. Tho' mind you, ne'er overstep the bounds of sobriety." The old man spoke piously. "A judicious quantity of spirits is a man's great friend. More is his enemy, and the more so for the young. Why, there's a bantling in his lordship's household, I'll not say who excepting he's apprentice footman and not likely to stay so, I'll warrant, what with drinking in broad daylight and seeing ghosties and devils hiding in nooks and crannies. You must learn from others' mistakes, laddie, or life will be a sore hardship."

The driver took another healthy swig.

"Gor, but your feet are nearly longer than your legs," the driver said when he caught sight of the great black boots. "You'll be a rare tall one if your frame catches up with those feet, laddie."

The driver waxed philosophical as the miles slipped by beneath the coach wheels, commenting upon the ways of the gentry and how best to get around them. Brianna heard only half what the man said. She struggled with the reins until, her arms too tired to keep up their effort, she belatedly realized if she gave the pair their heads, they kept up a spanking pace and kept on the roadway too, without any need for human instruction.

Windsor Park's greensward stretched around the general's coach as it headed up the gravel drive to Windsor Castle itself, autumn still gentle to massed trees and late-blooming roses. The huge castle loomed ahead, stone terraces and towers edging the thick stone walls, banners floating in the wind, proclaiming the latest English victories.

"Look smart, me lad," the coachman said as he pocketed his flask and reached for the reins. "Those pennants are proclaiming your master's victories."

Brianna stiffened her back, her head still bent forward, as the carriage stopped.

"Get the step down." The coachman poked hard, and Brianna sailed off the side. She fell to the ground, her knees scraped as she landed on the gravel beside the coach. The coachman's aim was good—she was staring directly at the folded step. She pulled it down as the door above her head opened.

Lieutenant Morris tromped down onto the step and from there to the ground. He turned and waited for his commanding officer, giving the thin boy an idle glance that soon turned into shocked recognition. Samuel stared dumbfounded at his sister.

"Lieutenant?" the great Wellington queried as he stepped out and saw the young officer's expression. "Something amiss?"

"I—" Samuel wrenched his eyes from his sister. "I'm sorry, your lordship, what?"

"Is something amiss?"

Samuel stared at the nation's war hero. Lord Wellington was built on a heroic scale, of good height and broad body, with a regal nose and the face and curling locks of a Roman statue.

"Nothing, sir, sorry," Samuel replied. Resolutely, he turned on his well-polished heel, leaving his crouching sister behind and on her own as he followed the general toward the waiting royal footmen.

In the confusion of Lord Wellington's greeting, Brianna stole to the back of the coach. The side of Windsor's wide front terrace beckoned, and she raced for it, her feet chafed by the ill-fitting boots. She fell forward under the cover of the ancient stones, pulling herself as close as she could get to the wall and crawling forward, her heart in her throat. She inched her way around the building, stopping when she saw movement ahead.

Two men traversed the north terrace, one in a blue coat and a hat that flapped over his eyes in the wind. Thin and stoop-shouldered, the man moved rapidly, his long white hair blowing behind him, his arms flailing wide as he spoke, his words taken by the wind and thrust back behind him, unheard by the crouching Brianna.

His companion kept apace, his hands clasped behind his back, murmuring agreement now and then.

"Yes, Your Majesty," Brianna heard the younger of the two say as the men passed her hiding place, walking toward an open terrace door and disappearing inside.

Brianna had heard tell the mad old king kept to his chambers whilst the Prince of Wales ruled in his stead. She looked around, frantic to find somewhere to run and hide until her brother came out and she could explain. The only hope she could see was the open door through which the king and his keeper had just walked. The sound of royal guardsmen coming closer along the walkway decided her.

Gathering courage, Brianna got to her feet and, still crouched over, sped toward the open door, praying none were near. None were. Alone in the room, she swiftly surveyed it for a quiet nook in which to hide. It was a large and empty parlor, an open doorway gaping wide forty feet ahead. She made for the door but pulled up short, eyeing an endless expanse of corridor ahead. Red-uniformed men with black-plumed helmets stood in pairs at either end of the hallway, giants ready to defend the realm and its sovereign.

Brianna stood within the large parlor, casting about for a hiding place. Seeing a gilt door across the room, she opened it gingerly, listening for sounds of habitation. She heard nothing and ventured forward, slipping into the smaller parlor. A cozier world of bric-a-brac and narrow gilt petit-point-cushioned chairs met her wary eyes. The undertone of distant conversation hummed in the air as she moved with careful steps farther into the room, seeking anything she could use as sanctuary.

There was a surfeit of furniture in the small parlor, but every piece was spindly-legged and delicate, it would never hide her. The murmur of voices rose and fell. Brianna caught a hint of her brother's deep voice and stepped closer to the far wall.

"Yes, thank you, Morris. Now then, in that instance, your highness, the upstart was deployed along the ridge, as can be seen here."

"Ah, yes, yes, we see. Emmmm . . . Well, then, my dear

Wellington, have you determined your next course of action?"

"It depends upon the wily Jonathan's own movements, sire."

"Jonathan?" the regent queried, perplexed. "Who is this Jonathan?"

"I am sorry, your highness, I was speaking of Napoleon."

"Why do you call him Jonathan? It is not his name, is it?"

"No, sir. I have been pitted against him for a great many years, and I am afraid I have gotten into the habit of calling him a Jonathan Wild."

"Ah, yes. I see." The regent smiled. "Jonathan Wild. Very good, General, I like it."

Wellington prudently did not add that the full title he had given the upstart was Jonathan Wild the Great.

"The little colonel who crowned himself king and emperor. What a sad farce."

"Yes, your highness."

"The man is a madman, thinking a commoner may crown himself. Ridiculous. And he has wreaked havoc upon the civilized world. We must bring him to heel, Wellington."

"Yes, Your Highness."

"We count upon you to bring this usurper swiftly to justice. We said the very words to York and the others."

Hearing the regent refer to the men who had hamstrung his choice of staff at every turn rankled. "I could do much more for your highness's cause if I had more control over my men and our provisions."

"Yes, well, my brother York is determined to ensure that every item needed is procured."

"And every jot and tittle haggled over," Wellington said darkly.

The regent chose not to hear the great general's words. He continued in his bluff and friendly manner. "Now that you have the upstart on the run, it will not be long until the end. We always had faith in you."

"His ill-advised Russian campaign is more to be thanked than I. He helped our cause enormously by indulging in such folly."

"Enough modesty, General. Our generals have no need of it, they must be of firm mind and stout will."

"As you, yourself, would be, should you lead us in battle, your highness."

The regent's prodigious sigh carried through the wall to Brianna's ears. "If only we could spare ourself. We must admit it has been our secret desire to lead our own troops in battle, as our ancestors did in days of yore. But," he sighed again, "bearing as we do the heavy burdens of state, and with our father so gravely ill, we are not allowed to follow our heart, for fear of what would happen to our people."

"Nor would your subjects allow Your Highness to so endanger himself. They would be up in arms against such a course." And so, Wellington said to himself, would he. The thought of the overweight and petulant regent of England foisting himself onto the battlefield boggled the imagination.

"Our thoughts go with you," the regent was saying, "as you leave to join our troops and end the madman's rule."

Brianna listened to the regent's heavy movements as he stood up and bade Wellington Godspeed. The regent left the room as Wellington and Samuel collected their papers.

"Your lordship, if I may . . ." Samuel's words were fraught with misgivings, which his commanding officer heard.

"You've been looking squeamish all morning, Samuel. Out with it. What is wrong?"

"I mentioned a family matter—my young sister," Samuel said in gloomy accents.

"Go on."

"Yes, your lordship." Samuel's words began to tumble out over each other. "If you recall, I mentioned our housekeeper can no longer care for her. She must be transported to our guardian's estate in Sussex before I leave, since she has nowhere to stay."

Samuel's words sent icy daggers through Brianna's thumping heart.

"How long will this family business take?"

"No!" Brianna gasped, the word escaping her lips before she could stifle her surprise.

The two men in the next room turned toward the sound. "What . . . ?" General Lord Wellington was asking, but Samuel was already racing to the small door. He wrenched it open in time to see his sister dash through the far door to the hall.

Brianna careened outside and plunged into the startled arms of a very large man dressed in royal purple.

"What the devil?" Prinny exclaimed as what seemed a dirty young boy landed against his stomach, knocking his breath away.

"No," she cried out, as if he had attacked her. Tears blurring her vision, she pushed herself away from the man's soft belly and rushed past him down the corridor.

Prinny was totally nonplussed. He saw Samuel racing toward him. "Is it anarchists?" Prinny asked as Samuel raced past. Wellington came swiftly behind.

"Who *is* that urchin?" Prinny asked, but none stopped to answer.

"Guards!" Wellington shouted.

"Brianna," Samuel yelled.

Lord Wellington caught up with his aide, stopping the young man's reckless flight through the palace corridors. "Lieutenant!" Wellington spoke as royal guards raced past them. "What the devil is transpiring here? Do you know that urchin?"

"That urchin is my sister Brianna, your lordship."

"Great God," the great man exclaimed, his face a study in disbelief.

Brianna made it to the end of an intersecting corridor, ducking under the arm of one astonished royal guardsman and zigzagging around three others, into and out of parlors and antechambers. Behind her streamed an ever lengthening line of pursuers, most of whom were shouting for her to halt on the spot.

She made it to the west end of the long palace corridor before, guards in front and behind, she was caught between the legion of king's men. She fought off the first two who reached her, kicking one in the shins and biting the hand of the other, but she did not fare as well when three more launched themselves at her, two in front and one behind.

Brianna went down in a flurry of shouts and blows, her cap coming off in the process. Long red curls hit the face of one of her captors.

"What the bloody hell?" he exclaimed inelegantly.

"It's a *girl!*" another shouted.

"I don't care if it's the Queen of Sheba, hold onto her until we get to the bottom of this!" the captain of the guard shouted as Samuel arrived. They were hauling Brianna to her feet.

"I demand you let me go," she informed the shocked officer in imperious accents.

"You demand, you little baggage? And just who the devil are you to be demanding anything?"

Samuel reached for his sister. "I'll take her, Captain."

"I'm sorry, Lieutenant," the guardsmen said, "but I am charged with their highnesses' safety, and this one is headed for gaol."

"There is no danger to anyone's safety. Other than mine and her own," Samuel said grimly. "You are holding my sister, Miss Brianna Elizabeth Morris."

"Your—" The guardsman's shock was quickly stuffed back inside his mouth.

"You may release her, Officer," Wellington told the captain.

"Yes, your lordship." The captain saluted. "As you say, sir," he added with a gaze full of sympathy directed toward Samuel. "Is she loosed from Bedlam, Lieutenant?"

"No, but she may be headed toward it," Samuel threatened.

The moment the guard let go, Brianna ducked under her brother's arm. Before she could start away she was stopped, a man's hand grabbing the scruff of her neck, catching hold of her begrimed shirt and hauling her aloft.

"Morris!" Wellington thundered, holding the girl with her

toes dangling an inch off the floor. The general eyed the urchin, up one side and down the other, before raising his gaze to meet Samuel's.

With sinking heart, Brianna's brother faced England's war hero. "Yes, your lordship."

Wellington handed over the girl. "Take care of this *immediately*."

Lieutenant Morris swallowed. "Yes, sir."

"You are quite sure this is a female."

"I'm afraid so, your lordship."

Wellington shook his head. "Frightful," was his final comment upon the subject.

Once she was let down, Brianna stamped her foot and opened her mouth, prepared to defend herself. She found her brother's boot holding her foot down, his hand quickly wrapping around her open mouth. All that came out past his fingers were garbled sounds of struggle.

"Egad," the regent said from behind them. "Are there now female anarchists?"

"The modern world is undisciplined and lax-moraled, but we shall never sink as low as that, Your Highness," Wellington assured his ruler.

Prinny peered more closely at Brianna's blackened eyes. "You're quite sure it is female?"

"I'm not an it!" Brianna managed to get out before her brother's hand clamped harder across her mouth.

"Aye, she's female, Your Highness," Samuel answered. "She is also an undisciplined, ungrateful, irresponsible child! Your Highness," Samuel added in a quieter tone.

"Whyever did you bring her to Windsor?" Prinny asked.

"We did not bring her, your highness. Finding out how and why she came is the very first course I am determined to pursue."

"The second, one would hope, is to find her proper attire. If you're sure she is of the feminine gender," Prinny repeated doubtfully.

"That I will, Your Highness," Samuel said grimly. "As soon as I've delivered her into the hands of our guardian."

"Is he a strong man?"

"He is a distant cousin of our late mother's."

The regent looked dubious. "We wish him luck of her," he said before he walked away, surrounded by his guards.

Brianna attempted to object, but her words could not get past her brother's firm hand. Before she knew what was happening, she was hauled out of Windsor Castle and thrust, headfirst, into a waiting carriage. She tried to scramble out the other side, only to be stopped by guardsmen already prepared for her attempt.

"I shan't stay with any old guardian, I shall run away the moment you are gone," she told her brother. "You cannot abandon me to such a fate!"

"It is a better fate than being sent to prison," Samuel replied grimly.

General Lord Wellington spoke as he shut the carriage door. "We leave at first light, I cannot give you more time than that."

"I'll be back in time, your lordship, thank you."

The door closed with the resounding sound of a gaol to Brianna's ears.

"You can't do this," she sobbed as her brother rapped on the roof, giving the order to start out.

Samuel glared at his sister. "You have disgraced us both. Must you make this worse by your interminable bawling?"

Brianna brought her fist to her mouth, trying to quell her sobs. "You hate me."

"Most excessively," Samuel agreed. He saw her eyes slide toward the nearest door. "If you make one move toward that door, I shall have you tied and chained."

"You never would!"

Visions of his career in tatters hardened Samuel's words as he stared at his recalcitrant sister. "Don't tempt me," he said in brutal accents.

Brianna sensed the depth of her brother's anger and fell back against the thick carriage squabs, turning her head away from his relentless gaze and closing her eyes. One day he would be sorry of his perfidy, she told herself. Exhausted from the early morning ride to London and all that had transpired since, quiet tears slipped down her cheeks.

As the miles clip-clopped away beneath the carriage, Brianna fell into an uneasy sleep, and her brother worried about the interview ahead.

Chapter Four

At Ashford Hall, deep in the wilds of Sussex, a dreary afternoon had turned into blackest night. A steady rain beat against the windows and thick stone walls, obscuring the countryside and the faraway stars.

A lively fire warmed the duke's study, the masculine room filled with well-worn books and hunting dogs. The books inhabited floor-to-ceiling bookcases, the dogs lay in front of the fireplace, dozing at their master's feet.

A mantel clock struck eight P.M. in the quiet room. One of the spaniels lifted its head, sniffed toward the door and then laid its head back on its paws. The master's study was at the rear of the huge Stuart house, and so Andrew Ormsby did not hear the coach pull up the drive.

He was reading the weekly post from London when a loud pounding intruded on his thoughts. He looked up, one of the dogs beginning to bark.

"Quiet, Daisy." She quieted until a loud thud brought her master to his feet. "What the devil!" He strode to the door, trailing three barking dogs.

Daisy, Rowdy, and Byron raced down the hall ahead of their master, jumping up at the stranger, their barks blending with high-pitched screams and the shouted conversation of two men, one of whom was Harding, the duke's estate manager. The other was a stranger dressed in a rumpled uniform and carrying what seemed to be a squirming, screaming, dripping, and decidedly filthy urchin.

"I can't hear you!" Harding shouted over the dogs' yaps, the urchin's screams, and the noise of the storm.

"Quiet!" the Duke of Ashford commanded.

Harding turned toward his master, the dogs subsiding into whines as the young rain-soaked soldier in the open doorway stared at the tall and obviously angry nobleman. Even the baggage slung over his shoulder was quiet for a brief instant.

"What is the meaning of this?" the duke asked in angry accents as the noise began anew. Daisy barked, jumping at the loud package that wiggled and squirmed and demanded to be let down.

"Let me down this instant or I'll never speak to you again, Samuel Morris!" Brianna shouted, nearly deafening her brother's left ear.

"Enough!" the duke roared, sending the dogs scurrying away.

"I'm terribly sorry, sir," Harding said in the sudden lull. "I can make neither heads nor tails of what the man says, with all the noise."

The duke glared at the soldier. Rain was gusting in through the open doorway and dripping from the young man and his burden.

"Who are you and *what* is that?" the Duke of Ashford demanded.

"I've come to speak to the duke on a very private family matter," Samuel said.

"Private! With this noise? Family, did you say? Whose family?" Ashford demanded.

"I must speak to the duke," Samuel insisted.

"You *are* speaking to him!"

"He says his name is Lieutenant Morris, your grace," Harding interjected as Samuel looked, dumbfounded, at the nonpareil before him.

"You are our guardian?"

"Guardian? I've never clapped eyes on you before this moment!"

"I'm Samuel, your grace. Mary Morris's son," he added desperately. "My grandmother and your mother were cousins, I believe, and this is my sister, Brianna. I—I expected you to be older."

The duke stared at the uniformed young man as if he were demented. He perused the grimy backside the soldier carried.

"Who told you such a confounded thing as that?"

"I applied this afternoon to your solicitors, and they said you could not travel to London."

The sixth duke grimaced. "Which is the truth, but hardly because I am too ill or too old, as can plainly be seen. Did you say that baggage is your *sister?*"

The sister in question was beating her fists against her brother's back and yelling to be let down. "I won't stay with any miserable old duke! I won't, I won't, I won't!"

"Could you possibly manage to quiet your sister long enough for us to have an intelligible conversation?"

"I'm not quite sure how to do so, your grace," the young man replied.

"Improvise," he was told.

"Brianna, please—" Samuel began.

"Let me down!"

"Let her down," the duke echoed.

Against his better judgment, Lieutenant Morris released his sister. The moment her feet hit the floor she took off down the hall. The dogs gave chase, yapping and barking.

"Harding, take care of it," Ashford said.

"Yes, your grace," Harding said in doleful accents.

Samuel watched the man take off after Brianna. "Perhaps I should help," Samuel offered worriedly.

"Harding will take care of it. Where does she think she is headed?" the duke asked.

"I would venture to say . . . away . . ." Samuel answered hesitantly.

"Thank you, Lieutenant, for that enlightening reply," Ashford said dryly. "People usually meet me before they flee my presence."

"I must apologize for our precipitous arrival, your grace. And for my sister's bad manners."

"I imagine you are forced to do a prodigious amount of apologizing for that relative. You and I shall continue this interview in my study, where it is quieter."

"I really ought to try to help your man."

"First you will explain your presence here. She'll go nowhere in this storm. If she does, she'll either die or drown, neither of which seems as dire a consequence as her continuing to shriek at the top of her lungs. The land for miles in all directions is mine, so she shall be found one way or another." The duke led the way to his study and rang for the butler. He poured himself a medicinal dose of an excellent port his grandfather had laid down, and after a moment's reflection poured an additional glass for the young soldier.

"I'm afraid my stay must be brief," Samuel told the duke.

"Please, do not apologize. I look forward to your departure, young man, straight upon your explaining your arrival."

"I had been informed that you were named in our parents' will as our guardian," Samuel said, as he had in the hall.

"Your guardian," the duke repeated as his butler entered. "Ah, Twinforth, there you are. Please inform anyone whose ears have not already apprised them—we have somewhere in our house the presence of a slight problem. It is a ragamuffin banshee, purported to be both female and human. Please see that it is caught and brought to me, bound and gagged if necessary."

"Yes, your grace," Twinforth replied. He did not by so much as a flicker of an eyelid deign to recognize any impropriety in the request.

As Twinforth left, the duke handed the glass of ruby port to the lieutenant.

"I take it that graceless hoyden also purports to be part of my family."

"Your mother's family, your grace."

45

Ashford shook his head. "Thank God she is not here to see what her relatives have spawned."

Samuel looked anything but happy at the duke's words. "I take it your mother is not in residence."

"Here? Good Lord," was the duke's reply.

With sinking heart Samuel continued. "You are not by any chance married, are you?"

"I beg your pardon?"

"No," Samuel said, further confounding his host. "I was afraid you weren't. That complicates things miserably. And you not even knowing of our existence . . ."

The duke's penetrating blue eyes regarded his confused and confusing young relation. "My dear boy, having never before clapped eyes upon you, I have no knowledge of whether all this noise and confusion is normal behavior in your household, but I must assure you it most decidedly is not in mine. Arriving uninvited and unannounced, late of an evening, with an insane relative slung over your shoulder, is, to put it quite bluntly, beyond the pale. It is simply not done. I live a quiet life, I hope I am making myself clear? The next time you choose to visit, if you do so choose, I expect proper advance notice and an entirely unexceptional entrance."

Samuel gulped down the port. "Yes, your grace," he said nervously.

"Good. Now, why have you come?"

"To leave my sister with you."

Rain poured down outside. The fire crackled in the grate. Distant sounds of pursuit, and the clicking of the spaniels' nails nearer by, came toward the two silent men.

"You expect to leave your sister," the duke said in a strangled tone. "With me."

"I thought you knew you were named our guardian."

It took Andrew a moment and a fortifying swallow of port before he could reply. "I was aware of a technicality, that is to say, my solicitors were informed years ago that my father had agreed to such a provision, and I accepted his duties upon his death. Years ago," he emphasized. "And never a word from your parents since. Surely you cannot mean to deposit this undisciplined hoyden upon my threshold and depart."

"I'm afraid that's very much what I do mean to do. Your grace," Samuel added belatedly.

"But you cannot!"

"We are forced upon your mercy," the young officer said dramatically.

"Upon my *mercy?* You do not even know if I possess such a virtue. I would as lief clasp a viper to my bosom!"

"I would never willingly have descended upon you in such a ham-handed fashion, but things have quickly come to an impossible head, and I must depart with General Lord Wellington for the Continent at daybreak. I am left no choice in the matter," the lieutenant defended.

"Of course there is a choice," the duke replied loudly. "There is always a choice. You must continue to do whatever it is you have been doing with her."

"Such is no longer possible."

"You cannot leave a child of—of whatever age, upon my doorstep."

Samuel almost told Brianna's true age, but thoughts of Hobby's admonitions were loud in his ears. A young woman couldn't live alone with a single man without forever ruining her reputation. "I don't suppose you have a sister?"

The Duke of Ashford stared at the young soldier. "I beg your pardon?"

"An aunt or some other female relation living with you?"

"No. Why do you ask?" The duke scowled. "How old is the chit?"

Samuel swallowed. "A mere child," he temporized.

"How mere a child?"

"Brianna is, ah, fourteen, your grace. And young for her age," he added.

Their conversation was interrupted by the arrival of Harding. Behind him Twinforth, and Dennis, the head stableman, hauled Samuel's furious young sister into the study kicking and screaming.

"Your—guest, your grace," Twinforth announced calmly, if loudly, over her noise.

The duke came toward the girl, glowering fiercely. Brianna saw he was as old as she had been told. He was at least thirty, his face set into ugly menacing lines.

"I won't stay with this ogre, I won't, I won't!"

"Good," the large man said coldly. "Now, on that singular note of agreement, are you prepared to silence your flapping tongue, or shall I have you locked away where none can hear you until the conclusion of my interview with your brother?"

"You wouldn't dare!" she told the aged ogre in front of her.

"Do not tempt me," came the warning reply. The duke looked toward Harding. "Take the urchin away until I ring."

"I'm not an urchin!"

"Again we agree, and I stand corrected, Miss Morris. Urchin is far too kind a term for what you are."

"Where shall I take her, your grace?" Harding asked.

"I have no idea. Find a place," the duke snapped.

Brianna looked defiant and more than a touch triumphant when Harding departed. Her triumph was short-lived as he returned, scant moments later, the housekeeper in his wake. The young girl took one look at Mrs. Potts and knew she had met her match.

"Ah, Mrs. Potts," the duke said as Brianna again tried to bolt. Samuel grabbed for his sister, but it was the duke who caught the seat of her oversized breeches and hauled her back.

"How dare you," Brianna demanded. "Unhand me!"

"If you are not extremely careful, I shall give your backside the melting it so richly deserves," the duke replied. He handed her over to the redoubtable Mrs. Potts.

"Clean her up and find her something decent to wear while she awaits. She seems to be a relative of sorts."

"Yes, your grace." Mrs. Potts's firm hand held the girl fast as Brianna tried to twist away. Unlike the men, she did not let go. Brianna wrenched her arm, nearly pulling it out of its socket.

"Owww, you've broken my arm!"

"Not I, but yourself, young miss. Best stop before you hurt yourself, dearie," the housekeeper said with unshaken placidity. "Where do you wish me to take her, your grace?"

"Don't ask." He scowled at the child. "Clean her up and lock her in somewhere until I send for her."

"I'll not be ordered about," Brianna declared. She looked toward her brother for help but found Samuel being discreetly silent.

"If she gives trouble, haul her down to the dungeons! I don't want to hear her noise."

Since the house boasted no dungeons, his threat was useless, but Brianna did not know this small fact and so was cowed enough to allow her captors to propel her forward. Vowing never to speak to her brother again, vowing to run away at first opportunity, she went with sulky face and nasty disposition upward through the huge house.

An hour later Samuel had consumed two more glasses of port and explained the entire situation to his distant cousin. The duke was not best pleased, but he could see no way around the duty his father had agreed to long years ago when it seemed the most unlikely of circumstances that his wife's young cousin would predecease him.

"Lord Wellington is awaiting my arrival, your grace. We set off immediately for the Continent," Samuel repeated for the seventh time in the clipped conversation. "I must be off," he finished. "Please tell my sister that I shall write and beg her forgiveness."

"Her forgiveness?"

"I feel it might be best if I don't go up. . . . I wouldn't want to disturb her further."

The duke glared at the soldier. "You, sir, have walked into my home and cut up all my peace and quiet. Let's not put too fine a point on it—you are afraid to face that shockingly undisciplined child."

"Yes, sir, that too." Lieutenant Morris backed toward the hall door. "She will be ever so much better when she's had a chance to calm down and reflect upon her situation."

"Go, go," Ashford told his young relative in peeved tones. "But I cannot guarantee your sister will be alive when you return."

Samuel Morris beat a swift retreat before the duke could change his mind. He hauled the general's driver from a warm nook on the side porch and jumped up beside him, handling the ribbons himself and traveling post haste through the pouring rain. The driver grabbed for his flask and held onto his swaying seat as Samuel negotiated the long Ashford drive, the way lit only by the wildly swaying coach lights.

"Is the devil himself after us, Lieutenant?" the driver managed to ask.

"Aye, and the devil to pay if we're late to the boat!"

Inside the sixty-room mansion Harding tiptoed back into the duke's presence, waiting quietly at the door until his employer looked up.

"Yes?" Andrew scowled.

"Your grace, what are we to do with her?"

"How the devil should I know?"

Totally unenlightened, Harding turned around, the duke's next words greeting his steward's back.

"Inform Mrs. Potts the little baggage is to get no food until she stops caterwauling and asks for it quietly. Damn and blast!" he bellowed, irritated past endurance. "I suppose we shall now have to advertise for a tutor for the wench, although I'm damned if I know what bloody good it will do. She's a little heathen, and she'll probably be the death of us all before that rapscallion brother returns!"

"Yes, your grace," Harding said feelingly.

The duke threw his paper aside and thrust himself to his feet, stomping out past Harding and down the wide front hall of his ancient family home. He climbed the curving main stairs, grousing about relatives that have impossible children and then have the bad grace to die young, leaving the raising of the little monsters to men who have better things to do than play nursemaid.

"At least I have not yet inflicted any brats on the rest of

humanity!" the duke thundered when he reached the master's suite sitting room.

"Your grace?" His valet, James, came out from an adjoining room. "Did you call?" he asked calmly.

"Listen to that," the duke demanded, "do you hear that uproar?"

"Yours, your grace, or the girl's?"

"Hers," the duke fairly shouted as he thrust an arm heavenward. Thumps and bumps came from the floor above. "What *is* that noise? Find out what is happening up there!"

James left, to return five minutes later. The duke had already divested himself of his coat, waistcoat, fobs, and watch. He was wearing only his ruffled white shirt, doeskin breeches, and tall boots.

"It would seem your young guest is throwing about everything that is not nailed down," James told his master.

"That is the outside of enough," the duke declared. He strode out to the hall and up to the next floor in his shirt-sleeves.

James trailed after his master as he made his way to the third-floor nursery. "She's got good lungs," was James's opinion. "It must be a family trait. Reminds me of you when you were young," Andrew was told.

The duke ignored his valet's words. "Mrs. Potts, unlock the door!"

The housekeeper did as the duke bid, starting in after him, only to be thrust back outside. She questioned the valet with her eyes on one side of the door whilst inside she heard the duke relock the door. Brianna watched as he pocketed the heavy iron key and turned around to face his unwelcome charge. She backed away from him.

"I'll scream—"

"Scream all you like," he replied. "Scream until you're too hoarse to croak."

"I'll—I'll—" She backed up until her back was against the windows. "Don't you dare!" she cried.

"Your grace?" Mrs. Potts's worried voice was muffled by the door.

"Go away," he replied.

Brianna saw the angry man's expression. "If you murder me, they'll hang you!"

"It will be worth it," she was told.

The duke stared at the defiant and dirty little face that glared up from just below his shoulder level. She now wore a plain white borrowed shift much too big for her. The thin muslin chemise was covered with a blue wool shawl that belonged to Mrs. Potts's own wardrobe, but the duke was not aware of its pedigree. As he watched the girl, she gulped, her little chin beginning to quiver. Her stormy green eyes glittered with liquid that started to spill down her pale cheeks.

"I—I want my bro—my broth—" she hiccuped, and suddenly she was sobbing. "I want my brother!"

Andrew Ormsby looked down at the little chit, vastly uncomfortable. His anger gave way to irritation mixed with pity; she obviously did not want to stay, any more than he wanted her there.

"I don't blame you for crying," he said in a conciliatory tone.

"I'm not crying," she cried out between sobs. "I have something in my eyes!"

The duke fought a smile. The child had pride, he gave her that. "In both eyes too," he agreed. "That can be most serious. But you must understand," he said awkwardly, "I've no experience dealing with children, so you must help me out."

"I'm not a child!"

"Then why are you acting like one?" he asked quietly.

Her pride nettled, she took prodigious great gulps of air, trying to stop her tears.

He handed over a handkerchief. "For the something in your eyes," he said diplomatically.

She reached for it and wiped her eyes, her thin little shoulders still rising and falling with her gulps of air. When she handed the lace-edged linen back, he was amazed to find it clean.

"Here, let me get that dirt off. Mrs. Potts was supposed to clean you up—"

"She did," Brianna said sourly.

"Why did you not let them wash your face?" he demanded.

"My face is clean!"

He reached for her chin, tipping her head back before she could stop him. "Your face is black with—good grief, what is it?"

Brianna tried to turn away.

"You have two black eyes." The Duke of Ashford was positively dumbfounded.

"I know, and that dirty Ned Finch has a split lip, and he'll never call me a pasty-faced girl, nor will any others unless they want to get theirs too!"

"Incredible," Andrew murmured.

She stared up at her captor. "Sammy's gone, isn't he?"

"If you are referring to your brother, the answer is yes. He said he would write."

"You don't want me here." Suddenly she looked like what she was. A very tired, very frightened, little girl. "Nobody wants me."

"Here, now," Andrew interrupted, afraid more tears would soon spill. "That's no way to talk."

"It's true. Hobby got herself engaged to marry that old Jed Stout and all his brats and Sammy won't take me with him to war and the regent wouldn't even let me hide long enough to escape and the general nearly threw me in the carriage and sent me here, and you don't want me either."

". . . You seem to have led a rather colorful life for your young years. As for going to war, your brother had no choice on that head."

"I'd make a better soldier than any of them!"

"Miss Morris, I am prepared to swear that you are perfectly capable of single-handedly bringing Napoleon to his doom. However, we have not yet sunk so low as to send our girl-children off to do men's battles." Brianna watched him turn away. When she realized he was headed for the door, she ran past him, blocking his progress. "What now? More fisticuffs?" he demanded.

"No, sir," Brianna said meekly, changing tactics. "I'm sorry if I upset you."

The duke frowned. "What's this?"

Brianna looked up at him with wide innocent eyes. "You see, I have been kidnapped, sir."

"Kidnapped."

She thought fast. "In truth, I am a Gypsy child, stolen from my people at birth, and if only you will find it in your heart to free me, I shall go back to them."

"I see," the duke replied. "That seems a capital plan."

"It does?"

"Absolutely. But I'll not have it said any are ill-treated in my household. Can't have Gypsies spreading bad character about me, now can I? You'll get farther if you start in the morning with a hot meal and a good night's sleep behind you. I misdoubt you can want to walk from Sussex to Kent in this night's weather."

Brianna's eyes glowed with newfound hope. "You'll let me go?"

"Of course," he replied easily, his hand on the door latch. "In fact, I shall do better than that. I shall find your Gypsy parents and bring them here to claim you."

"Oh no! That is, you—you cannot do that. You'll not be able to find them."

"Of course I shall," the duke informed the girl. "I have all the means at my disposal to do anything I wish, including dealing with a troublesome fourteen-year-old. If I cannot find your people, how then could you?"

"Fourteen?" she asked as Mrs. Potts rapped on the door.

"I've a bit of sustenance for the child," the housekeeper said, bringing the duke to unlock the door. She bustled in with a tray of steaming hot chocolate and buns as the duke left.

"There now, I've brought you some sweets. Your throat must be ever so parched and painful after all the yelling."

Brianna wanted to ignore the woman and her offering, but

the nursery was cold and the smell of the rich hot chocolate invaded her nostrils and made her mouth water. Her throat *was* dry and she was ever so hungry.

"There's hot cross buns, and a bit of fresh bread and cheese too," Mrs. Potts added. "Just in case you feel the need to keep your strength up. Nellie, come here," she called to the doorway, and after a minute a shy-faced young maid peeked into the long unused nursery.

"Yes, ma'am?"

"Come in. It's all right, Miss Brianna won't bite, now will you, dearie? This is Nellie, and she's brought a dress that's near your size. We need to measure you, so we can find something decent for you to wear. You mustn't be entertaining gentlemen in your shift, no matter they're old enough to be your father. Did you make the bed up?" Mrs. Potts asked Nellie.

"Yes, ma'am."

"And put the hot brick inside the sheets?"

"Yes, ma'am."

"Good. We don't want our young guest to catch cold after all this running about in damp clothing, now do we?"

Mrs. Potts fussed over Brianna, the young girl responding to the womanly kindness. She yawned as she let them lead her into the bedroom off the nursery.

Still determined to make good her escape, Brianna let them try on the plain blue gown, suffering their nips and tucks and pins and comments. When at last they were done and she slipped between the toasty sheets, she gave a contented little sigh. Mrs. Potts pulled the covers up around Brianna's shoulders, the girl's eyes closing no matter how hard she tried to keep them open. Mrs. Potts picked up the blue gown and told Nellie to check the fire and put out the bedside lamp before she left.

Nellie worked across the room, putting more coal in the grate. When she was done, she wiped her hands on her apron and tiptoed nearer the bed. "I'll put out the lamp, shall I?"

"Yes," Brianna said sleepily.

"You must do as he says, miss."

". . . What?"

"You must do as he bids," Nellie said urgently. "Me dad has worked for his grace for ever so long, and he'll tell you, you must not cross him or you'll be fearfully sorry. He's got a fearful temper as can make great men quake in their boots for fear of upsetting him. Ferocious he is, miss, so you'd best have a care."

Brianna twisted away, her back to the young maid. Nellie turned the wick down and scurried across the shadowy room to the hall door, scraping the key in the lock. Behind her the young newcomer closed her eyes, promising herself she would rest for just a few minutes before finding a way to escape.

Tears filled her eyes, spilling down her cheeks as she lay alone in the strange and lonely room. She had cried herself to sleep almost every night for all the long, lonely years since her mother died, but tonight the pain was a fresh wound. She was alone, her parents gone to heaven, her very own brother leaving her behind, even her faithful Hobby running off with Jed Stout and his fat children.

Everyone had left her. But she would show them all. She would run away and join the army or perhaps a wild Gypsy band, as she fibbed to the old duke earlier. Or stow away to the South Seas and become the first female pirate.

Her arms hugging her pillow close, she drifted off to sleep, lulled by the steady rain to dreams of sailing ships and gold doubloons and Black Bree, the terror of the seas.

Chapter Five

An enormous thunderclap woke Brianna, the rain slamming against the windows and pouring down the walls in torrential streams. Deep night held sway; only the sputtering grate was alive in the darkness. Brianna lay still, listening to the storm as it slowly lessened. She turned over in her bed, her eyes going sleepily to her window. It wasn't there.

The young girl's eyes flew open. Panicked, she sat up in the strange bed, staring around herself until she remembered where she was and why. There was a window on the opposite wall, and outside, the rain pattered softly now, the storm's worst dying away.

The duke said he would let her go tomorrow, but adults could never be trusted to keep their word. Even Hobby, who had sworn to stay with Brianna forever when her mother died, had deserted her word. If she could not trust her own dear Hobby, how could she trust an elderly relative she'd never met before this night?

Samuel would sail in the morning. If she could reach her brother's ship and stow away, if they did not find her until they were far, far away, they would have to let her stay and fight. All she had to do was steal away from the house, find her way back to the London road, and then beg her way onto a passing coach. She could tell them a perfectly heart-rending tale of needing to reach her sick grandmother, then find her way to the harbor, where any there would know which ship would carry the great Lord Wellington's party.

The more she thought on it, the more convinced she became that her only course was to force her brother to take her with him. Women went with the army. She'd heard tell of women camp followers; Old John had said that's what she would be if she went off to war with the lads. Anything another female could do, she could do. Just because she was a mite younger did not mean she could not best them all.

The chill night air dampened her enthusiasm a bit, but she resolutely pulled the sheet off the bed. Folding it, she covered her head and bare shoulders, letting it drape down around her chemise. She tied the blue shawl tight around her shoulders and back around her waist to keep her makeshift hooded garment in place. She had gotten up from a sickbed, she would tell whatever coach she flagged down, and they would be ever so anxious to help a poor waif return to her family. Fortified with this vision, she started out.

Her first disappointment was that the door to the hall was locked. She tried the connecting door to the nursery schoolroom. It opened. As she crossed the floor her bare feet chilled. She would have to find her boots. Crossing her fingers behind her back, she reached for the hall door and tested the brass handle. It creaked. She froze. She heard nothing except her pounding heart. The door fell open. Then her eyes befell her second disappointment.

A young footman was stationed outside the door, a pallet laid on the floor for his comfort. He was sitting with his back against the wall, his head bent forward. His chin to his chest, booted feet stretched to the opposite wall, he dozed, blocking Brianna's exit. She hesitated, about to step over him, when he stirred and mumbled something incoherent. She jumped back, shoving the door closed. It banged shut. She stood perfectly still, hearing his movement outside and then someone else coming near.

"Ronnie, watch what you're about, making such noise at this hour." An older man spoke.

"I didn't make no noise," he defended.

"And didn't I hear your bloody great boots fall to the floor? Have a care what you're about lad. I'll spell you a bit if you want to relieve yourself or shake out your upper works."

Brianna backed away from the door, standing in the middle of the room and thinking hard. Her eyes went to the window. It was a very long way down to the ground. The rain pattered softly when she opened the window and leaned out to get a better look. There were fluted edges and carved curlicues that could give her feet purchase. It was also cold and wet. Brianna looked out over the window ledge and back at the warm bed. She hesitated and almost turned back.

The thought of her brother fighting the horrible monster Napoleon stiffened her resolve. If she were not there to keep him safe, he might die and she would be all alone in the world, with none to care. This old duke didn't want her, he would ship her off to the foundlings' home or the poorhouse the first time she displeased him. And, glumly, Brianna admitted to herself that displeasing people seemed her very own particular talent.

There was nothing for it. Go, she must. She stepped out onto the ledge that ran beneath the windows and crouched down to grab hold of the molding before she could change her mind. The stone ledge was slippery, her legs hampered by the chemise and the sheet she wore. She reached back up for the window ledge, straightening up on the foot-and-a-half-wide ledge. Grabbing the loose ends of the sheet, she tied two ends together around each leg, the chemise bunched up inside her makeshift pantaloons.

Moving carefully, she hunkered down, her hands grabbing the molding as she slipped one bare foot off the ledge and dangled it down, rubbing it along the fluted corbel, feeling for a safe place to wedge her foot. She found a niche and then closed her eyes, letting her other foot over the edge and down. Nicking her shin, she found another niche and then another, scooting down, her hands reaching for the next lower bit of molding, her feet squirming one at a time down the fluted corbel.

Ten minutes later there was nothing beneath her feet. She felt around with her right foot, her eyes useless. The stone corbel ended two and a half stories above the ground, her foot swinging inward to find only smooth stone facing. Her arms aching, she gritted her teeth. A soldier never gave up, she told herself. She brought her foot back to its niche, placed more of her weight on her two feet, and leaned her head enough to look upward.

Raindrops fell into her eyes. It was over twelve feet back up to the ledge, and once she reached it, she would have to have the arm strength to heave herself up on it. She took a deep breath and hugged the corbel hard, reaching out with her left foot to test the wall. A ledge met her foot. Narrow, six inches at most, but a ledge. She brought her foot back, held on tight and slowly inched her left hand out. Her hand found a six-inch depression in the wall. It was a window, she was sure of it, a window almost as tall as she.

Leaning as far as she could while still holding onto the molding, Brianna found a bit of worn mortar between two of the mansion's huge thick stones and angled her fingers around it, holding on for dear life. Saying a silent prayer, she let go with her right hand and reached to grab the left-side molding. Her equilibrium in danger, she swung her left foot onto the ledge and then, her body in an X shape between the ledge and the stone corbel, she let go with her left hand and searched across the glass to the frame, to the other side, to anything she could grasp.

She found nothing and was about to panic when she felt the window give way. It came open and nearly sent her reeling. She grabbed for purchase, her hand catching the inside of the window frame and hanging on for dear life. Her heart in her throat, Brianna pushed hard, shoved herself away from the stone corbel and around the near edge of the open window frame, her right foot following her left. Her balance lost, she fell forward into the dark room and landed on something soft, only a foot or two beneath the bottom of the four-foot-square window.

It was a huge bed, the comforter she landed on nearly swallowing her in its thick folds. The room was warm and silent. Her heart still stuttering, she lay still for long moments, trying to gather up strength. She had to quit this room, she had to race to London before her brother left. But she was so very tired. The cloth that covered her was soaked and clinging miserably against her skin, making her shiver. Wet and cold, she couldn't move freely. She tried to kick off the offending weight but it wouldn't budge.

Tired, Brianna reached to untie the makeshift pantaloons

and the wet blue scarf. The smell of the wet wool curled her nose, and she cast it over the side of the four-poster bed. The clinging wet sheet went next, the oversized chemise last.

Exhausted, wet, miserable, and naked, Brianna moved under the thick warm comforter, her dripping hair splayed out across a pristine white pillow. Her brain foggy with sleep, she realized the bed and the room were warm. Warm meant human habitation.

In all the scores of bedrooms in the huge house, there could only be a very few that were inhabited. In point of fact, she had seen only the duke and his staff. Nary another family member. Perhaps the others were already abed when she came, she reasoned sleepily. Perhaps she could enlist the aid of his wife or sisters or whomever in the morning.

Brianna snuggled up against the thick pillows and drifted off to sleep dreaming of lovely ladies who looked exactly like her mother and who would rescue her from all harm.

". . . It is not the odious duke, my dearest Brianna, who is your relative, it is I, the friend of your mother's bosom, who am related to you and that dastardly brother of yours who left you in my husband's evil clutches. How very brave of you to jump off the roof and go in search of your brother. Just the thing your mother would have done."

Her dreams comforted the sad-hearted child in the huge bed. She stretched out in her sleep, one small hand flung down toward the floor, the other arm up around her pillow and then stretched wider as, in her sleep, she greeted her subjects.

"The king has come to his senses and proclaimed you the bravest lass in all Christendom, Brianna Elizabeth Morris, bravest since the Great Elizabeth led our armies into battle. You have led us into victorious battle alongside the great Lord Wellington and his able aide, your brother, unlike our poor stay-at-home regent . . ."

All looked toward the defeated and sorry-faced dumpling of a man who, with woebegone expression and clenched fist to his forehead, did proclaim his perfidy.

". . . If only I had been kind to the waif," he said with tearful eyes. "I thought her an anarchist, and female to boot!

How could I know she would lead our great country to victory over the French . . .?"

Brianna turned in her sleep, her arm falling to the regent's snoring shoulders. Shoulders do not snore, she informed the regent. Turning, he mumbled in his sleep, Brianna's hand sliding from his shoulder to his hairy chest.

"I did not know rulers snored," Brianna Elizabeth informed her people. They cheered her anyway.

"There are things I do not know," she told her fellow countrymen. "Not important ones," she hastened to assure them, "but nevertheless, there are those odd bits of information that I am still learning. When you elect a sovereign who is a scant fifteen, even if she has saved the country from the horrible Napoleon, you must expect a bit of discombobblement before all is set aright again."

They cheered and the regent snored.

"Enough," Brianna Elizabeth commanded.

Andrew Ormsby was used to feeling naked female flesh against his own. Never wearing nightclothes, he discouraged his sleeping partners from entangling themselves in the masses of attire each had to wear when awake. Asleep, his long well-muscled arm found his restless sleeping partner and imprisoned her, falling across her chest, its weight keeping her quiet until dawn.

During the stormy night a sleepy James awoke and left his bed in his narrow room next to his master's. Shivering at the drafts of cold night air, he found his way across the huge master bedroom, to find one of the two large windows open. He pulled it closed, latched it, closed the drapes, and stumbled to the fireplace, where he heaved a fresh log atop those already smoldering in the grate and prodded them all until the fire blazed bright. The valet saw his work catch hold and left, asleep almost before he hit his pillow.

The temperature in the master's chamber slowly warmed, the thick goose-down comforter warmer and warmer with each passing quarter hour, until it was much too hot for the sleeping duke and the girl who unwittingly shared his bed. In his sleep the duke thrust it aside, a double thickness landing on top of the unsuspected and unsuspecting Brianna. Brianna herself squirmed under the heavy covers, trying to push them off.

His sleep disturbed by movement beneath his arm, Andrew came half awake. He yawned, opened an eye toward the dawning light outside, and saw a young girl lying beneath his arm. His eyes opened wide, shock chasing all hope of sleep away. The Duke of Ashford was accustomed to the warmth and comfort of well-experienced and willing female flesh beside him in the night, but the sight of a girl-child naked in his bed left him stunned. He stared at the bedside table, looking at the full decanters of water and brandy, racking his memory for an answer as to how the child had arrived in his bed.

While he worried, he moved. Exiting the bed, he reached for his satin-trimmed night robe, wrapping it around his tall, lean frame as he moved. He stood near his bed, staring down at the chit of a sleeping girl.

Upstairs, Mrs. Potts opened the door to the nursery bedroom, worried about the wee girl who had fought so valiantly until she succumbed to fear and exhaustion. She was a rare one, Mrs. Potts had told Cook before she ventured above-stairs; she could have been a chip off the master's own block if he'd married and had a girl-child of his own. When she found the nursery bed empty, Mrs. Potts sounded the alarm, albeit a quiet one since the duke had not yet called for his morning tea. When he did, he would have to be told of her disappearance.

It was decided James was the logical bearer of sad tidings, and the staff waited for the valet to come below-stairs. It was nearly quarter past seven when he stumbled, sleepy-eyed, down to the kitchens for a cup of strong tea.

"Perhaps, it's for the best," he opined when he heard of the girl's disappearance. "His grace is not the man to raise children. Although I fear he will be most displeased at a guest going lost. He does so like an orderly house."

James went up the servants' stairs, carrying his master's morning tray of strong tea and hard biscuits. He entered the master suite sitting room and stopped to tap on the bed-chamber door before he opened it and went inside. The duke was not a morning person. Six mornings out of seven he had to be roused from his bed.

"Good morning, your grace," James said in a cheery voice. He placed the breakfast tray on a bedside table and made his way to the windows. Thrusting open the drapes, he turned toward his master's bed. "It's past seven and I'm sorry to tell you but the girl's gone missing, your grace, I don't know—" The valet's words strangled in his throat. The girl lay atop the master's bed, and from what he could see of her bare arms and back, she was stark naked.

Andrew Henry Arthur Ormsby, sixth Duke of Ashford, spoke from a wing chair in the morning shadows across the room. His valet jumped at the sound of his voice.

"She has thrown off her blankets each time I have covered her." The valet turned toward the sound of his employer's voice, his relief writ large across his plain features. The duke sat beside the cold fireplace, bare legs peeking out beneath his robe. "You'd best cover her again before you wake her," Andrew told his man.

The valet did as he was bid, averting his eyes as he covered the girl. "Mrs. Potts reported the girl missing."

"Is that my tea?" the duke questioned, bringing his valet and his tea tray to his side.

"What is she—" James started and stopped. "That is, is everything . . . to your liking?"

"Hardly to my liking," the duke responded sharply. "I've been up for hours, sitting in this miserably uncomfortable chair while that chit has occupied my bed. How did this happen?"

The valet stared at his master as if accused of a crime. "Are you asking me, your grace?" James looked shocked.

"I left orders for her door to be watched," the duke told his valet. "I want to know how she got past."

"Yes, your grace. I'll find the culprit."

"The culprit," the duke said, "is in my very own bed. I want to talk to the idiot who let her escape the nursery."

Their conversation was interrupted when the culprit herself stirred, stretched, yawned and sat up. Sleepy-eyed, she looked toward the two men.

"Oh!" she gasped when she realized she lacked clothes. She grabbed for the covers.

"Well?" the duke demanded, his brow beetled. "What have you got to say for yourself?"

Brianna looked toward the windows and then back at the men across the room. "It's gone morning," she replied in a dispirited voice.

"Morning does follow night," the duke informed her.

Brianna's head curved over her body, her fingers picking at the thick goose-down comforter. "They have sailed," she said, her soft words smiting at the duke's well-protected heart.

"You are speaking of your brother," the duke clarified.

"I could have stowed away," Brianna said. "I would have been with him in battle."

The duke spoke with exemplary calm. "Would it be too much to ask how you managed to land in my bed?"

Again Brianna looked toward the windows. "I couldn't get down any farther."

The duke saw the direction of her gaze. He rose from the wing chair and strode to the windows. He unlatched one, opened it, and peered out. And up. When he turned toward the chastened child, his expression was a mixture of disbelief and admiration.

"You could not possibly have shinnied down that stone facing," he told her.

Brianna's head rose, angered by his condescending tone. "And why could I not?" she demanded.

Andrew stepped back from the window, his bare heel tramping on Brianna's damp and discarded shawl. Beneath it lay the sheet and chemise. The duke looked down and then looked up at the wide-eyed but belligerent girl.

"Your brother has left me responsible for your safety. I *shall* live up to that responsibility, no matter the cost to either of us. Do I make myself clear?"

Brianna said yes, the lone word buried deep in her throat, her head ducked toward her hands as they wrung the coverlet.

"I beg your pardon?" the duke said.

"Yes," Brianna said more loudly, a touch of defiance back in her voice.

"Good," the duke said placidly. "James, please see to more appropriate covering for Miss Morris before she is escorted to her quarters."

James did as he was bid, Mrs. Potts arriving to take charge of Brianna whilst the valet helped the duke bathe and dress for the day. Andrew suffered his valet's silence until he could stand it no longer.

"Well?" the duke demanded.

"Your grace?" his valet responded.

"Out with it."

"Out with what, your grace?"

Andrew grimaced. "Whatever it is that is fairly dancing off your tongue!"

"I'm sure I don't know what you can mean, your grace. Except that I feel a mite sorry for the girl, young as she is. And such a brave little thing."

"Foolhardy is more to the point."

"Left here with just us, I can't imagine what's to become of her," the valet said.

The Duke of Ashford grimaced. "I am much more concerned with what's to become of *us.*"

Chapter Six

After young Brianna Morris's spectacular entry into the Duke of Ashford's establishment, in the next fortnight the duke would have been hard put to prove she was within Ashford Hall's stout stone walls. She ate her meals in the nursery and spent her days and nights in that same nether region of the house, far removed from him.

James and Twinforth were for once in rare agreement against the rest of the staff that it was neither proper nor sensible to have the duke sit down to his meals alone with a prattling schoolmiss. Indigestion was bound to immediately occur. To both parties, James added, earning a quelling glance from the butler.

Mrs. Potts, as housekeeper, spoke for the rest of the staff, mainly female, as Twinforth later disparagingly told Harding. Misplaced motherly concern, in Twinforth's estimation, made the understaff complain about the poor child being left so alone.

"Poor child, indeed!" Twinforth reported he had replied, and said it again for the estate manager's delectation. "Any impecunious young relation allowed to live in such luxury as ours should be on her knees thanking the Almighty for her good fortune. Instead, Mrs. Potts is determined to turn the household upside down to better please the child. Did you hear of her actually scaling the ramparts?" he asked, scandalized.

Feeling sure the butler meant the girl the night she arrived two weeks past and not the rotund Mrs. Potts later attempting the same feat, Harding admitted quietly that he had. "Repeatedly," he added, hoping to forestall yet another opinion upon the girl's behavior. His hope was short-lived.

"The audacity!" Twinforth allowed himself to exclaim before he quickly brought his tone down to his normal decorous accents. "The duke's patience has been sorely tested."

"Here, here," Harding agreed in great fellow feeling for his employer. The estate manager's own patience was being sorely tested by the various staff members' speaking silences and impassioned defenses on the subject of how best to handle the girl.

Harding managed to dismiss the butler, and escaped the house with his lordship an hour later. They rode to East Ashing village and onward to the Wallingford estates. They were ostensibly in search of prime horseflesh, but in truth each was glad to escape Ashford Hall and all talk of the child who had so unceremoniously landed on the duke's doorstep.

By the end of the second fortnight a dispatch from the Continent had arrived for Brianna from her brother Samuel, and the first of several applicants answered the advertisement for a governess Harding had placed in the *Times*. Brianna ignored her brother's missive. It was placed upon the dresser in the small nursery bedroom and lay unopened even after Mrs. Potts herself attempted to cajole the child into finding out what her brother had written. While Mrs. Potts met with no success in the nursery, one floor below, the duke was meeting with little success in his efforts to obtain a governess for his new charge.

Each applicant's written qualifications fell short of the duke's mark. One's language was deplorable, another's handwriting, he objected to the tone of a third and the ages of the fourth and fifth, one being too young, the other too old. Andrew threw the fifth atop a cherrywood table in his dressing room as James trimmed his hair.

"Damned nuisance," the duke muttered.

"If your grace does not wish his ear nicked, he will sit still," James informed his employer. His words met with silence, and the valet went back to his task, working for several minutes before the duke again began to fidget.

"What's to be done with her?" he asked rhetorically. "She cannot continue to run wild."

"It's early times," James soothed. "She's only just arrived."

"Just arrived?" the duke scoffed. "It has already been a month!"

"You'd hardly know the wee girl was about, she never leaves her rooms."

"They are not her rooms," Andrew corrected a bit peevishly. "And her presence permeates every conversation in this house. Is she eating, is she ill, is she unhappy, is she comfortable, is she—"

The duke's diatribe was interrupted by Twinforth with the news that a young lady had arrived by hired carriage. Andrew Ormsby frowned blackly at his butler. "Are you daring to tell me we now have *another* child on our hands?"

"No, your grace," Twinforth quickly corrected. "This young lady says she has arrived in response to your request."

"I have requested no arrivals, young ladies or otherwise," the duke thundered. He pulled off the towel James had placed around his neck and threw it on the dark-patterned oriental carpet beneath his shaving chair. "And by God, I'll tell her so to her face!"

The Duke of Ashford strode out of his chambers and down the upper hall. He took the steps of the wide, curving stairway two at a time, his boots thudding against the red mahogany. Their loud reports carried his wrath before him down toward a young woman who stood in the front hall, looking upward. Her hand was to her hat, a few dark windblown curls peeking out from beneath it.

"What the devil is the meaning of this?" the duke demanded loudly.

The woman waiting below did not cower. Her back stiffened and her words were to the point.

"Please inform the Duke of Ashford of my arrival. I am Miss Constance Powell and I am here in response to his request for a governess."

Andrew was at a momentary loss for words. "You're too young," he replied bluntly.

"I am not too young," she replied calmly. "Nor is that your decision to make. I demand to speak to the duke himself."

"I *am* the bloody duke," Andrew snapped.

There was a slight pause in which Miss Powell very plainly allowed her surprise to show. When she spoke, her tone was entirely neutral.

"Please accept my apologies, your grace. I have never before met a member of the nobility who had such a— unique manner of expressing himself. Am I to instruct a child in proper manners or are you, yourself, to be my charge?"

A strangled sound escaped the duke's throat.

Twinforth's perfect composure slipped, his eyes widening as he stared at the young woman with the calm face and the most shocking cheek. As the butler struggled to maintain his equanimity, above his head at the top of the stairs the duke's valet was grinning. James went back along the hall to his master's chambers, whistling softly.

The duke turned on his heel. "Follow me," he said gruffly. He led the way to his private study. Once there, he dismissed Twinforth and turned to face Miss Powell. She was not above five feet, four inches tall, her figure slim. Her heart-shaped face and large gray eyes were totally inappropriate for a governess; she was much too comely.

"How old *are* you?" he asked without preamble.

"I have just celebrated my twenty-fourth birthday."

"You look younger."

"Thank you," she replied.

Nettled by her politely questioning expression, he waved her toward a narrow couch. "Sit, sit . . ." The duke himself moved to his grandfather's intricately carved desk, putting the ebony and rosewood between himself and the very determined-looking young lady. "I must apologize for the manner of your greeting," he said briskly.

He was rewarded with a brief smile.

"However," he continued, "you must have realized you were going beyond, completely beyond, all *mannerly* bounds by appearing on my doorstep without invitation. Since I have not yet replied to any of the letters of application, I have *not* invited you. And prevaricating to my butler is not in the way of being the best of manners either."

"I did not precisely prevaricate. That is to say, I am a governess. I told your man you were expecting me, as you had advertised for a governess. Nor could you have replied to my letter of application since I sent you none."

The duke frowned. "None?" he repeated, as if he misbelieved his ears.

"That is the truth of it," she replied easily.

Andrew's eyes narrowed. "You are nothing if not direct."

"Would you prefer circumlocution?"

"I would not." He let the silence grow between them while he watched her fingers twist nervously around the reticule she held.

Constance Powell looked down at her hands. She lost some of her composure during the lengthening silence. Finally she removed a folded envelope from the small handbag. When the duke opened it and began to read, her voice faltered. "I have very good references—most satisfactory, as you can see. I am proficient in Latin, Greek, and Italian, and not only have taught these subjects, but have translated religious texts for my father. I managed the rectory's accounts from the age of fifteen. At twenty, when my father died, I took a position with Lord Rushmorton's household."

"Rushmorton . . ." Andrew searched his memory.

"When Lord Rushmorton removed his establishment from Surrey to his York holdings, I was forced to ask my cousin for temporary quarters," she said in dignified accents.

"Your cousin?"

"Evelyn Marshant, as she was before she married." Her next words came more slowly. "She is now the wife of the Duke of Hensley's second son."

"I see. You were forced to look for employment upon her marriage."

71

"No. That is to say, she was already married when I accepted her hospitality. I—I only now am seeking to make my own way—"

Andrew looked up from the paper to see Miss Powell blushing furiously. "Oh, I say—am I to understand there were, ah, later problems? Family problems?"

"Her husband is none of my family," Constance Powell said quickly. Resolutely she met the duke's eyes, still blushing. "There were no actual . . . problems, but the—the situation has become intolerable and I must again seek my own fortune. As you can see, it would have been difficult to explain my circumstances without speaking in person."

"I can see it would have been dashed difficult to consign them to paper," he agreed.

Miss Powell's back stiffened. The duke scrutinized her from her toes to the tip of her hat. Her half boots looked to be of good leather but were well-scuffed. Her pelisse was not new but was of good cut and cloth. Made of a conservative deep green, its brown fur collar and cuffs matched the fringe of coffee-brown hair that peeked out from beneath a green-ribboned bonnet. Except for a little too much prettiness, she seemed altogether quite unexceptional in her mode of dress and manners, which was a high compliment in the duke's roster of opinions. Miss Powell had presence and sense, and she certainly seemed to have determination, which would be crucial if she were ever to control Brianna Morris.

"I suppose you are familiar with proper etiquette," he said.

"Intimately," Constance replied firmly.

She waited for the duke's decision. He walked to the bell pull, rang, and waited in silence for Twinforth. When he saw the young woman's pensive expression, he relented.

"You might do."

"Thank you."

"What I mean to say is, I am not adept at hiring governesses, having never done so before. But since you are here, you might as well stay for a fortnight or so and see how things get on."

"Oh, your grace, *thank* you," Miss Powell said with much more fervor. "You will not be disappointed, I assure you."

"Yes, well, that's as may be. You have yet to meet your charge," he added darkly.

"And your wife," Miss Powell added.

"I have no wife."

Miss Powell was startled. "I am sorry if I have intruded upon a recent bereavement."

"What the deuce are you talking about? None has died. The child you are being hired to instruct is not mine but a distant relative who has recently been given into my care."

"Oh . . . oh, I do see. How old is the child?"

"Fourteen."

". . . Did you say . . . fourteen?"

"I did."

"Years," the young governess clarified as Twinforth discreetly knocked before admitting himself.

"Of course years, what else? Oh, Twinforth, send the hired coach on its way and collect Miss Powell's bags."

Twinforth gave the young woman a frosty glance. "The bags in question have already been conveyed to the outer porch, your grace."

"Well, bring them in and pay the man."

Miss Powell spoke. "He is already paid. He has in fact already left. I took the liberty of dismissing the coachman when I arrived."

The duke turned on her with a darkling look. "Oh, you did, did you? A bit too sure of yourself, were you not?"

"No, your grace. Only of your generosity of spirit," she told him demurely.

"You may go, Twinforth," Andrew said. "And you, Miss Powell, may soon regret your impetuosity. I might as well inform you straight away that you have your work cut out for you. Mind, I do not expect miracles of erudition from the girl. What I *do* expect is for her to be taught manners and decorum, that she be kept clean and clothed as befits her position, that she learn not to shriek like a banshee and not to climb up and down the walls."

He was rewarded with an expression of such mixed parts as to make him smile grimly.

"If you can add anything in the way of learning sums or the female arts of sewing or whatever, I shall be appreciative, but do not waste your time on such details until you have civilized the child."

"Is there something amiss with her . . ." Miss Powell searched for a polite word.

"Upper works? Other than being spoiled past rotten, I would venture to say no. You'd best meet her and decide for yourself."

"I look forward to it," Miss Powell agreed in a faint tone. Her thoughts went to the child's possible reactions to a new person. If the girl were as wild as her protector stated, a new governess might need a space of time in which to win over the child. Miss Powell could not afford to lose the position before she truly gained it. "But I think our first meeting should perhaps be alone, nothing so very formal, so as not to intimidate your charge."

"Alone? Agreed," the duke said with obvious relief. He rang again for Twinforth. "Miss Powell, I warn you, you are liable to find her most—unusual. You will need to be strict with the child. In fact, I insist upon it. I do not want my household in an uproar. I want my peace and quiet back. If you can manage that, you may keep the position. I will expect a weekly report upon your progress. And if you meet with any success, you will be amply rewarded for however many weeks or months your presence is required."

"Weeks?"

The Duke of Ashford shrugged his wide shoulders. "She will not remain long in my household."

Twinforth arrived, the duke making no effort to explain his prior words. The butler was told to conduct the young governess to her rooms and from thence to her charge.

"And afterward you'd best introduce Miss Powell to Mrs. Potts and the staff," Andrew said as Twinforth bowed and followed the young woman from the study. When he was alone, Andrew Ormsby allowed himself the luxury of a deep sigh. He fervently hoped Miss Powell would prove adept at working miracles.

Miss Powell's own thoughts were not far off the same mark as she followed the stately butler up to the nursery. She had nowhere else to turn, and was determined to make the best of the situation, no matter how uproarious the child might be.

But the child Miss Powell met a few minutes later seemed sad and spiritless and hardly capable of the kind of noisy and disruptive behavior the duke had described. The girl was tall for her age and very thin. Thick red curls cascaded across her shoulders and down her back. She sat in a window seat, her unhappy eyes gazing out at the brisk October day. The wind that had nearly taken Miss Powell's bonnet gusted leaves against Ashford Hall's stone walls and whistled against the windows.

"Good day to you, Miss Morris," Miss Powell said, but the girl did not look away from the window. Constance Powell came nearer. "Might I join you?" She received no answer. "My name is Miss Powell, Miss Constance Powell, and I am to be your new governess. My friends call me Connie, and I hope we shall be great friends." She waited. "May I call you by your first name?"

"It is Brianna." The reply sounded woebegone.

"So I was told. And is that what you are called?"

Brianna sighed and looked deep into the woman's kind gray eyes. "At home all called me Bree."

"Then so shall I," Miss Powell promised. "How is that?" When she received no reply, she spoke softly. "You do not like to be here, do you? It is not a very pleasant place?"

A tiny ray of hope sprang into Brianna's jade-green eyes. "Oh, Miss Powell, nor shall you. Nor could any! Can you already tell how unspeakable it is? How perceptive of you! How could one be happy with a guardian who imprisons one?"

Miss Powell looked properly shocked. "Imprisons?"

"They lock the doors so I shan't get out of these two rooms. The duke does not want to know I am in the house.

All must tiptoe about or chance his wrath," Brianna said, warming to her subject. "He will most likely imprison you too."

"He most definitely shall not! Nor can he keep you locked in. A child needs air and sunshine, and even if you are practically grown, you still need the roses brought to your cheeks. Did not your former governess insist upon your needs?"

Brianna looked solemnly into her new governess's concerned gaze. "I have had none."

"None? No governess? Not ever?" Miss Powell looked at the girl in shock.

"Not ever. Nor have I left these rooms since the day I arrived," the girl reported honestly.

Connie Powell was fast becoming incensed. "How long has he kept you thus?"

"For years and years," Brianna said dramatically and quite inaccurately, although each day had seemed a year to the young girl who kept to herself in Ashford Hall's nursery.

"It is not possible," Connie expostulated. "No one could be so horrid as that."

"The last time I tried to leave these rooms I had two black eyes," Brianna said dolefully.

"He wouldn't dare! I would as lief work for a devil as a man who was so base as to handle his household by fisticuffs, let alone as to strike blows at children."

"No, no," Brianna said hastily. "I did not precisely say that he himself hit me—"

"No matter who carried out his commands, he is the master of this household and is responsible for his servants' interpretations of his orders," the governess said emphatically. "And such behavior cannot go unpunished. No matter it costs me this position, I must inform the duke I will not tolerate such mistreatment of any in my charge!"

Brianna threw herself at Miss Powell's feet, her hands clasped together, imploring her newfound friend not to say one word. "Oh, please, do not mention this, please—"

"Child, child, calm yourself. None shall harm you while I

am in this house," the young woman promised the girl. She found Brianna's hand and gave it a reassuring squeeze.

"Please promise you'll never bring up what I said, please—"

"You have no need to fear," Connie said instead.

"You cannot go to him!"

"But don't you see I must?"

"No!" Brianna objected. "I shall never talk to you again, never trust you, if you abuse my confidences!"

"I do not wish to abuse your trust, I want to help."

"You do not want to help me!"

"I do, I promise you, I do. I very much want to be your friend."

"Then you will never speak to him of what I have told you," Brianna insisted. She grabbed for the woman's hands, tears springing to her eyes.

"Calm yourself, child. If you feel so very strongly about it, then yes, I agree."

Brianna hesitated. "Does that mean you promise not to say anything?"

"Yes, I promise you. And I also promise that you need fear no more. Black eyes indeed!" Seeing Brianna's panic, Connie Powell spoke briskly, turning their conversation away from Brianna's trials and tribulations. "Will you help me list what we shall do together?"

"I would like that above anything," Brianna fibbed meekly, giving further lie to the duke's disastrous description of the poor child in Miss Powell's opinion. "I am ever so eager to learn everything there is to know in all the world."

"That might be a bit more than any of us can do, but we shall make a start," Connie promised her young student.

Later that afternoon Miss Powell was introduced to Mrs. Potts and the kitchen staff. At supper with the housekeeper at the kitchen head table that same night, the new governess delicately broached the subject of Brianna's pallor.

"The child seems not to be receiving enough exercise. I do so believe in sunshine and fresh air for children."

"Lord love you, dearie." Mrs. Potts patted the younger woman's smooth hand. "Exercise in the sunshine! Except her attempt to climb down these old stones, the girl's not been out of the nursery. And that was in the dead of night, and raining enough to drown a fish. I hope you have better luck getting her outside."

Thinking the well-meaning Mrs. Potts had just confirmed Brianna's wild tale, Constance Powell spoke with great certitude, a very determined expression upon her face. "I shall, Mrs. Potts. Believe me, it shall be my first occupation."

"Good," Mrs. Potts said contentedly. "Have a bit more lamb, dearie, and here's a dab bit of Cook's own mint jelly."

Constance Powell accepted the round little housekeeper's ministrations absently, her thoughts on much greater matters.

Chapter Seven

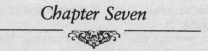

November brought chilly rain to the south of England, and the news of Bonaparte's defeat at Leipzig. The *Times* was full of the news of Holland throwing off its yoke, of the Prince of Orange leaving his English exile to return to Amsterdam in triumph. And above and beyond all else, the air was full of the news of England's glorious victories.

The army was Wellington's in the public mind, no matter that the Duke of York parsed out the pennies for its keep. No matter which generals might be involved, it was General Lord Wellington above all whom they cheered when the news kept growing brighter and brighter.

England was full of bunting and banners and flambeaux lit to the honor of her fighting men. It seemed every village square had Wellington and Victory spelled out in garlands of colored lanterns. Throughout the countryside postmen rode into towns and villages, their hats covered with ribbons denoting the latest victory as they brought news of Ciudad Rodrigo, of Badajoz, Salamanca, St. Sebastian, and Toulouse.

Miss Powell subscribed to a monthly ladies' journal in which the governess tried to interest her young charge. Brianna was a good and bright girl; her teacher would have defended her to any who dared say her nay. And the young Miss Morris had more than a passing basic education, disproving yet more of the duke's disparaging comments.

She bent to languages with an eager ear when Miss Powell spun fairy stories in Latin or Italian, she already knew her sums, and could plain sew and embroider, even if her stitches tended to become a bit ragged when she was bored, which did not take long, truth be told.

But while Brianna gained in knowledge, she seemed not to find any interest in clothing other than whether it kept her warm in the drafty old house. Connie poured over the magazines trying to find something that would interest the girl. Nothing did until the military craze that was sweeping the nation also swept through female fashions.

Suddenly there were military epaulets decorating coats and new short jackets called spencers. The drawings of what the London ton were wearing showed morning dresses cut in imitation of the cossack mantle.

For evening, ladies were advised to wear Prussian helmet caps of canary yellow frosted with silver and ornamented with a diadem and tassels and a curling ostrich feather.

Brianna skipped through the drawings of fancy evening clothes but became fascinated with the military epaulets and braiding of simpler high-waisted daytime gowns and overcapes.

"You must have a proper wardrobe," Connie declared. She cast a disparaging eye at the plain gray dress Brianna wore. It had been cut down and tucked in from one of Nellie's dresses after the young maid was promised a new gown when material was bought for her mistress's wardrobe. Whatever style it might once have had was lost in the translation to shorter hem and sleeves. "You would be amazed what a new gown can do for one's disposition."

"Then you must have one also."

Connie smiled at the sweet child. "We all shall have, you and I and Nellie all together, what do you say?"

"All with braid and epaulets," Brianna added hopefully.

"At least some," Connie agreed.

James tapped on the schoolroom door before peering in to inform Miss Powell the duke wished her presence below-stairs, his words surprising her.

"Have his guests departed for London?" she asked.

The valet winked at Brianna. "No, nor shall they this night. The weather's too heavy and going worse. Be a good night for one of your climb-downs, girl. Reminds one of the last time."

"James!" Constance Powell remonstrated. "That is not a laughing matter."

"And who's laughing, may I ask?" He winked at Brianna again. "Best have a care, miss, or he'll nail bars up to the windows."

"Thank you, James," Connie said in dampening accents. "I shall be down directly," she added, dismissing him. Once the duke's valet left the schoolroom, Connie reached for her young charge's hands. "You must pay no attention, Bree, none will place bars on these windows."

"He might," Brianna objected. "He cannot maintain control of my lands and my wealth if I manage to break free of him. If you promise never to tell any others, I shall tell you the true story of my birth." Brianna lowered her voice to a whisper. "I am truly a love-child," she said, and seeing her governess's wide-eyed consternation, continued. "Of someone quite royal, that's why I am so very rich and why I am not supposed to know, but I heard my ancient nurse speak of it before they sent her away. I am doomed," Brianna declaimed. "Doomed to live thus forever whilst all I long for is a small little room of my own with a few of my very own things from my true home." Brianna raised her hand, closing it into a fist and resting her forehead against it as she drooped forward in dramatic fashion.

Mrs. Potts came through the doorway and caught her breath. "Dearie, what's wrong? Is it the stomach ache?"

Constance Powell rose to her feet, her hands running down her skirts, smoothing her second-best blue dress as resolve grew within her breast. "Mrs. Potts, would you please stay with Miss Brianna until I return. The child is very upset."

"Dearie, now whatever has happened to put you into such a state? You mustn't make any scenes while his guests are here, my girl. He'll not be liking it if you do."

"I can well imagine his chagrin," the governess said. If Mrs. Potts or Brianna had been better acquainted with Constance Powell they would have been sorely concerned with the firm note of determination in her voice and the stubborn lift of her chin. As it was, Brianna had already forgotten her histrionics and was busy showing Mrs. Potts fashion pictures when Miss Powell sailed out of the schoolroom to do battle with the duke.

A clap of thunder startled one of the young maids busy in the guest chambers. The giggling of her companions could be heard in the stairwell as the governess passed the landing and continued down. More thunder rumbled in the distances outside, presaging rain as the November winds whipped in off the sea. Twinforth sent footmen scurrying to light early fires throughout the parlors, warding off the chill that was already seeping through Ashford Hall's ancient walls.

On the ground floor a large florid man paced beside a shorter and wider man. They walked from the duke's study to a large front parlor.

"I still do not comprehend why Ashford insisted on meeting here," Lord Rossmore said quietly.

"It was Prinny's decision, I believe, not Ashford's. There was some talk about a rather disreputable duel," Lord Barnstable responded in low tones.

"Aye, I know, but it's nonsensical for Prinny to banish Ashford from London because of a duel, disreputable or otherwise. By Jove, he could not cause Prinny more grief with Parliament than Prinny's own brothers already have."

"There you've hit the heart of it, Rossmore. Prinny wants Ashford to continue on the War Committee but he can't afford another scandal. The opposition to his policies grows with each new tidbit. Thank God the war's going well in the Peninsula—that goes a long way to balance out accounts."

"The reports I read said Bonaparte's lost Portugal and Spain."

"And 138 cannon they left behind when they fled back across the Pyrenees. It's the beginning of the end of that French devil, I'll warrant," the florid Lord Barnstable was saying as they passed near the stairs.

"Our lads even got their ammunition," Rossmore chortled. "By gad, I should have liked to see that usurping weasel Joseph Bonaparte fleeing with nothing but the clothes upon his back."

"I have a dispatch with me that tells of Jourdan even leaving behind his marshal's baton," Barnstable added. "Speak of rats deserting their ships!" Their laughter carried down the hall as they entered the front parlor and joined the duke and his old friend Lord Effingham.

Miss Powell heard the duke speaking as she descended the stairs.

"What say we send Wellington off to the Americas now that he has Boney on the run?"

"Andrew, are you serious?" Lord Effingham asked his host.

"Prinny would be better off sending York," Barnstable put in. "Since he'd be far away from the blandishments of the fairer sex and the selling of promotions."

"The Americans have taken Fort St. George, lest we forget," Andrew added.

"Yes, but surely anything that happens here and on the Continent is much more important than any American war could ever be," Rossmore declared. "I say, let the bloody rebels fight it out with their wild Indians over there. Perhaps they'll kill each other off."

"Is that what you're recommending to Prinny?" Barnstable asked Rossmore.

Andrew handed them each a brandy. "Here's to Prinny regaining the colonies his father lost."

"Andrew," Effingham said. "I begin to think you are actually serious on that head."

"Only partly," the duke admitted. "Well, then, here's to good Farmer George's son, our prince and regent."

"Hear, hear," the others agreed loyally.

Andrew saw the governess stop in the hall outside the wide double doors. "If you will excuse me, I have some estate business I must attend to—I shall send Twinforth in to show you to your rooms and see to your comfort."

The Duke of Ashford joined Miss Powell in the hall and led the way to his study. After he called for Twinforth and settled down the spaniels who had raced to him at his entrance, the duke turned to Miss Powell and the subject at hand.

"I wished to hear your weekly report, of course, but I am also in need of your advice concerning the girl."

The governess said nothing. The duke gazed into her impassive eyes, and when she maintained her silence, he continued.

"This beastly weather has forced my guests to stay the night, and therefore they will join me at dinner. In your opinion, do you think the girl capable of behaving in a proper manner if she were invited to join us?"

"Do you dare to invite her?" the governess responded.

"Miss Powell, that is precisely what I am asking your opinion upon. Dare I do so?"

"I'm sure I cannot advise you concerning your friends," she replied stiffly.

Andrew mistook the meaning of her stiffness. "You need not chastise yourself if she is still giving a great deal of trouble. You have had, as yet, very little time with her."

"She is not giving trouble, she is an *angel,*" Connie responded sharply.

The governess's vehement defense of the girl brought a sharp bark from Daisy and took her listener by surprise. "Then I am at a complete loss as to understanding your recent moods," the duke told her flatly. "In these past weeks you have seemed ever less than happy each time you have reported on her behavior and progress."

"On the contrary, I have told your grace how well she is doing in her studies."

"I am not speaking of the girl's progress. I am speaking of your attitude. In point of fact, each week you have seemed more and more dissatisfied. I assumed it was due to the inherent problems of dealing with the girl, and I have been most concerned. I must tell you things have been so much more settled since you arrived, I have been most satisfied with your efforts. I should hate to have you so unhappy as to give notice."

"And leave that poor girl alone in this house with you? I never would!"

The duke's face was a study in shocked disbelief. "What the devil are you implying? I assure you, Miss Powell, I have never been less than a gentleman in my entire life, and I might add I enjoy the most sterling of reputations." The thought of the rumors after his duel with young Standish harshened his tone. "Any female is safe under my protection, and I'll challenge any who deny it! Daisy, be quiet," he warned the dog.

Rowdy was growling, as if ready to protect his master. Byron opened one eye but otherwise did not bother himself with the human disagreement.

"Ah-ha! Violence yet again, I see!" Connie said, remembering Brianna's tale of black eyes.

"Woman, how dare you bring up such a subject," Andrew demanded, thinking she referred to the duel. "I was worried about your leaving my employ, but perhaps I should worry more about your remaining. You may not be well-bred enough to be able to train an untutored girl. Nor do I wish her around those so prejudiced as to form such harsh opinions without having unbiased knowledge of an event. If there is gossip being bandied about in my household, I demand to know of it!"

"Or you will do what?" Connie demanded back. "What is

there left for you to do? You threaten to send me away, the one friend she has made? How fitting of you to be so cruel, you who have already stripped the girl of her family and her wealth, kept her under lock and key since she was a tot, and resorted to fisticuffs when all else failed!"

The Duke of Ashford stared at the obviously demented female. He was momentarily so confused by her senseless words that he fastened only upon the last. "Fisticuffs?"

"Ah-ha, and so you do not even deny the charges. Well, sir, let me assure you there will be no more black eyes!"

"Black eyes," he sputtered, his voice rising in volume. "How dare you speak to me thus?"

"How dare *you* treat the poor child in such a fashion? Even if she is from the wrong side of the blanket. Have you no shame, no honor? She is *still* of the blood royal!"

Andrew Ormsby's normally curbed temper flared hot. The woman glared at him, her arms akimbo, her face blazing with indignation. He took two long steps toward her, towering over her with beetled brow. "Have you gone quite mad?" he demanded angrily.

"Don't try to intimidate me," Miss Powell warned the man who loomed over her. "I shall scream and shout to all of your perfidy."

The Duke of Ashford grimaced. "It seems screeching is all any of you bloody females can do. Blood royal, is it? Well, let me tell you, the last time it was Gypsy blood."

"You make no sense," Constance told the duke.

"*I* make no sense!" He stared at the woman. *"Harding!"* he bellowed, and then bellowed again.

The sound of his shouts astonished his guests in the front parlor and brought the estate manager into the study at a trot.

"Is something wrong, your grace?"

"Nothing has bloody well been right since that little vixen first arrived!"

"How *dare* you call me a vixen?" Connie Powell demanded.

"Not you, *her*. Although, Miss Powell, if the boot fits, I say wear it!" Angrily, he turned toward Harding. "Tell this—this *female* when that girl arrived."

"Miss Brianna, your grace? It was evening, as I remember—"

"The month, you fool."

"Why, it was September last, your lordship . . . Miss Powell." Harding was not sure to whom he was supposed to direct his answer. "She's been here going on to three months now."

"Who delivered her hence?"

"Her brother, Lieutenant Morris. Samuel Morris, your lordship."

As the duke queried and the estate manager answered, Miss Powell's expression slowly lengthened, her reddening blush blooming across her cheeks and staining down her neck.

"And where is that mendacious hoyden's brother?"

"I do not precisely know, your grace. On the Continent with General Lord Wellington, I would imagine, as he is his lordship's aide. Perhaps in one of his letters to Miss Brianna—" Harding glanced toward the mortified governess. "Perhaps if Miss Powell could convince Miss Brianna to open her brother's letters, he might have mentioned his whereabouts."

"That is all, Harding. No, wait, before you leave, one more item." The duke's tone was cold as ice. "Please be so good as to inform Miss Powell of the girl's exact appearance when she arrived. If you remember."

Harding looked from the angry duke to the obviously distressed governess and spoke slowly. "It would be hard to forget, your grace," Harding opined. "Miss Brianna was carried inside the hall—upside down over her brother's shoulder, in point of fact. She was shrieking loud and continuous invectives. Some of which were more . . . colorful than one would expect a young miss to have knowledge of. . . . She was dressed, I'm sorry to say, as a lad, in disheveled shirt and breeches. She had dirty feet—bare, if I remember correctly—and unkempt hair."

"*And?*" the duke prodded.

"Yes, well . . ." Harding glanced toward the silent governess. "I am very much afraid she also sported two black eyes, of which she was exceedingly proud."

"Bla-Black eyes?" Connie Powell whispered.

"It seems she had rather soundly trounced a village lad—the day before, as I believe—and gave rather worse than she got, from what she said."

Harding said no more. He watched the duke turn his full attention to the abashed governess. Being called upon for no further information, the estate manager departed the room rather more quickly than propriety would allow, leaving the duke and the governess alone and silent in the study.

"I— My apologies are, of course, not enough to assuage my—my comments. I shall pack immediately," Miss Powell assured the duke.

"Damn and blast your soul, do you dare to tell me that after all this, you now intend to add injury to insult and run away from your duties?" he demanded.

Connie was still blushing scarlet. "You have as much as already given me notice. I would like to leave at first opportunity. I feel the utter and complete fool."

"And so you should. And so she made you, that good little 'angel' of yours. Now, are you going to pack up and decamp or shall you stay?"

"I can hardly credit that you would wish me to stay. You said you did not."

"I said no such thing. We were talking at cross purposes in any event. Of course I want you to stay," Andrew informed her harshly. "If you leave, I shall have to go through all this again with someone else. Do you wish that fate on me? Or her, for that matter?"

". . . No," Connie said slowly. "I would not wish it upon anyone."

"And you have already said you like the girl."

"I did," Connie replied meaningfully.

"At the very least, she stays quiet for you. She hasn't shinnied down the walls lately or landed in my bed."

"I beg your pardon?"

"You heard me correctly," the duke said grimly. "I must say I did consider bars on the windows, but I was afraid she might then find a way to tunnel through the floors."

"You need have no fears on that head."

"One cannot be positive of anything with that child, least of all what she may say or do next. I own, I would not be surprised to find she was a changeling. But my duty is clear and so is yours. Now, as to the more immediate problem at hand and why I called you down. Again I must ask you about the dinner hour. If it were merely Effingham and myself, I would not concern you, but with Lords Rossmore and Barnstable here, I am fixed upon the horns of a dilemma. They are in the habit of having female companionship at dinner, without which I am positive we will be sunk in politics throughout the meal and thus do our digestions infinite harm. I had thought of having you bring the child down so that the dinner hour might be a bit more pleasant. However, I have no wish to shock members of the king's cabinet with outlandish behavior that would soon be the talk of all London. Nor do I relish her whispering more wild tales behind my back."

"If you wish her presence, I guarantee she shall behave and she shall not invent any more fictions this day or any other," Connie informed her employer.

"Are you quite sure you can manage her?"

"I am *entirely* sure," Connie Powell said firmly. "She owes both of us a very great deal more at this juncture than merely good manners, and since you allow me to stay, I shall ensure that she learns the folly of prevarication beginning this very day."

The duke hesitated. "Very well. We will assemble in the green parlor before dinner."

Connie hesitated.

"Yes?" he asked.

"Your grace, since you are allowing me to continue my work with her, there are a few small changes I would like to make in Miss Brianna's circumstances as soon as possible," Connie told his lordship.

"Anything within reason," he replied. "All I ask is that she be polite and entirely unremarkable this evening, and that you remove her immediately if she seems on the verge of becoming obstreperous."

"I do promise, your grace, and thank you." Miss Powell gave her employer a brief curtsey before she turned and left.

Andrew Ormsby reached to scratch Daisy's head, Rowdy crowding near. Byron watched to see no further human interruptions were at hand before he roused himself from his comfort by the fireplace and came wagging his tail to his master's chair.

"Royal blood," the duke told his dogs. "And a bastard at that . . ." He shook his handsome head. But a grudging smile played around his eyes and lips as he thought about the chit of a girl. The smile left as he thought ahead to dinner.

Chapter Eight

*B*rianna was in alone in the nursery when Nellie came flying in ahead of two young footmen.

"Miss Brianna, you are to be moved!"

The young lady in question backed away from the intruders.

"I shan't go to the dungeons," Brianna cried out.

Ronnie, the youngest of the footmen, stared at the girl he had been patrolled to watch the night she arrived, his eyes as round as saucers.

"She's windmills in her head, she has."

Nellie looked from Ronnie to Brianna. "No, she's not, she's just a bit touched, that's all. She's royalty, she is."

"Royalty," Tom, the older footman, scoffed.

"All know the royals are a bit touched," Nellie defended. "Just look at the king."

Tom pulled linens from the dresser drawers. He looked toward Brianna and then toward Nellie, smiling hugely.

"She's royalty, all right, Nellie-me-girl, and you're the bleeding queen."

"Let her be," Nellie defended. "He don't mean nothing, miss."

"I'll not go!" Brianna fairly shouted.

Miss Powell came in from the schoolroom door. "You will do precisely as you are told."

"Oh!" Brianna saw her friend and ran to her gratefully. "They want to take me somewhere and I'll never see you again!"

"Stuff and nonsense," Connie said. "I have made these arrangements myself."

Brianna's eyes widened. "You?"

"I," her governess confirmed. She looked toward Nellie and the footmen. "It's little enough she has. What is the difficulty?"

"Nothing, miss," Nellie said hurriedly as she and the two footmen retrieved the few linens and toiletries Brianna had accumulated under the watchful eye of Miss Powell.

The rooms Connie led her pupil to were on the floor below and on the opposite, western, side of the huge house. A small sitting room, done in gilt and apple green, led to a bedroom of peaches and cream, and both looked out upon a near prospect of green lawns edged by wide-branched ancient oaks. In the distance the sea roared toward sheer cliffs that ran straight down into the foam.

Brianna's steps slowed as she entered the sitting room, her fingers trailing over the top of an elegant and dainty rosewood table. Gilt edged the delicate tables and the picture frames that surrounded soft-colored oil paintings of Ashford Hall, of a curving coastline, its beauty bleak and bare, of cottages that hugged the lee side of distant golden hills, purpled moors a vague haze in the distances beyond.

Wandering from wall to wall, Brianna was lost in a deluge

of riches. The carpet beneath her feet bled from darkest forest to lightest apple green, woven through with golden threads, hints of umber casting shadows in its depths. Delicate gilt tables and tapestry chairs led to a doorway into a bedchamber that gave the young girl pause.

Inside the large inner chamber a canopied bed was covered with thick cream-colored embroidered lace. Matching hangings dripped delicate filmy tendrils from the ceiling and flowed down past thick lace-encrusted pillows to touch the peach colored carpet.

"It's beautiful." Brianna turned to her benefactress. "I can never thank you enough."

"You must thank your guardian," Connie replied.

"Oh, Miss Powell, I have no compunctions on that regard. I cannot imagine how you cajoled him to agree to all this, but I know it is you I should thank. None other but you could have warmed the cockles of his heinous and elderly heart."

"The duke is not elderly," Connie replied, but Brianna was bubbling over with happiness and did not hear the warning tone that lurked beneath her governess's words.

"You have worked miracles," Brianna enthused.

"Hardly."

"But you have! You have done exactly that. For he hates me, and only you can make him be kind."

"He does hate you," Connie replied in a deceptively soft voice.

"He must be in love with you."

"Brianna!"

"But Miss Powell, Connie, he must, don't you see? Or he'd never succumb to your blandishments."

"He has succumbed to nothing."

"He has allowed me to leave the nursery," Brianna said.

"Not allowed. Awaited the very day."

The governess's words gave Brianna momentary pause. "I do not understand."

"No? I should think you would."

"I am at a complete loss as to what you can mean."

Constance Powell regarded her pupil with calm gray eyes. "His grace has awaited the day he could return you to your people."

". . . He has?"

"Most decidedly. And, thankfully, that day is now at hand."

"It is?" Brianna asked doubtfully.

"You must be thrilled."

"I must be? I mean, that is to say, I suppose I *must* be. . . . Could you perhaps tell me why? That is, why precisely I should be so thrilled this particular evening?"

"Why, because the Royal Herald is at this very moment within these walls."

"The Royal Herald?"

"Yes," Connie said as if she had explained all.

Brianna frowned in concentration. "The Royal Herald."

"Yes," Connie said again. "The very gentleman who has recorded all births—on both sides of the blanket. Forgive me for being so blunt, but as you, yourself, have told me of your history I feel we can be perfectly honest with each other."

"Of course," Brianna agreed weakly.

"He has come to take you back to your rightful place."

". . . He has?"

"Most definitely," Connie assured her pupil. "He has demanded that you have proper rooms, and he has insisted you dine with him, the duke and the Royal Gaoler."

Brianna swallowed hard. "Gaoler?"

"Nothing for you to worry about, dear Bree. It is just that there are the most wretched sorts, liars and malcontents, running about the countryside telling the most lurid stories about the royal family. The herald has come because he has heard a relative is being kept against her will and stripped of all her wealth. The gaoler has come because often such stories are falsehoods, and when they are, he must throw the mendacious person into imprisonment as a warning to others who would take the royal family's name in vain. Just a formality."

Brianna plunked down upon the ivory and cream lace coverlet. "I have the headache. I shall never be able to attend their royal—royalnesses."

"You must not worry. I shall tell them to come directly here this moment so as to end all these formalities and have you on the way to your palace."

"Miss Powell!" Brianna reached for her governess's hand. "You must not bring them hence."

"But I must. As a good and loyal subject, I am sworn to do my duty."

"It's not true!"

"What is not true?"

Tears began to fill Brianna's dark green eyes. "About my being a royal personage . . ."

"No?"

"No . . . you see, I was afraid to tell you the truth."

Miss Powell sat down beside her charge. "Which is?"

"I *am* a princess, but not of the royal family. You see, I am a Gypsy princess, stolen while a mere babe and—"

"Enough."

Brianna was momentarily startled by her governess's ringing accents. "But—"

"I said enough." Constance Powell eyed the girl grimly. "Enough fabrications, enough whiskers, enough lies."

Brianna jumped to her feet, her small hands clasped to her breast. "He has won you over to his side!"

"No."

"Yes. You no longer believe me! Why else would you doubt me?"

"The estate manager, the butler, the valet, the housekeeper, the cook, the maids, your very own brother bringing you here three months ago, not years and years of a lonely childhood—"

"Stop!" Brianna raised her hands to her ears. Blushing furiously, she lowered first her eyes and then her head. "I did not mean any harm. I only wanted someone here to be on my side."

Connie heard the true loneliness in the young girl's voice,

and her heart went out to the child in spite of herself. "Liars never prosper. And all here are on your side. There is no other side.

"Brianna, the duke only wants the very best for you. And that his peace and quiet not be disturbed. That's not so very much to ask, is it?"

". . . No."

"He has invited you to dinner."

"To throw me to the gaoler!"

Constance Powell smiled. "There is no Royal Herald here, nor a gaoler, royal or otherwise."

"Do you mean you prevaricated?"

"Brianna," Connie said warningly, "I fought fire with fire. I hope you have learned your lesson."

"Yes, Miss Powell."

"Good." Connie stood up. "We have our work cut out for us. Within the next two hours we must make ourselves and our wardrobes presentable. And, my young friend, I must impress upon you how important this evening is to us both. The duke intends to observe your manners and bearing, and if he feels you have accomplished naught or little, I shall be summarily dismissed."

"I shall not fail you," Brianna promised dramatically.

Connie Powell gazed at the girl, fondness and worry vying for place. It was impossible not to like the child. It also seemed impossible not to be scandalized by her behavior.

"I would feel ever so much better about this evening if your promise was a touch less fervent and a touch more demure. The highest compliment a well-brought-up young woman can receive is that in society's eyes she is entirely unexceptional. A lady does not draw attention to herself."

Her words were met with a bright smile, Brianna's natural high spirits once again rising to the surface.

"I pledge to be at my best. My *very* best," Brianna assured her governess. "I shall do you proud."

Brianna's assurances did nothing to assuage her governess's fears, but there was no time for worry. Mrs. Potts and Nellie were called into duty, along with a pair of velvet drapes from the long-unused mistress's sitting room, after an urgent conversation between Mrs. Potts and the duke's valet.

The men assembled in the red parlor were prepared for a long, dull, country evening, and teased their host about his lack of cosmopolitan luxuries.

"If you did not keep such an excellent cellar, I would have chanced the storms and the roadside inns over such a dull evening as we have ahead," Lord Rossmore informed the duke from over the top of a crystal glass.

Effingham accepted the glass Twinforth offered as he smiled at the regent's minister. "It is his only concession to civilized life," Francis Effingham confirmed.

"Hardly that," the duke defended.

"Well, it's a damn fine one," Lord Barnstable opined. "Much better to be safe and warm than jumbled about in a coach hurtling through the natural forces, I say. I, for one, prefer a comfortable backside."

"And that you have," Effingham told him, laughing.

Barnstable joined in the good-natured laughter. "A bit of extra girth never hurt a man."

"Nor rusticating into a veritable vegetable?"

"Francis, as always, you exaggerate," the duke chided his friend. "I have my lands to survey by day and my library and my wines to keep me company by night."

"And how are we to be kept from utter boredom this evening?" Francis Effingham asked his host with mock severity.

"My dear Effingham, my most fervent hope is that you all shall perish of boredom before this night is over."

"I beg your pardon?"

Barnstable helped himself to more wine. "Look at the bright side, Francis, we're here alone so Andrew can at last tell us of the duel."

"There's nothing to tell," the duke interrupted.

"Come now. It's said she's vanished from London. I thought we might find her here, and you in the throes of the most compromising circumstances."

The duke seemed not to hear this slur upon his reputation.

"Barnstable, leave it alone," Rossmore said.

"Why? Aren't you curious? I heard he fought for another."

"Enough," the duke said firmly.

"Ah, we've hit a sore point. Now, is it the bit of muslin or the unknown friend that brings up his ire?" Barnstable asked.

His question was never answered. Lord Rossmore's, "Oh, I do say," interrupted the conversation as Rossmore sprang to his feet. "I think you'd best change to a more acceptable subject."

In the doorway stood a lovely young woman dressed in an Empire-styled gown of ice-blue velvet. Her dark hair was piled high in Grecian curls, held in check by an ice-blue velvet ribbon. One long ivory arm held a child in its curve, a child dressed in identical ice-blue velvet. The young girl's masses of auburn curls were held back by a matching velvet ribbon, her eyes demurely lowered.

The duke stared at the vision in the doorway. "Miss Powell, thank you for accepting my invitation."

Constance Powell hesitated only a moment before giving Brianna a small push forward. Brianna came toward the men, dropping a deep throne-room curtsey and straightening slowly, her eyes still modestly downcast.

Barnstable looked from the girl to the woman to the duke, his questioning eyes finally coming to rest on Effingham. For his part, Effingham could only give back a most enigmatic expression.

"Permit me to introduce Lords Effingham, Rossmore, and Barnstable," the duke was saying. Each of them bowed in turn. "My ward," Ashford continued, "Brianna Morris, and her governess, Miss Powell."

Effingham stared at his host and then gave the young woman a thoroughgoing perusal. "Would I had had such a governess," he said into Barnstable's ear.

"My dear Miss Powell," Rossmore was saying. "I cannot tell you how pleased I am at your arrival."

"We are all pleased," Barnstable put in, "pleased and, may I add, astounded. My dear Andrew, what have you been keeping from us all?"

"Yes," Effingham agreed. "You mentioned nothing of this when last we met."

"I mentioned nothing because I knew nothing," the duke replied, scowling at Brianna. Unfortunately, his disapproving scowl was wasted since she did not see it. Miss Powell led her charge to a small red-brocaded settee where the young girl sat down with proper decorum and kept her eyes on her hands.

"How very odd," Effingham said. While Barnstable and Rossmore bent their attention toward the governess, Effingham's gaze was on her pupil. "Does she speak?" he asked the duke.

"One might call it that," the duke answered ambiguously. He looked toward Miss Powell. "I believe the child has been learning a bit of history along with her other studies."

"Yes, indeed," Connie Powell agreed. "We have been studying the Roman emperors."

"And which is your favorite?" Rossmore asked indulgently, his attention more on the teacher than the pupil.

"It is hard to decide," Brianna answered softly.

"Yes, I suppose it would be," Rossmore replied, his interest elsewhere. The governess's eyes were wide and thick-lashed.

"But I think I should have to say Claudius."

"Claudius?" Barnstable interjected, staring at the girl. "I should have thought Caesar or Marcus Aurelius."

"Whyever would one pick the crazed Claudius?" Rossmore asked idly. "There is nothing about the man to recommend him."

"But he is like our own rulers."

The duke choked.

"Brianna," Connie said in quiet caution.

"What did she say?" Rossmore stared down at the chit of a girl. "What was that?"

"One could feel quite at home with him. Claudius, that is. It is true he was crazed, but our own King George is that, and all seem to hold him in high esteem. Claudius was quite the bumbler and definitely had too much appetite for his food and his drink, but isn't our own regent much the same?" Lord Barnstable was caught with a terrific coughing fit. "Oh, and Claudius had the most awful marriage, as all say Prinny does. Is it true, do you know?"

"Prinny?"

"My brother says all call him that," she added innocently. "Do they not?"

Effingham's amusement was bubbling over. "Not quite all," he told the girl. "Only his closest companions. But who is this brother of whom you speak, and how do you come to be at Ashford House?"

"Perhaps Miss Morris is growing tired," the duke said through his teeth.

"Not a bit of it," Francis answered, grinning. "She seems most alert."

"My brother is Lieutenant Samuel Morris," she told them proudly. "He is with Lord Wellington on the Continent, capturing Bonaparte."

"Singlehandedly, one would suppose," Barnstable said dryly.

Brianna's brow puckered. "I don't believe so, your lordship. I think he has a deal of help, at least I hope so, because Old Boney is a terror."

"An astute observation," Barnstable replied.

"I am intrigued by an acquaintance of Wellington so vast that you speak of the regent as Prinny," Rossmore said, frowning.

"You see, I— Not precisely vast," Brianna admitted after a swift glance at the woman by her side. "I heard the name mentioned, and it seemed to fit."

"Then you do not know the regent as well?"

"I've run into him," Brianna answered truthfully.

"Brianna," Connie said sharply.

"But I *have*. Truly. You may ask Samuel, he will tell you. That's why they sent me here. Lord Wellington said he could not afford to have me causing international incidents within his household."

Effingham grinned. "That I can well believe."

Constance Powell rose to her feet. "Brianna, I think you may be tired."

"I'm not a bit of it," Brianna told her governess earnestly. "And I've been ever so good. I've only told the truth and I've said nothing bad and I've not even brought up anything about the baby Princess Sophia wasn't supposed to have or Prince Ernest killing people or—"

Choking sounds of surprise and suppressed laughter came from the men around her, stopping her words.

"Miss Powell!" the duke thundered.

"Brianna!" Connie cried as she drew the girl to her feet. "Come along!"

"Oh, please don't go," Effingham said over laughter that brought tears to his eyes. "I was so looking forward to the girl's dinner conversation."

"Get her to her room," the duke demanded.

"What did I do?" Brianna asked from the hallway as Connie Powell swept her out of the parlor and toward the grand stairwell.

"Good Lord," Rossmore murmured.

"Where did you find the child?" Barnstable asked.

"She was carried over my threshold by main force. Francis, stop laughing!"

"I'm sorry," Francis Effingham said over unrepentant laughter. "How long is she to be your ward?"

"Only until her brother returns," Andrew answered grimly.

"You'd best hope for a short war."

"Francis!"

"I'm sorry . . . but of all people to be saddled with a precocious and, dare I say it, *outspoken* child—you?"

Twinforth came to announce dinner, the highly diverted Effingham leading the way, Rossmore and Barnstable behind. Twinforth leaned circumspectly toward his employer and spoke softly.

"I took the liberty of removing two of the place settings, your grace."

"Good."

Effingham waited at the doors to the dining room. Andrew walked toward him. "It's not funny."

"But Andrew, it is positively droll."

"Enough about the girl," Andrew insisted as they walked forward to join the others.

"I agree," Rossmore said from his seat at the table. "The child needs training. What I want to know is wherever did you find the governess!"

"She doesn't seem very effective as a teacher," Barnstable interjected.

"Clifford, with her looks, she has no need to be effective."

"Did you see she wore no jewels?" Effingham put in.

"She had no need of them, she shines on her own. She's not the one you fought over, by any chance, is she?" Rossmore asked Andrew.

"No," the duke growled, ending the topic.

The next morning Brianna awoke to find the duke gone at early light along with his London companions.

"What do you mean, gone?" she asked when Nellie brought her morning tea and toast and gave her the news. Getting no proper information, she threw aside her covers. Her bare feet hit the cold floor as she raced out and down the hall to Connie's room, catching her governess at her morning ablutions.

"Connie, he's gone! Did you know he's gone?"

"Brianna, you are supposed to knock, and ask for, and *wait* for, permission to enter," Connie objected.

"But he's gone, and I thought he couldn't go to London."

"Perhaps he's gone somewhere else," Connie said as she finished buttoning her thin muslin morning dress.

"Nellie says James said a messenger came in the night, and it was urgent for the duke to leave for the capital."

Connie came toward the girl, reaching out for her hands. "Then he must have obeyed a summons of some sort."

"Whose summons? Why?"

"I have no idea. Brianna, why are you so upset by this?"

"Upset?" The young girl stared up at her teacher. "I'm not upset."

"You are racing around in your nightwear as if the house were afire."

Brianna pulled her hands back, shaking her head a little. "I'm not upset. . . . Why should I be upset?"

"I'm sure I don't know."

"Neither do I," Brianna said firmly. "And I'm not."

Chapter Nine

November stretched into December, Ashford Hall slumbering through the dreary winter months. Brianna waited for the duke's return with as much concern as did the spaniels, leaping at every sound. She flew to windows whilst they sniffed at doors, all to turn back in dejection when the duke did not appear. She denied she was ill, but it was apparent to Connie that something was wrong.

The girl bent over her needlework, attempting to learn the patience necessary for small, even stitches. She perked up a bit at her history lessons, asking questions, her eyes aglow with the tales of distant heroes. She allowed Mrs. Potts to direct her in the finer arts of cooking and dining.

"None knows where you'll find your calling," was Mrs. Potts's opinion. "Best to be ready to take care of yourself in the world, dearie. A little knowledge of cooking has made the difference between wife and spinster more times than not. Move your rump, Byron," she added to the dog, who now found shelter most winter days in the warmth of the kitchen.

"Where is your husband, Mrs. Potts?" Brianna asked as the housekeeper attended to the dog, the cook, and the girl.

"Bless you, he's gone on to a better place. I think she needs to add a bit more sugar, what do you think, Eunice?"

"A smidgen more won't hurt," the cook replied.

"You mean he's in heaven?" Brianna asked.

"What? Oh, no, love, he's in the Americas searching out a fortune."

Brianna thought about this news. "Are there fortunes to be had in the Americas? I thought they only had Indians and wars."

"Aye, there are fortunes to be made by the first and the smartest, and Mr. Potts is that, he is."

Brianna was lost in thought, the smell of burning sauce alerting Mrs. Potts. "Stir to the bottom of the pan, girl, stir to the bottom."

They made Christmas pies, Brianna helping Eunice and Mrs. Potts, even Connie taking a hand in the baking. Brianna asked if the duke would be home for the holiday, but none could tell her. Twinforth would only say he lacked knowledge one way or the other. Brianna discussed presents with her governess. "If he comes and we have nothing for him, he will be very disappointed," was Brianna's opinion. "And if he doesn't come and we must give them to him late, think how mortified he shall be that he did not attend us."

Brianna seemed to take great comfort in the idea of a mortified Andrew Ormsby.

"The very best present you could possibly give him would be to pay attention to your studies and your manners, Brianna."

"Emmm . . ." Brianna responded, her thoughts on other things.

The week before Christmas a carriage came trundling up the long drive just past noon of a Tuesday. Brianna heard the carriage wheels and the horses and ran to the library window to look out at the snowy landscape. She disturbed Daisy's nap, bringing her bounding to the window, looking up at Brianna for the news.

"He's home!" she shouted to her teacher.

Daisy began to bark at the sound of clawing at the closed door.

"Brianna, come away from the window this instant. Now look what you've done. Rowdy, stop that this instant."

"How can you tell it's Rowdy outside?"

"Because Byron would not be so ill-mannered. Pick up your books," Connie said sternly.

Brianna bent to retrieve the volumes she had dropped to the floor. Daisy nuzzled the girl and then went to the door, whining to get out.

"Treating the duke's library in such a fashion," Connie scolded. "Have you learned nothing in these past weeks?"

"I have learned ever so much, my dearest Connie, I truly have," Brianna replied as she let the dog join Rowdy outside.

"Close the door and come back here. And do not think to bamboozle me with flattery. I own at times I think we are making progress, and then you return to such hoydenish behavior as not even a farm girl would employ. One would think you had been raised by wild Indians."

"Hobby—she was our housekeeper . . ." Brianna explained. A shadow of sadness passed through her emerald eyes, then was banished most forcibly. "Hobby used to say I'd grown up like a wildflower instead of like an English rose. No pruning, no human hand in the process."

"I can see what she meant," Connie said in repressive accents.

"Old John—he took care of the stable and whatever fell apart—a great deal fell apart after Samuel took off for the army, I must say. Old John was forever called away from one thing to get busy fixing something else. It was most aggravating for him. He had a wonderful vocabulary."

"I can almost hear him."

"Yes, well, he said wildflowers were just as pretty as roses, sometimes more," Brianna added a bit defiantly.

Connie watched the girl's blushing cheeks. "And well you should color. A proper young miss does not go about giving herself compliments."

"But I'm not, dear Connie, I'm not going about at all, and the compliment was his, not mine."

"Nor does she go about repeating compliments given her."

Brianna collapsed upon the chair across from her teacher, her forearms flopping down onto the round fruitwood table between them, her expression as woeful as the sigh that escaped her young lips.

"Nor does she throw herself about in disarray across the furniture. She sits with her back straight . . ." Connie waited for her charge to straighten. "And with her hands folded in her lap—and never greets a remark or a situation with such a sullen expression as that. You have no time to lose, Brianna. Most young ladies of your age are already well-versed in etiquette."

"Perhaps we could sew ramrods into the backs of my gowns," Brianna suggested helpfully. "For I shall never remember not to slouch if I am thinking of something else, and my hands go any which way they feel like before I can call them back."

"You will learn. It is merely a matter of practice. Rigorous practice."

"Connie?"

"Yes?"

"It doesn't seem that proper young ladies are allowed to have any fun or freedom. I think I should rather like to be an improper young lady."

"Brianna!" Connie Powell was scandalized. "That is just the sort of remark you must refrain from in civilized company. You mean nothing amiss, but it will be taken in the worst kind of manner and you shall harm your chances before you've found them. You must look forward to your future. You have no inheritance, you have no means of support except the kindness of your relatives."

"My brother will take care of me," Brianna insisted. "When he comes home."

"Life is not so simply decided. Many soldiers do not return and—"

"He shall," Brianna interrupted sharply. "Nothing shall happen to Sammy."

"I don't mean to upset you, child, I mean to make you face the reality of your circumstances so that you can appreciate the very great favor the duke is doing you. I sincerely hope your brother survives the horrors of war, but he may not. And if not, are you to remain a spinster poor relation living off your distant cousin?"

"I should die first! But he will come home," Brianna added stubbornly.

"And when he does, he will eventually marry and have his own family, his own wife, who will not want a sister-in-law in charge of her home, so you will again be the poor relation, relegated to a life of begging alms from your brother instead of your cousin."

Brianna's stubborn little chin thrust out in defiance, her eyes dancing with anger. "I did not ask for the duke's largesse, and I shall never beg his nor any other's. If Sammy wants some cork-brained light frigate that hangs after the army, I say let him have her, I shall survive on my own!"

Constance Powell stared at the lovely child whose sweet face was pulled into angry lines, heard the high young voice mouthing words straight from a soldier's barracks and was struck dumb.

"I shall," Brianna added when she saw Connie's amazed expression. "You think I cannot?"

"I know you cannot if you do not arm yourself with enough learning to command a genteel position in life."

"I am trying. You are looking most strangely, Connie."

"I am discovering a very low opinion of the brother who would introduce you to such language."

"What language?"

"I shall not repeat your words," Connie told her flatly.

"Then how shall I know which ones you mean?"

"You know exactly which words I mean."

A polite tap at the door preceded Twinforth's entrance into the library. He bore two letters on a silver tray. "The mail has arrived, Miss Powell, with some Christmas boxes Mrs. Potts is seeing to."

"Thank you, Twinforth."

Brianna was disappointed. "The duke did not arrive with the boxes, I suppose."

"You suppose correctly, Miss Brianna," Twinforth replied as he left.

One of the letters was from Samuel. Connie handed it to Brianna, who placed it on the table without opening it. "Is that from him?" Brianna asked.

"If you are referring to the duke, yes." Connie opened the folded page, reading quickly down the short note, but not quickly enough to suit Brianna, who prompted for information as soon as Connie began to read.

"Well? Is he coming? Does he say when? What's keeping him away?"

"Let me finish, child . . . He has sent the boxes to wish us all a merry holiday, he has been visiting in Kent and will be going with friends for winter hunting in the shires."

"Winter hunting? He can do that here, we've all the snow and deer and rabbits and whatever right here."

"He is with friends," Connie said quietly.

"Well, he could bring them here too, we've got rooms enough for a regiment."

"Brianna, he has made other plans. You cannot come to depend upon his presence. At fourteen you are no longer truly a child, and must learn to be independent and self-reliant."

Mrs. Potts arrived to hear Connie's last words. "Bless me, but don't be telling the girl such things. A man wants a docile, depending kind of female when he weds. One who'll do his bidding and see to his needs with no talking back."

"All girls do not wed, Mrs. Potts. And those that do not must earn a living."

"And those who do must earn a living too, one way or another," the housekeeper agreed. "Meself, for an instance. But still, a bluestocking isn't what a man wants to cuddle up to, of a cold night. And you, little one, you're growing up to know the truth of the world soon enough. Why, I was hardly older than you when I married Mr. Potts. Sixteen, and not the youngest bride by far. The duke should be seeing to finding a proper young man for you, is what I say."

"No proper young man will have a young lady who lacks manners, poise, and address."

"Aye, well, the Quality do have different ways, that I know," Mrs. Potts agreed. She smiled at Brianna. "It looks to be a quiet Christmas with the master gone, but we'll still have our Christmas pudding and cheer."

"I'm sure I couldn't care a fig where he is," Brianna said with a haughty tilt of her unruly auburn curls. "And I shall be sixteen in March," she added mutinously.

Connie gave her charge a quelling look. "Brianna, you simply must stop making up stories."

"None would believe you anyway, Miss Bree," Mrs. Potts told Brianna. "You're too spindly and small, you've got no figure yet at all."

Brianna blushed, but her eyes were resolute when she faced her teacher's disbelief. "You may think what you wish about my looks, and I have no delusions about being pretty, but I *did* turn fifteen last March . . ." Bright tears lurked in her large eyes, turning them stormy green. "And I am not a child."

"But his lordship told Twinforth you was naught but a child barely turned fourteen."

"He was wrong," Brianna insisted.

"Why did you not correct his lordship, child?" Mrs. Potts asked. "Dennis told as how your brother himself said you were fourteen."

Brianna bit her lower lip. "Samuel fibbed, and I didn't know until after he left. I didn't think it mattered."

Connie reached for the girl's hands. "Brianna, it makes all the difference in the world. A fourteen-year-old playing pranks and climbing down walls into the duke's bed is frowned upon and called a hoyden, a young woman who is halfway to being sixteen is called much worse things for the same actions."

Brianna blushed scarlet and would not meet her tutor's gaze. "I don't know what you mean," she prevaricated.

"Miss Bree, the whole house knows of the duke and James finding you in his lordship's bed," Mrs. Potts told the blushing girl.

"I was trying to get away!"

"Everything you were doing was beyond all bounds. I am afraid I shall have to be much more strict with you, Brianna." Connie turned to Mrs. Potts. "We shall take our meals in the dining room from this day forward, Mrs. Potts. And," she added as she turned to Brianna, "we will dress for dinner and we shall attend to the proprieties. *All* of them," she emphasized for Brianna's benefit.

The girl's lowered head gave no glimpse of her rebellious eyes. "May I go to my room, please?"

"Yes, I think that a very good idea. Don't forget your brother's new letter." Connie handed Samuel's letter to Brianna. "And while you are in your room, you can use the time to meditate upon your situation. If you are indeed fifteen, you are no longer a child, Brianna, nor shall I treat you so. You shall get your wish and a very great deal more."

"Yes, ma'am," was the very subdued answer.

Mrs. Potts spoke as the dejected girl left. "My heart goes out to the poor child."

"She is a young girl, not a child, it would seem," Connie corrected, "and I must write to the duke. I shudder to think what the duke will say when I inform him of this turn of events."

Mrs. Potts stared at the tutor. "Inform him of her age? Whatever for?"

"Mrs. Potts, it is entirely outside the bounds of propriety for a single man to keep a girl of marriageable age alone in his household."

"But you're here, and I, and the others. And you can see he's gone as much as he's here."

"As a governess and tutor to a child, it was at least proper if a bit strange not having female relatives present. I must tell you I was quite overset when I arrived and learned there was no wife, mother, or sister in the establishment. If my situation had not been so dire, if I had not already dismissed the coach, I might have turned straight 'round and gone back in search of other employment."

"Still and all, you're here."

"Mrs. Potts, you and I and all who are here are in the duke's employ. We could be dismissed for any interference in the duke's decisions. In the eyes of society, we cannot take the place of a proper chaperone."

"His lordship would never take advantage of the girl! Or

any other, and I'd like to see the one who'd say he would," Mrs. Potts defended stoutly.

"Unfortunately, no matter how proper the duke may be—which could be argued from what polite society says—the fact of our belief in his propriety makes no difference. The situation is improper of itself. She'll never marry one of her station, nor even so much as receive a proper reference to work as a tutor or governess, if her reputation is sullied. She *must* be made to realize that society thinks the worst of any who deviate from the accepted norms." Miss Powell looked decidedly worried. "I don't know what he will do, but I am sure the duke is not going to be pleased."

"But, Miss Connie, what good will it do to tell his lordship? He can't just send her away. The girl has no place to go."

"I do not want to inform him, Mrs. Potts, I simply have no choice. It is my duty."

"Look on the practical side. She's already here, so the damage, such as it is, is already done."

"But she will be sixteen in a very few months!"

"And we shall cross that bridge when we come to it. We don't have to bother his lordship now. And by the time we have to, spring will be here and her brother probably back and nary another problem for the poor wee girl."

Connie Powell wanted very much to believe the housekeeper's words. Mrs. Potts saw her advantage and continued speaking of the poor lonely young girl and what was to become of her and how there really was no problem, the duke was not even in residence. "Well," Connie said slowly, "perhaps we could wait just a bit before telling him."

"There's the ticket," Mrs. Potts said encouragingly. "We'll just wait a bit and see what happens."

As the two women worried over Brianna's fate, Brianna herself was sitting on the middle of her bed, Daisy at her side. The young girl held the small packet of unopened letters from her brother, putting the newest on the bottom and staring at them glumly.

Daisy nuzzled for attention. Brianna absently petted the

dog as she picked at the red ribbon that banded the growing pile of envelopes. When Nellie brought fresh coal for the fire, she saw her mistress engrossed in reading.

"Is that your brother's letters, miss?"

Brianna looked almost guilty. "What?"

"Is that the letters from your brother, then?"

". . . Yes."

"I'm ever so glad you're finally reading them, miss. Mrs. Potts was worried you was still angry at him."

Brianna made a face. "I am still angry with him, but there's not much point when the object of your wrath is so far off he doesn't even know it."

"What he did, he did for your own good, Miss Bree. Bringing you to the duke, I've heard James say as much. And he can't help being away miss, it's Old Boney who's making all the trouble." Nellie came toward the bed, looking down at the open pages. "Would you like to read them out loud?" Nellie asked shyly.

Brianna shoved Daisy aside and made room for Nellie beside them on the bed.

"Well," she said doubtfully, "there's ever so much to read."

"We could start with the first one," Nellie said helpfully.

Brianna looked at the paper in her hands. "That's what I was just doing. His first letter is full of apologies about leaving me here. . . . He says he would have been shot if he'd tried to hide me as a soldier. I wouldn't have wanted him shot, no matter how angry I am at him. He'd only just arrived, and said they had a stormy crossing and were all sick aboard ship. The next letter is about a battle at a place called Leipzig—what a strange name—and how Boney was thoroughly trounced. Whyever would he want a place so far away it's called Leipzig?"

"I'm sure I don't know, miss."

"Well, anyway, he says it's another sign the tyrant will soon be gone." She picked up the newest letter. "Now he says Lord Wellington is very pleased with Holland throwing off its French yoke."

Nellie's forehead pursed. "Holland who?"

"It's a country, like England or France."

"I never heard of it," Nellie said.

"Well, the ruler is a man called the Prince of Orange and—"

"Prince of *Oranges?*" Nellie objected. "Whoever heard of such a thing?"

"He says he's been living here but now he can go back to Amsterdam, that's in Holland, because he's their king."

"He's king of oranges and Holland? Foreigners have ever so funny ways, Miss Bree. . . . Whatever was he doing here?"

"Hiding from Old Boney, I suppose," Brianna said.

"Not much of a king to have to hide, is what I'd say. Our king would never do such a thing! It's no wonder you didn't mind waiting to read your letters, with such goings-on in them. I think you'd like James's letters from London better. They're ever so much more interesting, all about his grace and Lord Effingham and all the ton, not about orange princes." Nellie giggled. "Do you suppose he's colored orange too?"

Brianna's head had come up. "James writes of the duke?"

"Oh my, yes, and they have such wonderful parties and all. I told James as how I wanted to work someday in a grand London house, and he said he'd write and tell me all about what goes on so's I'd know when I came to London."

Twinforth knocked on the door. "Excuse me, Miss Brianna, I'm looking for— Daisy! Nellie," he said disapprovingly, "Daisy is not allowed on the beds. Nor are the staff."

The dog jumped up at the sound of its name and pattered toward the butler in search of its dinner. Nellie jumped too.

"I'm sorry, Mr. Twinforth."

Twinforth was stern. "If Miss Brianna is through with your services, there is other work to be done. You can help get the dogs ready for travel."

"Yes, Mr. Twinforth." She gave a little curtsey. "Are you through with me, Miss Bree?"

Brianna watched Twinforth usher Daisy out the door. "Why are the dogs traveling?"

"The duke intends to hunt them, miss. His instructions came with the packages."

Twinforth left the room, Nellie picking up her forgotten coal bucket.

"Is there anything else, miss?" the little maid asked.

"I should enjoy reading your letters from James, Nellie. I imagine he talks of all the duke's friends."

"Oh yes, miss. Especially Lord Effingham and Lady Beryl."

"Lady Beryl?"

"Oh yes, Miss Bree." Nellie cast a quick glance toward the doorway to make sure Twinforth had gone ahead down the hall. "Lady Beryl Cavendish," she whispered. "She's the most beautiful lady in London, and she's the duke's favorite. James writes of her ever so much, and describes her dresses and how all say she is of the very first stare. Did you know the ton call our master the Bachelor Duke? They say if any can catch the Bachelor Duke, it is Lady Beryl. Mayhap he shall marry her and we will have grand parties and all of the London ton coming here, or even the duke might want us to move to London." Nellie's eyes danced with the visions of such glamorous happenings.

"You'd best find Twinforth," Brianna said dampeningly.

"Yes, miss."

Nellie skipped out of the bedchamber, happily unaware of the gloom into which she had cast her young mistress.

Chapter Ten

*T*he Duke of Ashford planned to return to Sussex in mid-December after his hunts in the shires, but Lady Beryl Cavendish convinced him to stay on in London and escort her to the famous Cavendish Christmas party her uncle gave each year. Andrew revised his plans, accompanying Beryl to all the holiday festivities, and decided to leave for the country the day after Christmas. But there were New Year's invitations and Twelfth Day parties that Beryl had, most innocently of course, accepted for them both, and so he was still in London when the weather took a decided turn for the worse.

Stages were halted; not even the mail came or went except by special messenger. In London a freezing white fog devoured light and distorted the sounds of the horses, which slipped and slid on frozen streets, isolating those who ventured out. In the first days of January, society and commerce came to a halt, the duke spending his nights with his spaniels in front of a roaring fire. As the month lengthened, he ventured out for short forays to his club and to the regent's bidding, icy nights succeeding cold frosty days, all covered over with dense fogs well into February.

On one late February night the Duke of Ashford's valet woke to hear his employer arrive at the London town house just before dawn. His grace of Ashford stomped up the stairs, muttering to himself about the perfidy of the female race, banged his shin against the bedstead in his bedchamber and began to swear.

In a small room off the master suite, James got to his feet, yawning as he came to help his master undress, only to find that Andrew had already fallen asleep sideways across his bed. The faint sound of his alcohol-soaked snoring accompanied the valet's efforts as he covered the sleeping duke, banked the fire, and went back to his warm bed.

Later that morning the bleary-eyed duke woke to find James attempting to undress him.

"What the devil are you trying to do?" Andrew barked.

"I'm trying to get you out of your evening clothes, your grace."

"Well, stop it."

"Yes, your grace." James kept at his chore.

"What time is it?"

"Just after ten, your grace."

"Good God, leave me in peace!"

"Yes, your grace. As soon as I've removed your shirt." James finished his work, leaving the duke to turn away and go back to sleep. He was still in his smalls, but James decided against attempting to get his employer into his nightshirt.

After tossing and turning for another hour, Andrew finally rang for his tea. With it came a tall glass full of a strange concoction and the post, which he stared at with bleary eyes.

"I want no invitations for the next six months," he informed his valet.

"Yes, your grace."

"Society. Bah! Nonsensical females making inane conversation to your face and gossiping behind your back. I don't know why I even considered coming back to London."

"I believe it was because of the—I believe you said, infernal racket and upsetting turmoil caused by one lone chit of a girl."

Andrew groaned. "My head is splitting. The last thing I need to be reminded of is my newfound ward."

"Yes, your grace."

"I never want to see another female as long as I live."

"I take it the opera was not a great success," James said as he handed the tall glass to his employer.

The duke pushed it away. "Last night was an unmitigated disaster. Lady Beryl spent the entire evening flirting with

Rossmore, whilst Lady Rossmore chose to inform me, at great length and in repugnant detail, of her former liaison with the regent. One of the opera dancers kept sending such saucy glances in the direction of our box that the entire audience began to peruse Rossmore and myself, and all the while Signora Rosselli managed to sing both loudly and off-key! I don't care what it is, decline them all."

"And the one from Carleton House, your grace?" James asked as he proffered the glass again.

"Will you stop sticking that horrible concoction under my nose? Tell Prinny I have become ill unto death and shall never leave Ashford House again."

"If you drink it straight down, it won't be so very bad," the valet soothed his extremely put-upon employer.

Andrew sniffed at it, his nose wrinkled. "You can't possibly expect me to drink this."

"You always say that, your grace, and you always end by drinking it."

Andrew screwed up his nose, looking very much like a recalcitrant child, and opened his mouth, forcing down the milky brew. "Ugh," he shuddered as he thrust the empty glass away. "It had better work."

"You always say that too, your grace. Your mother has sent you a message."

Andrew groaned. "You are full of miserableness this morning. Waking me to this thundering head, forcing ugly brews down my gullet, and now you tell me my mother is writing. Where is she and how far is she indebted?" he asked, lying back against his pillows and closing his eyes before he took the news. "You'd best read it to me, my eyes are not up to focusing yet."

James opened the letter carefully and read:

> "Dearest Andrew,
>   I shall be leaving Ireland by the end of March if the weather permits. Please see to the town house being readied for my arrival. I was shocked to hear of your duel with the brother of a certain young woman of

questionable virtue. I have ever warned you of the wiles of women, especially those met at such places as Vauxhall and Raneleigh. I am glad you did not lose your life over someone not worth the candle. I would have come immediately when I heard of your plight, but winter engulfed the country and I could find no one with enough perseverance to accompany me. Even Tinsdale was so weak-spirited as to come down with the influenza. Patience is a virtue that must be striven for all one's life. Tinsdale is better and sends her love, as do I,

your mother"

Andrew groaned several times throughout the reading. James was not sure whether the duke's discomfort was due to his mother's words or the current state of his aching head.

"Shall I see to a headache powder, your grace?"

"No," the duke said irritably. "After that plonk you had me force down, it will simply heave up. I suppose it could be worse," he added, thinking of his mother's plans. "She most likely won't be arriving until mid-April. Make sure you have everything packed for the country before she arrives."

"Before her grace arrives, m'lord?"

"Of course before. You certainly don't imagine I will stay on here once she arrives."

"It has been a deal of time since you saw her grace, m'lord."

Andrew Ormsby reached for his brocade dressing gown without answering his valet. Annabella Ormsby, the dowager Duchess of Ashford, was a formidable lady with very definite opinions concerning the future welfare of her only child. Unfortunately, her opinions and her son's desires did not agree, and therein lay the reasons for their polite, loving, but often strained relationship.

In the dowager's often expressed opinion, the future duchess should be of impeccable lineage, have excellent health, and be, above all things, malleable. Andrew's response was that the description fit a brood mare. His mother went on to say she should not be pretty enough to attract other men's attention nor should she be of a curious sort, for they always ended by getting into trouble of one stripe or another.

"Where the devil are you going?" Andrew demanded as James started for the door.

"To get the headache powder, your grace."

"I don't want it. I prefer to suffer as I am. What else have you got there?"

"Miss Powell's progress report on Miss Brianna, your grace. And a letter from Miss Brianna herself."

Andrew's eyes opened. "Good God, she's been climbing the walls again!"

"I hardly think so, m'lord."

The duke glowered at his valet. "She must have done something abominable if she thinks she must write and explain herself. You'd best read me the tutor's letter first."

"Yes, your grace," James replied as he opened the missive.

"My dear Lord Duke,

I have the pleasure of informing you Miss Brianna is working most diligently upon her study of Latin and history. The artistic merit of her watercolors is quite exceptional and her craftsmanship is becoming more presentable. Her touch upon the pianoforte is also improving. She has asked to be taught the finer points of horsemanship, as I believe she already has some little knowledge of riding. I am not adept at the skill, but Mr. Harding has mentioned that your stable is both fine and extensive and that you have staff who could suit the purpose when the weather turns better, if you were inclined to allow her the liberty. If you will advise as to your wishes, I will inform Miss Brianna. There is another matter of which I feel I must speak, but I am persuaded it will be best discussed in person.

Sincerely,
Your Servant, Constance Powell."

"Ah-ha," Andrew said, "I knew it. Something that cannot be discussed by letter. Good God, I hope the house is still standing."

"I think we would have heard if it were otherwise," James replied dryly. "Do you wish me to read Miss Brianna's letter?"

"Hand it here," the duke commanded. He took the letter, opened it and began to read out loud.

"'Dear Cousin,'" Andrew read, his valet's brow rising at the salutation, but Andrew apparently seeing nothing amiss. "'I am writing to you as Cousin instead of as Duke—'"

Andrew looked up. "Of course she is, the little vixen, she's trying to soften me up before the blow."

He looked back down at Brianna's letter. "'. . . because what I must say is very very personal. It is said that your life is a degenerate and dissipated one . . .'" Andrew trailed off, astounded. James attempted to look impassive as the duke continued, his expression stiffening as he read. "'*Which,* I must inform you, is the worst possible thing for one's health at your *advanced* age.'" He looked up at James. "So much for any hope she has yet learned diplomacy." His eyes returned to the scraggly handwriting.

"'It is much better to stay at home at your age. Perhaps you could engage your time by reading religious tracts. Hobby, our old housekeeper, had many of them and said they were a great comfort to one who would soon *meet their maker.* Only watch you do not overwork your eyes . . .'" Andrew's tone hardened. "Now I've failing eyesight!"

He looked back at the letter. "'. . . and you must get to bed early to conserve your health and ensure that your digestion is in good order. It is most especially wise to stay away from simpering females, especially beautiful London ones!'" Andrew threw the letter to the bed beside him. "Bah, she's beyond redemption!"

"Is that all she wrote, your grace?"

Andrew gave the innocent-seeming James a darkling look. *"All?* No, it's not all, but it's *enough."* Regardless of his own words, Andrew snatched up the page before James could reach for it.

"'I am sorry to inform you,'" his grace of Ashford continued, "'that even from this distance I can foretell the trouble you are being led into by Lady Beryl Cavendish and all others of her ilk. Beware! But most particularly beware of this Lady Beryl. Looks are not everything, your grace, and are most deceiving as to one's true virtues. If you feel the need of companionship in your waning years, you should look closer to home. To one who is long-suffering, brilliant, dutiful, and kind, and whom you are leaving to languish alone, to pine away with none to keep her company all the way out here in Sussex!'" the duke ended. "James, what are you laughing at?" he growled.

"I'm not laughing, your grace."

"You are most definitely smiling!"

"I'm sorry, your grace. I was merely trying to imagine who she could mean."

Andrew stared at Brianna's letter. "The girl is daft," he pronounced. "There's no other explanation. She's touched in the head. Perhaps it runs in the Morris family; Samuel showed no sense the way he handled her situation."

"One could say he showed quite good sense, bringing her to safe harbor, so to speak, before he left."

"Safe harbor, is it? Well," Ashford said grudgingly, "you may well have the right of it. She would surely have been shipped off to Bedlam by any sane person not bound by familial duties. James, send this, this—*page*—back to Miss Powell and tell her the girl obviously has too much time on her hands. And ask where the bloody hell she's learning all this London gossip. While you're at it, tell her the girl's handwriting is execrable!"

"Immediately, your grace."

"Oh, and James, since the weather has lifted a bit, send the dogs back to Sussex. And pack for a prolonged journey."

"Are we following them to Ashford Hall?"

"And deal with that chit's nonsense? No, thank you. Two family seats, and between my mother and my ward, I've not got a home to call my own," he grumbled. "We shall tour until my mother leaves London for her next destination."

"She might be in London a great while, your grace."

"I have a great many friends to visit."

"What with the war in Europe, it could be months."

"Thank you, James, for that hopeful assessment. But you underestimate the dowager duchess. Mere wars have never stopped mother from going where she pleased. I wish Napoleon luck if he takes her on."

The day following the duke's receipt of Brianna's homily, Daisy, Byron, and Rowdy arrived home in a hired coach. Even Byron roused himself sufficiently to howl happily as he jumped down onto the wintry drive and trotted around the side of Ashford Hall's sedate facade behind the careening and yelping Daisy and Rowdy. As the dogs headed for the warmth and the familiar delightful smells of their own kitchens, one of the young stablemen came out to greet them.

"So you're home, lads and lassie," Dennis said, sinking to his haunches as they threw themselves at his arms.

While the happy scene was going on in the cool wintry sunlight, inside the grand mansion Twinforth took the packet of letters from his lordship. He placed the packet on a long cherrywood buffet in the entrance foyer and marched regally to Harding's small office at the back of the house, the hired coachman trailing behind.

"Mr. Harding, the London coach is here for your instructions," Twinforth announced, and withdrew. The coachman, his cap twisting in his hands, waited on the estate manager as Twinforth went back to the front hall.

Miss Powell was in the library, correcting Brianna's written translation of a portion of the *Ars Poetica* when the butler disturbed her concentration to announce a missive from the duke.

"The coachman is with Mr. Harding, should you wish to send a reply," he informed her.

"Thank you, Twinforth." She opened the letter whilst he waited, skimming through the duke's brief note and then reading Brianna's scrawled letter, her expression more and more aghast.

"Is there a reply, miss?"

"No," she said forcibly. "Where is Miss Brianna?"

"I believe she is with Mrs. Potts in the laundry, miss."

"Thank you," Connie said in frozen accents.

Twinforth watched the young woman stalk down the hall toward the green baize door to the servants' hall.

In the laundry the smell of boiling linen, of bars of soap and starch, hovered in the warm air over the ironing table, flatirons, and airing rails. Brianna was at work with a flatiron, Mrs. Potts directing her as she ironed embroidered linen handkerchiefs.

"You must know how it is done in order to teach your own staff properly one day," Mrs. Potts told the perspiring girl. "Between Miss Connie and meself, you shall be able to do any man proud."

Brianna tucked a dampened curl back behind her ear, her disheveled hair tied back with a thin white ribbon, her white muslin workdress damp from the warmth.

"Brianna." Connie Powell came in from the cobblestoned back courtyard. Her tone of voice warned Brianna before she turned around to see her tutor's hardened expression.

"Is it my Latin paper?"

"Come with me immediately," the governess ordered crisply.

Mrs. Potts gave Brianna a reassuring smile and called out to the governess, telling her how nicely Brianna was learning her household chores. "It's better to be good at something useful than talk a dead language, I say." But she said it to Nellie after teacher and pupil were gone.

Brianna followed her teacher across the cobblestones to the trellised rose garden on the south side of the mansion. The rambler roses were cut back, the vines seemingly lifeless in the wintry weather. She kept a prudent silence, awaiting the scolding she knew was in the offing.

"I tried my very best," she said timidly when Connie stopped on the bricked walkway lined with bare-branched rose bushes.

"Your Latin is perfectly acceptable," she was told. "Brianna, you are like these roses. You show a lovely face in

121

summer and lure people to like you, never showing your nettles and thorns. And then you leave cold hard branches behind, hurting all those who care for you past measure."

Brianna regarded her teacher soberly. "I have been trying my very best—"

"Your very best?" Connie thrust Brianna's letter toward the girl. "Is *this* your very best?"

Brianna glanced down and then blushed.

"And well you might blush," Connie said. "Take it. Take it and *read* it."

". . . I know what it says . . ."

"Then read this."

Brianna took the parchment and, with sinking heart, saw the ducal coronet and seal. Brianna read:

Miss Powell,

I will not comment upon the enclosed message from your pupil other than to say that I trust you will see your duty and do it. Besides scurrilous slander and the most ill-mannered of comments, it shows a want of delicacy on your part in allowing the child to while away her hours amongst gossips. It also shows that her handwriting is execrable. One would hope, however dense or backward the child may be, she might be capable of at least learning the bare rudiments of good penmanship *and good manners*. As to the riding, I see no point in teaching a girl-child the finer points of horsemanship, but if she feels this would be a reward for proper behavior, by all means, try it. I am for anything that will make a civilized person out of your heathen charge.

Brianna did not look up. "I think he is most awfully upset with me."

"With *us*," Connie corrected coldly.

"Not you," Brianna cried. "You have done nothing."

"I am sure his lordship shares your opinion. That I have done nothing thus far and he is wasting his money employing me."

"Connie, he is not! I will do anything you say. I couldn't bear it if you left me."

"And I cannot bear to look into the duke's revulsion when he returns and I must face him."

"Revulsion?" Brianna cried. "Whatever for?"

"Brianna, he of course assumes I put you up to this."

"But you didn't! I shall write and tell him—"

"You will not write him again. If you want me to stay one moment longer, you will never again mention pining females nor send one word at all until he returns."

"I promise!"

"And I do not trust you."

Brianna heard the brutal words and knew she deserved them. She hung her head. "What do you wish me to do?"

"Nothing."

"But my studies—"

"You may do as you wish this day. I will repair to my room and make a decision whether to go immediately or to await the duke's return before leaving."

"Please, please don't leave me . . ." Brianna's eyes darkened with tears. "I promise to do all you say. I don't want you to leave me too. . . ."

Connie Powell looked away from the motherless girl. Fatherless too, her brother gone; even the Mrs. Hobson she spoke of so often had married and left Brianna behind.

"We shall talk at dinner," Connie said.

Brianna watched her teacher walk toward the house, and then Brianna herself escaped to the stables; the smells of oil and leather, of horse flesh and spaniels, comforting in the cold wintry air. The dogs romped around her feet, oblivious of the cold and so happy to be home they quite erased her grave expression. Her natural high good spirits came to the fore as she reached to scratch their necks and wheedle Dennis into letting her help groom the horses.

Chapter Eleven

During the frigid beginning of the new year, the prince regent became bored to distraction and proceeded to drink himself under the table more nights than not, until finally, one late night, he went into a fit. The Dukes of Ashford and Kent were with His Highness, ringing immediately for help. The government was thrown into terrible alarm, but not a word of the emergency escaped to the papers. The headlines and news were full of the successes of Wellington and his allies.

By the end of February a rumor roared through London that Bonaparte himself had been killed. The truth of that was soon known. Whilst all but a select few were unaware of the problem, Prinny was on the road to recovery, to the great relief of his cabinet and close associates. The old King was gone completely mad, and none could imagine what would have happened if the regent had gone daft too.

The first inklings of spring finally arrived in the capital and brought with them a thaw in the weather and the news of the capitulation of Paris. The prince regent wasted no time in resuming his social life, and appeared with Lords Ashford, Barnstable, and Effingham at Lord Rossmore's establishment for an evening of cards and drinks in early March. The regent was in fine fettle, something oddly boyish about his aging face as he beamed across the table at the Duke of Ashford. The gentlemen having abandoned their dinner jackets, unbuttoned their waistcoats and gambled the night away.

"My dear Andrew, we seem to have lurched our opponents yet again," Prinny said with a grunt of triumph.

"Your luck has undone them, your highness," Andrew agreed.

Rossmore motioned to the footman at the door to bring more brandy while glowering at Effingham. "You are the most atrocious gambler, Francis. I can't imagine why you pursue it."

"I gamble because one *must*. A gentleman lacks choice in certain matters unless he wishes to be ostracized by polite society." He sighed a great theatrical sigh. "It is my duty to my social position to gamble away my family fortune." He earned the laughter he sought, the men puffing on their cigars and raising their goblets for more brandy.

"Gamble away, if you must," Rossmore said with bad grace, "but if you are truly a gentleman, you will not foist yourself upon unsuspecting partners."

"You are not unsuspecting, Harry. You know I am a miserable player. Can we please change the subject to something more interesting? For example, we could discuss Andrew's governess."

Prinny stared at the duke. "Andrew, speak up. You can't tell me you have a governess at your age."

"Francis is speaking utter nonsense." The Duke of Ashford scowled at Effingham. "I have been handed the charge of seeing to the welfare of a young relative, and have employed a tutor for that intent. It is an unimportant subject."

"Andrew's young cousin may be unimportant, but she is certainly diverting," Rossmore put in. "She even claims to have run into you, Your Highness. Quite literally."

Andrew was aghast at the thought of Brianna's lies being bandied about London, but before he could reply, the regent spoke.

"What did you say?"

"And she's an acquaintance of Wellington's, as she tells it," Rossmore added.

"Her brother is an aide," Effingham corrected.

Prinny stared into the fire for a moment and then frowned. "Hoydenish juvenile with a mop of red hair? Runs about like a mad puppy destroying furniture?"

All three men at the prince regent's table were astounded, the most so Andrew.

"That description is most apt," Andrew agreed when he finally found his voice.

"Miserable child," Prinny opined. "Sorry for you, Andrew."

"Thank you, sir," Andrew said feelingly.

The duke was saved from more conversation on the topic by the arrival of Lady Rossmore and her daughters, home from the theater. The men, except Prinny, quickly stood, only to be waved back to their chairs by Lady Rossmore's black lace evening fan. "We did not mean to interrupt your evening," she said as she curtsied toward the prince.

"Not a bit of it, pretty ones always make us play better."

"If His Highness plays any better, we shall all be in debtor's prison before the night is out," Rossmore said.

The girls curtsied and were sent to bed, the hour past one in the morning. Andrew watched them go, wondering if Brianna would ever have the good manners and easy grace, let alone the refined looks, of the Rossmore girls.

Lady Rossmore saw the direction of his gaze and misread the wistful expression. She lingered for a moment beside her husband's chair, a proprietary hand on his shoulder as she ordered coffee and sweets to be served. The regent had gained a great deal of weight over the dull winter months, and divided his attention between the sweets that arrived with the coffee and his buxom hostess.

"How was the play this evening, my dear Lady Rossmore? Did your girls enjoy it?"

"Most prodigiously, your highness. As did the Princess Royal, I believe."

At mention of his daughter, Prinny's face fell momentarily into unhappy lines, since his darling daughter had visited her mother this week against his express wishes. Lady Rossmore, seeing the regent's expression, continued brightly.

"The evening was a fête for Mr. Sheridan." As she spoke, Lady Rossmore's gaze went to the handsomest man there, some said the handsomest in London. The others, even the prince, looked a bit disheveled and more than a little dissolute at this late hour, with their jackets off and waistcoats unbuttoned to display their rotund bellies. Andrew, however, seemed merely nonchalant and devilishly good-looking, his stomach flat without the need of artifice, his long legs extended toward the fire. Lady Rossmore wondered how much of the duke's obviously magnificent body dear Beryl had already intimately charted.

"Sheridan," Prinny said. "Now there was a writer."

"Agreed," Andrew added. "Not like that boring twit Byron who only quotes and talks of himself."

"Andrew named one of his hounds after Byron," Francis put in.

Prinny smiled. "Boy has more passion than sense," was Prinny's opinion. "Do you think it all true? All the talk of Byron's affair with his sister Augusta?"

Effingham answered. "If not, she seems to be the only one he's missed."

Lord Rossmore did not look pleased at the turn in the conversation. "Really, Francis, that's the outside of enough with a lady present."

"Sorry."

"Yes," Prinny added. "We must beg pardon of your sensitive ears, Lady Rossmore."

"I have heard many speak of swooning over Byron's smoldering gaze," she replied, her eyes on Andrew. "Lady Beryl told me he made her feel quite faint."

"I suffer from the same malady around that simpleton," Andrew said dryly.

"I do so like his poetry, especially when he declaims it himself."

"Which he does at every opportunity."

"One would think you were jealous, Andrew."

"One would be wrong."

Lady Rossmore smiled and excused herself, leaving the gentlemen to their conversation. After another round of drinks, the prince called for his carriage. Rossmore said the night was still young, but the prince was set to go. Effingham agreed to partake of another libation with his host, putting the long forgotten ivory and ebony gaming chips into their rosewood box as Ashford accompanied the prince toward Carleton House.

Inside the royal equipage the prince took a sip from his hammered silver flask, his mood swinging darker. He spoke after a long and subdued perusal of the dark streets the carriage was clattering through.

"We love our people."

Lulled into a half slumber by the coach wheels, Andrew roused himself. "Of course, Your Highness."

"Did you read what they said of us this week in the papers they call news? They had the audacity to call our assemblies at Carleton House promiscuous beyond bounds. Said they were filled with notorious midnight bowers and miscellaneous companionships. Miscellaneous companionships, I ask you!"

"It is probably the doing of the Princess of Wales's advocates, your highness."

"Would we had never married the ugly strumpet. How dare she talk of us, whilst we pay for the establishment she's filled with back-stabbing malcontents and her Blackheath lovers!" The Duke of Ashford commiserated in silence with the unhappily married prince. "You've never married, Andrew, and by gad, you've the right of it, we think. We told young Devonshire the other night to emulate your example if he wished a contented and worthwhile life. Did you know he's deaf?"

"Many are when it suits them, Your Highness," Andrew said diplomatically.

"Egad, you've the right of it again," the prince said, smiling and gaining back some of the fine glow of comradeship he had felt earlier. "We should like to develop that sort of deafness ourself at times. You have no idea how tedious it can be to rule a nation, Andrew. It quite did us in last month."

The Duke of Ashford kept a prudent silence on the topic of Prinny's last illness, and found himself sharing yet another final libation at Carleton House before he could finally leave for Ashford House and his own bed.

When he arrived home, he shrugged off his many-caped greatcoat, heaving it at the waiting, sleepy footman. Wide awake, he glanced at the invitations that filled a small sterling silver tray on the hall sideboard, familiar crests evident as he idly rifled through. Putting them back, he saw his own crest in the middle of the pile and reached for the envelope. It was from Harding, and one look at its contents sent him storming up the staircase, shouting for James to attend him. The sleepy-eyed valet rose from his bed and rushed into his master's room dressed only in his smalls.

"What's wrong, your grace?"

"She's gone off shooting pigeons with one of my fowling pieces and got Will Tupper instead!" Since these words were given without preamble, it took the valet a moment before he realized their import and attached Brianna to the pronoun.

When he digested the information, James Tolliver went ashen. "Your grace—has she killed him, then?"

"No, blast her, her luck held. She only blew his hat off his head." The valet delivered himself of such a huge sigh of relief, his employer eyed him even more sharply. "Do I detect a note of sympathy in all that sniveling?"

"Oh, no, your grace. It's just that I am much relieved she has not done harm to your family name."

"How could she, she does not share it."

"But she is your ward, your grace."

"Don't remind me," Andrew said darkly. "Call for my phaeton and the fastest pair. You'd best pack for overnight."

"We leave for Sussex, m'lord?"

Andrew Ormsby eyed his valet. "At first light," the duke confirmed. "Unless you have a better plan for leashing my incorrigible relative."

James Tolliver delivered himself of a blinding smile. "Not I, your grace."

"If I didn't know better, I would swear you are pleased, James Tolliver."

"I am always pleased to do my master's bidding," the valet replied with remarkable diplomacy.

His grace of Ashford watched James leave the room, a scowl marring the duke's patrician features. He knew there was something amiss in James's reactions, but he was too tired to pursue the matter. Tomorrow would be soon enough.

The next day the duke arrived at Ashford Hall as Brianna and Constance sat down to their accustomed, quiet dinner.

"Your grace!" a startled footman blurted out as he ran forward toward the arriving phaeton.

"Your grace?" a surprised Harding questioned as he came out of the stables and saw his employer alight from the carriage.

"Your grace," Twinforth said with perfect equanimity, as he bowed the duke toward the main dining room and opened the double doors. "His grace," the butler intoned as the duke entered.

Brianna and Constance Powell looked up to see a very serious-looking Andrew enter the room. Travel-stained and more than a little put out, he scowled down at the tutor and her charge.

"Please continue," he said. "I trust you will forgive my appearance."

"Of—of course, your grace," Connie stuttered. "We were not expecting you."

The footmen bustled about bringing him food as Connie cast a swift and accusing look toward her charge.

"I didn't write," Brianna told her teacher, but it was the duke who replied.

"And why did you not?" he asked. "You seemed eloquent enough these weeks past concerning my failing health."

Concern flooded through the young girl. "Are you ill?" she asked.

"No. Merely decrepit and aging fast."

Brianna blushed crimson and saw Connie turn her attention upon her plate. She wouldn't look up. Brianna's stomach was doing some very disturbing flip-flops as, her heart in her mouth, she steeled herself to meet the duke's steady and decidedly unfriendly gaze.

"I did not mean precisely that," she answered belatedly. "And I beg your forgiveness if I said anything that caused you discomfort. We're awfully glad to have you home, your grace," she continued, trying to change the subject. "If you had let us know you were coming, we would have waited dinner until your arrival."

Andrew grimaced. "Very pretty. However, I could not apprise you of my arrival since I myself did not know I would be coming until I received Harding's message concerning legal actions being taken against me by a certain Will Tupper."

At the duke's words Connie looked up and a torrent of information, explanations, and apologies issued from both his ward and her tutor, all aimed at ensuring his grace was fully apprised of the exact circumstances of Brianna's encounter with Will Tupper.

"It wasn't what you think," Connie said forcibly. "It was entirely an accident."

"He said he'd be my target for a kiss," Brianna burst out. "I told him I wouldn't and then he tried to get the gun away and kiss me anyway and it went off and hit his hat but his hat was on the ground, not his head! He tried to grab me and I floored him and he got nasty and said he'd be my ruin!"

Andrew Ormsby heard a chorus of explanations that did nothing to soften his opinion until he heard the last of Brianna's disclosures. At her confession, he rose from his chair, nearly upsetting the footman who was pouring his wine.

"He did what?" the duke demanded of Brianna.

The girl was taken aback by the ferocity of his question, not to mention the vision of the six-foot, three-inch giant suddenly looming over her. "He said he'd be my ruin," Brianna repeated, looking up into the blue eyes she remembered, and finding them stormy with some unknown intensity that frightened her.

"He kissed you," the duke accused.

"He never did," Brianna replied. "As if he could best me!"

"Your grace," Connie interjected, "it truly was not her fault." Lord Ashford momentarily turned his attention upon his ward's tutor. When his accusing eyes met hers, she wilted back upon her chair. "Although of course she should not have taken the gun without permission—"

Brianna sprang from her chair and faced her benefactor squarely. The fact that she had to tilt her head back to see his face a foot above her own did not deter her.

"You may think what you wish, but Will Tupper is the sloppiest blacksmith I ever saw, and he is a lout and a cad to boot, and I wish I had shot him in the heart, which I could have, as I am a crack shot!"

"A crack shot," the duke repeated disparagingly.

"If your grace would care to test my prowess, I stand ready."

Andrew Ormsby stared down at the chit of a girl who had the unmitigated audacity to challenge him. "I hope you will indulge my doubts."

"I will *not* indulge your doubts or your irritating arrogance or Will Tupper's either," Brianna informed her benefactor with eyes sparkling with unshed tears. "Will Tupper is a sore loser and I will *not* apologize!"

"You, my girl, will do as I tell you," the duke informed his ward.

"Never!" she replied loudly.

"Never?" he demanded even more loudly.

"Your grace, I am sure Brianna does not mean—"

"I do!"

"She does!"

Constance Powell stared toward the two angry faces who were united in opposing her words. Miss Powell rose from her chair and gave the smallest of curtsies.

"I can see I am not needed," were her parting words as she left the room.

Once she was gone, the footmen who flanked the long

mahogany sideboard disappeared through the hall doors, and finally the duke and his ward were alone. Brianna swallowed hard, but she faced up to the tall duke, her small chin set forward in stubborn challenge.

"None has ever made me forsake my principles and none ever shall!" Brianna informed him.

"Well, bully for you."

There was a long moment in which silence stood between them. Brianna tried to gain the duke's measure, and Andrew tried very much the same thing as he gazed down toward the chit of a girl who had been left on his doorstep.

"I refuse to have my fortune squandered by solicitors attempting to stave off your adversaries," the duke finally told his charge.

"I don't blame you."

"I beg your pardon?"

Brianna spoke slowly. "I was in the right, but if I were you, I should say the same. I certainly would not want the likes of Will Tupper getting one farthing of my inheritance, if I had an inheritance, and I would castigate any relative who put me in such a pickle."

"You would."

"Yes. I would." Worry creased the young girl's brow. "He can't do that, can he? Make trouble for you?"

"He most certainly can and is," she was informed.

"Oh, Andrew," Brianna grabbed the duke's hand within both her own. "I am most dreadfully sorry!"

Andrew Ormsby looked down into green eyes the color of ocean depths, a queer feeling rising inside him when she called him by his given name. She looked up at him with such pleading honesty he forgot to be angry at her. Her hands clasped his, the warmth he felt at her touch adding to his unease. He had been prepared to lecture her upon her unfeminine and dangerous actions, but found himself staring instead into the most beautiful eyes he had ever seen, the words gone from his mind. Bemused, he realized the girl was different than he remembered. Something about her had changed.

"Andrew?" Brianna questioned. "I mean, your grace," she said when the silence between them grew.

"What?" he roused himself.

"I am most desperately sorry for worrying you, I didn't mean to and I'll never do it again," she promised, her trusting eyes never leaving his.

"Never do what again?" he asked softly.

"Worry you."

Andrew stared down at her upturned face. "That's a promise I'm very afraid you can't possibly keep."

"I shall try very hard."

She wore a muslin round gown figured with tiny embroidered clusters of yellow flowers and green leaves. The neckline was high and frilled, the bodice molded around curves that declared the girl no longer a child. For one mad moment he contemplated kissing the lips that curved full and pink beneath her adorable upturned nose. He was leaning forward when he realized what was happening and gained control of himself and his fancies, his face hardening into sharp lines. He withdrew his hand from hers so abruptly he startled her.

"If you mean what you say, you will cease all your hoydenish activities." Fighting himself, the words came out more harshly than he realized, until he saw bright tears spring to her eyes. They were quickly quelled, Brianna's pride softening his heart as she straightened her back and gazed straight at him.

"I shall never distress you again!" She pushed past him, a chair flying backward as she ran from the room. The side door opened at the sound, a footman peeking in and quickly withdrawing after one look at the duke's unreadable expression.

Alone, and stunned with the reactions she had brought forth, Andrew sank to a chair and studied the food that was growing cold upon the table. She was a mere child, he told himself, he must be demented to have thought of kissing her. When Twinforth looked in, he saw the duke sitting with his head in his hands, his food untouched.

"Your grace?"

"Send for James. Tell him we leave immediately."

Even Twinforth was startled by this pronouncement. And when he repeated it to James Tolliver, he was privy to some colorful language on the subject of men who didn't know their own minds.

Chapter Twelve

Once back in London, Andrew Ormsby threw himself into his tasks and his pleasures, spending long hours in war-room meetings at Carleton House and Parliament and even longer hours at White's and various gaming hells known for their high stakes and loose morals.

He escorted Lady Beryl to the opera, to the theater and assemblies, routs and card nights. But most evenings after he deposited her at Cavendish House, he went on in pursuit of less savory pleasures.

James Tolliver was worried, and some inkling of his worry came through the words he wrote to Nellie in Sussex. But when he broached the subject to the duke, he was told quite firmly to mind his own business.

"Nothing is wrong," Andrew insisted. "I'm healthy as a horse. Thanks to my mother, we shall soon be forced away, and I intend to partake of the city's pleasures whilst I may." The mention of the dowager's expected arrival sent the conversation upon another tack, and James soon found himself alone in the master suite, his grace of Ashford finally pleased with his cravat and out the door to his nightly rounds.

Two hours later at Cavendish House, the duke leaned forward and kissed the tip of Lady Beryl's bare ivory shoulder. They stood in an alcove off the ballroom, music floating in the air around them, the sounds of laughter and conversation coming back through the velvet curtains that hid them from general view. In the reflected candlelight Lady Beryl's elegant blond curls seemed spun of purist gold.

She wore a gown designed for a Grecian goddess, its simple white folds clinging to her hips and breast and bound in place by thin golden cords. Gold-encrusted pearls circled her neck, her wrist, and the high waist of the gown that fell straight to her ankles.

"We must return to the others," she murmured.

"They've not yet missed us." His lips found a shell-like ear to nuzzle.

She shivered and then playfully pushed him away, a languid smile accompanying her sideways glance. "Don't be a naughty boy or I shall have to seek a hero to protect me."

"I thought I was your only hero," Andrew whispered into her ear.

She tapped the shoulder of his exquisitely cut evening jacket. "Fie, you simply toy with my affections, as all my other friends say."

"Friends? Or beaux?"

Beryl gave him a brilliant smile. "Do not sound jealous, dear Andrew; you have no claim on me."

Her words for some inexplicable reason made him think of Brianna's homily on grasping women. He had been thinking a great deal too much of that young hoyden in recent days, and irritated with himself, he drew Beryl closer.

"You are very nearly undressed."

Her laughter was silvery. "But only nearly, my pet." She made a pretty moue and pushed him back, walking away toward the curtains slowly enough to give him an ample view of her luxurious figure. She wore only a thin chemise under the daring gown of sheer muslin. It clung to every soft curve, teasing the eye and inviting it to closer examination. She stopped in the draped archway, looking back over her shoulder. "You shan't make me return to my uncle's guests alone, shall you?"

He frowned as he came forward. "I fear you are turning me into a tame puppy."

"I am doing no such thing," she told him, laughing again.

She placed an affectionate and proprietary hand on his sleeve. "Come along and you may get me a champagne punch. I am positively parched."

"I don't want to get you a champagne punch. I want to get you alone and away from all my competition."

Beryl batted her eyelashes provocatively as he held the velvet drape aside for her. "Perhaps after my uncle's guests are gone we can find a quiet moment by ourselves."

Heads turned when the tall dark duke led the petite blond beauty across the dance floor. The handsome couple were the talk of London; there were wagers in more than one gambling establishment as to when or if he would pop the question.

"Ashford," Lord Barnstable called out as he joined Andrew at the tables heaped with refreshments. "Have you done it yet?" The portly older man picked an apricot tartlet and popped it into his mouth, washing it down with champagne.

"Done what?"

"I've a bet on, you'll speak to her uncle before the year is out. Don't figure you'll be able to hold out much longer."

"Hold out?" Andrew said politely, only his eyes revealing his irritation.

"Against female blandishments, old boy. Beryl's a widow and getting a bit long in the tooth. Best not keep her waiting, with all these young dandies to choose from. Best get a move on."

Andrew's back had grown stiffer with each word from Barnstable's mouth. "I hardly think your words either proper or fitting when discussing a lady of quality and virtue."

"No need to go up in the boughs. I say widows are the best of wives, already broken in, if you see what I mean."

"Excuse me," Ashford said in freezing accents. He walked away toward the orchestra as others came near the table.

"Can't hold out forever," Barnstable said to his back.

Beryl sat with her aunt near the chamber orchestra. Andrew threaded his way through the crowded ballroom, angry blue eyes discouraging any interruption. Barnstable was a fool, but he had the right of it and Andrew knew as much. Beryl was becoming a bit distant lately, more and more finding previous engagements on her calendar when he suggested a night's entertainment. He knew she expected him to propose; he expected himself to propose. It just never quite seemed the proper time or place.

"You look so very grim, Andrew. Whatever has cast you into such a fit of the blue devils?" Beryl asked as he handed over the tiny china plate heaped with sweets and fruit.

"Nothing," he replied, but after a few minutes of polite conversation with her aunt, he drew Beryl aside. "We must talk alone."

"We just have."

"I'm serious."

"I can see that by your scowl, and so can the entire assembly. You will have them thinking we are on the outs, dear heart."

"Are we?" he asked.

"Are we?" she asked back. Before she could stop him, he was pulling her into his arms. "Andrew!"

"Waltz," he told her as, one arm around her back, he reached for her hand. They moved together well, the music sensuous, the air warm with people and candlelight. He looked down at the creamy skin that escaped her daringly low neckline, her swelling breasts barely contained by a narrow strip of thin fabric.

"You are naughty tonight," Beryl teased. "I fear I shall have to teach you some manners."

"Teach me manners?" Andrew repeated. He thought of the young hellion causing havoc at his Sussex estate. "I assure you, you have no idea to what lengths bad manners can be taken."

He spoke so feelingly she gave him a curious little glance. "Whatever are you talking about?"

"Nothing. I was thinking of something else."

"Someone else?" she asked archly.

"No," he said too quickly. "Well, yes."

"Who is she?"

"Someone who is driving me toward Bedlam."

Beryl stiffened. "Perhaps you should be dancing with her."

"No, no, it's nothing like that. Actually, that's one of the things I wish to discuss with you."

"What is?"

"Children."

Beryl stopped dancing. "I *beg* your pardon?"

"I don't mean this moment, but there are certain situations, considerations, in my family that impinge upon my way of life, my arrangements, at least for the near future."

"I suddenly feel the need of air," she told him. Beryl Cavendish kept a sweet smile on her face whilst inwardly cursing the beast. Next he would tell her he had a by-blow and expect her to raise the creature. Andrew Ormsby was rich, titled, and good-looking, and Beryl was determined to become the Duchess of Ashford. No matter he was next to impossible to bring up to scratch, no matter his mother's objections were so violent they had reached Beryl's ears all the way from Dublin, thanks to mutual friends.

"I'll have no grasping widow in my family," the dowager duchess was reported to have said.

"Are you feeling unwell?" Andrew asked as they reached the terrace.

"A bit of the headache, from the heat, I expect," she explained. The back of her pink-gloved hand went to her smooth forehead as she sighed.

The Duke of Ashford looked down at the vision of frail and feminine beauty. Backlit by the bright room behind them, her body was once again outlined to perfection through the thin dress. The pink satin ribbons along her sleeves fluttered in the evening breezes that caressed the terrace.

"You are too beautiful for words," he told her.

"Thank you, kind sir."

"I'm not one for giving those pretty, meaningless compliments you seem to enjoy."

"I don't seem to enjoy them. I do enjoy them. All women do."

A slim dark-haired young man came out through the

terrace doors. Dressed in the most romantic coat of softest black velvet, his snowy cravat artfully cascading down his chest, he appeared pensive and very, very young. "Lady Beryl?"

She turned at the sound of his voice, her smile widening. "My *dear* Lord Byron, I cannot believe my eyes!"

He came straight toward her, reaching to grasp her hands and leaning to kiss each wrist as he brought it upward to his lips. "Dearest lady, you remember your poor friend."

"None could forget the immortal Byron. Andrew, isn't it wonderful he could come this evening?"

"Thrilling," the duke said, looking positively put-upon.

"I'm most dreadfully sorry, Ashford," Byron said. "But in the presence of such sublime beauty, all else, even manners themselves, fly away, and one is left with only the vision of such perfection as to make even the angels in heaven weep with jealousy."

"I'm getting a drink," Ashford said. Beryl's tinkling laughter carried toward him as he marched inside Cavendish House, nearly running over Lady Hunnicut.

"Lord, have a care, Andrew," she said with a deep, throaty laugh. "You're much too big to go barreling about with your thoughts in the clouds. Or on Beryl."

"Sorry, Pamela. Where's Hunnicut?"

"I have no idea. My husband went to the loo tables, but from thence onward he seems to have become lost. I thought to look for him on the terrace."

"He's not there. That fop, Byron, is out there quoting himself to Beryl."

"And you're leaving them alone? What a trusting man you are."

"I have a dog who whines in the very same tones," Andrew snapped.

"It would seem he is *irresistible* in some quarters. The man, not your dog," she replied, smiling.

"If she wants the likes of that—that—*poet*, she's welcome to him."

"Do I detect a note of disharmony in paradise?"

"Pamela."

"Andrew, I'm not a gossip. But if you ever want a shoulder to cry on, I stand ready." Pamela Hunnicut was tall and, at thirty, in her prime. Her thick brunette hair was swept up off her neck with gold ribbons, her cloth of gold gown a touch less daring than Beryl's but equally revealing of her charms. At this moment her hazel eyes were smiling meaningfully into Andrew's stormy eyes. "In point of fact," she said softly, "you can have much more than my shoulder if you like. Hunnicut is very understanding of my friendships."

Andrew grimaced. "I'm sorry, Pamela, I've no pretty replies. I am so deuced confused, I am sincerely considering life in a monastery."

"You? Good Lord, what has she done?"

"Cut up all my peace of mind, that's what, and for absolutely no sensible reason in the world. She is a reckless hoyden who hasn't an ounce of sense nor a hint of propriety, and I think I am losing my mind."

"Andrew, whom are you speaking of?"

"What?" Confused eyes of the deepest blue looked down into Pamela's questioning gaze.

"I thought we were speaking of Beryl."

"Beryl's on the terrace," Andrew said. "Excuse me. I've got to find her blasted aunt and do the pretty before I leave."

Lady Pamela Hunnicut watched the upset Duke of Ashford walk away, a perplexed expression furrowing her brow. She watched his strong, straight back and long, well-muscled legs until he was lost in the throngs. Then she positioned herself near the terrace doors and waited for Lady Beryl.

Lord Byron escorted a smiling Beryl Cavendish back into the ballroom a quarter of an hour later, stopping to speak to Pamela as they entered. Beryl lost her smile when she found out Lord Ashford had quit the premises.

"Oh, he's been gone an age, dear," Pamela said as she walked beside them to the whist tables where her husband and the Barnstables sat.

"Gone?"

Byron looked abashed. "Have I caused you grief, dear lady? Do you wish me to go after him for you?"

"Of course not. Andrew had mentioned he was not feeling well," Beryl said smoothly, hiding her displeasure under a sweet smile. "Come along, dear Lord Byron. I wish to have your opinion upon my uncle's newest acquisition."

Lord Barnstable watched Beryl conduct the poet away from the card room. "Cavendish's newest, eh? Art or mistress?"

"Clifford, really," his wife remonstrated.

"He's just upset," Hunnicut put in. "Worried about his bet."

Pamela looked up from her cards. "Bet?"

Barnstable looked uncomfortable. "Whose bid is it?"

"Clifford? What is this about a bet?" Lady Barnstable demanded.

"He bet Ashford would come up to scratch this season, but it seems someone's thrown a spoke in the works."

"This year," Barnstable corrected irritably. "And you needn't look at me that way, Bedelia, all of London has bets on the Bachelor Duke remaining a bachelor."

The next morning Polite Society was treated to the information that Andrew Ormsby, the Duke of Ashford, had announced himself to be quite done in by the exigencies of fashionable life. It was also widely reported that he had called for his phaeton with alarming haste, considering his supposed weakened condition. He even insisted upon handling the ribbons himself, and even as they spoke, was heading toward his country estate.

In point of fact, Lord Ashford was not on his way to Sussex. He was driving at full tilt out the London road, Lord Francis Effingham racing just ahead and trying to keep Andrew's equipage from catching up to his new high-perch phaeton. While the two friends raced toward Lord Effingham's Oxfordshire estate, and London gossiped about the possibility of Lady Beryl losing his grace of Ashford's attentions, Brianna sat cross-legged upon her bed. Her chin in her hands, her expression pensive, she listened to the most recent letter from James.

"'We're to leave for the shires and hunting at Lord Effingham's,'" Nellie read from the valet's letter. "'I've no idea when we shall return, but give my best to all, James Tolliver,'" Nellie finished.

"Just fancy, he's actually boxed with Gentleman Jackson," Brianna said in awed tones as Nellie folded the letter. "Oh, if only I were a boy."

"I would be so frightened if I were Lady Beryl."

"Whatever for?" Brianna demanded.

"Why, for his getting hurt."

"Fudge. Gentleman Jackson knows better than to deck any of the nobs who subscribe to his athletic club. Why, he'd have no clientele at all if he went around beating them up."

"Still and all, it has to be dangerous."

"I'll bet it was fun," Brianna admitted. She heaved a great sigh. "Gentlemen have all the fun in this world."

"Oh, I don't think so, Miss Bree."

"Of course they do. They get to go off on crusades and wars and become highwaymen and acrobats and anything they please. It's a man's world, and that's the truth of it."

"For my tuppence, ladies have the best of it," Nellie declared. "If you're lucky enough to marry well, you have all sorts of pretty clothes and get to decorate your very own house all nice like, just the way you want. And taking care of a big brute who's all your own, what could be lovelier?"

An errant thought of the big brute of a duke, tall and dark and strong, crossed Brianna's mind at Nellie's words. His eyes were the most amazing blue.

"Miss Brianna? Is something wrong?"

"No, I was just wool-gathering, that's all." Brianna felt her cheeks flushing and was thoroughly put out with herself for being so silly.

"Don't you ever think of the man you'll marry, Miss Bree?"

"I shall never marry."

"Oh, Miss Bree, don't say such a thing!"

"Nellie, you are a positive romantic."

"Am I, Miss Bree?" the maid asked with rounded eyes. "I never knew I was much of anything. A romantic, am I? Fancy that. Just wait until I tell the girls." Reminded of her duties, she jumped up from the floor and stuffed the letter into her apron pocket. "I'd best get below before Twinforth comes looking for me. He's the most scariest person when he gets upset."

"He's not the scariest," Brianna said, but she did not elaborate. After Nellie left, Brianna sat fingering the coverlet that lay beneath her, thinking of the duke's precipitous leave-taking. He couldn't stand the sight of her, that was plain. Tears sprang to her eyes at the thought, and she wiped them away. He didn't have to like her, she comforted herself. She had not wanted to be left with him in the first place.

And it was his fault her dreams were filled with visions of a tall, blue-eyed prince. He wore a black satin cape and rode a huge black stallion and came charging at her to sweep her up off her feet, but just as he reached for her, he disappeared, the horse racing away riderless as Brianna stood alone on the empty plain and stared after it.

Chapter Thirteen

Ashford Hall slipped into a new routine as the master remained away. A much more subdued Brianna bent to her studies, trying to please her teacher and fill up all the empty spaces when her mind drifted toward London and the beautiful women who filled the duke's life.

Mrs. Potts and Connie spent the spring creating a small but neat wardrobe from the Christmas packages of fabric and accessories the duke had sent. It was a most practical array and he had been most generous, Constance said, but

Mrs. Potts was of the less charitable opinion that the duke had left the purchases to some man of business who knew nothing of young girls and what might please them.

For her part, Mrs. Potts had created a forest-green riding habit from some of the material as her Christmas gift to the girl who was the staff's darling, even if she was the rue of her teacher's, and the bane of her guardian's, existence.

Brianna had fallen in love with the riding habit the moment she saw it. It spelled freedom and fun—and she was wearing it to tatters, Mrs. Potts told her with ill-concealed pleasure.

Now that the weather had changed, Brianna escaped the house each spring day as soon as she put away her studies. She flew to her room, changed to her riding habit, and raced outside, careening down the rose-trellised path that led along the side of the house to the stableyard behind. She slowed to examine particular buds, urging them into full bloom, drinking in the warm spring air that floated with the soft scents of early flowers.

Her goal was the stable, her hope that in exchange for help and sometimes in exchange for merely getting her out from underfoot, Dennis would allow her to ride one of his charges. The spaniels waited for her at the turn of the path, already accustomed to their new daily routine, Daisy and Rowdy chasing along ahead, beside, and behind, Byron waiting patiently for his head to be stroked before he lay back down, his head between his paws, soaking up the afternoon sun.

"Have a care, Miss Bree," Dennis sang out as she came through the main doors into the cool dimness of the stable. A huge chestnut stallion was cross-tied, the head stableman trimming his hooves, Dennis and Jeff soothing him when he tried to buck.

"Does it hurt him very much?" Brianna asked, her brow knitted with worry.

"Not a bit of it," the head stableman told her without looking up from his work. "He's just a might nervous, he don't take to being tied up."

"Nor should I," Brianna told the chestnut soothingly. She

skirted around their work and headed back toward Dark Star's stall, calling to her softly. The mare's head came up, her ears flicking back and then held upright and alert when she recognized the familiar voice. She came toward Brianna, reaching her head over the stall door to nuzzle Brianna's shoulder.

Brianna patted the animal's elegant nose, Dennis coming alongside and watching them.

"She's taken a shine to you, she has."

"I suppose she's already been exercised . . ."

"Well now, as luck would have it, I've not had a moment to see to her yet today." He grinned at Brianna's gratified expression. "And I thought she might have a friend stopping by. Mind if you take her out for a run, you must groom her when you get back, no running off because Mrs. Potts is calling you to dinner."

"I promise!"

"If you do, I'll be the one in trouble for letting you take her and you not getting back in time."

"I never shall," Brianna promised. "I am learning to be most awfully punctual and dependable, I truly am."

"What bouncers you tell," Dennis said. But he smiled as he let Brianna lead the mare outside. She was a lovely shiny black with four snowy feet and a pure white star on her forehead.

Dennis gave Brianna a leg up into the sidesaddle he insisted she use and handed her the reins. He watched, his hand cupped over his eyes as he watched her trot sedately down the drive. Daisy and Rowdy barked in chorus as they chased after the mare, racing to catch up.

Dennis was whistling tunelessly as he went back into the stable and returned to his chores. He knew the mare would get a dandy workout once Brianna was beyond the elms that lined the curving drive. She would wait until she was out of sight and shouting distance of the house before she urged Dark Star into the gallop they both wanted.

Brianna had ridden all her young life, and after half a year cooped up inside Ashford Hall's elegant confines, she was bursting with restless energy. It was spring and she would soon be sixteen, new feelings bringing laughter and tears by turns as her body changed and she grew toward womanhood. She trotted through the gate at the end of the drive and then turned off the road, letting Dark Star have her head. They flew across the unplanted fields, the dogs in close pursuit and yelping with joy as they headed for the sea.

It wasn't really the sea, it was actually a great bay that gave onto the English Channel, but the water went on forever. The duke's lands ran all the way to the high cliffs that edged the bay—smugglers' cliffs, Dennis had warned her solemnly. Cliffs pockmarked with caves that hid forbidden treasures.

She wasn't sure she believed his romantic tales, but the huge bay that led to the sea fascinated her. She drank in the salt air that swept in over the cliffs, looking down seventy feet to the water that frothed and pounded up against the rocks and a patch of stony beach. Squinting in the bright sunlight, Brianna tried to see beyond the bay, to see across the English Channel to France as Daisy and Rowdy searched through overgrown bushes for some sport of their own. All Brianna could see were the curving arms of the huge bay and a glimpse of silver glittering in the distance beyond. A sudden longing for her brother washed through her as she stared toward France.

Behind to the east, vistas of clouds drifted over the distant downs, flocks of sheep grazing in nearer fields. Spring plowing was under way, the black overturned earth dark amidst the vivid green of the surrounding meadows. The budding trees were sparse enough to the west that a glimpse of the rooftops and chimneys of the whitewashed village of East Ashing could be seen, the spire of the village church rising toward the white-clouded blue sky.

Brianna was alone with the sounds of the sea and the wind and the dogs' occasional yelps as they raced back and forth, sniffing out surprises. Dark Star pawed at the ground as her rider dismounted with the aid of a good-sized boulder. She walked the horse along the edge of the cliffs, a grove of elms and maples beyond. A squirrel, surprised by the dogs, scurried up a tree into the protection of its uppermost branches. It sat still and alert on its haunches, its small dark eyes darting glances all around, watchful and waiting. Far below, Daisy and Rowdy jumped up at the tree trunk, barking for the animal to come down and play.

When Brianna remounted the mare and turned her toward the road that led to the village, she realized the sun was dipping lower in the sky.

"Daisy, Rowdy, come, we're late!"

The dogs responded to her urgency, racing ahead and alongside and finally behind as Dark Star galloped across the fields to the road and raced back across the huge Ashford estate. Brianna was unaware that she had yet to ride far enough to be off the duke's property.

At the stable Dennis was watching for her. "I thought I'd have to come after you," he said over the din of the barking dogs.

"And just where would you have found me?"

"To the sea cliffs, looking for pirates." He grinned. "Where else would you be going?"

"It's all a bamboozle, isn't it? You've been funning me all along!" As she spoke she dismounted and walked the warm horse, finally tying its reins.

"Never would I do such a contrary thing," Dennis said innocently.

She took the dandy brush and the curry comb from him, working to remove the dried mud before she reached for the body brush. Dennis watched her with approval as she used a sweeping circular motion, following the direction of the hair and working slowly toward the back. Every few strokes she stopped to run the brush across the curry comb, dislodging the dirt.

"Don't forget under the mane and the inside of the pasterns."

"And under the tail and between the legs," Brianna retorted.

"What's that noise?" Dennis said, looking toward the curve of the drive. The horses whinnied as the clatter of hoofbeats and carriage wheels came nearer. The dogs barked and ran off around the drive, yapping frantically. "It sounds like an army," Dennis reported. "Jeff! Mr. Sly!" he called to the head stablemen as he ran toward the drive. Brianna stayed where she was, brushing out Dark Star.

One carriage, then two, then a third, clattered up the drive, closer and closer. They did not lessen their pace at the front of the house but came around to the back, Mr. Sly and Jeff joining Dennis at a trot as two high-sprung phaetons drawn by pairs and one huge black coach and four came to a stop in the cobblestoned stableyard.

The stablemen went forward to help, Brianna staring at the large black coach as Mr. Sly put the step down and James Tolliver stepped out upon it. At the sight of the duke's valet, Brianna's breath caught in her throat. She gaped as London dandies and ladies stepped out onto the cobblestones. Their loud conversation and peals of laughter carried to the house where Twinforth and Harding both heard and hurried back toward the side terrace.

"Ashford, you cheated," a young blond dandy challenged.

"Henleigh, you're a sore loser," Francis Effingham said.

Brianna could not hear the reply over the din of the other voices and her pounding heart. He was here. Footmen were loping toward the large coach piled high with luggage.

Andrew stepped out of the front carriage, laughing at something his companion was saying. He reached back and Brianna caught a glimpse of a gloved hand, and then the most beautiful creature imaginable stepped out of the duke's carriage. She was everything beauty demanded. Petite, with a heart-shaped face, large blue eyes, ivory skin, and blond hair that framed the angelic face.

"It is not true," Andrew was protesting, "I did not run from London, Beryl. Francis and I drove to Oxfordshire to hunt as we do every year. I was pleased as can be when you and Jane and Henleigh arrived."

"You wished to rush off here without us," Beryl pouted.

"No," the duke said, more than a little uncomfortable. "I merely felt you would be bored to tears staying so long in the country."

"No such thing, I want to know more of your life, Andrew."

Lady Beryl wore a riding costume made of exquisite pale blue wool. As Brianna watched, Beryl tucked her arm into the duke's. The handsome couple walked toward their companions, the spaniels dancing around their feet and barking wildly.

"Pamela, tell him he cheated," the young blond dandy called out to a tall brunette dressed in a wine-colored pelisse. She laughed, the sound shrill to Brianna's ears, and turned toward a man whom Brianna recognized as Lord Effingham. Effingham's pale good looks receded between the dark duke and the blond dandy who leaned over a third young woman with dark honey curls.

"Henny, you're a poor loser," Andrew called out.

"Jane, you tell him," the Marquess of Henleigh said. Dressed in the most fancy of finery, he was the picture of a London gentleman, complete with quizzing glass to his eye as he wrinkled his patrician nose.

The disparity between the two men was evident in their attire. The blond was a tulip of fashion, his yellow and white waistcoat of striped toilinette worn over a lemon-yellow shirt and under a green coat of corbeau cloth cut with exaggerated shoulders and narrowed waist. His breeches were of an impractical white Angola cloth, his hunting boots black with white tops. Attached to this finery were gold chains, a watch fob, a scent pendant, and his quizzing glass.

Beside him the duke towered inches taller, the cut of his coat of charcoal superfine and buckskin breeches simple, his waistcoat a sober dove color. The points of his white collar were stiff but not exaggerated, his snowy cravat tied with artistry but not flamboyance.

"Admit it, Andrew."

"Of course I admit it, dear Henny, I was behind when we reached the drive," Andrew countered easily, grinning.

"What cheek! Do you hear your hero, Beryl? Pamela? Jane? He dares to admit his perfidy."

"Andrew dares much . . . in many areas," Pamela said, smiling. She received an appraising glance from Beryl.

"And how do you know such a thing?" Beryl asked sweetly.

Henleigh said something Brianna could not hear, and they all laughed, the dogs joining in with happy yelps and jumps in the direction of the duke. He leaned to scratch their ears as he introduced them to his guests.

"And this," Andrew said, "is the only Byron worth his salt. And Rowdy and Daisy too, the best hunters you can imagine."

Most of the conversation was unintelligible at Brianna's distance, words spoken over other words and the laughter of all. Effingham was bored, his indifferent glance finding the black mare. Indifference turned to curiosity when he spotted Brianna. Trying to hide, she ducked her head and went back to her work. The Marquess of Henleigh saw the direction of Effingham's gaze and lifted his glass to his eye.

"My word, Andrew, are you hiring females to attend your mounts?"

Andrew made a sarcastic retort as he glanced toward the stable and, seeing Brianna, stopped in his tracks.

"That is a female, I suspect, under all the dirt," Henleigh continued. "I would almost swear to it."

"Shall we go inside?" Effingham asked the women when he saw the duke's astounded expression.

"What nonsense are you spouting now, Henny?" Lady Jane asked.

"A female?" Pamela questioned, looking toward the dirty urchin beside the black mare.

With each question the duke's expression darkened.

"A female indeed," Beryl scoffed, and her eyebrows raised in exaggerated horror. "Andrew, what is the meaning of this?"

Andrew stalked toward Brianna, a muscle working in his jaw. He looked ferocious. The girl wore a bedraggled green dress stained with mud and muck, her face smudged with dirt, her curls spilling every which way. In four long strides he reached her side, the dogs pattering along beside him.

"I'm not dressed like a boy," she said hopefully, presenting him with a heart-melting smile. "And I'm ever so glad you've come home, Cousin Andrew. Your grace," she added belatedly with another dazzling smile.

"Andrew, don't *touch* her, she reeks of the stables," Beryl cautioned from a little distance away.

"He knows how to handle her," Effingham said.

Beryl heard him and turned, her eyes narrowing as she searched his face. "Francis, you sound as if you know something about this creature."

Effingham did not answer; he was looking toward Andrew, who had Brianna by the ear and was dragging her forward, the dogs jumping up beside them, trying to join in the game.

"Careful, don't let her touch your clothes," Henny called out in horror. He put his perfumed handkerchief to his nose as they passed.

"Harding," the duke fairly shouted at the man who was coming toward them along the side terrace. "See to my guests!" Andrew was past the small group of Londoners, pulling Brianna toward the kitchen doors.

Pamela gave Beryl a long, arch look. "Do you suppose there was a reason he didn't want us to accompany him here?"

She received no reply for Harding interrupted, giving a polite little cough. "This way, if you please, ladies, gentlemen . . ."

James Tolliver watched his master haul Brianna toward the kitchens as the Londoners followed Harding in the opposite direction toward the side porch where Twinforth waited. The valet turned toward the head stableman. "Our girl good with the horses, is she?"

"She's a rare one, Mr. James, and full of pluck. I hope his lordship's not hard on her."

"He'll give her an earful, I'll warrant, what with those London henwits laughing at him."

"He's always had a temper, our master. When he was a lad, I remember the days when he'd mill anyone down for looking cross-eyed at him."

James remembered them too. He took off after his master at a trot.

Near the kitchen's back door the scullery maid looked up from her sudsy pots to see the duke himself barreling inside, dragging Miss Bree behind. Startled, the maid dropped the heavy iron skillet she was washing, the sound so loud on the flagstone floor, the cook nearly jumped out of her skin.

"Betsy, you scared me out of ten years' growth, be more careful or—" The cook saw the duke coming toward her, Miss Bree by the ear, and barking dogs behind and beside.

"Let me go, you great brute!" Brianna shouted as he hauled her past the cook and up the back staircase. James came inside at a quick trot, trying to catch up with his master.

"Whatever has the girl gone and done now?" Cook asked as he passed.

"Made a cake of him in front of his friends," James said as he passed.

Ahead of him up the stairway Brianna managed to wrench out of the duke's grasp and race for her room, banging the door shut and holding it closed. The sixth Duke of Ashford stopped in the middle of Ashford Hall's wide upper hallway and bellowed at the top of his lungs for Miss Powell.

"Your grace," James said as he reached his master's side.

"I want Miss Powell!"

"She'll be coming, your grace, never fear. You could call the devil out of hell with those lungs. The girl did nothing wrong. A little honest work is all—"

"I don't want to hear it," Andrew warned.

Constance Powell was in the library downstairs when she heard the duke's summons. She ran past Twinforth as he ushered the Londoners into the red parlor. She hardly gave them a glance as she flew past and up the stairs toward the waiting duke, reaching his side out of breath.

"Your grace, I'm sorry, we had no word, we weren't

expecting you," the tutor said in a rush of words. She gave a brief, belated curtsey. "You . . . rang?"

"I did not *ring*. I bellowed!"

"You are still doing so," she pointed out.

"Come with me," he ordered. He marched to Brianna's closed door and turned the brass knob. It stuck. He pushed, and a chair that had been wedged against the door fell forward, the door banging against the inside wall and bouncing back, the sounds echoing in the silent house.

"Tea?" Twinforth asked the guests downstairs.

All eyes but Twinforth's were on the ceiling.

"I think sherry might be wiser," Lord Effingham told the butler.

Upstairs Brianna was making a valiant but futile attempt to stare down the angry Duke of Ashford. "One in the breadbasket, that's what you'll get if you come near me. I'm no Gentleman Jim, paid to turn the other cheek to nobs," she warned in as menacing a tone as she could muster. Since she was a foot shorter than her adversary, she was definitely outclassed, but her chin jutted out and her hands were balled into fists in front of her. She saw her tutor behind the duke. "I didn't *do* anything, Connie, I swear it," she defended.

"I suggest you look in a mirror," Andrew said in frigid tones. He turned his back on her and stared down Miss Powell. "Is she the daughter of a servant? I was asked. Is she a bit off in the upper works? I was asked. Are you hiring female grooms? I was asked. The girl is as disheveled and dirty as a street urchin, and you tell me I was not expected. Is this filthy costume her normal attire?" he demanded.

"It's my very favorite!" Brianna blurted out.

He gave her a withering glance. "No doubt."

"I'm sorry, your grace, this is entirely my fault," Connie told her employer. "You agreed she could ride, and I thought to make her responsible for her mount."

Andrew still stared at the tutor, his face an angry mask. For some inexplicable reason the woman's rational answer irritated him further.

"I don't want her filthy," he snapped.

"I'll see that she changes, your grace."

"I won't have her making a laughingstock of herself," he said with such force he surprised even himself. He saw his vehemence affect Miss Powell, and turned away from her puzzled expression, meeting Brianna's indignant gaze and feeling more foolish by the minute.

He had an almost overwhelming desire to spank the girl, and knew none of it was her fault. Without saying a word, she had made him see how shallow his friends were, and he wanted to punish her for making him see a truth he did not want to deal with. He also wanted to knock the supercilious smiles off Henleigh's and Effingham's faces, and he wasn't feeling much more kindly toward the ladies who had laughed at Brianna, including Beryl.

"Your grace?" the tutor questioned.

Without replying, he turned on his heel and stalked out of the room.

James awaited him in the hall. "There's no need to get yourself into such a pucker—"

"A pucker?" Andrew bellowed. "I'm not in a pucker! I'm dashed *angry.*" He stalked into the master suite sitting room.

"And I don't blame you, your grace."

"You don't know what you're talking of!"

"Of course not," James soothed. "Although you shouldn't let your mother upset you so."

"What in the name of heaven has my mother to do with any of this?"

"I don't scruple to say I think you very wise indeed to repair to the country instead of going back to Ashford House whilst she is in London. But I see no reason to take out the inconvenience, and your natural ire, on the wee damsel," he added placidly. He disappeared into the duke's bedroom before his employer could throw anything in his direction.

A reddening Andrew glared at the empty doorway. He considered firing his disrespectful valet as, unable to stay still, he began to pace his sitting room. He pulled off his coat, throwing it across a wingback chair, his waistcoat soon following. He pulled sharply on his shirt buttons, sending the top two flying across the room. Swearing to himself, he pulled on the next one, sending it skittering, and gave up, the white Egyptian cotton gaping open across his massive chest. He ended at the tall multipaned window that looked out over the west lawns, jamming his hands into his pockets and staring stonily at his own domain.

He had known better than to bring Beryl and the others to Sussex. He had tried to talk them out of accompanying him, but in the end he let them override his objections. He had hoped to introduce Brianna in controlled circumstances and quickly banish her back to her schoolroom.

He had no intention of allowing his ward to become a London laughingstock, nor for her to be hurt. He realized how worried he was about the reckless chit, and the thought shocked him. He could not understand the hold she had on his thoughts, or his unwarranted concern when she herself seemed not to give a fig about others' opinions. Andrew finally decided his reactions were due to a natural protectiveness and his anger due to his friends' lack of manners and to his mother's imminent arrival. Annabella Ormsby was enough to throw anyone off his stride. Satisfied with the explanation, and a great deal calmer, his grace of Ashford went toward his bedroom and allowed his valet to help him dress for dinner.

Chapter Fourteen

Dinner was served that night at eight. The duke was agreeably surprised by the miracles his staff had wrought in the kitchens upon such short notice. A rack of lamb was placed on the ivory damask-covered sideboard, Twinforth doing the honors of carving whilst footmen brought platters of veal and skate, new potatoes and fresh string beans. Savories and soups, light wines followed by clarets, were served and removed.

Finally dessert wines, fresh apples and pears, cheddar and Stilton cheeses were placed around the heavily chased-silver candelabra that held court in the center of the long mahogany dining table. All was done with elegant precision by the watchful Twinforth and his well-trained minions. The butler took quiet pride in seeing his grace's visage visibly lighten as the meal progressed. Twinforth held that a well-served meal could calm the most ruffled feathers, and felt he had proved his point as the night wore on.

The fact that Brianna and her tutor were not invited to table did not escape Lord Effingham's notice. Francis kept up his end of the conversation, engaging in a rather bored flirtation with Lady Pamela as he surreptitiously watched his host lean toward the lovely Beryl, whispering near her ear.

"You did not answer me, Francis," Pamela told the preoccupied Effingham.

"Emmm? Anything you have to say, I would willingly agree to, my sweet, if it would sway your nays to sweet surrender . . ."

"And would that stop your eye wandering so often in Beryl's direction?" she asked in a light tone.

Francis gave Pamela his full attention, smiling languidly. "If I detect a tinge of jealousy in those dulcet tones, I am most pleased, dear lady. But my thoughts were not of dalliance with another, but merely of the mysterious Andrew."

The worldly brunette caught at the note of teasing knowledge in her companion's tone. "What are you hinting at, you fiend? I shall expire of curiosity if you do not divulge your meaning."

"Did you not see the lovely creature who ran past when we arrived?"

"What lovely creature? I saw only a filthy urchin."

"Outside, yes. But inside there was another to whom Andrew gave the most urgent summons."

"Summons?" Pamela demanded loudly enough to be heard by the others.

Jane looked up the table. "What?"

"Pamela?" Beryl looked up.

"I was simply wondering about the lovely creature who seemed so eager to reach our host's side earlier." Pamela gave Andrew a winsome smile.

"Andrew," the Marquess of Henleigh said with mock sternness, "are you hiding a lovely creature about the house?"

"No."

"Sorry to disagree, old chap," Effingham said, "but they will inevitably see her."

Beryl frowned. "See whom?"

"No one," Andrew said again. "Francis is speaking of a mere tutor, if you must know, an *employee*," he stressed.

"Lord Rossmore was quite taken with her beauty when last we were here. He mentioned her to Prinny," Francis added innocently.

"Who and where is this paragon?" Beryl asked with none too friendly a tone.

Andrew looked down the table, exasperated. "Francis exaggerates as usual. He is prone to building Banbury tales out of pure air."

"I'll not say another word," Effingham agreed meekly.

Beryl took up the cudgels, Francis restraining a smile as he sipped at his wine.

"And did this 'paragon' come to table when last you were here, Francis?"

"Of course not," Andrew interjected.

"Well, she was to dine with us, Andrew," Francis corrected. "Until her charge got herself into trouble with her tongue."

"That's enough," the duke said, his words clipped and his tone testy. Vastly irritated, he glared at his friend. "If you must know, I have a distant relative, the child you saw earlier, who has been left in my care until her brother returns from duty with Wellington. The female Francis is so enamored with is her teacher, and I made the unmitigated mistake of allowing the child and Miss Powell to join us before dinner."

"You have a ward?" Henny asked, surprised.

"You mentioned nothing of a child," Beryl told Andrew.

"It was—and is—of no moment," he insisted.

"Is that the pretty young thing in the stables?" Lady Jane asked from the other end of the table.

"Pretty—" Beryl began and stopped. "Jane, that dirty urchin was full-grown!"

"She is not an urchin," Andrew all but thundered. "Nor is she anywhere near full-grown. She is fourteen in years, but she is nearer *twelve* in sense, and in manners she is a babe in swaddling clothes!"

"She looked older than fourteen," was Jane's comment. "And I thought her quite pretty, even if the poor dear does have red hair."

"Totally unfashionable," Pamela agreed.

"She has no need to worry about fashion," Andrew growled.

"Surely all have need of being fashionable," Henleigh said into the silence that followed his host's words.

"Henny, you can't see beyond your own self-satisfied nose," Andrew declared.

"Well, I do say!"

"Andrew, really—" Francis put in.

Beryl reached for Andrew's hand, bringing a frown to Francis's brow as she looked down the table at Henleigh and the others. "Andrew, as usual, has the right of it. Poor relations have no need of being fashionable, they are happy to receive any largesse from their betters."

"Their betters?" Andrew stared at Lady Beryl as if she were demented. "The girl has no betters."

Pamela met his eyes. "Andrew, we of course mean no disrespect to your relative."

Beryl watched Andrew through narrowed eyes. He flushed and looked away, focusing on Pamela's understanding expression. "Brianna will end by marrying some local swain if her brother does not soon return, and the lovesick fool will be welcome to her, I say. God help him if he tries to tame her."

None but Pamela seemed to hear his lordship's strange choice of words.

"A hellion?" Henny asked, suddenly interested.

"An innocent," Andrew said quickly. "An undisciplined, stubborn, hard-headed, vexatious *child.*"

"She sounds positively diverting." Pamela gave a sly sideways smile to Francis and then turned toward her host. "You must let us meet her."

"I doubt I shall have any say in the matter," he said grimly.

"I beg your pardon?" It was Henny who spoke.

"She seems to interject herself into situations no matter what she is told," Andrew explained. "But you are forewarned. All of you. She is a shocking imp who has grown up as wild as the wind and twice as insistent."

Beryl put her fork down with a decided little ping, ending the dinner as if she were already the duchess. Her displeasure was momentarily visible before she cleared her brow and smiled at Andrew.

"Shall we?" she asked them.

"Of course," he replied.

A footman sprang to attention behind Beryl's chair, pulling it back for her as she stood and swept her satin half-train back, sailing out of the dining room, with Jane and Pamela following in her wake. A sigh of relief escaped Andrew's lips as the double doors to the hall closed behind them.

"Now," Henny said, leaning forward, "tell us all."

Andrew's gaze was fastened on Francis. "I swear your mouth is bigger than your brain."

Francis shrugged and tried to look properly chagrined. "The subject was bound to come up. It's better they know than to run into her without knowledge."

The duke grimaced. "You have a point, they might have been shocked senseless."

"Not the girl, the governess," Francis corrected. "No one

would ever mistake her for a governess if they did not know it to be the case. I have done you a favor by preparing Beryl for the inevitable meeting. I wonder you didn't think of it yourself."

"I must see this paragon," Henny said into the silence that followed Effingham's words.

"You are making a piece of work about nothing," Andrew informed them. "Twinforth," he continued, the butler coming forward and giving a slight bow. "*I shall have my brandy and cigar in the green parlor.*" The duke looked from Effingham to Henleigh. "Any gentleman who is not preoccupied with the subject of my household arrangements is welcome to join me."

Henleigh watched Andrew stalk from the room before he turned to his companion. "I think you tried his civility a bit too high, Francis. He is definitely up in the boughs."

"He has been since we arrived," Francis pointed out. "I, for one, think he protests a bit too much."

Henleigh arched a brow, his quizzing glass falling to his chest. "What do you mean?"

"Henny, think on it a moment. Do you remember how adamant he was we not accompany him? And how he finally bowed to Beryl's insistence because he could not marshal a good argument against our traveling on with him? If you had a guilty secret running about the house, would you want to bring your lady-love near her?"

"Are you speaking of the child or the governess?" Henleigh wanted clarified.

"The *governess,* of course," Francis snapped.

"Oh . . . Oh . . . I see. I think . . ."

Francis ground his teeth. "Good grief, man, it's as plain as the nose on your face."

Henleigh stood up. "I'm joining Andrew." He waited for Francis to follow. As a footman opened the double doors, Henleigh glanced at Francis. "I don't believe a word of it, you know."

"What?" Francis stopped his fork in midair.

"Andrew's a gentleman. He would never take advantage of a servant. Nor is he a fool. He'd not have brought Beryl within a league of here if anything havey-cavey was going on. Which way is the green parlor?" Henleigh asked, adding exasperation to the other man's irritation.

"Bloody idiotic Bond Street exquisite," Francis said after he gave the instructions and Henleigh had left. He stuffed the last of his trifle into his mouth and shoved his own chair back, ignoring the footman as he stalked out of the dining room.

Upstairs, in a guest chamber sitting room, Beryl's maid was repairing her mistress's elaborately coiffed hair. The mirror over the inlaid fruitwood dressing table reflected her face and the two women who sat sipping sherry behind her. Their laughing conversation drew Brianna nearer the door to her tutor's room. Connie watched her pupil's distraction.

"Is something amiss with you?" Connie asked.

"Oh, no," Brianna said quickly. "I was just—" Her eyes hit upon their dinner tray. "Just about to take our dinner tray down."

"There is no need. Nellie will fetch it."

"But there is so much for them to do, with all the guests and no notice." Brianna already had the hall door open and was coming back to reach for the tray. "Poor Nellie is probably dead on her feet, racing from room to room and seeing to everything for their comfort. I should hate to think I made her day any harder."

Connie doubted Brianna's intentions were quite so benign, but she did not stop the girl. She was glad of a moment alone in which to collect her thoughts and decide upon the best way to approach her unwelcome task. She had to inform the duke of Brianna's true age, it was her bounden duty. But she dreaded his reaction. He was not in the best of moods, that was plain to be seen, and Connie knew there was the possibility he would decide the girl could not stay in his establishment, which meant not only Brianna's banishment, but hers as well.

While Connie worried over where Brianna might be forced to go, the object of her concern had divested herself of the dinner tray and sped back up the stairs. Beryl

Cavendish had been given the largest guest quarters. Her rooms were next to the long-unused mistress's suite, which drew Brianna to its door as a loud peal of laughter traveled through the walls.

"Don't laugh, Pamela," Beryl said into the dressing-table mirror as Brianna slipped inside the dark room next door. She felt her way carefully around the Holland-covered furniture toward the wall between the two sitting rooms. "It's not beyond the bounds of credulity," Beryl insisted.

"It's bootless to consider the possibility of Andrew being involved with a servant," Pamela said.

"Beryl, Andrew would be the last to stoop to such a liaison," Jane said sensibly, her voice carrying clearly through the wall. "But even if it were true, you would never get the right of it."

"He is not the type to chase after a governess," Pamela declared.

"Any man is capable of chasing a light-skirt, dear, you should know that better than any," Beryl said waspishly.

Beryl's words rankled the more because of their truth. Lord Hunnicut's flirtations were at least as legendary as Pamela's own.

"You should know, dear," Pamela said sweetly. "As you were one of them."

"Oh, fie, you can't hold that against me. You were busy elsewhere," Beryl replied. "And if you dare tell Andrew about Hunnicut or about Francis, I shall never speak to you again."

Brianna gasped so loudly in the next room, the sound was audible to Jane, who was resting her eyes and letting the two cats have at each other. She turned her head toward the wall beside her.

"Did you hear something?"

"What?"

". . . Nothing, I suppose. Are you ready yet, Beryl dear, or shall we spend the entire evening watching you curl your hair?"

Beryl waved her maid away, gave herself a final check in the mirror, and rose from the tapestried bench.

"Did either of you get a good look at the woman? Is she competition?"

"Of course not," Pamela soothed. "But a satisfied man is less likely to be thinking of tying the knot, now is he? I am on your side, entirely, dear," she prevaricated blandly.

The women left the upstairs sitting room, their progress down the hall accompanied by the soft rustle of their skirts. Their high-pitched voices floated down ahead of them to warn the gentlemen of their approach. They lifted their skirts with one hand, trailing down the stairs chattering pleasant inanities.

In the dark and chilly mistress's suite Brianna sneezed and sneezed again, disturbing more dust as she moved toward the door. She stumbled over a chair leg, righted herself, and found the doorknob. Going back along the hall to her teacher's room, she was sunk in gloom.

Connie Powell looked up from her book when Brianna entered, a quizzical smile playing around her lips. "Have you been helping in the kitchen all this time?"

"I—" Brianna raised her glum face to the older woman. ". . . Not precisely."

"I did not imagine Mrs. Potts and Eunice would allow the kitchen to become quite so dusty."

Brianna looked down at her skirt and sneezed.

"Are you catching cold?" Connie asked innocently.

Brianna caught the gleam in her teacher's eye, a slow smile spreading across Brianna's freckled face. "You know," she challenged.

"I can't imagine what you mean."

"Oh, Connie, they are beastly, they truly are."

Connie's expression changed. "You mustn't speak thus of your guardian's friends."

"But you didn't hear them. They are brittle and cold and without conscience or honor—"

"Brianna!"

Brianna stamped her foot. "It's true and worse." She flounced to an overstuffed chintz chair and threw herself into it.

"Sit up straight," Connie said, going back to her book.

"Why? I don't want to be anything like them, with their fancy manners and their cold hearts." She lapsed into an uncharacteristic silence. After long quiet moments passed, Connie looked up again.

"Brianna?"

The girl looked at her teacher with such a sad expression, Connie felt genuine concern. "You must not let them sink you into a fit of the sullens."

"It's not them," Brianna replied, "it's *him*. Connie, what are we to make of it if he has such shallow friends?"

Connie closed her book upon her place mark and stood up. "We are to make of it that it is none of our business. And you, young lady, are to get ready for bed. A tired mind builds all sorts of strange fancies. And you are fanciful enough when you are rested. Come along and we shall find Nellie."

Brianna bounded to her feet, looking much brighter and entirely more hopeful. "Are we going down?"

"No, we are not," Connie said firmly, dashing the young girl's hopes.

Brianna knew her teacher's moods after all the long winter months the two had shared; she knew when Connie had spoken a final word upon a subject, it did no good to wheedle. With bad grace Brianna allowed her teacher to call for her maid and tuck her into her bed.

It was only after she was alone, after the lamps were low and the upper floors quiet, that Brianna strained to hear the sounds of his lordship and his guests far below. She fell asleep to troubled dreams of her Black Prince. He seemed to be ensnared by a female dragon, and no matter how hard she tried, Brianna could not free him.

Chapter Fifteen

*L*ady Beryl Cavendish's curiosity over the duke's household arrangements grew as day followed day, Andrew pretending to be oblivious to the lovely Beryl's more and more direct hints. He did not want to face the mixture of consternation and hilarity—and the inevitable gossip—that would result from Beryl meeting Brianna before Constance pronounced Brianna ready for the test.

To that end, he avoided Twinforth's several messages that Miss Powell begged a private audience at his earliest opportunity, sure she wished to petition for her charge and ever more sure the girl needed more time before she was submitted to Beryl's scrutiny. The child in question, however, was nowhere to be seen, and by the third day he realized the young heathen herself was giving him a wide berth. He felt positively grateful until, at week's end, he found his thoughts continually wandering toward how the child was managing to stay so totally out of sight.

He told himself his only concern was that his friends would dine out for months on the story of when Beryl met the riotously ill-mannered Brianna. As he thought about this sorry turn of events, he realized his thoughts were once again dwelling on the child.

Irritated at first, it was suddenly obvious to him he had taken the wrong tack and must immediately change course. Instead of forestalling the inevitable confrontation between Beryl and the girl, he should welcome it. Get it over, like bad medicine quickly swallowed.

The news of the duke's decision was brought to the top-floor nursery where Brianna had spent the greater portion of her waking hours since the night of the duke's

166

arrival. Connie was with Brianna when Nellie came running with the news that Mr. Twinforth said Miss Bree was to join the duke and his guests at tomorrow's midday meal.

"Just imagine," Nellie breathed, her eyes wide as saucers. "And his lordship says you're to wear your best gown, miss, and Twinforth is to bring you family jewels! Oh, and you too, Miss Connie."

"Oh, dear," Connie fretted when Nellie had left. "He has avoided me all week, and now this. Why is he suddenly requesting your presence? He suspects the truth!"

Brianna had wandered to the windows, her back to her tutor, her eyes on the darkened vista of the home forest.

"Then why would he worry about jewels and fancy gowns?" Brianna put in. "I've heard them pestering my cousin, they are expiring of curiosity about you."

"Me?" Connie was astounded. "Whatever for?"

Brianna turned to face her best friend. "Because you are too lovely by half—do not stop me, I am quoting—and Lady Beryl feels you to be the reason he has not yet offered for her hand."

Constance Powell opened and then closed her mouth without uttering a syllable. A thousand thoughts assailed her bewildered brain, not the least of which was that Brianna was demented.

"That is the outside of enough," Connie finally managed to say. "Brianna, months ago you attempted to thrust me in his lordship's path, for what reason I have no idea. Unless you thought to consolidate those you depend upon, which is entirely unnecessary. Your guardian will never fail you, nor shall I."

Brianna came away from the window and sank down on the floor at Connie's feet. "I know you have little reason to trust me, but I swear I am telling you the truth. They have done nothing since they arrived but speculate upon your position here and tease him unmercifully about my being here and your being my tutor. I have heard them, and all the staff will tell you the same. Connie, we must *do* something to help him!"

"Help him?"

"Yes. He must escape her clutches."

"Her clutches?" Without the benefit of Nellie's letters from James, Constance Powell was at a complete loss.

"Lady *Beryl's,"* Brianna explained none too patiently. "Have you not listened to a word I've said all week?"

"You have waxed eloquent upon the subject of your distaste for Lady Beryl, you have heaped calumny upon the duke's guests, but you have failed to grasp one simple truth. Like finds and follows like. Each fault you find in his friends, you extend to him."

"Never!" Brianna defended. "He is not like those—those fops and fribbles who are shallow and vain and stupid beyond endurance."

"Then how can you think he will be swayed by such?"

"Well, he *has* been," Brianna pointed out. "He is already in Lady Beryl's clutches."

"Perhaps that is precisely where he wishes to be."

Brianna dismissed the notion with a toss of her thick auburn curls. "He is a man," she explained patiently. "What he wishes and what is good for him are rarely the same."

"I beg your pardon?"

Brianna came toward her teacher, reaching for her hands. "Dear Connie, you, yourself, have taught me this in the books of history you quiz me on. Their value is not in the names and dates of who did which to whom." Brianna spoke with all the passion of untried idealism. "It is the *whys* and *hows* of history that, once learned, teach us the truth of what we are and what we should be."

Constance Powell stood up. "Brianna, what are you saying? No, don't answer that. Whatever you are saying, you are interfering in issues that are none of your business. You are presuming to know what is best for the duke, over and above what he wishes for himself. That is totally unconscionable."

"Oh, fustian."

"Brianna, for all our sakes, you must promise me you will do nothing to bring attention to yourself when you join his guests."

Brianna smiled brightly. *"Dear* Connie, I shall be an angel, I swear it!"

Beryl had decreed the next day's luncheon would be a picnic, and the weather was obediently warm and mild. The footmen, under Twinforth's watchful eye, carried tables and chairs to the lawn gazebo as Mrs. Potts inspected Nellie's cleaning, giving the lacy, white-painted room a final swat with the broom.

It sat two steps from the lawn, in the midst of the gardens, its wide latticed arches looking out upon the home woods and the great south facade of Ashford Hall itself, seen past the luxuriant blooms whose perfume spiced the warm spring day. Mrs. Potts made way for the arriving footmen, nodding to the butler as she came down the steps to the garden path.

"A lovely day for a picnic, Mr. Twinforth."

Twinforth regarded the sunny blue sky sprinkled with chalky white clouds that chased each other south. "I think the weather may hold," he replied grandly.

Mrs. Potts repeated his words to Cook a few minutes later as she sampled a bit of the cold ham. "I told him of course it would hold, it would hardly defy Lady Beryl."

"Aye, and she seems bent that none will, including our master," was the cook's opinion. "And it's only right and proper he marry, it's past time he was settling down and thinking of a family. Since Miss Bree has come, he must have often thought how good it would be to have a family and young ones about."

"If he marries Lady Beryl, we'll see little enough of him or any family," Mrs. Potts said firmly. "She'll lead him a merry chase, mark my words, and the chase will be in London, not all the way out here. I wonder she's not after him to leave this very minute."

In the small blue morning parlor Lady Beryl was saying very nearly the same words to Francis Effingham. They were alone, awaiting the others, and Francis had come to the window where Lady Beryl stood. Her back was to him, his hungry eyes looking down at the nape of her neck beneath her pale blond curls.

"You must help me convince him to leave," Beryl said. "I shall expire of boredom if I must spend another day in this godforsaken place."

He leaned to kiss the tip of her ear. "What a bad girl you are! . . . I could find ways to end your boredom."

Brianna came down the hall ahead of Connie and so heard Lady Beryl's throaty peal of laughter. She slowed, reaching a hand back to stop Connie as they neared the parlor door. Connie was about to lecture her charge on the evils of eavesdropping when the words inside the room stopped her speech.

"My darling Francis, you are the most adroit of lovers."

"Then end this farce with Andrew and come away with me."

"Come away with you where? To a season in Italy perhaps, since the abominable Bonaparte is finally imprisoned? And then what? My dear Francis, you are a married man."

"I shall leave Emma," he declared passionately.

"Then you shall do so without me," Beryl told him. Her voice lowered to a silken murmur. "Dearest Francis, I have no intention of ruining my reputation or yours. There is no need for such a calamity. Can't you see that all is as it should be? I shall marry Andrew and you shall stay married to that dear little mouse of yours whom we never see, and we shall go on being the best of . . . friends."

"I don't like deceiving Andrew, you know."

"But darling, deception is the spice of lovemaking. Admit it, you adore the intrigue just as much as I. You know I have the right of it." Her words ended in a whisper and a lingering kiss.

Brianna hauled Connie back from the door, saw Lady Jane and Lady Pamela descending the stairs with the Marquess of Henleigh and spoke brightly and a bit too loudly.

"I am ever so excited, Miss Powell, but you must help me a moment . . ." Brianna propelled Connie with her into the library across the hall.

"What are you doing?" Connie hissed, confused and upset, but not wanting to be overheard.

"I couldn't think of what to say," Brianna explained as they heard the others pass by to enter the parlor across the hall.

"I don't wonder," Connie replied. "Of all the odious, contemptible felines I have ever met!"

"Shhhh . . ."

"I will not go in."

"Connie, we must. Now can you see why we must help him?"

"No," the governess answered firmly. "Whatever our opinions, it is none of our business."

"But we must warn him!"

"Absolutely not. Aside from which, a man besotted with such a creature will not hear your words. There is nothing to be done." Brianna was staring at her teacher with a most bemused expression. "Brianna?"

The girl reached to kiss Connie's cheek. "As always, you are absolutely correct."

". . . I am?" Connie asked suspiciously.

"Absolutely. He would not hear our words. Come along, we must not be late." And, so saying, Brianna opened the library door and sailed forth into the blue parlor.

Connie thought about heading directly back to her room, but propriety won out over her emotions and she followed Brianna into the blue parlor.

Pamela was giving Francis an arch and questioning look, Jane and Henleigh speaking to Beryl when first Brianna and then Connie appeared in the doorway and came forward.

Beryl glanced across the room. She saw a slim young girl in a high-necked, high-waisted, long-sleeved gown of jonquil yellow, ruffled at neck and cuffs. A strand of pearls was the red-haired girl's only accessory. Behind the girl a dark-haired beauty entered. She wore a stark morning gown of dove gray relieved only by an edging of white lace at collar and cuffs.

"How do you do," Brianna murmured sweetly. Her eyes

cast down, she dropped a deep throne-room curtsey. Her eyes rose slowly, meeting Lord Effingham's as she straightened. "And how good to see you once more, my lord."

Something about her tone alerted Beryl. The girl looked innocent and very young, but the eyes that greeted Francis seemed to hold a secret both knew.

Francis himself stared back at the girl, a little disconcerted. Finally he gave her a brief smile and introduced pupil and teacher to the others.

Connie found herself the object of the Marquess of Henleigh's quizzing glass and stiffened her back, her face set into a faint polite smile. Brianna reached for Connie's hand, giving it a reassuring squeeze as the Duke of Ashford appeared in the doorway.

"Sorry, I'm late," he said without entering. He was dressed in riding clothes. "Harding and I have only just got back. Twinforth will see you to the tables and I shall join you momentarily."

With that he was gone, and Twinforth appeared as if by magic, bowing slightly and with very proper address preceding the small group down the hall and through the west doors onto the wide stone terrace.

The spring breeze was laden with the scent of roses as they reached the gazebo. Within were two tables covered with food and four footmen waiting to serve. Chairs were placed within the large open-air room and about the green expanse that circled the white building. Radiating out from the lawn, like spokes in a wheel, were meandering garden paths that led through the rose gardens.

Jane took a deep breath, drinking in the sweet-smelling air. "How very lovely."

"Thank you, your ladyship," Twinforth said.

"I think this is the largest rose garden I've ever seen."

"It is one of the largest in England, I am told on good authority," Twinforth responded, bowing slightly.

Pamela dropped into a wicker lawn chair, holding out a hand for Francis to sit next to her. He looked toward Beryl, found her attention on the child, and dropped to the seat Pamela patted.

"Naughty boy," Pamela said softly. "What have you been up to?"

A footman arrived with a tray bearing iced champagne, rescuing Francis from having to reply.

"Brianna, is it?" Beryl said across the lawn. "What an unusual name." As she spoke she glanced at and away from the tutor who stood beside Brianna, as if dismissing Connie from notice.

"It is a family name," Brianna replied sweetly. Her hands were clenched into little balls hidden in the soft folds of her straight skirt.

"I wasn't aware of it, an Ormsby name? Of course I wasn't aware of you either, dear. Andrew had said nothing about you."

Brianna's eyes widened innocently. "I have thought it odd too, Lady Beryl. Do you know he had never even so much as mentioned your name in passing conversation? Have you known my cousin long?" she asked in such a docile tone, any who knew her would have been forewarned.

Henleigh choked on smothered laughter. "Sorry," he managed to say as he grabbed for an iced champagne from the footman who approached. He handed it to Beryl and reached for two more.

"How very gallant," Brianna admired as he handed Connie a goblet. Brianna reached up to take the second one.

"Are you quite sure—" he began, and then shrugged, turning to take yet another for himself.

"Brianna—" Connie began in a warning tone, but was stopped by her pupil turning toward her with a dazzling smile and a wink unseen by the others.

"Dear Miss Powell, you and my cousin are so united in being strict with me, but this is a special occasion. We have guests we may never again see."

Pamela looked past Francis toward the young girl in the beribboned yellow dress. "I can assure you, you will see a very great deal of Beryl, my dear."

Beryl smiled. "Pamela, you mustn't tell tales out of school. I'm sure dear Andrew will choose his time and place."

The man in question came around the gazebo. "Andrew will chose his time and place for what?" he asked as he came to a stop beside Beryl.

"For whatever he wishes," Beryl said smoothly. She smiled up at him and was a bit irked to find his attention was on the girl and Miss Powell.

Andrew glanced approvingly at Brianna and then gave an encouraging smile to Connie, warm with gratitude for Brianna's unexceptional appearance.

Beryl saw the warmth and misread it, her eyes narrowing. She glanced away and saw Pamela watching her, a malicious little smile on her face.

"Well, Miss Powell," Andrew said heartily, "thank you for joining us." He looked around the assemblage. "I'm famished," he told them all before he headed toward the relative safety of the gazebo. "Let's see what we've got, shall we? This is all informal, absolutely informal, today," he repeated. Perhaps, he hoped, in such an informal setting any of Brianna's social gaffes would go unremarked.

"Andrew?" Beryl asked in a mildly startled tone as she was left behind.

Andrew stopped in his tracks and looked back, reddening. "Sorry," he said, coming back to offer his arm. "My mind's wandering."

"I should say it is," she told him. Then she smiled up into his distracted eyes. "One would think we were an old married couple." She tapped him lightly with her closed fan and then let it fall from the ribbon attached to her gown as she laughed merrily and called to the others. "Come along. If dear Andrew is going to behave in such a fashion, then so shall I and act the hostess, how is that?"

"Oh, we couldn't *presume* upon your kindness, dear Lady Beryl." Brianna spoke as swiftly as she moved away from Connie and around the chairs in which Pamela and Francis still sat. She was in front of the startled duke and tripping lightly up the steps and inside the gazebo. "After all, you are our guest," Brianna continued brightly. "And my cousin would think me remiss if I did not attempt to do my duties."

Andrew felt Beryl stiffen, but his attention was on the girl. She was obviously determined to prove herself worthy of inclusion in the gathering; perhaps Miss Powell had indeed worked wonders. One could always hope, he told himself.

"Wouldn't you, dear cousin?" Brianna asked as he came inside with Beryl, the others following.

"I am *depending* upon your performing your social duties," he told her with such feeling that only Brianna and Connie understood his meaning. To the others his words sounded very much like an attempt to put Beryl in her place.

Pamela smiled at the young girl, hugely enjoying herself. "I think it most kind of you, dear Brianna, and I hope we can be wonderful friends."

Not bloody likely, Brianna thought, but her smile remained in place as she informed the Londoners of their choices and spoke of the recipes and ingredients, ordering the footmen to cut a little more here please, and give dear Lady Beryl a bit more of that.

"I can decide my own, thank you," Beryl said coolly. Her smile was tight. "One would think you had cooked the food yourself."

"Not today," Brianna replied breezily. "But you must try a bit of the chicken. It's poached in wine, butter, and its own broth, with special ingredients I cannot divulge. The pears are from our—from my *cousin's*"—she underlined the change, ensuring all heard her first proprietary pronoun— "own orchard. Only the ham and the cheddar are not Ashford grown and made."

"We do have quite an extensive larder, thanks to Harding's sensible management," the duke agreed, unconsciously including Brianna in his statement.

Pamela walked back to the lawn chairs alongside Beryl. "Are you feeling well, Beryl? You look a touch peaked."

"Is something wrong?" Jane asked, coming behind.

Beryl shot Pamela a murderous look as the others remarked upon her pale color. Brianna thought about adding a comment about Beryl's pinched lips but decided against it as Andrew was at that very moment walking beside Connie and telling her how pleased he was with Brianna's behavior.

Brianna glowed and waxed eloquent upon all the beauties of Ashford Hall and its estates. Lady Beryl was silent, barely listening as she watched the progress of Andrew and the governess.

Chapter Sixteen

*T*he footmen had arranged low tables beside each lawn chair, bringing more champagne, wandering about the picnic party offering more food from the heavy silver trays they carried. Beryl sank gracefully into a chair, Francis plopping down beside her. Pamela saw Andrew coming near with the governess and moved to the chair on Beryl's other side, not looking in Beryl's direction as she sat down. Andrew handed Connie into the chair beside Pamela and then sat in the empty chair beside her, his attention on Brianna and Henny's conversation as they came forward from the gazebo laughing about something he had not heard.

"Everything all right?" Andrew asked anxiously.

Beryl frowned seeing Andrew's obvious concern.

"Mustn't frown dear," Pamela said softly. "Does horrific things to the face."

"I'm not speaking to you. You knew I was saving that chair for Andrew. If I didn't know better, I would say you were dangling after him yourself."

"Whyever do you think you know better?" Pamela replied, further cutting up Beryl's peace of mind.

Beryl ignored the others, turning toward Francis with a melting smile. "When all others desert me, shall you still be at my side?" she asked coquettishly.

"Always," Francis affirmed. "Music arises with its voluptuous swell when such soft eyes look so loving."

"That's not right," Henny put in from beside him.

"Francis can do no wrong in my eyes," Beryl replied, raising her voice a bit and including Henny in her flirtatiousness. Andrew was still maddeningly deep in conversation with the governess, who looked up at him with so earnest an expression Beryl wanted to dig her eyes out.

"I don't think he's noticing, dear," Pamela said.

Francis leaned to see Pamela. "What am I missing?"

Pamela smiled with an arched brow. "How much Beryl relies upon you, my pet."

Henleigh turned to Brianna. "Do you know Byron's work?"

"Only by reputation," Brianna replied. She half listened as he quoted, her attention on Connie and the duke.

> *"Music arose with its voluptuous swell,*
> *Soft eyes look'd love to eyes which spake again.*
> *And all went merry as a marriage bell."*

"But I truly must have a moment's private conversation, regarding Brianna," Miss Powell was saying earnestly to the duke, but his attention had wandered.

"Henny," Andrew interrupted the governess, frowning at his friend. "Whatever do you think you are doing?"

"Correcting a quotation," the marquess responded.

"Byron's not the thing one discusses with a child."

"Hardly a child," the marquess retorted, and earned a genuine smile from Brianna.

"Actually," Pamela put in, "you've not finished it. It continues: 'And all went merry as a marriage bell. But, hush! Hush! A deep sound strikes like a rising knell.'"

"Pammy, must you be so literal?" Francis complained.

"Where did you ride this morning, Andrew?" Beryl asked, changing the subject.

"Hmmm? Harding was in need of some direction regarding the spring planting."

"I beg your pardon?" Henny raised his quizzing glass.

"Do you mean to say you are actually involved with the agriculture?"

Andrew frowned. "I don't understand the question."

"Don't tell us you're a farmer at heart, dear Andrew, for we know you well enough to disbelieve," Beryl said.

"I don't know as I'm a farmer at heart," he agreed.

"Oh, I can quite see you in the fields," Jane told him, smiling. "I'll wager you'd be the most smashing farmer."

The duke grinned at the good-hearted Jane. "Flatterer."

They laughed and the others smiled, except Henleigh and Beryl. Beryl watched the governess lean slightly toward the duke, determined to get back his attention.

"Well I, for one," Henleigh declared, "cannot imagine Andrew mucking about in the dirt."

"He leaves that to Cousin Brianna," Beryl said gaily, laughter from the Londoners following her words.

Brianna blushed, Connie looked with concern toward her pupil, and Andrew frowned. "I beg your pardon?"

"You surely can't have forgotten our arrival."

There was more laughter. Connie gave Brianna's nearest hand an admonishing squeeze.

"What a sight I must have looked," Brianna said ruefully. "I had ridden across the fields, the very ones you cannot imagine my cousin mucking about in," she said truthfully. "And my horse lost her footing in one of the irrigation ditches." She avoided her tutor's eyes. "I landed in the dirt, the wind knocked clean out of me. I was so worried about Dark Star, I walked her home, and was trying to make amends with the poor thing when you arrived. I was mortified," she ended honestly enough, remembering being hauled by the ear across the cobblestoned stableyard.

Andrew looked concerned. "Why didn't you tell me?"

"You didn't give me a chance," he was told quickly.

"Good Lord, you could have been hurt."

"I was more afraid for Dark Star," she said piously.

"Oh, I do say, I am deuced sorry I laughed," the marquess told her. "You could have been *killed.*"

"Brianna, dear," Beryl said. "I can hardly credit falling off a horse in an open field."

"Oh, Lady Beryl, I am sure you cannot. I am positive you would never commit such a breach of etiquette."

"Touché," Henny said, laughing. "The kitten has claws, Beryl. You'd best be on guard."

"Well-taught girls do not glare at their betters."

Brianna bounded from her chair. "Thank you. In future, if and when I meet my betters, I shall follow your advice."

"Brianna," Andrew said warningly. "Sit down."

"Never!"

"What a rebellious little child you are," Beryl commented. "I can hardly believe you are fourteen."

"I am not fourteen."

"Brianna," Connie said warningly.

"What did she say?" the duke asked.

Connie cast Brianna an exasperated look. "Your grace," she said, "I have attempted to speak to you since you arrived about this—this small matter. It seems her brother made a bit of a mistake about her age when she arrived."

"He didn't think you'd take me in if you knew my real age," Brianna defended.

"She is not fourteen," Andrew repeated, making sure he understood what the woman was saying.

"No," Connie said unhappily. "I'm afraid she is not."

"Egad," Henny put in. "How old is the girl?"

"I was just about to ask the very same thing," the duke said carefully.

Connie hesitated. "Brianna is fifteen."

"Sixteen," Brianna corrected in a small voice.

"Sixteen?!" a chorus of voices responded. Brianna saw the duke's shock, but it was only Connie's surprise she answered.

"Brianna, do not make this worse than it is."

"But Connie, you made me promise to tell the truth, and yesterday was my birthday," she admitted to her teacher.

"But you said nothing!"

"Because you said he wouldn't let me stay once I was sixteen!"

"Andrew," Beryl said incredulously, "you cannot presume to house a sixteen-year-old female under your roof without inviting the very worst kind of assumptions. Girls of her class are married by sixteen."

"What do you mean, of my class?" Brianna demanded.

"Although the duke has been kind enough to put a good face on this—situation—no doubt to spare you pain, it is obvious that you cannot possibly be a relation of the Ormsbys."

"Beryl," Andrew began, but his words were drowned out by Brianna's.

"You are a liar and a sneak and you don't give a fig about my cousin Andrew, and all here know it!"

"Brianna!" the duke reprimanded.

"You've said I should speak only the truth, and speak it I have!" Her voice trembled as she dropped a swift curtsey in his general direction. "If you do not wish to hear it, I am heartily sorry!" She ran off down the garden path, and Connie moved to follow as the Londoners teased Beryl and Andrew stood up and started away.

"Andrew, surely you're not going after the little baggage," Beryl said.

The duke did not answer.

"Beryl, dear," Pamela said as the duke strode away. "I think you've put your foot in it."

As Pamela spoke, Andrew overtook Miss Powell on the path and told her to go back.

"But she is very upset, your grace, and she'll need me. She's lost everyone; father, mother, her brother gone to war, even her Mrs. Hobson left her . . . She's frightened."

"Miss Powell, *please* go back," he said again. Unwillingly, she watched him stride past. Brianna was far ahead of them across the lawns, her skirt raised as she fled toward the spinney.

"She had good reason," Connie called out after the duke.

The spinney was cool, wild violets growing shadowed by the ancient oaks. Out of breath, Brianna ended her headlong flight, leaning against the rough bark of a huge gnarled tree. Behind, she heard footsteps. "Go away, Connie," she called in a voice breaking with tears. "I'm sorry, but she was being deliberately hateful and I won't—"

But it was the duke who turned her 'round and looked down into stormy green eyes. Tears spilled down her cheeks and she tried to pull away.

"I won't apologize," she told him fiercely. "You can beat me if you like, you can send me away, but I won't say I'm sorry to her when I'm not!"

"I know," he told her softly.

"I can't possibly— What did you say?"

He reached to wipe away the tears that spilled down across the dusting of freckles across her upturned nose. "I hope you will show better manners than they have and apologize for your share of the proceedings."

"Will she?" Brianna asked rebelliously.

"I rather doubt it, but I was not aware you wished to use Lady Beryl as a role model."

"She is mean and spiteful and I won't have them teasing Connie, for they're not worthy to kiss her hem. I do not like them."

"You've only just met them. But in any event, they shan't be here. We leave at week's end."

"But you've only just come," she told him, and he could see her disappointment.

He tipped her chin upward, looking deep into her eyes. "Have you missed me?"

"Yes," she told him, unaware of the effect her answer had on him. "Don't you want to stay?"

"Oh, little one, I think I had best run very far, very fast."

"I don't understand."

"Nor do I," he said softly. "And you were the very model of a proper young lady this morning—until you ran away. Miss Powell has worked miracles. I am very proud of you."

Brianna stared up into eyes so blue they seemed to rival the sky above, her own shining at his praise. "You are?"

"I am," he confirmed. "You are changing almost before our very eyes."

"Are you truly pleased?" she asked in a small voice.

She had never looked so sweet. His heart softened as he looked down at the orphaned girl. "Truly."

"I wish you would stay."

"I shall be back."

"When?"

She was growing into a beauty, those wide-spaced eyes the green of ocean depths, and lips whose color needed no rouge. "Perhaps you and Miss Powell may come visit me one day in London."

"When?" she asked again.

"You are a determined little wench." He saw her disappointment and leaned forward to give her forehead a gentle, avuncular kiss. "Don't look so upset, little one," he said softly. He wanted to comfort her, to hold her near and tell her she would never be alone again, that there was nothing for her to fear. "I shall send for you one day," he promised, but even as he said it he thought of his mother's sojourn in London and how very long it might be before he was in a position to make good upon his promise.

But Brianna knew nothing of his mother's visit and was wide-eyed with excitement. "Oh, Andrew, you shall be ever so pleased, I shall be the very soul of propriety! Thank you, thank you!" Brianna reached upward and wrapped her arms around his neck, going up on tiptoe to kiss his cheek.

He felt the tug of her young arms and allowed her to bend his head downward. Her soft lips were warm upon his cheek, and then with the exuberance of youth she pressed closer, her gratitude rising up and spilling over. And then her feelings turned into something much different. As she leaned against him, his hands went to her shoulders, ready to gently push her away. She strained upward to kiss him again on the cheek, and then her lips met his. Lightning as jagged as heaven's bolts coursed through her, shocking down her spine and setting fire to the pit of her stomach.

The girl's kiss upon his cheek had sent a flood of unexpected warmth through Andrew's veins. His arms went around her protectively and then her lips were pressed against his; he could feel the change in her course through his own blood. Her hands slipped from behind his neck and moved to cradle his cheeks in wonderment. He reached for them, pulling them away but unable for the moment to let go. He stared down into eyes as deep as the sea and saw her awakening to her senses, saw the unasked and unanswerable questions.

"My God, you are so sweet." He heard himself speak aloud his thoughts.

"I feel so strange." Her voice was small, her words simple. Her arms reached to cling to him and, his eyes closing for a brief moment, he didn't stop her. She was a child, Andrew reminded himself, a schoolroom miss, but the body that pressed against him was not a child's, nor were the lips that reached upward to mold themselves against his own. His arms went around her, folding her close, his tongue touching her lips and sending shivers down her spine. She clung to him, her lips opening. A small moan escaped her as his tongue sought out the soft warm depths of her mouth, and then she gave herself over to her senses, floating in a place that held no time but the beating of their hearts. Experiencing for the first time the emotions that flooded through her, she was bereft of sense. All that existed was the world of their bodies touching. His tongue left her mouth and she sought it out, shyly touching her own tongue to his, tentatively exploring his mouth. She felt him shudder, realized he was feeling what she was, and nearly drove him insane as she became more insistent. She wanted to be close, closer, closer still, forgetting to breathe as he responded to her, reality spinning away.

Her body pressing against his, her arms and mouth searching to be closer, she was making his flesh harden. He tightened his arms around her waist, drawing her up, her feet inches off the ground. He cradled her in his arms, one arm below her waist to the curve where her body met her thighs, the other against her back, his hand lost in the confusion of thick red ringlets, crushing the hair that tangled through his fingers. Holding her captured in his arms, he tasted the sweetness of her searching kisses.

"Andrew Henry Arthur Ormsby!" a female voice thundered out behind him. *"What* is the meaning of this?"

Chapter Seventeen

At the sound of his mother's voice, Andrew stiffened and looked past Brianna to see the dowager duchess standing on the path directly behind them. Beside her was her longtime companion, Martha Tinsdale.

"I'm sure this can be easily explained," Martha soothed as Andrew released Brianna. She slid down the length of him, his face a mask against the exquisite pain she caused until her feet hit the ground and he could thrust her back behind him. "Andrew will tell us how this has happened."

"Martha, be silent," the dowager duchess snapped. "Well?" she demanded of her son. "What can you possibly have to say for yourself?"

Brianna stared at the two tall women, one regal and angry, the other diffident and kind-looking.

"I wasn't expecting you, Mother."

"That much is obvious," Annabella Ormsby snapped. "I heard the most ghastly rumors in London and decided to come visit and squash them. I arrived to have Francis Effingham and the others point me in this direction and suggest the most shocking things, and now with my own eyes I find they are justified." His mother's attention turned to the girl. "What's your name?"

"Brianna Morris, your grace." She gave a swift curtsey as Connie came running down the path.

"Don't think to butter me up," the dowager told the girl sharply.

"Your grace," Connie said to the duke as she stepped around the women. "Thank you for watching Brianna. I shall take her back to her studies."

"Watching her? Is that what you call it?" the dowager demanded. "And just who, pray tell, are you?"

"Constance Powell, your grace. I am Brianna's teacher."

"It looks to me as if my son has taken over that function!"

"Brianna had been upset—" Andrew began.

"He was being kind," Brianna interjected.

"He was being more than kind," the dowager snapped.

"I'm sure there is a simple explanation for what we saw," Martha Tinsdale said.

"There certainly is, and it's as old as time," the dowager said tartly.

"Mother," Andrew overrode the others, "you are jumping to ridiculous conclusions. The child was upset and I was merely trying to calm her."

"Child, you say?" She reached for the black ribbon that held her quizzing glass and brought it to her eye, giving Brianna a thorough going-over. "How old are you, young miss?"

"Sixteen," Brianna answered truthfully, one look at the dowager convincing the girl she had best not lie.

"Good God." The dowager dropped her quizzing glass. "Sixteen and carrying on alone with my son!"

"She was not carrying on," Connie defended. "And his grace thought her to be fourteen until today. She's only just turned sixteen."

"You're not making things better, Miss Powell," the dowager said. She eyed her son. "And what was your present to be?"

"Mother, I resent this on all our behalfs. Miss Powell is accurate, I did not know her true age until a few moments ago."

"Whereupon you immediately took advantage of the girl."

"He did not!" Brianna put in before Andrew's own reply.

"I did no such thing." But he did not sound entirely convinced of his own words.

"Well, Tinsdale? We can't stand out here all day," she complained as if Martha Tinsdale were dawdling. "You'd best see to our things, and if any ask, Miss Powell was with the girl. Young woman, you and this girl come with me. Andrew, make yourself scarce."

"I beg your pardon?"

"You heard me. Take a ride, chop wood, do something to work off your appetites. And stay out of sight until you come back up the front drive as if you've been somewhere else. The entire household is talking about you running after this girl. Wait. Before you go, aside from our own staff, who knows she has been living here alone with you?"

"She has not been living here alone with me," he said, so exasperated his voice rose with each word. "You make it sound as if—as if—I know not what! I myself only just arrived Tuesday, and I came with Pamela Hunnicut and Beryl Cavendish, so she has not been in the house alone with me! I have not even been in Sussex since November."

"Andrew—" Brianna began, only to be forestalled by Connie and the dowager duchess.

"Brianna—" Connie said, shocked, but Annabella Ormsby's voice overrode all else.

"Andrew?" the dowager repeated. "How dare you call my son by his given name? Are you determined to shout your indiscretions to the four winds? I tell you, this is the very outside of enough, I won't stand for such behavior!"

"She may call me what she pleases!" Andrew bellowed, startling them all. "Brianna is your cousin Mary's child, and she has the right to call me as she pleases." As he spoke, his indignation rose. "Her brother brought her here as my ward when he left to fight with Wellington, and by God, none will say I've done her ill!"

"Are you through?" his mother asked mildly.

"For the moment!"

"Good. Now, as I understand it, none can prove I have not been here throughout."

Andrew stared at his mother. "You?"

Connie hesitated. "Your guests," she mentioned to the duke.

"This week, yes."

"In November . . ." she reminded.

Andrew grimaced at his mother. "The tale-tellers, no

doubt, who filled your ears with utter nonsense. Rossmore, Barnstable, and Effingham were here overnight in November. They caught a glimpse of the girl."

"All right," his mother said, "now go. Martha, why are you still here? Come along, all of you—except you." She scowled at her son.

Tinsdale took off up the path at a swift trot, Connie bringing Brianna to walk beside the dowager.

"I'm sure there was no harm meant," she was saying as she left. "His grace has ever been the soul of propriety and always a gentleman . . ."

Andrew heard the governess defending him and wondered what she would be saying if she had been the one to find him kissing the child. Child, she's a child, he reminded himself. He watched his mother maneuvering Connie and Brianna back up the path. Brianna looked back once, her eyes soft as she gave him a tremulous smile. His mother yanked the girl around unceremoniously and urged Connie to walk faster.

Andrew turned on his heel, frustration and anger in his every stride as he debated disobeying his mother and finally recognized the sense of her demand. He stalked off toward the home woods on foot, wanting no horse beneath him. He might kill the poor beast.

The Londoners were gathered in the green parlor when the dowager reached the house. "Simply follow my lead," she said just before they reached the footman who opened the door for them. They walked inside and toward the curving stairway. Their steps were heard, Francis Effingham appearing at the parlor door and looking down the hall. "Dear aunt Belle, I couldn't imagine what was keeping you."

The dowager changed tactics, bringing the girl with her toward the parlor, Connie following dispiritedly behind.

"Is there a glass of sherry to be had?" she asked. "Hello, Beryl, Jane," she said as Francis went to fetch her drink. "Henleigh, how's your mother's back?"

"Much better, your grace."

"Good, good. Brianna, child, you can tell me more of your progress in my absence after dinner. Run along with Miss Powell now. I intend to have a glass of sherry and retire to my rooms, assuming Tinsdale has organized our baggage."

"Are you back from Ireland then, dear lady?" Francis asked as Connie and Brianna left. He brought the dowager a small crystal glass filled with pale sherry as she settled into a parlor chair.

"Ireland?" She looked astounded. "I went up to London for the week to shop."

Lady Pamela carefully watched the dowager. "All thought you to be in Ireland."

"I was until last fall when dear Brianna's brother needed me back to chaperone my ward. She's led such a sheltered country life," the dowager was saying blandly as Brianna and Connie left the room.

They did not see Beryl's suspicious eyes on the dowager duchess. "You have been here, then, through the winter?" Beryl asked.

"Hmmm?" Annabella Ormsby took her time. She raised her quizzing glass and used the quite considerable force of her personality in the appraising perusal she gave her questioner. "Beryl, dear, you must have a hearing problem. I've just told you I went to London to shop for the child."

Francis sat down beside her. "You seem to have taken a very great deal of luggage for a week's sojourn in London, dear lady. The hall is overflowing with baggage and boxes."

"Francis Effingham, your logic is as poor as your schoolwork used to be. What you see is not what I took with me but what I brought back. There is a great deal of shopping to be done when a young girl is about to come out," Annabella said blandly.

"Come out?" Beryl said, shocked.

"Oh, your grace, are you bringing the child to London?" Jane asked innocently. "She is such a pretty little thing. I'm sure she'll take."

"Yes, even with that mop of unfashionable red," Pamela agreed sweetly.

"Do you mean to say the chit is truly a relative of yours?" Beryl demanded.

"Who did you think her to be?" the dowager asked back.

"Did you find Andrew?" Henleigh said.

"What a goosecap you must think me," the dowager replied, dismissing the marquess with a wave of her hand. "You are a naughty boy and I should take you to task. You love to gossip, you're just like your father, but don't put yourself into queer stirrups again by repeating such fustian to others as you spoke to me, Albert Henleigh. You nearly gave me the vapors with your wild tale of my son chasing after some Gypsy girl, and here you were speaking rubbishy poppycock about my very own ward."

"But he did go after her," Beryl insisted.

"They may have gone off in the same direction but to different ends. You must have seen them both heading for the stables. She was seeing to her birthday present; she is simply in love with that horse."

"The one she fell from?" Jane asked innocently.

"Oh, dear, when did she fall?" Annabella Ormsby covered her surprise with a note of alarm.

"The day we arrived," Jane explained.

"And where then is your son, might we ask?" It was Beryl who spoke.

"Busy with estate business no doubt."

"He was seeing to the planting this morning," Henleigh put in.

Beryl gave Henleigh a decidedly irritated look. "He didn't rush off in the middle of our picnic to go plant crops."

"Such a deal of work, running a vast estate," the dowager put in. "And the more so since he's been gone all these months. I can tell you there are things that only a man can handle, I have quite given up the attempt."

"So you have suffered through the entire winter out here?" Francis asked, not so innocently.

The dowager's attention turned toward Francis, her dark eyes riveted upon his face.

"My dear boy," she calmly lied, "you saw me in November, where could I have gone in all the beastly weather between then and now?" Francis stared back as she continued. "Did you ever find that fob that went missing?"

"I—I—no, I rather think perhaps it was caught up in Rossmore's or Barnstable's mish . . ."

"I trust it wasn't too valuable?"

Francis Effingham looked into his godmother's fixed expression. "A mere trifle."

"You didn't mention you were here in the fall," Beryl accused Francis. "You knew of the girl all winter?"

"Does Francis tell you everything, Beryl? I wasn't aware you were so close," the older woman said, looking from the suspicious Beryl to the nonplussed Francis.

Pamela smiled at Francis. "Are you, you two dears, and none the wiser?"

"Of course not," Beryl snapped when Francis did not seem to be able to summon words. "I just thought it odd nothing was mentioned to me. To any of us," she corrected.

The dowager finished her sherry and placed her glass on the small delicately inlaid ivory and ebony table beside her chair. "I intend to rest before dinner," she told them. As she left the room she gave Beryl a parting look that was half questioning, half disparaging.

"I don't quite understand your preoccupation with my ward, dear. Or why you think Francis spends his time gossiping about my household." The dowager fixed upon Francis a bright smile. "I have known him since he was in leading strings, and I've never before heard him accused of bearing tales. I can assure you there are no gossips amongst my associates. I consider them beneath contempt and never accurate, for they are not in search of truth, but of creating a sensation. Imagine what a mean, small-minded person might do with the idea of a young girl living in a bachelor's household, no matter how many chaperones attend!"

On that note she left the room.

"I don't care what she says," Beryl said in low but definite tones. "Something is going on."

"I'm sure you're right," Pamela said. "But is it with Andrew?" she asked with a pointed glance toward Francis.

"What do you mean?" Jane asked.

"Nothing . . ."

"No, really," Jane said. "Have I missed something?"

Beryl gave a warning glance to Francis and a withering one to Pamela. "I believe I have a touch of the sunstroke from our outing. I am going to rest until dinner."

When she left, Francis soon followed. Pamela sighed and stood up. "I suppose there's nothing but sleep to keep one occupied until dinner. I don't know why people say the countryside is refreshing, I find it tiring and tedious."

"I think of it as restful," Jane said.

"If you feel so rested, what would you say to a rubber of two-handed casino?" the marquess asked her.

"I say yes."

"Capital! I shall ring for cards."

In the mistress's suite the dowager was not the least bit tired. "Watch for my son and bring him to me the moment he returns," she told Tinsdale as she supervised Mrs. Potts and Nellie. "Best put the Holland covers in the dressing room so that none of those busybodies see them."

When Andrew arrived, Martha had unpacked and the sitting room was in fair order, Mrs. Potts and Nellie still working in the bedroom. Martha went to close the door between the two rooms.

"What now?" Andrew demanded. "I must change for dinner."

"Is that any way to greet your mother?"

"I seem to remember a rather loud greeting an hour ago." He threw himself into a chair by the window and stared moodily out at the darkening sky.

"We have to talk about the girl."

"There is nothing to discuss."

"There is everything to discuss. In the first place she cannot stay here."

"She can stay. I shall leave in the morning."

"Be that as it may, it has no bearing on the situation. She cannot stay alone in a bachelor's establishment, particularly one so far removed as to invite inevitable gossip. By the way, I told Francis I was here in November and he agreed.

Don't give me scowls, something had to be said. The girl is a young woman and obviously cannot stay here. Obviously again she has nowhere else, and I am aware your father took on the responsibility for Mary's children, although it was years ago and I fail to understand why we heard nothing of them before now. However, that's neither here nor there at the moment, so I propose to remove to London and take her with me."

Andrew's head jerked around, his expression incredulous. "What did you say?"

"I can hardly leave you with the girl, particularly after what transpired this afternoon."

Andrew flushed. He saw Martha turn to her packing with renewed concentration. "You have my word such a lapse will not happen again."

"Good. I accept it. Now then, I propose to stay in London until her next birthday, whereupon she can be presented to society and hopefully gain a suitable offer."

"But that's an entire year in London," Andrew objected.

"I know my duty," Annabella said firmly. "By the look of things on the Continent, it is unlikely her brother will return in the near future. If he has not returned before the Season begins, you shall be called upon to do his duties."

"I?"

"You. This is assuming I can do something with her hair and her manners. She obviously needs a great deal of town polish before she can hope to make a respectable marriage."

"Marriage?" He rose to his feet. "She's a mere schoolroom chit!"

"She is obviously grown enough to attract suitors," his mother said dryly. "And she must marry, and marry quickly enough to dispel all this talk. You have acknowledged her as family, do you suppose you may now send her out in the world to earn her keep as a governess or some such? If so, you are being foolish beyond permission."

"Of course she must marry. Someday," he said gruffly. "And the quicker she's off my hands, the better."

"I quite agree," his mother answered.

"In a way, I shall be sorry to find her a husband."

Annabella gave her son a penetrating look. "In what way, pray tell?"

"I'm thinking of the dastardly trick we'll be playing, foisting her upon some poor unsuspecting fop."

"That will be his problem, not yours."

"Thank the Lord. . . . Perhaps then my life can get back to its normal peace and quiet." As Andrew said the words, he thought of his mother staying in London for the year and groaned.

"Are you unwell?" she asked.

"No. I'm perfectly fit." He leaned to dutifully kiss his mother's forehead. "I must change."

"You have no real—interest—in the girl?" she asked as he reached the door.

"Of course not. She is a taking little thing, but she has a nasty temper and the most unorthodox of manners." And, with that, he left his mother alone with Martha Tinsdale.

"I thought to save my son from that odious Beryl Cavendish, and arrive to find I must save him from himself. Men, bah. They never know what's good for them."

Chapter Eighteen

You promised," Brianna told the frightened Nellie later that night. "It's a matter of life and death!"

"That's what I'm afraid of, Miss Bree. The master will kill me dead."

They were in Brianna's room, whispering beside the window that looked out on the sparkling night sky as a thousand stars spangled the blackness. Brianna pressed folded bits of paper into Nellie's hands.

"But Miss Bree, I'll be caught for sure!" Nellie wailed.

"It doesn't matter if *you're* caught, you are simply carrying out a guest's request. If *I* were caught, everything would be ruined."

"R-Ruined?" Nellie tried to thrust the papers back. "Oh, Miss Bree, I just know I'll never be able to do it right."

"Nellie, please." Brianna, impassioned by her cause, reached for the maid's arm. "I am being taken away, and tonight is the only chance we shall have to save his grace from Lady Beryl."

"He doesn't seem to want saving, Miss Bree."

"He may not know it, for he is much too fine and decent to realize what a horrible witch she truly is, but he will one day thank us. Not that he will ever know," Brianna added hastily as she saw Nellie blanch. "Go on." She opened her door and gave Nellie a gentle push. "Hurry," she urged in a loud whisper.

Brianna watched Nellie cross the hall to Lady Beryl's door. The maid hesitated, looked back, saw Brianna motioning her forward, and quickly knelt, shoving a piece of paper under the door.

"Stop," Brianna called out in a hoarse whisper. "Is it the right one?"

The sounds of the after dinner party came up the stairwell as Nellie snatched back the note and, with trembling hands, opened it. She shook her head, thrust the other paper beneath the door and jumped to her feet, running to Lord Effingham's door and tucking the second note underneath. She fled on down the hall, racing for the green baize door to the servants' stairs before Brianna could ask for anything more.

Brianna closed her door with a small satisfied sigh and went back to the window, looking out at the night sky. Before dinner the dowager duchess had informed Brianna she would leave for London in the morning. There would be many lessons in comportment and manners, and at the end there would be a grand party where Brianna would be presented to society. And, hopefully, find a suitable husband. The dowager had explained she did not wish thanks, she was merely carrying out her duty. Connie had given

Brianna a very speaking look, and Brianna had expressed her thanks most excessively, according to the dowager.

The truth was, Brianna's heart was so full she did not hear much of what any were saying to her. Her thoughts were filled with the duke and the memory of his startled look when she kissed him. The sensation of his arms holding her safe while his mouth searched hers had overwhelmed her with sweet longings that nagged at her still.

She turned away from the window and caught sight of her reflection in the oval mirror over the dressing table. She sank to the vanity bench, staring at herself in the lamplight, the room behind blurred by shadows. When he looked at her, what did he see? she wondered. She saw unfashionable red hair that went its own way no matter how it was combed, freckles that marred the milky complexion of her cheeks. A whey-faced child, she'd heard someone say once; that's what she was. She was hopeless.

She was too thin, already taller than Lady Beryl and growing still taller. But he had let her kiss him, and then he had kissed her, and in that wondrous moment her entire world changed. His arms had grown strong around her, lifting her up; his lips had become demanding, and his tongue—she shivered with the memory. Closing her eyes, she was back in his arms, his mouth searching out hers.

Sounds in the hall startled Brianna back to the present as the dowager duchess and the London ladies passed by her room, calling out their good-nights. Behind them came the gentlemen, the flurry of noisy good-nights, tromping footsteps, opening and closing doors, soon over as Brianna waited with baited breath, her heart thumping against her rib cage.

In Lord Effingham's room his lordship saw the folded piece of paper the moment he closed his door. He reached down to the Axminster carpet and retrieved it, glancing quickly and then reading more slowly.

Dear One,
   I was a beast to you and am thoroughly miserable.

Meet me in the gazebo when the others are abed and I
shall prove my feelings.

Francis Effingham was both surprised and pleased and
more than a little flattered. Finally Beryl was coming to her
senses and realizing Andrew would never come up to
scratch. He debated whether to change, decided he'd best
start to undress in case any should happen upon him as he
slipped outside. He could put a coat over his nightclothes
and say he hadn't been able to sleep and decided to take a
turn around the grounds. None would assume a gentleman
was going to an assignation in the gazebo in his nightclothes.
Whistling softly to himself, he began to undress.

Lady Beryl did not see the note placed under her door
until long after she entered. The paper had caught in her
skirts as she passed over it. Later, as her maid helped her
start to undress, it dropped to the floor.

"Mae? What is that?"

"I don't know, your ladyship." Mae fetched it for her
mistress and Beryl unfolded it, beginning to read.

"You may go."

"Do you want me to come back to help you undress, your
ladyship?"

". . . No, unfasten my dress, please; I shall do the rest
myself."

Mae did as she was bid and soon left the room, whereupon Beryl looked back down at the note.

My dearest,
   As you desire me, you must destroy this as soon as
you have read it, as a pledge of good faith. I cannot wait
another moment to declare myself. Make yourself ready
for my approach. Come to the gazebo after all are
asleep. I can wait no longer!
P.S. Remember to destroy this.

A look of triumph filled Beryl's pale blue eyes, her victory
so sweet she did not give a moment's thought to why

Andrew would be so adamant about the note being destroyed. Planning quickly, she disrobed and went to the clothes press, pulling out fresh linens.

As Beryl changed, across the hall Francis and Brianna both opened their doors a crack and carefully peered outside. Their rooms on the same side of the hall, neither saw the other. Francis was looking for signs of lamps being lowered, but still saw light coming out from beneath the nearby doors. He went back to lie upon his bed, waiting impatiently for the others to retire.

Burning with curiosity, Brianna was still debating with herself about sneaking out to see what was happening when Beryl's door opened. Brianna jumped back, closing her door and then prizing it open a crack to see Beryl tap lightly on Jane's door and slip inside. Sure something was amiss, Brianna scooted out into the hall, fairly dancing with worry. Looking up and down, she tiptoed nearer Jane's door, where she could hear their voices but not their words. She leaned closer, her ear against the wood, as Jane spoke again.

"But Beryl, why would I be wandering the grounds in the dead of night?"

"Darling Jane, he'll not think to question you, and even if he did, you could say anything you wished. Say you had a tryst too."

"Thank you, dear Beryl, for gratuitously ruining my reputation along with your own!"

"Andrew will hardly be in a position to cast stones. Nor will he be able to delay further. He'll be forced to do the honorable thing and marry me. I shall have him, if only you will help." Beryl's eyes lit with another idea. "Do you suppose there is any way we could wake the old harridan for her to see for herself?"

"Beryl!"

"I suppose you're right, there's no way we could tell her in advance without being much too obvious. But you will do, and if you make tons of noise, perhaps she will awake. I shall be so flustered I shall blurt out the most suggestive comments and he will have to offer for me."

"Noise?" Jane repeated, shocked by everything Beryl was saying. "What noise do you mean? Do you expect me to shout like a banshee?"

"I suppose you cannot do quite that, dear. I shall help, shrieking at our being caught and him compromising me and all that until everyone hears."

"Beryl, this is not wise. He's bound to see through it, and I shall feel the most utter fool yelling my head off when I can perfectly well see it is only Andrew and not some attacker."

"Nonsense. You'll say you could not see him at all, only a man attacking a woman, and then you realized it was Andrew and myself and you were stunned past speech." Beryl smiled triumphantly. "He shall have compromised my virtue in front of one and all. Jane, dear, you are looking at the future Duchess of Ashford."

"By trickery—"

"Darling, you know perfectly well he loves me. He simply has been a bachelor too long and we must help him over the hurdles, that's all."

"I suppose, after all, he did request that assignation. And you love him, of course."

"Of course I do," Beryl said smoothly. "And I shall be so grateful to you, I shall owe you." Beryl laughed. "I shall owe you, and the duke shall pay when the bill comes due!" She opened the door to the hall and started through it.

Brianna jumped back, flattening herself against the wall in the dark corridor and looking as guilty as she felt. Beryl was so caught up in her musings she never looked behind as she went the few short steps to her door and let herself inside.

A long sigh escaped Brianna's lips as Beryl's door closed.

"Are you feeling unwell, dear?" Martha Tinsdale asked, startling Brianna into an upright position.

"Oh!" She turned to face the woman coming through the green baize door, a teapot in one hand and a lamp in the other.

"Do you need help? I saw you leaning against the wall."

"Oh, no . . . I—I thought I heard—noises."

"It must seem there are many strange noises with so many about after having been here alone so long." After the words were out, Martha looked around at the closed doors with a guilty expression of her own. Annabella would flay her alive if she gave the game away. "You must excuse me, her grace is waiting for her tea."

Brianna walked down the hall beside the tall woman. "Her grace is still up?"

"A veritable night owl," Martha confirmed.

Brianna stopped at her door, smiling up at the warm-hearted woman. "Good night, Miss Tinsdale."

"Please call me Martha, dear. I hope we shall be fast friends." She continued down the hall, the lamplight wavering around her.

Brianna went inside her room, her mind racing over the possibilities of the dowager somehow becoming involved in this night's activities. As she thought about it she heard movement outside. Very carefully, very quietly, she opened her door in time to see Francis Effingham holding a candle close, his hand around the flame as he sneaked toward the stairs.

Next door in the master suite James was still up. The spring night had turned chilly, and the valet tiptoed across his master's chamber with an extra blanket. The duke was snoring lightly as James shivered and looked toward the open window. Knowing his grace preferred fresh air James decided yet another blanket might be needed. Lamp in hand, the valet went to the dressing room next door and then crossed the hall to the linen room.

As James headed out the dressing room door, Brianna slipped into the master suite sitting room. A soft glow from the banked fire lit the room with a shadowy gloom. She saw the inner door and made for it, pausing on the threshold to gather courage. In for a penny, in for a pound, she told herself, she had done more dangerous things by far. It was for his own good, and it must be done this night, before she was gone and unable to protect him from the odious Beryl.

Still, her heart was in her mouth as she crossed the huge chamber toward the carved bed that sat upon a dais and dominated the room. She looked toward the open window, remembering her climb in the freezing rain; it had been so many long months ago, it seemed as if years had fled in between. A strange sound came from the bed, and then another.

The duke was snoring. Slowly, she came nearer the bed, looking down at him. A lamp glowed on the night table, its wick turned low. In its soft light she could see his dark head turned away, one arm flung outside the covers. Brianna swallowed and reached to touch the arm. As she shook it, she heard footsteps coming near. Panic brought her heart to her mouth. If she were caught, there'd be the most awful row and probably Beryl and Francis would hear the uproar and all her plans would come to nothing.

The steps came closer. Brianna grabbed the thick quilt and dove underneath, pulling it over her head as James crossed toward the bed. She held her breath, listening as he came close and something heavy landed on top of her. The duke mumbled and turned, his knee grazing hers as she suddenly found her head buried against his soft cotton nightshirt. James still moved about the room, but the feeling of being close to Andrew's beating heart drugged her senses. She leaned her cheek against his chest and sighed, her eyes closing and then opening, alarm ringing through her brain. If she slept, she would be found here, and Francis was meeting Beryl at perhaps this very moment. Andrew's entire future happiness depended upon his seeing with his own eyes Beryl's true colors.

Brianna moved, intending to shake the duke awake. As she turned she realized she couldn't very well wake him until she was out of his bed. She raised the edge of the quilt and inched up and away. Her back touched against his outflung arm and it curved around her. She held her breath, waited, and then pushed her knees against his, trying to rise and turn. Andrew felt the change and responded, his movements drugged by the first deep sleep of night. The arm beneath her tightened, his other arm coming around to bring her close to his chest while his head dipped near her hair.

". . . Sleep," he mumbled.

Frightened of his waking, she knew she could not stay

where she was. She pressed her hands against his chest and pushed away. His arms tightened and brought her up toward his head. More asleep than awake, his lips found her cheek and kissed it. ". . . Sleep . . ." he said again, kissing her neck. His warm breath invaded her ear, sending heady sensations coursing through her blood and down her spine. She knew she should not be here, that she had to get away. His mumbled words warned her he was dreaming, but the sounds falling deep in her ear made her shiver with an expectation of something wonderful about to happen.

In his sleep Andrew dreamt Brianna was once again in his arms and he brought her close. The nearness of his body, the strength of his arms, liquefied Brianna's limbs. Her mind objected but her body turned traitorous, surrendering to her feelings and floating free, all willpower gone. He responded to the warm flesh in his arms, his mouth finding hers as his hand slid toward her breast. His lips crushed hers, his tongue thrusting between, and Brianna responded to the wondrous sensations, her arms going around his neck. She responded to his hunger, molding herself against him as he came fully awake and realized Brianna was actually in his bed.

"What the bloody hell!" he roared, lifting himself up away from her. He was about to thrust her from his bed when he heard James tap on the connecting door. "Your grace?" the valet asked as he opened the door.

Andrew fell forward, the girl beneath him. He grabbed the quilt, pulling it higher. "What?"

"Did you call?"

"No, go back to bed." The girl was pressed between him and the bed, his hips pressing down against hers. He could feel himself reacting and cursed aloud.

"If you're wakeful, I could get you some hot milk," James offered.

"Go back to your bloody bed!" Andrew barked, sending the confused James back behind the door.

Brianna lay beneath him, her breath shallow with his weight upon her and then caught in her throat as she felt the change in him, felt him hardening against her belly. Andrew threw off the covers and hauled the girl out of his bed, irritated with his body's arousal, his anger at himself as much as at Brianna. He hauled her toward the window.

"If you've been climbing again, I swear I'll break your neck myself so you needn't keep trying!" His angry words were said in a loud whisper, his eyes on the connecting door to his valet's room.

"I didn't climb in." She was still trying to sort out her confusion and his anger, the warmth in her belly and the change in his body. "I came to tell you to go to the gazebo."

In the faint lamplight from the table beyond, he regarded her serious young face. He looked down at the lips he had crushed against his and forced his eyes away. "You are a Bedlamite, there is no other possible explanation. You climb in my bed in the middle of the night because you want me to agree to an assignation in the gazebo."

"No, no, I want you to see one," she corrected.

"What did you say?"

"I—I saw Lady Beryl and Lord Francis, they're in the gazebo."

"You are mad."

"You already said that," she pointed out. "Are you afraid to confront them?"

He reached for his robe. "The only way to teach you to end these prevarications is to confront *you* with the objects of your calumny. You are going to be mortified by having to face them, but there's nothing else for it. You must learn to speak the truth."

Andrew reached for the lamp, raising the wick before he pulled the girl across his bedchamber and marched her out into the hall. His shoulders squared, he went to Francis's door, seeing no reason to wake Beryl at such an hour. There was no answer to his knock.

"He's not there," she whispered in a placating tone.

"He's sleeping soundly," the duke whispered back, anger in every syllable. He couldn't very well pound at this hour, so he opened the door and thrust her inside. The bed-table lamp was on, the bed empty. Without a word he turned and stalked across the hall. Brianna followed, watching as he hesitated and then carefully opened the door to Beryl's room. His lamp thrust forward, its light swept across the empty room. When he turned to Brianna, his face was a storm cloud in the murky light. "How do you know where they are?"

"I heard Beryl and Lady Jane," Brianna said, thinking quickly.

Andrew started for the stairs. Brianna ran after him, the stairs cold on her bare feet, but Andrew was marching forward shoeless and so she followed. Still trying to get his body to obey his brain, he willingly accepted the chill cold as he crossed the stone terrace and headed beyond the rose gardens to the gazebo.

"Go back," he whispered as they neared the gazebo.

Brianna did not answer and did not retrace her steps, but she did lag behind as Andrew walked forward to see Francis holding Beryl in a passionate embrace.

Her back was to Andrew as she pushed away from Francis. "Please, for the last time, you must go or you shall ruin all my plans!"

"You asked me here!"

"I did not! Andrew will be here any moment and I must be alone. Find Jane and come back with her, you both can find us here, but you must go before he comes."

"Beryl, I am besotted with you, but Andrew is my friend. If you marry him, it will be over between us. I will not make love to Andrew's wife."

"What's going on here?" Andrew demanded, startling them as he came up the two steps.

"Andrew, I can explain," Francis said quickly, only to be stopped by Beryl.

"Nonsense, Francis, there is nothing to explain." She smiled at the duke as if sharing a secret. "He couldn't sleep and was walking about. I told him I was waiting for someone."

"Yes? Who?" Andrew asked.

"Now, Andrew dear, there's no reason to keep up pretenses now—" Beryl saw Brianna standing on the grass and abruptly stopped speaking. With swift insight, and one look at Brianna's eyes, her tone changed. "I shall tell you exactly what has happened, dear Andrew, and I don't blame the dear, deluded child, I truly don't."

"What are you talking about?" Andrew asked while behind him Brianna's eyes lost some of their luster.

"You must have realized she has a—dare I say it?—*fixation* upon you, my sweet. She arranged this."

"Arranged Francis kissing you?" Andrew said in disbelief. "How clever of her."

"Too clever by half," Beryl said. "I received a note to meet you here. But Francis came, having a note he thought I had sent."

"Beryl," Francis began, but trailed off, as they were not listening to him.

"You see?" Beryl demanded, handing him the crumpled note. "You must send her away, Andrew. She is determined to come between us."

Andrew raised his lamp and read swiftly. "Brianna did not write this."

"She must have," Beryl insisted.

"I'm telling you she did not, the child's writing is illegible as Hottentot."

"Stop calling her a child!" Beryl stamped her foot. "She is not a child and she has set her cap for you!"

"Don't be ridiculous," Andrew snapped.

"If she did not write the notes, then her teacher did," Beryl insisted.

"And *that* is ludicrous," Andrew told her as Lady Jane came running past Brianna and up the steps into the gazebo.

"Why, your grace, what are you doing out here alone with dear Beryl at this late hour?"

"As we are hardly alone, I fail to understand your question," Andrew said calmly. "What are *you* doing out of bed?"

Confused, Lady Jane looked from the duke to Francis to Beryl and then back to the duke and Brianna, on the lawn behind him. Finally she turned back toward Beryl. "I don't understand."

"In that," the duke informed her, "you are not alone." He sounded thoroughly out of sorts.

"Beryl, what has happened?"

Beryl glared at Jane. "What are *you* doing here?"

"Why, you told me to come and—I mean—" She looked from Beryl's anger to the duke's unreadable expression and found no help even from Francis. She glanced toward Brianna. "I—I, oh dear, I don't know what I mean."

"If you'll excuse me, I think I'll head toward bed," Francis said. "My walk has done me wonders."

"I'll come too," Jane said quickly.

"Andrew." Beryl reached for his arm. "You cannot believe—I mean, I don't know what you believe. But you must believe I did not ask Francis to meet me."

"I can tell you this much," the duke replied. *"If* I believed this was Brianna's doing, then you, my dear Beryl, would have been laying a most unladylike trap, since you kept the note and then invited spectators."

Andrew turned on his heel and left the gazebo, spying Brianna on the lawn. "And you, young lady, are going directly to bed!"

Beryl looked daggers at the girl as she ran after the two of them, coming in just behind them as a red-eyed Twinforth forced back a yawn and asked if anything was amiss.

"No," he was told by his employer. At the top of the stairs the dowager duchess awaited, Andrew slowing at the sight. "I don't want to discuss it. Any of it," he warned as he pulled Brianna up toward her.

"Brianna leaves with me in the morning," the dowager duchess said quietly as Beryl started upward.

"Fine!" Andrew said, and thrust Brianna toward his mother. "Why not *tonight?*" He marched past and into his rooms, where James looked up from stoking the fire. "Don't you dare say one bloody thing!"

James said not one word.

Chapter Nineteen

The dowager duchess was as good as her word. The next morning a sleepy-eyed Brianna found herself up, dressed, and bundled into a coach with Connie, Nellie, Martha Tinsdale, and the redoubtable dowager. They were on the road to London before the rest of the household had finished their breakfasts.

Brianna sat tucked into the corner of the swaying coach seat, staring out the window at the endless grasslands of the downs. It was a mild spring day, sheep nibbling at the grass, the sun high in an endless blue sky. Brianna saw none of it; she sat in the coach, her thoughts on the appalling morning hours just behind.

At breakfast, as Lady Pamela questioned the dowager's leaving the day after she arrived, Lord Francis walked into the dining room, saw the dowager's expression, and turned to walk out again. His attempt was thwarted by Lady Jane and the duke coming through the door, the duke scowling when Pamela asked where Beryl was.

"How should I know?" he demanded.

When told Brianna and the dowager were leaving immediately after breakfast was over, he said nothing beyond telling the footman the scrambled eggs were cold and to bring him fresh.

They had left soon after, Pamela dying of curiosity and soon closeted with Jane and Henleigh. Francis followed the duke into his study, the door closing with a resounding thud as Francis tried to explain his actions of the previous night.

"Come along," the dowager had ordered Brianna, who lingered, hoping to at least say good-bye to the duke.

"Will he be coming to London?" Brianna asked.

"One never knows," Andrew's mother answered enigmatically.

Connie had protested they would need more time to pack, but the dowager took one look at Brianna's closet and informed Miss Powell there was no need to pack for the girl since she would need all new, from the skin out, once they reached London. Brianna helped Connie pack, clinging to her as if she were her last friend in the world.

When they were ready to leave, Annabella Ormsby had Twinforth inform her son and then started for the carriage. The Duke of Ashford appeared at the carriage door, giving his mother a perfunctory kiss, wishing them a pleasant journey and stepping back, having hardly glanced at Brianna and the others.

He did not smile once.

Now, with every mile, the carriage raced away from Ashford Hall and the duke. Brianna turned in her seat and saw Connie contemplating her. Nellie's head had drooped forward, bobbing with the coach's movements as she slept sitting up. Martha Tinsdale was sitting placidly, watching out the opposite window.

"You'll make yourself sick, looking out whilst riding backward," the dowager told her companion.

"It's never made me sick in all these years," Martha pointed out.

"There's always a first time, and we are not stopping until we reach the post house and change horses."

They came and went through villages, many men dressed in volunteer regiment uniforms, newly home from the wars. The horses threw up puffs of dust behind their hooves as they galloped up the post road, heading north.

Soon they were in open moorland. Endless undulating hills beyond hills, clothed in green and brown, receded into the distances. They passed through another village and the next before they slowed and pulled into an inn yard alive with ostlers and people.

The mail coach was readying to leave, overcrowded with luggage and people, and still more climbing up and clinging to the top after the inside was filled.

"Come along, we'll find some tea and biscuits, shall we?" Tinsdale suggested. "Stretch our legs a bit."

"You may stretch whatever you wish, but kindly refrain from discussing your limbs in public. You, girl—Nellie, is it? You want tea or do you want to sleep?"

Nellie yawned in the older woman's face. "I'm so sorry, your grace! I—I must have fallen asleep."

"I can see that for myself. Help me down. Brianna, come along."

Aware the dowager was displeased with her, Brianna trailed behind the duke's mother as they entered the inn, where Martha and Connie had secured a table. Early that morning the dowager had demanded Brianna tell her the truth about last night, and she had given the girl several long hard penetrating looks as the morning wore on.

Knowing she had been at the very least deceitful and most definitely meddlesome, Brianna said very little to anyone. She carried the secret of the rest of the night's happenings deep in her heart where no one would know. She saw Connie's saddened gaze and could only guess what the dowager duchess had told her. Her teacher looked vastly disappointed in her and more than a little hurt. Brianna knew they would be shocked to the core if they knew of her adventure in the duke's room.

Brianna stayed close to Nellie, the young abigail shivering at the thought of the dowager finding out she had delivered the notes that had caused all the furor and sent them headlong on their way to London. None knew the maid was involved, nor was there reason for any to find out. So the two young girls sat side by side and waited for their elders and betters to decide what next they would do.

While they waited, Brianna's thoughts drifted back to the night before, to before the duke had confronted Beryl in the gazebo. It seemed a dream, all that had happened in his room. It seemed impossible they had kissed. He had pulled her to him in his sleep, not knowing who she was. When he woke and realized what was happening, he had thrust her away as if she bore the plague. But his lips had borne down upon hers, and his tongue had invaded her mouth.

"Brianna? Are you feeling unwell? You are shivering." Connie spoke from across the table.

"I'm fine, thank you."

"Drink your tea, we've a long ride still ahead," Andrew's mother told the girl.

"Yes, your grace," Brianna said dutifully. She meekly did as she was bid, feeling the dowager's watchfulness and Connie's quiet rebuke, but none of it seemed as real as her memory of the feelings that welled up within her again as her thoughts drifted back to the touch of his lips against hers. New feelings had come surging to life within her, feelings that were achingly beautiful, making her long for more of his touch.

He was terribly displeased with her, and she was afraid he might never forgive her for last night. He had been so cold and distant earlier, as if he hated her for showing him the truth, and now she was racing miles and miles farther away with each turn of the coach wheels. Her melancholy sigh resounded in the traveling coach, the others glancing toward her bent head as she stared out the window.

"Come, come, girl, it's not as bad as all that," the dowager duchess told Brianna as if she had read the girl's mind. Brianna looked up, her heartbroken green eyes meeting the dowager's bolstering gaze. "This isn't the end of the world," Brianna was told.

"It feels very like it," she reported truthfully.

Connie was torn between sympathy and condemnation. "The pain you are feeling is the result of your allowing yourself to sink to deceit and meddling interference. Ill will and deprivation will ever result when one attempts to run roughshod over others' lives."

"I wouldn't be too harsh on the girl," the dowager said mildly, surprising her listeners.

"You wouldn't?" Martha Tinsdale spoke before she could stop herself. Annabella Ormsby was a formidable doyenne of advanced-enough years and high-enough social position to cut to the quick with her opinions. Her words often had the accuracy of a scalpel, and those upon whom she leveled her attention felt as if they had been viscerally attacked.

The dowager duchess of Ashford was given to sharp opinions, no nonsense, and a high regard for her own comfort. And so the bland exterior she presented as she spoke mildly to young Brianna Morris was dumbfounding to her longtime companion, Martha Tinsdale.

"That is to say," Martha added quickly, "I quite agree. After all, she is young and inexperienced."

"What she did was bad enough," the dowager interrupted, "but it was done in a good cause."

"A good cause?" It was Connie Powell's turn to be dumbfounded by the redoubtable dowager. "Your grace, there can be no excuse for meddling and deceit."

Annabella fixed her attention upon the young and pretty governess. "Is that what you have been teaching the girl?"

"Most assuredly."

"Balderdash."

"I beg your pardon?" Connie was shocked.

Brianna turned her head away from the window, Connie's rising voice intruding upon her daydreams. "Is something amiss?"

"I said balderdash," the dowager repeated placidly. "I do not believe in teaching the young platitudes that in truth do not apply. It's all very well and good to talk of honesty and all sorts of high-mindedness, but the truth be told, the race goes to the swiftest, the cleverest, and usually the most deceitful creatures alive."

"What race?" Martha asked into the silence that followed Annabella's pronouncement.

"Martha, you are the most exasperating, most literal person I have ever had the bad fortune to know. All races, the race of life, the attempt to get what we wish out of life. Life, my dear Miss Powell," the dowager continued to the silent and shocked young woman across from her, "is not a sweet nursery school. This child has all the makings of a leader of society—trained properly, of course. One must first learn all the rules before one can flout them with success."

Connie's reply came through pursed lips. "I may not be

the proper teacher for Brianna, your grace, since I cannot and will not condone such—such ideas."

"Yes, yes, I know I speak heresy to your young ears, but my dear, just like a good hound, you too will one day be blooded and your world will change."

Brianna stared at the dowager. "What did you say, your grace?"

Annabella turned toward the girl. "I said there are turning points in life, when all that went before is forever changed. Growing up is a matter of keeping your eyes and ears open, child, and your brain alert. One must learn by experience, and experience brooks no high-sounding platitudes."

Constance Powell could not believe her ears. "The human race rises from its gross beginnings through the striving after perfection. It is not enough to say we fall short of the mark, we must still strive to be better than our original natures. I believe in honesty and integrity! And I believe those at the pinnacle of society have a moral obligation to lead the way!"

"How very nice," Martha told Connie approvingly.

"How very young," the dowager added. "And how very disappointed you shall be when you meet those paragons of surface virtues, Miss Powell."

"Turning points in life," Brianna mused aloud. "When all that went before is forever changed . . ."

"What did the girl say?"

"Nothing, your grace," Brianna said hastily, her cheeks pink. She lowered her eyes, afraid her secret thoughts would fly out them.

Miss Powell sat stiffly, her hands clasped together around her reticule. "The duke wished me to continue my work with Brianna, but under the circumstances I shall send him my notice by mail."

"Whatever for?"

"I cannot condone the lowering of moral values," Connie said, her words as stiff as her back.

"I should hope not," the dowager replied. "But what has that to do with your leaving our employ?"

"I won't countenance actions such as happened last night by any pupil of mine," Connie said hotly.

"I sincerely hope you will insist such a contretemps never happens again," she was informed. "However, your work is not to be the girl's judge and jury. You are being hired to continue her studies and see to the care and feeding of her brain. Which by all signs is overactive in the extreme and can be put to good use filled up with some constructive learning."

"I shall speak my mind and shall never accept actions that go against what I believe to be right."

"Good. I can't abide milksops who forever yes one to death. Now, is that settled? Are you staying?"

"Oh, please say yes," Brianna interrupted.

Connie faltered. "I suppose I shall, if you wish it. But, your grace, I must tell you I will not condone bad actions just because they might lead to good results. The end does not justify the means."

"The end does not *always* justify the means," Annabella amended. "Last night it drove a spanner into a most disagreeable vixen's plans, and I must say I feel quite charitable toward our young heathen."

So saying, the redoubtable dowager leaned back against her traveling pillows and closed her eyes.

Connie saw Martha Tinsdale's encouraging little smile and tried to return it. She leaned back against the squabs and closed her eyes, listening to the sounds of the carriage wheels as the travelers bounced along the post road to London at a spanking pace.

Chapter Twenty

*B*rianna woke later, gazing out the window to find they had ridden into a starlit fairyland. "Look, Connie, look!"

Connie opened her eyes, the dowager already awake and frowning at the girl. "What's happened?"

She glanced outside at what entranced the girl and yawned. "Good, we have reached the city."

"There are thousands and thousands of lights. It looks as if the stars have come down to earth," Brianna rhapsodized.

Dusk had descended on London, a light fog covering the tops of the trees and hovering about the brightish dots of the new gaslights that stretched away down the boulevard past the swinging carriage lights in two lines that seemed to go on forever.

"A modern miracle," Martha pronounced. "What will they think of next?"

"They do not yield much useful light," was the dowager's opinion.

Their carriage was engulfed in the snarl of London traffic, the noise terrific as their driver maneuvered around the thundering coaches, curricles, and phaetons. A street seller was still calling out his wares into the night, hopeful one of the carriages full of reckless, laughing nobs would stop for a bit of pie on the way to their gaming hells. They'd be hungry enough later and foxed to the gills, in need of a bit of food before adjusting their coats and breeches and wandering off home to sleep away the day.

Footmen and grooms in the Ashford green ducal livery sprang to attention when the coach pulled in through the gates of Ashford House and slowed, the driver making the turn to stop under the vaulted roof of the main portico. The coach steps were flung down in place, the luggage unloaded from the far side as the near side door was opened and an extremely tall butler bowed to the dowager and extended his hand.

"Welcome home, your grace."

"Thank you, Coyne. Didn't expect to see me again so soon, I daresay," she replied as she descended from the carriage. Martha Tinsdale followed, then Brianna and Connie disembarked, Nellie last and moving slowly as she stared at the starched formality of the London staff and the yawning door that led into a marble entrance hall.

"This is Miss Brianna Morris, Coyne, and her tutor, Miss Powell. You, there, what's your name?"

". . . Nellie Nesbitt, your grace," the young maid answered, terrified of being the object of the dowager's attention.

"She is Miss Brianna's maid," the butler was told. "Have someone see to her and show my guests to, I think, the yellow suite. They will be with us until Miss Morris comes out next spring."

The tall butler nodded gravely, as if matters of state were being addressed. He raised one white-gloved hand and a green-liveried footman came forward, bowing low and preceding the guests across the black marble floor toward the wide staircase forty feet away and directly ahead. Off the three-story entrance hall they caught glimpses of elaborate reception rooms and the two broad halls that stretched back on either side of the central staircase.

Brianna looked up to the glass dome sixty feet above her head and then back down to the bright brass wall sconces that lined the entry with blazing light. Round marble pillars supported archways that led toward chambers ablaze with light and filled with treasures. A footman showed the way, only the sounds of their feet on the marble floor accompanying Brianna and Connie across the huge entry and up the wide staircase.

Nellie was shown toward a green baize door by another footman, his dismissive glance sending her into a fit of the dismals. She was afraid she might never find her mistress again in this huge house. In truth, Ashford House was not quite so large as Ashford Hall, but the Hall seemed warm and homely next to this London palace.

The yellow suite Brianna and Connie had been given consisted of six rooms: a sitting room that overlooked the north gardens, two bedrooms, two dressing rooms, and a room designed only for bathing. Lemon chintz splashed with white and green covered the overstuffed chairs, lemon-and-cream-striped wallpaper rose above the pale oak that paneled the lower portion of the sitting room walls. The carpet was a mossy grass green and thick to the touch.

Left alone while Connie oversaw the footmen delivering their few possessions, Brianna wandered from room to room in the corner suite of rooms. For Connie she chose the bedchamber that looked down on the gardens to the north and to the front had a view of the square. Brianna took the smaller bedroom, which had a small balcony high above the portico and looked out toward the plane trees in the square. She opened the double glass doors and stood outside in the chill night air until Connie came to fetch her for a light repast in their sitting room.

"You'll catch your death," Connie warned. "Her grace said you must be exhausted and are to have a good night's sleep and join her promptly at ten in the morning in her sitting room." The tutor felt Brianna's forehead. "I still think you're coming down with something. I am well aware your meekness and quiet can have little to do with remorse over your unconscionable meddling last night."

"I am sorry, Connie."

"I do not wish to hear it, I am completely out of patience with you. Only by your actions can you rectify my feelings for you. Words will not suffice."

"Yes, Connie."

Connie watched the girl's listless reactions as she took her seat and picked at her supper, more concerned than she cared to admit. Perhaps Brianna had learned something from her adventure. If not from all else, perhaps the duke's anger and coldness had made an impression on the girl. Connie could not imagine any man, let alone the duke,

taking kindly to being faced with his lover's lack of propriety, at the least, and infidelity at worst, in full view of the
entire household. Nor could he have fond feelings for the
chit of a girl who dragged him forward to see it.

Beryl Cavendish was beneath contempt, and the duke was
well rid of her but two wrongs did not make a right. Brianna
had no business interfering. Truth be told, there was a tiny
little part of Connie's heart that felt good about Brianna
showing Lady Beryl's true colors to one and all. But Connie
would never admit to having such a mean-spirited emotion,
and so it was a very subdued Brianna whom Nellie came to
undress after the dinner trays were removed.

"Miss Bree, I have the nicest little room all to myself, and
there's six maids and four undermaids, not counting her
grace's maid and me. I'm to have no duties except to see to
your needs and your clothes."

"You'll have precious little to do with my clothes,"
Brianna said, "since I've come with just this."

"Oh, her grace is going to buy you everything, I heard
them telling of all the orders flying about. And look what she
sent . . ." Nellie unfolded a soft nightdress of pale pink silk
and a wrapper to match. "Isn't it lovely? I hemmed it for
you," she said as she helped Brianna out of her chemise and
into the pale gown. "It's a wee bit big for you, but it's ever so
beautiful and I can take it in if you like."

"No, it's fine as it is." Brianna felt the loose silk move
over her bare skin. "It feels . . . free."

"Did you see the bathing chamber?" Nellie asked as she
tucked Brianna into the four-poster bed. "Everything is the
most modern, that's what Mr. Coyne says. He says Ashford
House is the finest house in Lunnon, saving the palace and
His Highness's Carleton House. Just imagine! We're going
to see them all with our very own eyes."

"Good night, Nellie . . ." Brianna closed her eyes and
willed the girl to be gone. It seemed to take an eternity
before Nellie finished with the fire in the grate and checked
all the windows and turned out all the lamps.

Finally Nellie was gone and Brianna was alone. She threw

the covers aside and stretched out, feeling the silken fabric slide across her breast and belly as she drifted off into a sleep that was filled with dreams of the duke.

In Sussex a restless Andrew Ormsby tossed and turned in his bed, evading the memory of young arms that seemed to come toward him no matter which way he turned. Plans were made for his guests to leave in the morning. Jane, determined to leave immediately, had forced Beryl and Pamela to agree and accompany her, as she could not travel without female companionship.

Beryl had been bright and witty all day; the duke had been polite. Pamela watched them as Beryl attempted to regain Andrew's good graces and the duke himself seemed not to so much as notice her. Francis was abnormally quiet, Henleigh and Jane carrying the conversation, replying to Beryl's witty remarks and gossip. Supper had been uneventful, and afterward the duke pled a disagreeable head, something he had eaten perhaps, and took to his rooms, leaving his guests to their own devices.

All but Pamela decided upon a game of whist. She wondered aloud if she could have eaten whatever had disagreed with the duke so violently. She felt a bit off herself and drooped in a chair by the parlor fire, finally going up to her room at the urgings of all.

At the top of the stairs she listened to the sounds of the voices below as the game continued. Smiling, she sped to her room, quickly undressed, and then pulled pillows and blankets awry. She stuffed the extra blankets and pillows down the center of the bed, covering them over with the thick coverlet. She went back to the door and raised her lamp, pleased with her work. If any looked in, she would seem to be asleep to the world.

Lowering her lamp wick until it almost flickered out, she crossed the hall and let herself into the duke's sitting room. The room was dark, lit only by a few embers in the grate and her flickering lamp. Cautiously, she moved to the open bedroom door and looked inside. The fire was still rising in the bedroom grate, the shadowy light outlining the huge bed.

She left her lamp on the rosewood table near the door and went forward across the bedchamber, her bare feet moving soundlessly, her bare arms chilled when a draft from the open window hit her. She wore only her chemise. Moving around the bed, the fireplace was behind her as she called out softly.

"Andrew . . ." Her voice was low but insistent. "Andrew, are you feeling better?"

The duke was lost in his thoughts but not asleep. Startled by the words, for a moment he thought he had imagined them. When she called out again, he turned toward the sound, unreasonable anger rising within him.

"Young lady, how the bloody devil did you—" He stopped. Brianna was in London. "What . . .?"

He stared at the outline of a ripe female body, backlit by the fire, her gauzy cotton chemise transparent. Full breasts, rounded hips, long legs were as visible as if she wore nothing.

"I worried about your being ill," she said, coming closer as she spoke. She stopped beside him, his eyes looking up at hers past her full, buxom breast.

"Pamela?"

She smiled. "Might I sit?"

"What do you want?"

A low throaty chuckle answered his words. She sank to the bed beside him. "Can't you guess? I thought I might calm your savage heart." Her hand reached to his brow, pushing back a lock of his thick hair and then lightly tracing the curve of his cheek until she fingered his ear.

"I don't know what you mean."

"Don't you?" Her finger traced across his lips and then dipped between them, touching the inside corner of his mouth. Leaning over him, her nearly naked breast grazed his chest. "Beryl wants your name as much or more than she wants you, dear boy," Pamela whispered. "Even you must see that after last night's debacle. She will never succumb without marriage."

"How can you think I would demand such behavior?" Andrew sputtered.

"Nor do you rush her to your marriage bed." He opened his mouth to object, but she leaned forward, softly kissing his lips before she continued. "It is your unnatural abstinence which lends your ward such appeal. A willing young miss can be irresistible to a virile man parched for lovemaking, but she can also mean the end of his good name. One should look for safe comfort with a woman who is safely married and free to do as she pleases. . . ." Her hand was running down his chest, rubbing across his belly.

"Pamela, Hunnicut is my friend."

Her laughter was soft and throaty. "Dear Andrew, you are such a stick, you know very well Hunnicut has his own set of . . . friends, as do I. We have a very companionable marriage, our lands march together and our families are happy. What we do for our private pleasures is our business, and so we keep it."

"This has nothing to do with me, Pamela, you have got the wrong of all of it. As to any interest in my ward, it is the furthest thing from my mind."

Her hand trailed down the covers to reach for the flesh between his legs.

"Pamela!" Andrew said, shocked, but the lady rewarded his amazement with a lazy smile.

"Your mind may not dwell upon the precocious Brianna, but your body is of another opinion," she informed him as his flesh stiffened. "Unless, of course, it is I who bring about such lovely changes in you . . ."

Andrew pulled her hand away and then reached up to kiss her, full and hard and long. When he let her go, his voice was gruff. "Does that answer your question?"

"No, but I should love you to keep convincing me," she teased.

"The others—"

"Will never know," Pamela said softly. As she spoke she unbuttoned the long line of tiny buttons down the front of her chemise, from neckline to waist. She watched his face as the chemise slipped off her shoulders, her breasts spilling out of its confines, naked only a few scant inches from his unreadable eyes. "A gentleman can hardly say no to a lady's free gift . . ."

He reached for her, burying his head between her ample breasts and breathing in the scent of female flesh. His mouth sought out first one nipple and then the other, pulling on them, his tongue caressing her as his hands pushed the chemise off her arms and roamed her bare back. She moaned beneath his touch and he responded, all the frustration that had bedeviled him since Brianna's kisses driving him toward this willing accomplice. He rose above her and reached to cradle her hips with his hands, bringing her up toward him. As he entered her he felt the hot moistness, and suddenly he was losing control.

All he could see was Brianna beneath him, her startled eyes when she felt him hardening against his will, her trusting young arms coming around his neck to plead for more kisses. He shuddered at the thoughts, trying to drive them away, driving himself deep into Pamela's flesh. He fought the battle between his body and his conscience and his body won, his closed eyes seeing Brianna beneath him. At the thought his movements gentled.

Pamela knew none of his thoughts. Luxuriating in the strength of his ardor, she slaked her needs, her experienced tongue seeking out his mouth and boldly plunging deep inside. The rhythm of their bodies matched as he exploded within her, her body reacting with shuddering paroxysms that faded slowly into a peaceful quiet. He fell back beside her, his long hard-muscled body stretched out, one arm across his eyes. She heard his shuddering sigh and turned to kiss him lightly upon the cheek.

"I must leave, my sweet," she whispered. "Do not trouble yourself about Beryl, she will allow you freedom if you give her your name. And I am ever your friend." She slipped out of his bed, leaving as silently as she had come.

Andrew turned on his side and stared into the dying fire, wondering if this were all part of some dream that had no meaning. He closed his eyes and searched for sleep, but visions of Brianna crowded away all else. He imagined her once more in his arms, her young body naked and vulnerable, and his body responded, giving him no peace. He fought his thoughts, trying to sleep and waking over and over again before dawn finally arrived to end his misery.

Chapter Twenty-one

*B*rianna's first days in London were spent in a blur of shopping and fittings. She needed everything, the dowager insisted. Once embarked upon a course, there was nothing for it but to see it through to its proper finish.

"Forget your politics, history, geography, and sums," the dowager commanded late one fine June morning. Brianna and Connie rode with Tinsdale and the dowager in the open carriage, headed for Oxford Street and yet more shopping.

"You have enough of it in your head already. If you can add household accounts, you are fit to be a housekeeper, not a wife. The only history you will need is a history of your friend's families and connections. This is most important, for men are vain and their mothers are more so. In future the only geography you need will be that of your own parlors and boudoir, all of which will come in due course."

Brianna stole a glance at Miss Powell's unreadable expression as the dowager continued.

"I find it lamentable you are so shockingly green at your age. You might as well have been raised in darkest Africa for all you know of polite society."

"I don't think I shall like polite society," Brianna said rebelliously, thinking of Lady Beryl.

"That's neither here nor there. You must learn the rules of any game you play, including the game of life."

"Is life then a game?" Connie asked disapprovingly.

Annabella Ormsby gave the young woman a faint smile.

"For those who are lucky, yes. For others it is a chore and a burden. Now, to purposes. Monday next I shall give a small tea party to introduce you to a few of my oldest friends, including Maria Sefton, who shall sponsor you for Almack's once you are out. I am afraid you will be sadly lacking in male companionship, my dear Brianna, until you are presented, but you will no doubt make up for it next year."

"I never want to see another male as long as I live," Brianna told the dowager forcibly.

The duchess raised her brow and her quizzing glass to better see the young girl. "I can sympathize with the feeling, but you shall find it, regrettably, impossible. They are underfoot no matter where you may go. What, may I ask, brought on this aversion?"

"I thought you quite liked Dennis and James, and there is the duke," Connie said.

"Men are a botheration," Brianna declared.

"Yes, well," Annabella glanced at Martha, "there's nothing to be done for it." A look passed between the two women that Brianna did not see. But Connie noticed the silent question and realized that Martha began to take much more notice of Brianna's rather grumpy reactions to all the presents and finery she was receiving.

Later at tea Martha tried to draw Brianna out about her life in the country. "Did you find many friends in the countryside?" she asked. "It must have been difficult so far away from other young people of your own station." This was said with a baleful look toward the dowager. "There should be more young people about to keep you occupied."

"She shall soon have more than her fill," the dowager promised.

"I suppose," Martha persevered, "you must sorely miss the friends you left behind when you left your home in Kent."

"I had none. The girls thought me unmannerly, and I bested all the boys."

"Bested?" Martha queried.

"I could mill any of them down. And did."

"Oh, dear." She was aghast. "Whatever for?"

"They called me names and said I had no parents."

The dowager grimaced. "I have never understood why so many adults think of children with some kind of roseate glow about the word. Children are, by and large, mean little animals." Coyne appeared at the parlor door to inform her grace that a Professor Garibaldi had arrived. "Ah, finally. Your dancing master," the dowager informed Brianna. "Run along to Professor Garibaldi, Miss Powell will chaperone you. Martha, come with me."

The dowager led the way to the privacy of her upstairs sitting room, taking the stairs slowly. Once inside the pale blue room, she turned to face her longtime friend.

"My son is leaving for Paris. He has sent word that the regent wishes him involved in the treaty negotiations. He will be stopping here overnight."

"He'll be gone so soon?"

"Not soon enough," the dowager replied tartly. She earned a quizzing glance. "I think it will be best if the girl does not know of his visit."

"Oh, dear . . ."

"I've instructed Coyne and the staff, but there is still the young maid Nellie."

"You need only tell her not to mention it."

"I can tell her, but anything that goes in that girl's ears is likely to come out her mouth. And then there is also Miss Powell to consider. I would have to give a reason."

"What is your reason, dear Annabella?"

"Martha, the girl's besotted with him, it's as plain as the nose on your face."

Since Martha Tinsdale had a remarkably large nose, this made it very plain indeed. "Yes, but surely, all young girls go through a phase of hero worship."

"Most never grow out of it," Annabella snapped. "That's not the point. I'm not worried so much about her as about him."

Martha's eyes grew round. "Surely you don't still believe the gossip we heard when we arrived."

"I didn't believe it then, nor do I now. But where there is smoke, you will very likely find fire." The dowager sat upon a very hard horsehair chair, her fingers fretting with a crocheted doily on the nearby table. "There is something between those two. I can plainly see he affects the girl, and I think the girl affects him, and that's what I'm worried about."

"She's much too young for him," Martha responded.

"Of course she is."

"He would never—well, you know—with a virginal young girl, you can't think that of him."

"Of course not. For all his rakish bachelor reputation, none has ever said he has acted as less than a gentleman in any circumstances. To the best of my knowledge his dalliances have all been with more than willing married women, some of whom can be so insistent, the only gentlemanly thing to do is comply with their desires. Other than that, and whatever pleasures he may pursue with the demimonde, his flirtations have all been both mild and brief. Except Beryl Cavendish." Annabella scowled at the thought of the young widow.

"One would think that was over."

"One would hope. In any event, he will be far from London and Beryl's clutches for these next months. But more to the immediate point, I don't want Brianna so enamored of my son that she'll not give her young suitors a chance at her affections. And that's exactly what's liable to happen if they are around each other."

"You can't very well lock her in her rooms."

"I thought of it, but that's merely making it all the more romantic. He will be arriving late and leaving early, he said. With any luck, she will be abed before he comes."

Luck was with the dowager duchess. And perhaps the duke's own disinclination to tarry too long with his mother caused him to arrive well after the supper hour. He went directly to his mother's front chambers, where he kissed her, making her nose wrinkle.

"You smell of horses."

"I felt the need of exercise."

"You rode from Sussex to London? Good Lord, I should think you will get more than enough exercise on the Continent. Tell me the truth, is the little monster truly deposed?"

"Safely on an island called Elba, never to be heard from again."

"Hmm."

"I speak the truth."

"Oh, I am sure he's on whatever that island is, as you say. But I am not convinced there will be any peace in Europe until he breathes his last."

"Bonaparte is gone, and we must rebuild the ravage he has made of the Continent. I shall leave at first light. James is procuring a hired carriage, since I see no point in having one of ours make the long trek back from Dover."

Annabella looked up at her handsome son, a bit of worry edging her smile. "How long will you be away?"

"Quite a few months, I should imagine. Negotiating reparations and treaties is bound to be tedious, since all Europe will be at the table one way or another." Andrew hesitated, looking a bit uncomfortable. "How is the girl managing?"

"Tolerably well for one so young."

"She is very young," he agreed.

"She could be your daughter," Annabella pointed out.

"I should have had to sire her at eighteen, and you would have early been a grandmother."

"Enough of that subject," his mother insisted. "You must get your rest, and if I do not see you before you leave, I want you to keep safe and come back in one piece."

"The war is over."

"I don't trust any island to hold that monster."

He kissed her brow. "I shall keep safe, I promise," he told her as he left.

Inside his own sitting room next door, Coyne was placing a leather bag upon his writing desk.

"This came from Carleton House, your grace."

"Ah yes, our instructions. Thank you, Coyne."

"Do you need anything, your grace, before Mr. Tolliver arrives?"

"No, I can manage, thank you." The butler was at the door, ready to leave, when Andrew spoke again. "Has my mother been in good health?"

"I would venture to say she's in fine health, your grace."

"And our young ward?"

"Miss Brianna has not complained of anything amiss."

"She, I imagine, is already abed?"

"Yes, your grace. She and Miss Powell are sharing the yellow suite," the worldly servant added.

"It's not important, I was merely curious," Andrew said quickly. "Good night."

"Good night, your grace." Coyne bowed and closed the door.

Andrew loosened his cravat, peeling off his jacket and waistcoat whilst he fought warring impulses. Finally he made up his mind and went down the hall to the yellow suite. He entered the dark sitting room and hesitated. Choosing the left one, he opened it and stood in the doorway, looking across the dusky bedroom.

Brianna lay sprawled across the bed, her covers thrown off. She wore a nightdress of pink silk that was much too big for her. She seemed still a child until his eyes followed down the curve of her exposed shoulder to where the gown fell, revealing one tender young breast.

He remembered coming awake with her beside him a fortnight ago. It seemed a distant dream. Anger at himself rose within his breast, and in that moment her eyes opened. She gazed directly at him and he stared back, mesmerized for a long moment.

". . . Andrew." It wasn't a question, it was as if it were natural for her to wake and find him looking down at her. She said his name again, caressing the sound with her lips.

He stepped back and closed the door between them.

Brianna's eyes closed, still seeing the vision in the doorway. Booted feet astride, long legs in doeskin breeches, his white shirt cut full around the arms and open to the waist, his dark hair wind-tousled. She couldn't see his face clearly, only a shadow pattern, and his eyes staring at her as if he were somehow both hungry and angry.

She drifted back toward sleep until wheels clattering on the drive below woke her. A carriage pulled up to the front portico in the middle of the night, and suddenly she sat straight up in her bed. She was not dreaming, he was here! She raced to the glass doors that opened onto her small balcony, stepping out into the cold and looking down. She saw James Tolliver speaking to a driver atop the coach, and her breath caught in her throat.

"Might as well get a bit of rest, his grace won't start out until dawn."

"Aye, I wouldn't mind a warm bed for an hour or two."

"We'll go 'round to the stables, and after you've seen to the horses, I'll see to laying on a bit of food and finding you a kip."

Their voices faded, the horses clip-clopping around the side of the house. Brianna ducked back inside her room, hugging her bare arms close against the cold. She looked toward her closed bedroom door. She had not dreamt him; he had truly stood in the doorway. Her heart skipped a beat and then stuttered. James said he was leaving again at first light. She wouldn't be able to even touch his hand or look into his sky-blue eyes. She had to speak to him, had to make him hate her less; the look in his eyes when he stood in her doorway showed he was embittered against her still. She couldn't bear the thought.

She reached for the blue cotton night robe the dowager duchess had bought her, the cotton gown that went with it falling to the floor. She pulled the robe on hurriedly and ran to the hall. A footman standing at attention beside the stairwell glanced back toward her, squinting through the gloom. She closed the door and ran back across her rooms to the little balcony. It was ten feet or more above the roof of the portico, and surrounded by smooth stone wall that gave no purchase.

The footman was lounging back against the wall when she came back out into the hall and started toward him. Near enough to see his sleepy eyes, she stopped and smiled.

"Will you please tell my maid I wish to see her?"

"Now, miss?"

"Or you can tell me where her room is and I can go fetch her," Brianna offered.

The footman hesitated. "I'm not to leave my post, and I'm to make sure none bother his grace until he leaves."

"Did his grace give such instructions?" Brianna asked with a sinking heart.

"Bless me, no, miss. Mr. Coyne gave them to me as he got them from her ladyship, herself."

"But who would disturb him in his rooms?"

The young footman scratched his head. "Aye, and I can't imagine who might."

"Perhaps she thought I might wish to ask him a question —or something."

"You, miss?" He looked scandalized. "Couldn't happen. Why, you'd be ruined."

". . . Ruined?"

"Miss, you must know it would beyond the pale for the likes of you to go to a man's rooms alone. And in the dead of night, why, you'd be a fallen woman for sure." He blushed to his towheaded roots. "A man could have his way with such a girl."

"Have his way? How does he do that?"

"Shhh." The boy looked around them in the silent corridor. Tapers burned at intervals down the entire length, shadows resting in the spaces between. "You mustn't talk about such things, miss."

"Whyever not? It seems to be a topic all others know about, even yourself." When he stubbornly refused to reply, she continued. "You've not told me where Nellie's room is."

"I don't know as you should be wandering about in the dark, miss, not knowing the house and being a lady and all."

"I could stay here and man your post whilst you went to fetch her," Brianna offered.

"If Mr. Coyne were to wake and find me gone, there'd be

the devil to pay. Begging your pardon, but I'd get a proper melting as how I wouldn't be able to sit down for a week."

"I only want to help," she told the boy, looking most innocent.

"Yes, I can see as how you do, miss, but it's not a bit of it you're being, begging your pardon again." He motioned toward the far baize door. "If you go back along the hall and through the door and up the stairs, she'll be along that hall that leads to the right, miss. I don't know which room, except it's not the first one." He didn't explain how he knew who occupied the first one, and Brianna didn't ask. "All the ladies' rooms are on that side, miss."

Brianna sped away before he could stop her.

Chapter Twenty-two

*B*rianna climbed to the top floor, the hallways narrower in the servants' wing and the walls thinner. A chorus of loud snoring greeted her ears as she crept along the hall and listened at the doors.

"Blow me down," a man's gargling voice rasped out nearby. Hopelessly off-key, burping between the words, he sang between swigs. ". . . roll me over and do it again . . . roll me over in the clover and do it again . . ."

"There's no rolling this night, Johnny, you're to go with his grace." It was a woman's voice talking.

"I'll," he hiccuped, "go along, all right. Just another wee one to stay awake . . ."

"You and your wee ones, I wash my hands of you. If you're not down, I'll tell them the truth."

". . . Tell 'em the truth . . ."

"If any looks at you close, you'll be tossed out on your ear.

You're to take the post coach back from Dover, and the money's here on the bureau."

". . . Money?" He perked up a bit.

"And no more of this," she said, taking his jug of rum and putting it on the bureau before she left the room.

Brianna hugged the pitch-dark hallway wall as the woman came out, looked back at the man and shook her head.

"I don't know why I put up with you," she said as she started down the narrow back staircase.

The man's door was open, the room lit by the lamp the woman had left behind. An old coat with several shoulder capes was thrown across the one chair, along with a wide-brimmed hat, the man they belonged to lying across his narrow bed. Every few minutes he coughed, sang a snatch of a song and then fell silent again.

As Brianna watched the man, a new idea caught hold of her. She abandoned her search for Nellie and tiptoed into the narrow room, grabbing for the hat and the coat. A long wool muffler fell to the floor beside the chair, toppling a pair of boots. She grabbed for them and jumped back into the hallway as the man began to sing again.

Carrying the stolen goods, she stopped at the top of the stairs and threw her booty down. Sitting on the top step, she shoved her feet into the boots and shrugged out of the blue robe. Donning the heavy coat, she got to her feet, hiking up her nightdress and tying it in place with the muffler. She thrust her hair underneath the floppy hat and started down the stairs.

The boots added an inch to her height, even if her feet did rub back and forth inside them. The coat was so long it came to the top of the boots, its shoulder capes giving her the wider look of a young man. The hat was greasy but broadbrimmed enough to hide her hair and face.

It wasn't until she neared the bottom that she slowed, thinking over what she had just done and how to make it help her cause. Her single purpose had been to disguise herself so that she could get near Andrew. But once near, what could she do? She knew only that none of the others must recognize her, that this must be a dead secret between them. While she pondered what her precipitous actions had gained her, sounds from above sent her forward, avoiding the kitchen and slinking past along the narrow passage that led to the back of the house.

Outside, the coach stood in front of the stable, the horses with their noses in feedbags. She had gotten this far, she told herself bracingly, she would find a way to talk to him and then return the way she came, change and be back in her room with none the wiser.

"You there," a voice called out. It was the driver coming near. "Are you Johnny, the one that's to come with us?"

Brianna nodded and mumbled yes in as deep a voice as she could manage.

"Young one, ain't you? What's the matter, can't talk?"

"Caught cold," she gargled.

"Well, make yourself useful and get the feed bags off, they've just sent word his lordship's leaving."

"Now?"

The man gave her a curious look, and she realized her voice would give her away. She ducked away around the horses and kept busy getting the feed bags off. The horses stamped their feet, impatient to be moving.

"Climb up and bring her 'round," the driver called out.

Brianna climbed up, grateful that old John had taught her how to drive the farm wagon. Nervous, she fumbled with the reins and then pulled, the horses jittery at the commands they didn't recognize. She pulled to the left and they leaned that way, walking a little closer to the house.

"Whoa," the driver said as he grabbed the nearest harness and stopped them. He climbed up onto the perch beside Brianna. "You've not much knowledge of horses, lad. Watch how it's done."

He brought the rig around to the front portico, Brianna ducking her head away from the lamplight as Andrew and James crossed the porch and climbed into the closed carriage.

"Help with the luggage, lad."

Hearing the driver, James said, "There's no need, it's been sent down ahead to the ship."

Ship. Brianna stiffened. What ship? Why wasn't he going back to Sussex? As the questions tumbled through her head, they were off down the drive, a sleepy green-liveried footman closing the gates and yawning behind them.

They took off at a spanking clip through the deserted streets, heading east through the city with Brianna holding on tight to her outside perch atop the coach.

"Looks like we'll be in for some weather," the coachman said when they finally left the city, the fog growing thicker with each mile. It swirled around the coach lanterns, the horses seeming to run ahead into a wall of it, the visibility less and less as they left the lights of town.

Brianna sneezed and sneezed again. "Where are they going?" she yelled, the wind making it hard to hear.

"To France."

"To France!" Her voice rose but the wind blew her words back behind. Suddenly she knew she would have no chance to speak to him. She could not very well jump down and advertise herself in front of the coachman and James and whomever he was meeting. He would be furious and would never forgive her.

Nor could he explain to them what she was doing there. Nor could she, come to that. What could she say to anyone that would not cause Andrew grief? There was only one course left, she had to get away without his knowing she had been there. Perhaps the driver was going back to London. Perhaps she could convince him to take her back. She could say she had wanted an adventure, that she had bet someone she could fool them, anything that a coach driver might believe.

The small box between Brianna and driver opened, James calling out from inside. "His grace says we'd best stop at the next inn and let the weather clear."

"Aye, we're making no time in this," the coachman called down, but it was another four miles before the lights of a wayside inn could be made out, a little village of whitewashed cottages tucked up dark and silent in the hours before dawn.

One disgruntled ostler was jostled awake by the innkeeper to see to the horses. "Have to be crazed, out on a night like this," he told the driver.

"Stubble it, you've got a nob inside and paying right pretty for the privilege," the coachman warned. "If you want to see a bit of the silver cross your palm, you'd best hold your tongue."

James Tolliver was almost to the inn door when he heard the coachman call up to his companion. "Lad, Johnny! What are you doing up there? Come down and see to your master's bidding." The valet glanced at the slight figure in the oversized coat who looked down toward the coachman. As she moved, her eyes met James's and then veered quickly away as she jumped back atop the coach.

"James?" the duke called from the inn doorway.

"Lad?" the coachman said at the same time.

Brianna saw the coachman coming toward her, saw James start back toward the carriage, and panicked. She scrambled to get off the far side of the perch, her hand tangling in the reins and spooking the horses the ostler was unhitching.

"Watch what you're about!" the ostler hollered, trying to keep hold of the nearest horse and keep him away from the other's rearing feet.

Brianna jumped onto the snorting horse. He reared up and neighed, his sounds met by unrest from the one the ostler still had hold of. The coachman was shouting at what he thought to be a crazed lad as the duke looked on in shock and James turned toward his master with a sinking heart.

"Your grace, I think that might be Miss Bree."

Andrew did not stop to ask how the valet knew or how the brat had come to be there. In the midst of the ostler's and the coachman's shouts, the shrill neighs of the other horses and the sight of the bucking horse rearing up again, he strode toward the melee.

"With my own two hands, I shall kill her," he yelled as he neared her side.

Unable to dislodge his cargo, the horse leapt forward, racing out of the cobblestoned yard and streaking across the road. There was a low stone wall directly ahead.

Swearing steadily, Andrew vaulted to the back of the second horse, sending the ostler skittering backward. He took off after the other horse, clearing the stone wall just behind and racing to catch up.

Behind him the ostler, the innkeeper, and the hired coachman turned to stare at James Tolliver.

"What's happening?" the innkeeper asked.

". . . A bit of exercise?"

"Exercise," the coachman thundered, "I'll not have nobs and their crazy ways endangering my horses! This will cost you!"

"More than you know," the valet responded glumly. "More than you will likely ever know." He ran toward the road, straining to see through the foggy dark as across the fields Brianna was letting the horse have its head. The thought she might be killed did not deter her. If she could get away without them recognizing her, she might be able to get back to London with none the wiser, though how, she was not too sure. But death was infinitely preferable to being caught, and so she urged the horse on, hanging onto its mane, her body curved close across against its neck.

Behind her Andrew saw the horse galloping madly into the wall of fog and assumed it was out of control. Praying she would not be thrown to her death, he urged the coachman's nag as fast as it could go, his whole intent upon saving her life, his own safety forgotten.

Brianna's mount was tiring faster than Andrew's, and so he was able to come alongside and grab for her.

"No, no!" she screamed, the mane slipping through her fingers as he pulled her off the animal by main force, landing her crosswise on her stomach in front of him. He slowed the coach horse, manhandling the loose harness the ostler had been about to remove when Andrew had thrust him aside, commandeering the animal. "No," she wailed, "you must let me *go!*"

"I'll let you go to perdition," he shouted, his relief at her safety supplanted by rising anger as he carried her back toward the innyard and the others. As they rode, Brianna implored him not to take her back.

"I only wanted to speak to you!" she yelled, but he did not answer and she could not see his face. "I'm becoming sick," she told him, near tears as her stomach pounded against the horse's back.

Andrew, meanwhile, was weighing his possible courses of action. She was right about one thing, none could know it was she. They rode back into the stableyard, James coming alongside first and then the stableman.

"What's happened?" James asked.

"Where's my horse?" the coachman demanded.

Andrew handed Brianna down to James. The hat slipped, and he jammed it back upon her head as he hauled her toward the coach.

"Send someone after it," Andrew snapped. "It nearly cost me my footman's life! These horses are fagged. Hire new ones, we return to London immediately."

"What about *my* loss?"

"I shall give you full measure for your horse," the duke said. He handed the half-undone harness to the coachman and marched toward the carriage.

Brianna straightened up inside to see him coming through the door and swinging it shut, his piercing look daring her to open her mouth. James closed the curtains and raised the wick in the lamp before he sat down opposite his employer.

"Is there any possible explanation?" the duke finally asked in frigid accents.

"I needed to speak to you alone."

"Not bloody likely."

"Your grace," James said softly, "it would be wise to keep your voice down."

A knock at the carriage door took James to open it, his body blocking the innkeeper's view of the interior.

"I've ale and roast chicken ready for your master."

"I shall tell him."

"Are you not coming inside?" The man looked perplexed, and James could not blame him. The fog had turned to a cold drizzle which was steadily growing worse.

"I, ah, the boy is ill."

"Then you'll be wanting some heat and some soup for his belly."

"No," James said hastily. "No, he, ah, can't eat. It's an old complaint. Box up the food and I shall be in directly to fetch it." Closing the door, he looked from the girl to the duke. "I'd best go or he'll be back."

Andrew was glaring at Brianna as James stepped down out of the coach, glad he was not the recipient of the duke's anger. What the girl could have been thinking of was more than James could fathom. Kicking up another lark, he decided; she was too high-spirited by half.

But inside the hired coach Brianna was dispirited and near tears.

"Take off that ridiculous attire."

She pulled off the hat, her tangled curls tumbling around her face and shoulders. The duke yanked the hat away from her, his nose wrinkling in distaste at its greasy feel. "Take off that coat."

"No."

Before she could explain, Andrew reached across the seat. In one continuous motion he grabbed her, yanked the filthy coat off, tipped her over his lap and raised his hand, bringing it down flat against her posterior.

"Ow!"

"You've been needing a melting your entire life, young lady, and now you shall have it!" He spanked her again, the report of his palm against her backside loud in the closed coach.

"Don't you dare," she screamed, squirming on his lap as his hand came down again. "I'll never forgive you, never," she told him as she struggled to break free.

He grabbed her waist and smacked her again, but as his hand came down, she slid down and the pink silk nightdress bunched up, uncovering the flesh that his hand smacked, shocking them both. He pulled the cloth down to cover her, yanking it so hard it ripped. She rolled off his lap and the torn gown fell from her shoulders, leaving her small young breasts and narrow waist naked, as it pooled around her hips.

Andrew found himself staring, and pulled his gaze away. Brianna crossed her arms on her breasts, shivering both from the cold and from the longing that stirred deep inside as his eyes drank in the sight of her. He grabbed his own cape of black superfine and thrust it toward her. She took it, his eyes averted as she wrapped it around herself. The door opened; James was half inside before he took in the sight of the girl on the floor, wrapped in the duke's cape, and the duke himself staring stonily at the cushioned velvet squabs across from his own cushioned bench seat.

"Your grace?"

"Get that blasted coachman and get us on our way," the duke barked, and James retreated, leaving the box of cold chicken behind.

It was pouring rain outside by the time new horses were hitched up and the coachman climbed up to his perch. James followed, opting for a seat in the rain rather than join the unsettled scene inside the coach.

"Is the lad daft, then?" the coachman asked.

"As queer as Dick's hatband," James affirmed, and in his heart he wasn't so very sure he was fibbing.

Hunkered down against the weather, fortified by the coachman's brandy flask, neither James nor the driver could hear anything beyond the splashing rain and the horses' hooves. For many miles there was nothing to hear as the silence inside lengthened between the dispirited girl and the irritable nobleman.

"Sit up upon the seat," were the words that ended it.

Brianna did as the duke bid, a flash of her legs visible as she moved.

"Cover yourself."

Brianna's shoulders drooped and Andrew's treacherous heart went out to her. "Whatever am I to do with you?" he asked softly. "You could have gotten yourself killed. Or worse. What if we had not realized you were there, what then? You would have been alone in the world, at the mercy of every scoundrel and highwayman from here to London. What could you possibly have thought you were doing?"

"I thought you were returning to Sussex, and I wanted to tell you—tell you—"

"Tell me what?"

"Tell you not to be angry with me."

"I am excessively angry with you," he told her, but the words were gently spoken.

"I didn't mean it when I said I'd not forgive you."

He groaned and turned toward the curtained window, opening it to see out into the storm. Andrew began praying the storm would lift and they could get her safely back before full day had arisen.

"I should like it very much if you would kiss me."

"What?!"

She shrank back away from him. "I was only asking."

"You, young lady, should not be allowed out of your rooms without two chaperones and a keeper!"

"But we have no chaperone, and your mother told me reputations could be ruined just by being alone with a man in a closed coach."

"Yes, but I can summon James if I need him to protect my virtue," Andrew said wryly. "You are the most exasperating wench it has ever been my ill fortune to meet. From the moment you were carried across my threshold I sensed you were trouble. I had no idea," he said feelingly. He saw her rising from her seat. "Stay where you are," he warned.

"But I shall be ill from sitting backward. Besides, I am already a fallen woman."

"You don't even know the meaning of the words."

"But we're alone in a closed coach. Besides, Nellie told me Mrs. Potts told her a woman that goes to bed with a man she's not married to is fallen, and I've fallen into your bed twice."

"Once from the window," he said dryly. "Don't you dare

come near me. If you are uncomfortable riding backward, we shall exchange seats."

"But Andrew, I am so very cold. If you would just let me sit next to you. Feel my hand." Before he could say no, her hand was on top of his.

"You are freezing," he said, surprised.

"Feel my feet." She brought his hand to the bare foot she extended to the seat beside him.

"Good Lord, you are going to catch your death. Come here."

Happily, Brianna complied, sitting sideways on the cushioned bench beside him. Her feet in his lap, Andrew chafed warmth into her toes as the coach rattled along the pitted road.

"I wish I were going to France with you."

He looked up, worried. "Don't even think it."

"No, no," she said hastily. "I just meant with you there. And Samuel . . ." Her words drifted away, her eyes closing as he rubbed her feet.

"Can you feel the warmth coming back?" he asked.

"Emmm . . ." She sighed as the carriage hit a bad bump, lifting her into the air.

Saving her from a fall, Andrew reached for her. Holding on tight, arms around his neck, Brianna ended up sitting on his lap, the cape skittering off and falling across his legs to the floor.

For one long moment after the danger passed Andrew held the bare body clad in silk close in his arms. "Brianna—"

Her young lips pressed against his, her tongue against his lips. She found the tip of his tongue with hers and felt him respond.

Andrew held back, telling himself to push her away. Telling himself maybe it was best to kiss her and end her curiosity. And then he recklessly crushed her near, deepening the kiss, teaching her willing lips and tongue. Every sensation was new to her, and she reached to feel more, letting him draw her tongue into his mouth, accepting his as little shocks of something wild and deep raced through her blood, her body melting against his. He felt her growing desire, felt a demanding insistence in the young mouth and arms that knew not what they sought.

She wanted to kiss him forever. She wanted the feelings never to stop, to go on and on and on. His hands roamed her back and then came around to cup her breasts, and she moaned at the touch, straining to be closer. Her movements on his lap excited him almost past endurance. His head dipped to kiss one perfect nipple, and she rained little kisses into his ear, calling out his name.

The carriage wheels muffled the sounds of their lovemaking, Andrew feeling himself ever closer to the edge of the precipice. Brianna writhed on his lap, and through the silk she felt the hardness she remembered and stopped moving.

He looked into green eyes that seemed as deep as the sea, so deep a man could drown in them and never care what happened thereafter.

"What do we do?" she whispered.

With superhuman effort he lifted her from his lap and placed her on the seat across. "We bundle you into your cape," he said, his voice ragged. "And we sit on opposite sides." She was staring at his lap. He ground his teeth. "And you do not do that."

"Do what?"

"Stare like that."

"You like it," she told him.

"I do *not* like it. You will drive me mad. You are the most diabolical temptress I have ever met, and you don't yet even know what you're doing. God help the men who meet you five years hence." He reached for the small opening in the roof and lifted its cover. "James," he barked, "stop the coach!"

James heard sheer terror in his master's voice. The driver heard it too. "The boy must have taken a turn for the worse," the coachman said as he brought the horses to a standstill.

The next moment the duke himself, with James's wet

overcoat protecting his shoulders, climbed up atop the coach. "I shall ride up here," the Duke of Ashford told the driver.

"I can well understand, sir. I've not much stomach for upchucking either. Best to let your man handle the boy."

For the remainder of the coach ride Brianna was confronted with a quizzical and then dozing James Tolliver. Outside, beside the coachman, Andrew was sunk in gloom as they approached Ashford House, wondering how he could manage to get Brianna to her rooms without giving her away.

His fears were justified. Dawn was up and so was the dowager when the coach clattered around to the back of the house and stopped.

"Andrew? I hoped you would realize you'd forgotten your papers." His mother came forward without batting an eyelash. Beside her a housemaid ogled the duke, wondering why he wasn't riding inside his carriage on such a morning.

"Henrietta, please take this poor coachman inside and get him something warm to eat, he must be frozen through." Annabella waited until the man lumbered off beside the maid before she hissed at her son to get inside and up the back stairs. *"Quickly,"* she ended.

James had the coach door open. Andrew grabbed the becaped Brianna and lifted her high, carrying her inside and up the back stairway, James trotting ahead. The dowager followed, stopping a servant who was about to enter the hall by blocking the kitchen doorway and telling her to go back and make up a tea tray.

"But I'm the scullery, your grace."

"Well, go tell someone who *does* do it," Annabella snapped, and the girl backed away.

James went through the green baize door at the top of the stairs ahead of the others, making sure none was about before he held it open for Andrew and his mother. He opened the door to the yellow suite, Andrew depositing the girl on the threshold.

Brianna caught at his hand as he turned to go, and he

hesitated, smiling briefly, before he left. He joined his mother in her sitting room and paced the floor until the tea tray arrived.

"Now," the dowager said. "From the beginning, please."

The duke unbuttoned his jacket and dropped to a chair, staring moodily into the fire.

"She wanted to talk," the duke said, looking up from his contemplation of the embers. "James is seeing to laying on one of our own coaches, I shall be gone within the hour."

"And that's all you have to say?"

"Yes." The silence lengthened, the duke staring at the dying flames, Annabella watching her son's face. "Mother, it's impossible to explain."

"You could try."

"She is headstrong and overemotional and . . ." He trailed off.

"And lacks manners, morals, and propriety?"

"She is a danger to society, racing about as she does."

"She seems to have cut up your peace," his mother agreed.

"You have no idea," he groaned.

"How far has this gone?"

It took a moment before her words sank in, and then he turned to face his mother. "What did you say?"

"I said, whatever is going on between you and the girl, how far has it gone? Don't look so shocked, and for God's sake, as well as hers and your own, tell me the truth."

"Nothing has happened between us!" As he said the words he realized they were not true. "That is, in truth a very great deal has happened, and I'm not quite sure how or why."

"The why goes without saying."

"Not with Brianna," he said with great emotion and more than a touch of tenderness.

"Let us begin with the night she climbed down from the nursery."

"Who told you of that? There was nothing to it, she was a child of fourteen and wanted to escape my clutches. At least I was told she was fourteen. She acted younger."

"Shall we move on to the day—and the *night*—before we left Sussex?"

Andrew looked sunk in gloomy thought. When he spoke, his eyes were on the fire. "Beryl and the others had upset her, she was grateful to me, and later she came to warn me of Beryl and was afraid James would catch her out, so she—well, she climbed into the bed." He cast a sidelong glance toward his mother.

"Grateful."

"Yes."

"So nothing whatever has happened."

"No. That is to say other than a mere trifle. A kiss."

"In the spinney or in your bed?"

"Well, actually—both."

"Andrew, is this a serious problem?"

He looked up from the fire, unhappily meeting his mother's quizzical gaze. "I'm most dreadfully afraid the answer to that may be yes."

Chapter Twenty-three

*B*rianna woke in the early afternoon to find Connie hovering over her. "Are you feeling well? Her grace said you were ill during the night."

"I'm . . . fine." Brianna sat up and looked outside, her expression as clouded as the sky. She had expected to be the object of everyone's anger, but it seemed the dowager had not yet informed Connie of last night's transgressions. A small sigh escaped her lips as she turned back.

"Brianna?"

She gave her concerned teacher a halfhearted smile. "I'm not ill," she answered truthfully. There was no way to explain the sadness that engulfed her or to tell Connie of its reasons. The duke was gone, riding to the coast and sailing far away, and her heart was with him, leaving her bereft and hollow.

Nellie came up to dress Brianna for her dance lesson, prattling of the mystery of the servants' hall last night.

"Some think there was a ghost about," Nellie confided. "But Mr. Coyne says only Johnny heard him, and he was too tiddled from shooting the cat to know what was what."

Connie looked horrified. "Shooting the cat?"

"Oh, Miss Connie, he was drunk as a lord, Cook says."

"But why on earth would that make him shoot a cat?"

Nellie looked confused. "I suppose he likes his drink, miss."

"It's a figure of speech," Brianna explained to them both. "Nellie's picked it up from the others. It's called London cant."

"London can't what?" Nellie asked.

Connie and Brianna stared at each other, suppressing sudden giggles. Connie tried to control hers as she explained, "Cant means a form of speech."

Nellie looked vastly surprised. "And here I always thought it meant you best not do something. A form of speech, you say. Well, if you ask me, people should say what they mean straight out, like I do."

Giggling agreement met her words, Connie hurrying away before her laughter bubbled over. Nellie began to fix Brianna's hair, Brianna finding the world not so terribly bleak until Nellie spoke of the duke's comings and goings. Neither she nor the others seemed to know the truth of what had happened; the dowager had spoken to no one yet. She probably wanted to confront the culprit first, Brianna reasoned, and she waited in dread all afternoon.

The call never came, and she did not see her grace until dinner, at which the redoubtable dowager was her normal self, correcting Brianna's table manners and carrying the conversation between the four females into edifying directions. There was not the smallest sign Connie or Martha knew of her adventure. Their hostess asked after Brianna's health once, leveled at the girl a long penetrating gaze, and after saying she should have a care about the night air, never again referred to the subject.

Summer came, and with it the arrival of the Russian Czar and the King of Prussia, all London abuzz with the gossip and news. Brianna heard of it from the daughters and granddaughters of the dowager duchess's friends, spending endless afternoons being polite through boring conversations about clothes and even more boring gossip about men and women she did not know.

But in the fall Brianna was rescued by the arrival in London of Lady Elaine Duttingham. She had come from her family's country estates for her first Season in London, and was just turned seventeen. Diffident, pretty, and the daughter of one of Annabella's godchildren, she was shy amongst the sophisticated city girls, preferring talk of her horses to talk of her clothes. In Elaine, Brianna finally found a friend.

They went to dance class together, listened as Connie read Samuel's letters to them, and wondered aloud about the lives they would lead and the men they would marry. Annabella watched Elaine's unstudied graciousness rub off on the rougher-edged Brianna and was happy to see some of Brianna's pluck and natural gaiety transfer itself to the shy Elaine. Altogether, they were good for each other, the dowager informed Martha Tinsdale, and, with Andrew far away across the sea, perhaps there would yet be time to rein in the impulsive Brianna.

"I think she has become your pet project," Martha told Annabella.

"Perhaps," the dowager said enigmatically. "I do so like to finish things I start. I received a lovely letter of thanks from her brother, by the by. It seems he and Andrew have run into each other in Paris or Vienna or somewhere. He is most grateful his sister will get a proper launch in society; he says she will owe her future to our good deeds."

"Thank goodness it will be next season and not this one," Martha said, and her friend agreed wholeheartedly.

There was altogether too much royalty in London this season, the Russians and the Germans descending en masse and cutting up poor Prinny's peace of mind by putting him out of sorts with his daughter, Charlotte. The reason was the Russian Czar's sister, the Grand Duchess of Oldenburg, who seemed to have come to London with the express intent of upsetting the regent.

She introduced Princess Charlotte to Augustus and Fredrick of Prussia, Paul of Wurttemberg, and Leopold of Saxe-Coburg-Saalfeld, all of whom were more desirable than her fiancé, the sickly Prince William of Orange. Charlotte broke her engagement and her father's heart, and Prinny blamed the grand duchess. They were polite on the surface, but there was terribly bad blood between them and it created tension throughout London's drawing rooms, parlors, and ballrooms, whenever they were to appear. The prince regent called the grand duchess platter-faced, and she pronounced him dissipated, disgusting, and obscenely fat, with a brazen way of looking where eyes dare not go.

Brianna heard all the gossip, made polite replies, and waited for Samuel's letters, which now and again mentioned Andrew. Brianna let Connie read the letters aloud and then would read them again alone. King Louis reigned in Paris, and Andrew was busy with Wellington and other diplomats, arguing over the Low Countries and the date of the second Vienna Peace Conference.

For months that never seemed to end, Brianna practiced her dancing and her watercolors, learned vast amounts of family gossip about those she met, and spent her time in sedate carriage rides with the dowager and long, protracted tea parties with the dowager's friends. Escaping when she could, she went riding with Elaine, the girls never alone, always chaperoned on their rides through Hyde Park or out to Richmond by Martha Tinsdale or Connie Powell.

The Vienna conference dragged on and on, and by December it looked as if the former allies might go to war with each other. The Bourbon throne was tottering, the French army wanted Napoleon back, and the King was more and more frightened. At winter's end, while the diplomats talked, Napoleon acted. He escaped Elba, and the King ran from Paris. Spring brought Bonaparte, determined to regain his domains, and Samuel and Andrew were in the thick of it.

Brianna could not get enough news, could not rest until she perused all the papers and learned of every battle and its outcome.

"Turn this way, please, Miss Brianna," a seamstress said as she worked in the yellow-colored bedchamber. "Her grace says we have no time to waste, as your birthday is almost here." The seamstress had been sent 'round from a well-known mantua maker in Bond Street, one of the dowager's favorite establishments, to fit first Elaine and then Brianna with gowns for the coming Season.

Brianna turned as the seamstress bid, listening to Elaine tell of news from home. "Persephone's foaled. I miss her so much, I wanted to bring her with me."

"Oh, I know. I miss my—I mean the duke's—Dark Star. She's the most wonderful black mare, and runs like the wind."

"Perhaps his grace will allow you to bring her to London and we can have some true rides."

"I doubt her grace will allow any true rides. Society seems to think cantering in Rotten Row is the only acceptable ride for a female. Can you imagine what they would do if we raced there? There would be nothing but expiring females falling to the ground in shock." Brianna grinned. "Wouldn't it be the most terrific fun?"

Although Elaine shared Brianna's enthusiasm for riding, she most definitely did not imagine it would be enjoyable to make a spectacle of herself in Hyde Park or anywhere else, and adroitly changed the subject to a letter her father had sent.

"The twins are off to school," Brianna was told. "My father says it's all terribly dull with us all away. He might come up to London." Elaine looked up. "Do you suppose if I wrote, he might bring Persephone up with him? Brianna? You look a thousand miles away."

"Sorry . . . what?" Brianna turned as the seamstress sat on the short stool, pinning up the hem.

"Are you feeling well?" Elaine asked.

"I'm fine," Brianna told her friend. She did not have the words to explain her emotions even to herself. She had not had a letter from Samuel in weeks, and his letters were the only contact Brianna had with Andrew. Her brother was unaware of how she longed for his brief asides when occasionally word came to him of Andrew's whereabouts or when the duke met with Wellington and spent a few moments in Samuel's company.

"I'm sure all is well with your brother," Elaine said when Brianna turned again for the seamstress and she saw her friend's pensive expression.

"Yes, it is. I would know if it weren't."

"How?"

The seamstress let Brianna escape from the pinned dress, helping her into a yellow silk wrapper over her chemise. The girls walked to the small balcony, a spring sun splashing light down across the grounds. Beyond the black wrought-iron gates the plane trees in the square caught the sunbeams in their branches, speckling the grass with light and shade.

"How can you know all is well? I would be terribly concerned if the twins were away and I heard nothing from them for weeks on end." Elaine leaned on the balustrade, watching the carriages that clip-clopped around the square outside the wrought-iron fencing.

"I just somehow know nothing is amiss. I cannot precisely explain it, but there's something inside my heart that would know if they were hurt or in danger."

"How odd," Elaine proclaimed. "Is it like magic?"

"A little, perhaps," Brianna answered softly.

"They? You said they, not he."

"It's too bad that horrible Old Boney escaped Elba and made everyone go back to fighting," Brianna said quickly. "Perhaps they'll catch him before the Season is over and Samuel will come home and you can meet him."

"Oh, I hope I can before I leave London."

"Leave?"

"Yes. After my Season I have no wish to remain in London. I want a quiet country life with horses and a husband who will be content with a quiet wife and a life far away from London and all its society."

Brianna turned to face her friend. "Whyever do you need a London Season for that? Aren't there any eligible young men in Surrey?"

"Bree, my dear, we are positively brimming over with them, but none suits my mother. She insists I have a Season in London so that I may know what I am missing. She is having the time of her life," Elaine said, smiling. "I don't mind so much since she's having all sorts of fun and reliving her first season, she told me the other night. Isn't that sweet?"

Brianna's brow wrinkled. "I'm not so certain. If she doesn't listen to what you want."

"Oh, tosh, I'll spend these months here with her, and then I can get home and get on with my life and everyone will be happy."

"Have you formed an attachment?" Brianna asked, her eyes alight.

Elaine blushed and looked away. "Nothing all that dramatic, I'm afraid. He doesn't even know I exist. He is most terrifically handsome, and my father gets along with him famously. They talk nothing but horses, so I know we should suit."

"And your mother?"

Elaine answered slowly. "His father was in trade, you see, and made his own fortune." Her head came up. "Which I see nothing wrong with," she added firmly.

"Nor do I," Brianna agreed. "It would seem to me a man who makes his own fortune is much more inventive than those who merely inherited theirs."

"What a good point, I shall remember it!" Elaine beamed. Her smile dimmed a little as she thought of her mother. "But, of course, he has no breeding, as my mother says. She says that's as important in humans as it is in horses if you're to have healthy stock."

"I suppose it is . . . But don't you occasionally need *new* stock in either?"

"Yes . . . Yes! You are entirely correct."

"Girls," Connie called out. "Come inside and change for Mrs. Enderby's tea."

"Oh, I don't know, what do you say I set a new style?" Elaine and Brianna watched Connie's aghast expression as she stared at the light wrapper. The girls giggled, their peals of laughter bringing a smile to Connie's face.

"Come along, we must see to your hair. Both of you," she added to Elaine, who had stayed the weekend. "Your mother will call for you at four," Connie continued.

The girls were still giggling. "This evening or in the morning?" Elaine asked.

"Not this evening," Brianna interjected, laughing. "She'll be much too busy at Carleton House parties *we* are not invited to because they are much too rakish for proper young ladies. Elaine, I fear we are being taught all the wrong things. If we do not learn how to become rakish, we'll never have any fun in London at all."

Connie suppressed a smile. "That is unbecomingly whimsical of you. I don't want to hear that kind of idle chatter at Mrs. Enderby's or it will be all over London that you have a fresh manner."

"Wouldn't you think they'd want a fresh manner now and again?" Elaine asked.

"Don't you start," Connie reprimanded, a smile playing around her mouth. "I don't want to have to chastise both of you."

"Oh, Connie, we shall be so excruciatingly prim and proper, we shall be the very pinnacle of social probity— absolutely boring."

"Stop this," Connie said, laughing, "or we shall all be censured."

"Oh, Connie, won't you join a bit of rebellion?"

"No!"

Nellie came through the bedchamber door carrying two new gowns.

"More gowns," Elaine said. "Where are you going to put them all?" A moment of disquiet sobered Brianna's expression. "I was only funning, Bree."

"What? Oh, yes, of course. Connie, is her grace in her rooms?"

"I think she is resting before the evening."

Brianna untied the yellow silk wrapper as Nellie asked what she would wear to the tea.

Brianna hesitated. "The cherry muslin, I think." She looked toward Connie for approbation.

"And your pearls."

"They're not mine, they belong to the duke," Brianna corrected quietly.

Elaine and Connie talked while Nellie dressed Brianna, finishing with cherry-colored ribbons entwined in her russet curls.

"They've always said pink and red didn't suit redheads, but I think you look your best in reds," Elaine told her friend.

"Some reds, not all. And green," she added absently. "Mrs. Potts, the housekeeper, made me a green riding habit." She looked toward Connie. "My very favorite gown ever was of blue. Connie, do you remember our blue velvet dresses?"

Connie smiled. "Made from drapes."

"Did you say made from drapes?" Elaine asked.

Connie smiled as Brianna explained.

"And old ones at that," Connie added.

"Only fancy all the gowns you have now."

Brianna moved away from the dressing table. "Your turn," she told Elaine. "I shall be back."

"Where are you going?"

"I have a question I need to ask her grace." And with that she was gone.

Nellie went to get the yellow gown she had laid out for Elaine, and when she left them alone, Elaine patted Connie's hand.

"There's no need for you to worry so about Bree."

"Am I so very transparent?" Connie asked.

"At times. And it is a most likable trait. But you must never fear, Bree is going to be the hit of the Season."

Connie bit her lip, her expression a bit distracted. "Yes, of course she is."

"Is that not what you were worried about?"

"Oh, I want her Season to be a success, of course, but I'm sure you're right, as none could help but like Brianna. But, that is, she does seem happy, doesn't she?"

"Never a sad moment," Elaine confirmed.

The young woman's words did nothing to lighten Connie's brow. "That is what concerns me, for I know she's worried about her brother's safety, and about the duke's, of course. But she never speaks of them or of her unease."

"We talk about Samuel all the time. We were just doing so a few moments ago."

"What does she speak of?"

"Everything. Their childhood and how she came to be here. But you mustn't worry, because she's perfectly sure he is safe. That both he and the duke are safe. She told me so."

"Perfectly sure?"

Elaine smiled. "Yes. She's quite convinced she would know if anything were wrong. And after all, that's not so very bad a feeling to have when someone you care about is far away, is it?"

"You are a very wise young woman," Connie told the girl.

"Not a bit of it . . . just practical."

"Is there someone far away that you care about, Elaine?"

There was a slight pause. "Only my father, Miss Connie."

"No young man?"

". . . There was one . . . at least so I thought until—until I came to London."

"And now?"

Elaine dimpled. "And now I see the wisdom of my mother's plan to introduce me to a greater selection."

In the dowager duchess's sitting room, Brianna was asking Martha if her ladyship was receiving visitors.

"You're hardly a visitor, Brianna, but she is napping. Perhaps I could help?"

"It's nothing, truly . . . I just wondered about my gowns

and all the rest. There is so very much of everything. I don't know how Samuel and I shall ever repay her generosity."

"I wouldn't worry about it, dear. She's enjoying herself. She always buys a little more than necessary, that's her way. If she can't decide, she'll buy both, if you see what I mean."

"It's just that I never expected—that is, I truly don't need all this expense and bother over me."

"Perhaps. Perhaps not. But why not enjoy it, I say."

"Oh, I do, I'm terribly grateful, I'm just—"

"A tiny bit nervous mayhap?" Martha smiled and squeezed Brianna's hand. "That will go away. Now run along so that I may change."

Brianna left, walking back down the vast, echoing hall, wondering why she felt so out of place suddenly, so very unlike herself.

Chapter Twenty-four

*B*rianna's birthday was chosen for the date of her official debut, the household preparing Ashford House from the cellars to the attics. In the midst of the happy confusion, Brianna seemed the calmest of all.

As the day lengthened toward night, she stood in the large dressing room off her bedchamber, feeling a strange sense of aloofness, of disconnectedness, as Nellie and Connie fussed about with her gown and hair. Her dress was of russet satin, high-waisted, with long straight sleeves that ended in points and were puffed at the shoulders. The neckline was square and modest, as befitted a young girl's debut into society. But it was low enough to catch a glimpse of the hollow between her breasts.

The gown was trimmed with gold braid, and more gold

braid was twisted around the thick russet curls that were caught up high atop her head.

Her grace appeared at the bedchamber doorway, coming inside with Martha just behind. "Let me see how you look," the dowager said, looking Brianna up and down from the golden braid in her hair to her gold satin slippers. "You'll do," the older woman said, quite satisfied with herself. "I have something for you," she said. "Tinsdale?"

Martha Tinsdale came forward with a small jewel box. Inside was a necklace of topaz and filigreed gold from which hung a large perfect pear-shaped topaz.

Brianna's mouth caught in a little oh of surprise and pleasure at the necklace's beauty. "I couldn't borrow it, I would be afraid something would happen to it."

"You're not borrowing it. It's your birthday present."

Martha placed the necklace around Brianna's neck, its drop pendant falling to the hollow between her breasts.

"Perfect," Annabella Ormsby pronounced.

Brianna looked at her reflection in the mirror, her eyes suddenly brimming with tears.

"Brianna?" the dowager questioned sharply.

"You have been so very kind."

"Pish and tosh," the dowager said, but her throat was a little constricted. "Now. It is time to go down and greet your guests."

"Where is Elaine?" Brianna asked suddenly.

"Right behind you," came the reply.

"You must promise to listen to my every word and correct me when I fail," Brianna told her.

Elaine laughed. "With all my vast experience of having come out last week? Come along, you must make a grand entrance, you know. Not too early, not too late, and you will have an endless line of well-wishers to greet who will shake your hand until it is puffed twice its natural size."

"I won't remember their names."

"No need. Just smile and nod and say how pleased you are."

In her suite the sounds from the front of the house could not be heard, but once out into the hall, the hubbub from below came up the stairwell toward them. Faint music edged around the laughter and conversations of the earliest arrivals in the marble entrance hall.

Brianna descended the stairs, looking ethereal, but in her mind's eye she saw the village children calling her names. She was the same and yet somehow she was different, and she was not sure why. Or even if she wanted to be.

The guests below greeted the dowager duchess and Brianna, admiring her, shaking hands and moving on. Carriages were lined up around the square and on out to Baker Street. As people arrived, were introduced, and moved on, the rooms filled with guests, snatches of music coming toward Brianna along with bits of conversation, all of it as distant as a dream.

"Why, my dear, Brianna," a familiar voice exuded sweetness, "I would never have recognized you."

Pamela Hunnicut spoke. Francis Effingham and a young man Francis introduced as his cousin Bertram, Earl of Pembroke, were beside her.

"How nice to see you," Brianna said mechanically.

Annabella began to worry about the girl and said so, quietly, to Martha Tinsdale.

"She's just doing as you've asked. She's being entirely unremarkable and decorous."

"Martha Tinsdale, there is a difference between being unexceptional and being dull."

"Is there?"

"Of course there is, and you very well know it. Look at me for example."

"Annabella, we've been friends for over forty years. I have yet to see the day you were ever *unexceptional*. I thought that was why you liked the girl so much."

"Who has said I like her?"

Martha did not reward the words with a reply. Keeping an eye on the doorway for new arrivals, she saw a uniformed young man talking to Coyne in the doorway. Excusing herself, Martha drifted toward them through the throngs.

"Coyne, may I perhaps help find someone?"

"A Lieutenant Samuel Morris, Miss Tinsdale."

Samuel Morris was overawed by the grand establishment and the throngs of people clotting the reception rooms.

"Miss Brianna's brother, how delightful you could join us," Martha cried.

"Miss—Tinsdale, was it? I'm terribly sorry, I didn't mean to intrude."

"Nonsense, Lieutenant, Brianna will be so happy you have come. I cannot imagine anyone she would rather see."

"If you will have someone direct me to her rooms, I will not—"

"Follow me," Martha said, smiling.

Samuel did as he was bid, while across the large parlor his sister was doing her level best to be polite as she extended her hand to Beryl Cavendish and quickly murmured a greeting, turning immediately to greet Lord and Lady Rossmore and their daughters. Martha brought Samuel near, but all he saw was a crowd of people who seemed to talk all at once to a gorgeous creature in a brownish satin gown. The creature glanced up, and in one and the same moment they recognized each other.

"Sammy!" she cried.

"Brianna?" Samuel did not believe his eyes. "It can't be you."

Etiquette and all else gone, Brianna flew to her brother's arms, shocking the people who filled the room. She shouted out his name as he lifted her high and spun around and around with her in his arms.

Lady Beryl smiled at the dowager. "I am *so* sorry, your grace."

"Why? What did you do?"

"I? Nothing! But it seems for all your effort, the poor girl cannot help remaining a wild heathen."

Annabella Ormsby raised her quizzing glass and studied the voluptuous Beryl. "I cannot speak for you, Lady Cavendish, but I for one, upon seeing my brother safe home from fighting Napoleon, would leap for joy even higher than dear Brianna is doing."

"Her brother, did you say?" the young Earl of Pembroke asked, his smile restored. "How capital for her!"

"Take your claws in, Beryl," Pamela Hunnicut said, smiling. "They are most unbecoming."

Standing a little apart from the others, Samuel and Brianna held each other at arm's length, studying each other.

"When did you grow so tall," he asked, "and how did you become such a beauty?"

"It's just the finery. I'm the same underneath, except an inch or two taller. You've lost weight, Sammy. Do they not feed you properly? When did you get back and how long can you stay? Are you home for good, have you been shot, why didn't you tell us you were coming—"

"Hush, enough," Samuel told her. He held her hands, grinning hugely. "I must say this is a better homecoming than the last, when I couldn't tell who you were from all the mud on your face. I cannot believe it. The last time I came home, I rescued two young boys from a mill in the pond, and now I come back and you're an elegant London lady."

"It will teach you, you'd best stay home, or next you'll come back and find me a doddering old lady."

"Not you. You'll never dodder," he informed his sister, and kissed her again, oblivious to the curious throngs around them. "Can you get away somewhere where we can talk?"

"Not quite yet. You see, the party is for me."

"For you?" He stared at her and then at the lavishness surrounding them. "Oh, good grief, I've forgotten your birthday again, haven't I?" He lowered his voice. "Do they know how old you really are?"

"Yes, no thanks to you. Why did you tell the duke I was only fourteen?"

"I didn't mean to fib, Bree, honestly I didn't. I said fourteen and then I remembered you'd had a birthday while I was gone, but Hobby told me you couldn't live alone with a bachelor, and I didn't see any women in his household, so I thought I'd best leave it alone. And it all turned out for the best, didn't it?"

"Yes . . . I suppose so."

Samuel glanced at the opulent room filled with beautifully dressed people. "It seems hard to credit, seeing you here."

"A fairy tale with you coming home to be with me. If only the duke could have come," she said wistfully.

"Isn't he here?"

There was a moment when Brianna didn't answer. She stared at her handsome brother. "I beg your pardon?"

"The duke. I was delayed with the packing of all the files and such, but he came back with Wellington a fortnight ago."

"Andrew is in London?" Brianna's voice was faint; Samuel almost didn't hear the words as the chamber orchestra began the next dance and other conversations rose and eddied around them.

"What? Yes. Didn't you know?"

"Brianna," Martha Tinsdale interrupted, "her grace wishes me to introduce your brother to some of your friends so that you may attend to your duties."

"I'm sorry," Samuel began, but Martha smiled and stopped him. "I really should leave."

"Oh, no," Brianna pleaded. "Please say you'll stay, I want to talk to you."

"If it's all right, I shall stay as long as I'm able. I have to get back and report in."

Brianna took her brother by the hand and introduced him to Andrew's mother. "Your grace, this is my brother, Samuel. Lieutenant Morris."

"Your ladyship," Samuel said as he bowed. "I tried to convey my thanks to you by letter, but I had no idea of the extent of your efforts."

Elaine brought Lord and Lady Duttingham to Brianna's side, introducing her father to Brianna as the dowager spoke in an aside with Samuel.

"I thank you, young man, but I must ask your help."

"Anything."

"Your sister has social duties to perform this evening, and so you and I shall have to help her do so by not taking up too much of her time. Are you in London long?"

"Hopefully, yes, your grace."

"Good, then an hour or two won't matter to you, but it will definitely matter to your sister's future. Do we understand each other?"

Before Samuel could reply, Brianna turned toward them, introducing the Duttinghams to her brother.

"Your servant." Samuel bowed to the lord and lady.

"Sammy, do you dance?" Brianna asked, earning a startled look from the Duttinghams.

"I'm afraid I should tread all over your feet, Bree."

Elaine smiled warmly. "Then we shall find you some ratafia and you may tell us about the French ogre. He has been fighting with Wellington, Papa, you will enjoy his conversation." As she spoke she moved away, taking her listeners with her.

Brianna stayed beside the dowager duchess, smiling and talking and shaking hands. But her eyes were remote and her heart heavy as she thought of Andrew back in London and not even letting her know. She gave the dowager a sidelong glance, wondering if her grace knew. Across the room Lady Hunnicut danced with Lord Rossmore, and Brianna looked for Beryl Cavendish between the introductions of even more guests, but neither she nor Francis Effingham were anywhere to be seen.

Music swirled around the rooms, coming from the grand ballroom. By ten the dowager declared Brianna had done her duty, and a few minutes later Brianna enjoyed her first dance of the evening with the Earl of Pembroke. Brianna was determined to enjoy herself despite her heavy heart, and by midnight a small cluster of young swains danced attendance around the lovely redhead who teased unmercifully and danced exquisitely.

Everett Barnstable, the young Lord Barnstable, adroitly cut in upon the Earl of Pembroke's dissertation upon racing phaetons and whisked Brianna away from the others' grasps.

"I have waited all evening and I must have this dance, I shall not take no for an answer," he declared.

She looked up into his determined brown eyes. "Do you

always gain your dance partners by highwayman tactics?" she teased.

"Only when they are as lovely as you and surrounded by other brigands."

"Are you all brigands, then? I had best have a care."

"Your reputation precedes you, my dear Miss Morris. I should say it is we who should be cautious of having our hearts cut up in ribbons over you."

Brianna's smile faltered. "What do you mean, my reputation?"

"I have it on the highest authority you are a nonpareil," he told the beauty. "My own eyes. I have watched you all evening, and I'll have you know I am a very good judge."

She laughed. "And very sure of yourself."

"But of course. When all of London is after one, it tends to bolster one's opinion of oneself. You shall soon know the feeling, and I intend to take you under my wing and protect you."

"You do?"

"Absolutely. We shall be seen everywhere together. The two most sought-afters in London will make a well-matched pair, wouldn't you say?"

"Your lordship, I have only just come out and—"

"Everett," he corrected as he moved with grace and dignity through the intricate dance steps.

"*And* I am quite sure it would not be correct for me to accept such a proposal."

"But I wish to steal a march on all my competition."

"You've just told me you had none," she said with a mischievous smile as the dance ended.

"Oh, I say, you are a rare find. You're not the least bit after my title, are you?"

"Hardly, since I have no idea what it might be."

"Sense of humor, no nonsensical chatter, where on earth have you been hiding?" Reluctantly he brought her back toward the dowager duchess and her waiting swains.

"In the nursery," she told him.

Annabella watched the laughing young couple approach,

heard the disparaging comments from his lordship's rivals and smiled in greeting.

"Everett, where's your mother?"

"I believe she is with Lady Hunnicut in the card room, your grace."

"No, Barnstable, they collected your father when they left for Carleton House."

Everett was disappointed. "I wanted you to meet my parents," he told Brianna, "they will convince you of my worth."

"Your worth?" the dowager asked.

"Yes, your grace. Your Miss Morris is not in the least impressed with me."

"How refreshing for you, Everett," the dowager told him tartly.

"I say, Barnstable, if Miss Morris isn't impressed with you, she shows exquisite taste," Pembroke put in as Elaine and Samuel came near with Connie Powell.

"I've introduced your brother to Miss Powell, Brianna, and she has been telling him of all your accomplishments since he's been away."

"More like all my transgressions."

"My lips are sealed," Connie told her charge.

"It is my turn to see just how very badly you dance, dear Sammy." Brianna placed her hand on his arm.

"You'll not be able to blame me if I march all over your feet," he warned.

"Of course I can," she replied as she led him toward the ballroom. "I'm your sister, I can do as I please."

Her unwilling victim made a valiant attempt to comply with her wishes, watching his feet more than the people around them or his partner. Before the dance was half over Brianna drew him out the open terrace doors they were near and ended his misery with laughter.

"You needn't laugh," he told her. "I told you I couldn't dance."

"I'm not laughing."

"You are so."

"I'm just so very happy you're home at last, safe and sound. You won't have to leave again right off, will you?"

"I hope to be posted here, but it depends upon the situation on the Continent and what his grace wants."

"His grace of Wellington. And to think we knew him when he was merely General Lord Wellington."

"I would hardly say you knew him, although in truth, he has never forgotten you. 'How is that little scamp of a sister?' he has asked upon occasion when your letters arrived. I daresay he wouldn't recognize you if he saw you now. I swear I did not."

"How could you, my face wasn't dirty and I wasn't windmilling anyone."

"And you weren't in boy's clothing," he agreed, grinning. "The duke will not believe you are the same girl he met upside down and backwards when he hears of your triumph tonight."

"Hears of my triumph?"

"I heard mention the Barnstables were joining him at Carleton House. Brianna?" Samuel asked as his sister's face collapsed into sad lines and sudden tears glimmered in her eyes. "What has upset you so?"

"Nothing, I'm perfectly all right."

"After all he's done for you, you're not *still* set against him are you?"

Brianna swallowed hard. "I am not set against anyone. I was merely surprised that he was in London and did not bother to at least call upon—upon his mother."

"It is strange you've not seen him. But I've heard he gives his mother a rather wide berth, perhaps that's the explanation."

Brianna forced her tears back, determined to speak in a neutral tone. "I should very much like to speak of something else. Shall we go inside? It's a bit chilly suddenly."

Inside, the rooms warmed by a thousand candles, people ebbed and flowed around the tables filled with delicacies. Their conversations rose in a din to the frescoed ceiling high above their heads where fat cherubs gamboled across a landscape of white-clouded blue sky. The musicians at the far end of the ballroom changed tempos, beginning a waltz, the first of the night. Only recently accepted into polite society, it was still thought a bit unsuitable by some, but Almack's allowed the sensuous dance, and a social gathering was no longer thought to be of the first water if at least one waltz was not played.

Brianna found herself near Connie and Martha Tinsdale. She was so distracted, she reintroduced Samuel to Martha and Connie.

"We met when your brother arrived," Martha replied.

Connie smiled at Samuel. "Are you enjoying yourself, Lieutenant?"

"Yes, thank you, Miss Powell. I had thought merely to pay my respects to her grace and see my sister to let her know I was back and safe."

"Oh, we knew you were safe all along," Connie told him, smiling warmly. "Brianna told us you were. We have shared your letters and your news from abroad, and I must confess I feel we had already met you, whilst we are all strangers to you."

"You are no stranger, Miss Powell. Bree's letters have been filled with all you have done for her."

Connie and Samuel settled into a happy conversation, and Martha Tinsdale watched Brianna slip away across the dance floor. Martha looked for the dowager and then looked back to find Brianna had disappeared from view in the crowded room.

Chapter Twenty-five

Outside, a few couples were on the terrace, the music carrying out the open doors and beyond to the gardens. Brianna skirted around the Earl of Pembroke, who attempted to catch her eye. She gave a perfunctory greeting to one of the dowager's many friends and slipped past the couples near the terrace doors. Drinking in the cool night air, she moved toward the edge of the terrace, staring out at the path that led past the flower beds to the sculpted hedges of the maze.

Brianna castigated herself for the tears she fought. She would not cry, she was no longer a child, she told herself. Silvery laughter met by a deeper chuckle came from behind her on the terrace, a couple dancing around the potted palms to steal a kiss. Brianna lifted her russet skirts, running down the wide shallow steps to the dark coolness of the garden.

She gulped air, her hands clasped tightly. She would have to return to her party, she would have to smile and dance and be polite until the night was over and she could escape to her rooms and cry alone.

"May I have this dance?" a deep male voice asked from just behind her ear. Chills went straight down Brianna's spine as she heard the familiar timbre. She turned and looked up into Andrew's eyes, treacherous tears spilling down her cheeks and turning his smile to an expression of deep concern. "Brianna? What's wrong?"

She swallowed hard. "Nothing, your grace."

He tilted her chin upward, staring intently into her emerald eyes. "Something in both eyes again?" he asked softly.

264

"Why didn't you let us know you were home? Why didn't you come to my party?"

". . . I have come . . ."

She had a hundred questions and as many accusations, but she could think of none of them as he reached for her waist. His other hand touched the shoulder of her gown.

"You have become a beauty," he told her as his fingers trailed down her arm and captured her hand. He held her for a long moment, until a waltz carried outside and drifted on the breeze. "May I have this dance?" he asked again in a husky voice.

He drew her closer, beginning the one-two-three rhythm, making graceful circles on the garden path.

"You have been back for a fortnight," she accused. Her words came out breathy as her body reacted to his closeness.

"Yes."

"You weren't going to come tonight," she managed to say as he drew her even closer, her breast rubbing lightly against his chest as their bodies swayed in time with the waltz.

"No," he admitted.

"Why?"

"Because discretion around you is far the better part of valor."

"Why did you come now?"

"I could not resist a chance to see the paragon of beauty all were describing."

"I don't understand."

"I was at Carleton House when Barnstable and Hunnicut arrived, glowing poetic about my young ward. Effingham said I wouldn't recognize you, and Beryl very nearly slapped him, so I was, of course, curious to see what had so affected them all."

"Beryl?"

"Hmmm?"

"Nothing."

They moved, one-two-three, one-two-three, Andrew's tall slim body grazing lightly against her breast and legs, sending shivers down her spine.

"Are you cold?"

"No." Hurt pride vied with true pain within Brianna, stiffening her posture and hardening her voice. "I'm sure you must be perishing to return to Lady Beryl."

"I shall survive," he told her dryly.

"In any event, you can see they exaggerated. I am still only myself."

"Ah, but what a beautiful self. They did not do you half justice. I saw you come outside with Samuel a little earlier. I imagined you might have asked after me, might have found out I was in London."

"I'm sure it is none of my business where you are."

Andrew ignored her tart words. "And then I saw you come back outside . . ." As he spoke he drew her even closer. When next he spoke, they were close enough to hear each other's heartbeats. "I wanted to tell you myself how very beautiful you are and how very pleased I am for you. I will soon have to stand in line amongst all your beaux to catch even a small glimpse of you."

Brianna felt herself melting toward him and fought the warmth that was flooding through her. She wanted to be haughty and cool, she wanted to deliver some appropriate bon mot and walk regally away from him before she began to cry. She could feel tears welling up again, her emotions in a confused uproar. She wanted to slap him for staying away, she wanted him to kiss her and never let her go. She wanted the feeling of his body against hers never to end.

Neither of them saw Martha Tinsdale step out onto the terrace and glance around at the couples, nor did they hear her little exclamation of surprise when she looked toward the lawns. The couples on the terrace looked to see what Martha saw as she hurried back inside toward the dowager duchess.

Andrew and Brianna were oblivious to any but each other as they made patterns of circles. Brianna's body at odds with her brain, she followed Andrew's lead effortlessly as they swayed one-two-three, one-two-three, nearer a kiss. His head bent toward her lips, her eyes shining up into his with the glimmer of unspent tears and something more. The music ended and their movements stopped, still in each other's arms.

"I *knew* the waltz should never have been accepted into polite society," Annabella Ormsby said in a loud clear voice from the terrace. The Earl of Pembroke stood beside her, staring out toward Brianna and the duke.

Startled, Andrew straightened and stepped back from Brianna, a slight flush on his cheeks, which could not be seen in the moonlight. A goodly crowd on the terrace watched him as his mother stood at the top of the terrace steps, her eyes fastened upon her son.

"Welcome home, Andrew, we were not aware you had arrived," Martha said from beside the dowager.

Brianna felt the loss of his hands as he dropped them to his sides.

"I have been unavoidably detained with government business," he said stiffly, "and cannot stay long this night. But I wished to pay my respects to Brianna upon her debut," he concluded in very polite, very correct, tones. "Now, if you will excuse me, His Highness awaits my presence." He bowed to Brianna, reaching for her hand and kissing it politely; then, shoulders squared back, head held high, he strode up the steps to his mother's side. He kissed her cheek, bowed to Martha, and pushed through the crowd of people, through the crowded house, and out to his waiting carriage.

"Brianna," Annabella Ormsby said loud enough to be overheard by the others. "I believe Bertram has been promised the next dance. And Bertram, I trust you will be more gracious than my son and, no matter how warm it may be, remain on the terrace."

"Yes, your grace," the young man said. He turned toward Brianna with a hopeful smile, and she accepted his outstretched arms, trying in vain to return his smile.

Brianna did not see the duke again for almost a fortnight. He was staying at his friend Effingham's, his mother found out. Brianna only knew he was in London and he was not home.

The round of parties and balls, at homes and assemblies, never ceased in the next weeks. Mornings were spent sleeping, early afternoons spent in calls and rides in Hyde Park, and the late afternoons used up with preparations for the nightly festivities.

Ashford House was inundated with cards and calls from hopeful young eligibles all vying for the young incomparable-in-the-making. All talked of her beauty and the wit and originality for which she was fast becoming renowned.

"I don't understand what they are talking about," Brianna confided in Connie and Elaine in the upstairs sitting room one afternoon as they rested before changing.

"You say exactly what you mean," Elaine replied. "You do it most politely, but you *do* it, and no one else does."

"And they think speaking one's mind is vastly clever?"

"It would seem so," Connie said.

"Why do they care?" Brianna asked her tutor. "Why should any of them give a fig about me in the first instance? I shall be gone from London soon and they shall never hear of me again."

"I doubt that," Connie told her.

"More to the point, *they* don't believe it," Elaine put in. "Brianna, you have a score of men vying for your attention, each more eligible than the last. Of course, they assume you will accept one of them. Whyever wouldn't you?"

"For the simple reason that I do not love any of them."

"Love grows between two people once they are married," Elaine told her friend. "My mother told me that is the way of it. You must decide with your head whom you will marry, and your heart will soon follow."

Brianna jumped up from her chair, pacing to the windows. Down below was the garden where Andrew had held her close. "I think you must have a very well-behaved heart if it will leap at your bidding. Mine will not respond except in its own way and time."

"Do you know what I think?" Elaine rose to come near her friend. "I think you have developed a tendré for your guardian."

"I don't know what you mean."

"Oh yes, you do. You were terribly worried when he was away, as worried as you were for Samuel, and everyone is talking of your debut and his sweeping you away outside. Come now, admit it," Elaine insisted.

"Elaine," Connie interrupted. "You must not tease upon such a subject, her grace will not like it, even in fun."

"Her grace is not here," Elaine pointed out, but she came away from the window. "All right, we shall talk about you and Samuel."

Connie blushed. Her head dipped toward the tatting she was working on, reaching in her sewing basket for her silver thimble. "I don't know what you can mean."

Brianna turned from the window, giving Connie a smile. "You two make the most adorable couple."

"All right, both of you, that's enough," Connie said primly. "Have you decided what you will wear tonight?"

Elaine answered and Connie determinedly drew Brianna into the conversation about their wardrobes, closing the books on the subjects of Samuel Morris and Andrew Ormsby.

That same afternoon, while the girls rested and changed, the duke appeared in his mother's sitting room at her request.

"How good of you to come," Annabella said dryly. "We see so very little of you."

"I have ever been the obedient son, I believe," he replied quietly.

"The entire town is talking of your staying at Effingham's. Amongst other things."

"What I do is none of the town's business." He moved from beside her chair to the fireplace to the windows and back, fingering the Chinese figures she collected on her mantelpiece.

"Stop fidgeting and sit down," she told him. "You are much too big to pace around a lady's sitting room. Be careful or you shall break those."

He replaced the small jade figures and dropped to the chair across the round fruitwood table from his mother. He crossed one long leg over the other, his mirror-polished black boot beating a tattoo against the carpet. "No, thank you," he said when she offered him tea.

"There is sherry if you prefer."

"I cannot stay long."

"Why?" She saw his expression and continued. "All of London thinks you avoid me like the plague. I think it is someone else you are avoiding. What I wish to know is precisely how long do you propose to keep up this avoidance?"

His eyes hooded over. "Until I leave for Sussex."

"Why are you avoiding her?"

"For ease of heart and peace of mind," he answered honestly.

His mother gave him a long, penetrating look. "Why then have you not already left London?"

"I—" He faltered. He had been asking himself the same question for days. "I shall be going in the very near future."

"Meanwhile you hover like a moth to a flame."

"I do not hover!" Andrew bounded up from his chair. "I really must be away."

"Well, before you go, you may as well know she has been behaving in a most unusual manner."

"For Brianna, the unusual is normal."

"She is unfailingly polite, but so distanced she might as well be on the moon. She has been the soul of propriety, except when dancing with *you,* and last Wednesday when she rode with young Barnstable."

"Barnstable?" Andrew looked grim as he came around the table to face his mother. "What did he do to her?"

"He did nothing to her. She challenged him to race and took off from Rotten Row, galloping away on her stallion so fast we thought it had bolted. Poor Everett tried to catch up and galloped across Hyde Park behind her at a fearful pace. After he had nearly winded both himself and his horse, he found out she was in no trouble whatsoever and was merely giving the horse a stretch, as I believe she put it."

The duke shrugged. "Is that all?"

"I know you are not concerned about the propriety of her

undertakings, or the gossip she engendered about her relationship with Everett, but are you not at least concerned that she might yet break her foolish neck?"

"Mother, I can tell you from personal experience, Brianna could best any horse in the kingdom. Now, if that is all—"

"That's not why I called you here. Young Barnstable has offered for Brianna." The dowager watched her son's displeasure.

"He'll never do. He gambles."

"All men gamble."

"Not like Barnstable."

"I think Pembroke is going to offer next," Annabella said. "You certainly can have nothing against the earl. He is the catch of the Season."

"I wish him joy of it. I owned that title for several Seasons and I had the very devil of a time with it."

"The earl does not foresee difficulty with it since he wishes to marry. He is not a gambler, nor a bon vivant. He is a simple young man with simple tastes for a quiet life."

"He'd bore her to distraction."

"He has a sterling reputation, one of the oldest titles in England, and is both handsome and wealthy. And young."

"You repeat yourself, Mother."

"Have you any objections?"

"Yes. I cannot imagine Brianna marrying someone named Bertram."

"This is a serious subject, Andrew."

"Ye gods, don't you think I know it? He's *not* offered for her yet, so we shall cross that bridge when he comes to it."

"You will find him coming to it soon," his mother warned. "And one more thing. I have received an invitation from Carleton House for myself and Brianna to accompany you to the regent's ball next month."

"That's not my doing. Wellington got on the subject of Samuel's sister with Prinny, and he remembered her. Blame them, not me."

"Did you agree?"

"I could not very well *not* agree. What could I have possibly said? I attempted to dissuade Prinny and had rather hoped I had succeeded. It seems I did not. You could of course demur."

"Tell the prince regent no? Don't be silly." She watched him look toward the square beyond the velvet-draped windows. "Is something amiss?" his mother asked.

"What? No . . ." He roused himself from his brown study, his brow creased with thought. "Perhaps I should take a bit more interest in her welfare. While I am still in London. After all, she is very young, and totally immature in these matters."

"These matters?" his mother questioned.

"Men falling about her feet and proposing Lord knows what all to her."

"Oh, that." The dowager duchess dismissed the subject with a wave of her hand. "That's none of your concern."

"I should say it is! I am, after all, her guardian."

"But her brother is home and I am here, you needn't worry yourself," she said lightly.

"My father was named her legal guardian, and that duty devolved upon me."

Ten minutes later Coyne showed a very pensive-looking Duke of Ashford out of Ashford House and to his waiting carriage. The butler shook his head as he came near the footman at the door.

"The strain of government work," he said gravely as he continued past.

Brianna was told of the duke's quick visit to his mother by Nellie, who innocently questioned why he was not living at home. That night and the next two days Brianna declared herself unwell and stayed in her rooms.

A score of ardent gentlemen presented themselves at Ashford House in hope of a glimpse of the Incomparable, but each was told she was indisposed and they were obliged to relinquish their nosegays and hopeful billets into the hands of the redoubtable Coyne.

The dowager duchess did not allow Brianna to wallow in self-pity a third day. She called for a private dinner in her sitting room Tuesday night just for the two of them, and over a light dinner of dressed lobster questioned Brianna's health.

"You look too pale by half," the dowager told the young woman. "And pining in your room will not help matters."

Startled, Brianna met the older woman's eyes. "I don't know what you mean."

"You know precisely what I mean, and I must tell you, I never took you to be a quitter."

"I'm not."

"Good. Then you will make every effort to look your best, and you will appear with all the young gentlemen and ensure that all of London, including my son, realize you are not an object of pity."

Brianna straightened in her chair. "An object of pity!"

"That you are a fighter and have your choice of any number of eligible bachelors."

"I am, I do!"

"It is not me you need to convince, my dear."

Chapter Twenty-six

The next afternoon Brianna accepted Lord Barnstable's invitation to ride and Lord Pembroke's request to accompany her and the dowager duchess to the opera. At the act break Lords Winston, Blethington, and Henleigh appeared in the Ashford box to pay their respects to the dowager and the young beauty. A few minutes after Henleigh arrived, the Duke of Ashford made an appearance, kissing his mother's cheek and bowing to a cool Brianna and a flustered Elaine.

"Won't Margaret be missing you, Henleigh?" Andrew asked when the marquess showed no signs of leaving.

"I hardly think yet," the marquess answered easily. "My sister is most understanding."

But the duke's glower soon sent Henleigh in search of more amiable surroundings. "He's much too old to be dangling after young girls," Andrew told his mother. "I'm surprised at you for allowing it."

"He's not alone," the dowager said.

"I think he is perfectly sweet," Brianna put in.

"Do you?" Andrew challenged. "He's old enough to be your father."

"But he's not. My father, that is. What do you think of the marquess, Elaine?"

"I?" She blushed. "I'm sure I don't know."

Andrew did not leave Brianna's side until the next act began, and spent the rest of the evening impatient with himself as his eyes kept drifting away from the stage to the Ashford box across the theater, where glimpses of Brianna could be seen when she leaned to listen to something the dowager said.

Early the next afternoon Viscount Winston arrived at Ashford House to find Brianna surrounded by suitors who turned pale at her slightest snub, who seemed cast into rapture by her smallest smile. They were each intent upon her smallest pleasure, diametrically opposed to the duke's reprehensible course of behavior, in which he did his level best to avoid her. When he did deign to pay his respects, he was disagreeable, moody and brusque by turns.

The Viscount Winston, if a bit portly, was the most ardent of her admirers and had come to ask if Miss Morris would consider accompanying him to the balloon ascents at Richmond that afternoon. He was most displeased when he found there were three other young men already dancing attendance and that Lord Pembroke had already insisted she go with him to Richmond. Brianna solved the dilemma by insisting they invite Elaine and all four attend together, along with Constance and Samuel. Her words were wounds to their hearts, Blethington and Lord Skye assured her, unless they were invited too.

"Oh, I say," the viscount began, trying to dissuade her from bringing any others. They were all sharing lemonade and conversation on the terrace, while Connie and Samuel took a turn around the garden with the dowager. Winston wore a long-tailed and perfectly tailored brown coat made by the famous Stultz, to conceal the beginnings of a decided paunch, his breeches a most fashionable pale yellow.

He sank ungracefully to one knee and grabbed at the hem of her green-sprigged muslin gown. "Brianna, I am your most devoted slave! You have no need of any others, you have only to say the word and I should be the most happy of men."

"My Lord Winston, please do get up from that awkward position. I assure you, I have no need for, no wish for, a slave."

"Then I shall be anything you desire, you have only to name it."

"Do you promise?"

"Upon my word of honor!"

"Then, dear Lord Winston—"

"You must call me Thomas," he interrupted.

"Lord Winston," she repeated sweetly, "if you truly wish to please me, you will get up and stop making such a cake of yourself each time we meet."

General laughter accompanied the chagrined suitor. He watched with worshipful eyes as she walked toward the dowager. "Isn't she wonderful?" Winston asked Lord Skye as he came close.

"She's wonderfully direct," he agreed.

"She is an original!" Winston declared. "An absolute incomparable!"

Within the hour the group had taken off for Richmond, and when the duke arrived at Ashford House, he found only his mother to greet him. She declared herself glad to see him.

"You can share tea with me, since Brianna and Elaine are gone to the balloon ascent with friends."

"Which friends?" the duke asked suspiciously. "You haven't allowed Henleigh to hang about, have you? I know his reputation, and he should not be around young girls."

"I thought he was a member of your set."

"That's neither here nor there."

"They shall be back early, in any event. We are to attend a musical evening at Lady Hobart's."

"I thought perhaps I might escort you this evening," the duke said diffidently.

"What a nice change that would be. The evening is to be highlighted, I believe, by the appearance of Signora Roselli, the Italian opera singer."

Andrew groaned. "The last time I heard her, my ears did not recover for a month."

"If you would rather not—"

"I'll go," Andrew said with none too good grace. "Actually, I was considering staying here until I leave for Sussex."

"Worn out your welcome with the Effinghams?"

"Of course not," Andrew said testily. "But I am to deliver a speech in the House of Lords next week, and my library and my notations are here."

"The house is of course yours, to do with as you wish."

"Precisely," the duke replied. He shared tea and biscuits with his mother and listened to her prattle on about all Brianna's suitors until he could stand it no longer. He could not understand why he was so irritated, but irritated he was when he left his mother's rooms and sent word around to Effingham's that James was to pack up and bring his belongings home.

Brianna arrived home accompanied by Connie, Samuel, Elaine, and her suitors amidst much laughter and high good spirits. Elaine saw the scowling duke upon the stairs, his expression striking terror into her shy heart, but Brianna chose to ignore his surly expression and wished him well, giving him a pretty curtsey and then turning her back on him as she bid her admirers a protracted adieu.

That night at Lady Hobart's, Andrew made good his word and sat between his mother and Brianna, his arms folded across his chest as he endured the warbling soprano with gritted teeth.

"Are you enjoying yourself, your grace?" Brianna asked when the signora paused in her recital.

"Do I look as though I am?" he demanded in an undertone.

"No, your grace."

"Then you have your answer."

"Yes, your grace."

"And stop your grace-ing me."

"Yes, your grace," she said impishly. Before he could form a devastating reply, she was up and away, a tall, loose-limbed young dandy with what looked to be a most uncomfortably high shirt collar escorting her toward the doors.

"Who is that with Brianna?" Andrew demanded of his mother.

"Let me see . . ." She brought her quizzing glass to her eye. "Oh, that's Blethington. Has Winston spoken to you yet? He mentioned he wished your permission to court Brianna."

"He's too plump."

"Andrew, really—"

"It's a sign of unbridled appetites in other directions, Mother. I happen to know he has barely a feather to fly with. And he frequents low establishments with his older brother. Not fit for Brianna."

"You mean he frequents the same low establishments you yourself enjoy?"

"That's neither here nor there," Andrew said. He stood up and went in search of refreshment, ending the conversation, his mother's amused eyes following him as he left.

The next afternoon the Duke of Ashford was in his library alone. Poring over notes for his upcoming speech, he tried to stopper his ears against the sounds of young people playing croquet on the side lawns. Finally he gave up the fight and shoved the pages aside, debating whether to join them. He walked to the window and then pulled a tall-backed chair around to face outside and sat in its comfortable depths, watching the gamesters with a pensive expression.

He did not hear the library door open until Brianna's voice froze him to his chair.

"They will miss us," she said.

"Just for a moment, dearest Miss Morris, one moment alone—"

"There you are, Skye," Viscount Winston said as he burst into the room. "I saw you try to make away with her!"

"Did you?" Skye said calmly. "Fine. Now go away."

"Never! Unhand her this instant—"

"Lord Winston," Brianna began, but Lord Skye cut off her words with his own.

"Now, really, old man, she'll not have you, you know. Not my fault she likes me better. No need to go off in a pucker."

"You've stolen a march on me!"

Brianna had had more than she could endure. She stomped her foot and called out sharply, rewarded by two pairs of adoring eyes turning in her direction. "I will not hear any more of this nonsense," she told them both. "I'll not belong to either one of you nor to any other, and that's flat. I am not a piece of furniture to be haggled over!"

"Forgive me, dear Miss Morris—" he said to her back as she stalked out of the room.

"Oh, Winston, shut up," Skye said irritably. "Now you've gone and done it."

Unseen across the room, the Duke of Ashford smiled to himself as the door closed behind the two bickering suitors.

However, late that evening he was not smiling when he made an appearance at Almack's. His mother had accompanied Brianna and sat with her bosom friends, Lady Jersey and Maria Sefton, as Lady Cowper and Countess Lieven came to join them on the narrow gilt chairs that lined one wall.

"Annabella, my dear, you've stayed away from London much too much these past years."

"Yes, and I want to know all that's happened while I've been gone."

"My dear, it will take hours just to discuss Byron and Augusta," Lady Jersey told her old friend.

"And Caro Lamb, don't forget," put in Maria.

"What's this I hear?" Princess Esterhazy asked as she came near. "Annabella, how good to have you back at

Almack's." They kissed on both cheeks. "It's been much too long."

"Just what we were telling her."

The dowager motioned toward Brianna. "Have you met my protegée, Miss Brianna Morris?"

Princess Esterhazy condescended to notice the young girl with a brief smile. "Very pretty, my dear."

"I hear you shall become the toast of London, my dear," Maria Sefton put in as Brianna curtsied and acknowledged the most powerful members of polite society.

"Good Lord, isn't that your son, Annabella?" Lady Jersey interrupted. "I don't believe it. And with Beryl Cavendish. I thought that was over and done with ages ago."

Brianna glanced toward the doorway where Andrew stood surveying the ballroom. His dark hair was combed forward in a fashionable Brutus style above the carved planes of his handsome face, his dark gold satin evening clothes making his chestnut curls ever darker and his azure eyes more blue. Beside him Lady Beryl was a blond and white confection in silk and lace.

Brianna turned away before their eyes met and smiled at Lord Skye across the room. He came quickly to her side, bowed low and kissed her hand before leading her to the floor. She was dancing when Andrew sought out his mother.

"Mother, you remember Beryl."

"She is quite unforgettable," his mother replied. "To what do we owe the pleasure of your company?"

"Beryl wished to meet an old friend."

Lady Beryl stared at him. "I? I merely mentioned the countess would be here this evening. You said you had family duties to attend to."

"Nonsense," the dowager said. "Andrew, run along and enjoy your evening."

"Since we are already here, we will stay," the duke told them both. He called to the Marquess of Henleigh and asked him to dance with Beryl whilst the duke offered his arm to his mother.

"Andrew," Beryl protested, but the duke was already leading his mother to the floor.

"I am pleased, Andrew, but amazed," the dowager said as they joined the other dancers.

"You were concerned about London gossips feeling we did not rub well together, Mother. This should end those discussions."

"You are ensuring none think you wished to slight your mother? How kind. But why are you with Beryl Cavendish and whom are you looking for?"

"No one," he said too quickly.

"Your eyes seem to wander everywhere at once."

"Nonsense. I was merely curious about the current crop of debutantes and their beaux . . . speaking of which, I don't see Brianna."

"She's dancing with Lord Skye."

"I don't see her."

"It's very crowded," his mother said complacently, hiding her smile as her son continued to search out Brianna and her partner.

He did not find them as, at that very moment, they were on the wide side porch. "You see how much cooler it is out here," the earl was saying.

"A bit too cool in this gown," Brianna told him. "I wish to go back inside, Alex."

"Give me a moment alone, you can't be so cruel as to deny me that after I've suffered through the throngs around you for weeks and weeks."

"I can be terribly cruel," she told him.

"You are much too beautiful to be cruel."

Brianna's sherry-colored curls were piled in ringlets, and her gown was of sea-green gauze shot through with silver ribbons.

"You look like a sea nymph," he told her as he pulled her closer. "Dash it all, you must marry me. I'll be a laughingstock if you say no, and I'll shoot myself."

Brianna, having been at first alarmed by such declarations, now laughed.

"I swear I will," he insisted, and so saying, he decided to prove his passion by trying to take her into his arms.

"Lord Skye!" Brianna snapped. "How *dare* you?" With

her closed fan she gave him a sound box upon the ear that made his eyes water. "I am ashamed for you," she informed the miserable young man before she stalked away toward the ballroom doors. Her companion followed slowly, rubbing his ear.

Inside, Brianna looked for the dowager duchess and then saw her dancing with Andrew. Their eyes met and Brianna's veered away as Lord Skye asked in subdued tones if she wished to dance.

"No," she told him, walking away toward the card rooms.

Andrew watched Brianna leave the ballroom and then saw Lord Skye going after her and missed a step.

"Andrew?" his mother questioned. "Is something wrong?"

"I'm not sure," he answered, unable to concentrate upon his dancing. He led his mother from the floor. "Let's look in on the card room."

"Whatever for? Won't Beryl be looking for you?"

"She's dancing with Henleigh," he replied absently, his eyes raking the crowded tables for a sign of Brianna. He saw neither Brianna nor young Skye.

To his mother's amazement, he began a thorough search of the entire establishment, opening and closing doors to side parlors, growing more upset by the minute.

"Andrew," she remonstrated, stopping his headlong hunt. "You are attracting attention."

"Are you not the least concerned that Brianna is nowhere to be found?"

"She is most likely on the dance floor."

"No, she's not. She's off somewhere with that young Skye."

"Poppycock. Come along with me and stop making a cake of yourself."

A grim Duke of Ashford followed his mother to the main ballroom and across to where Beryl Cavendish was looking decidedly piqued.

"Do you intend to thrust me off on others all evening?" she demanded in a low voice when he drew near.

"Andrew," the dowager interrupted and pointed.

He looked toward the far end of the room where Brianna was dancing with Pembroke, Lord Skye nearby and looking miserable.

"Andrew dear . . ." His mother leaned near his ear. "You are grinding your teeth."

With a murderous look at his parent, he bowed slightly and escorted a confused and displeased Beryl Cavendish out of the ballroom and out of Almack's. Annabella Ormsby settled herself comfortably upon a gilt chair beside Maria Sefton.

"Bella, dear," Maria whispered behind her fan. "Is something amiss with your son? He was storming about like a thundercloud."

"I think he's a bit smitten, that's all."

"Smitten? Then are the stories true?"

The dowager's ears perked up. "What stories?"

"Of Andrew offering for Beryl Cavendish."

"Rubbish," the dowager duchess replied. She watched Brianna's head turn toward where Andrew had disappeared and smiled. "Utter rubbish," she added contentedly.

When Brianna and the dowager returned home, they found the duke already there and pacing the long front hall.

"An early evening?" Annabella asked her son.

"Unlike yours," he replied. "Beryl felt ill and asked to be taken home."

"Directly from Almack's?" Annabella asked innocently.

"What? Yes. Why?"

"She seemed a bit out of sorts. I'm surprised you did not go on to your club."

"I didn't feel like gambling." He stared at Brianna. "I hope you enjoyed yourself with all those young suitors dangling off every arm."

"Oh, yes, your grace, I truly did. Thank you for your kind concern," she said sweetly. She dropped a swift curtsey and ran up the stairs.

"Good night, Andrew," the dowager said to her scowling son. "You really should get some rest. You look quite done in."

Chapter Twenty-seven

*I*n the coming weeks Andrew made it his business to escort his mother and Brianna everywhere they went. He drove them for afternoon outings in Hyde Park, for evenings at card parties, routs, assemblies, and Almack's. He danced the obligatory dance with Brianna and his mother, and then stood over their chairs casting a beady eye toward each of Brianna's suitors and ensuring they toed the mark.

By the end of the month both Brianna and Andrew found themselves looking forward each night to the dance they would share, but neither would admit it. All went well until the night of the Rossmore ball.

The Rossmore girls were entertaining a party of their contemporaries with a sprinkling of their parents' set, and Elaine and Brianna coaxed Connie to join them. Brianna appealed to the duke on Samuel's behalf and procured an invitation for her brother to escort Connie. They arrived to find the large Rossmore ballroom filled with young people and music.

Andrew stood with Lord Rossmore and Francis Effingham, watching the dancers pensively, when the Marquess of Henleigh arrived with Lady Beryl and the Hunnicuts. Beryl was cool and polite, Pamela Hunnicut warmly kissing Andrew and linking arms, demanding they have a dance and leading him toward the floor.

"Dear Andrew, you have been neglecting Beryl most dreadfully."

"Neglecting? How so?"

"Naughty boy, the entire town speaks of your deserting her to squire your young ward about."

Andrew stiffened. "The bloody town can go to bloody hell."

She smiled up into his troubled face. "Beryl had hoped you had forgiven her for that silly little scene at Ashford Hall last year. Especially since you seemed quite attentive to her when you first arrived back."

"Did she ask you to intercede on her behalf?"

"No, she'd never do so. . . . She's a mite bit jealous of any other females around you . . . even me." Pamela saw Andrew's discomfort and gave him another bright smile. "Never fear, I'm not about to seduce you, dear boy. I only do that once. After that a gentleman must court me if he wishes more favors."

He contemplated her warm smile and thought of Beryl. These women were what all the young girls around them, laughing in their suitors' arms, would become in not too many more seasons. Brittle, searching for light loves, unhappy no matter how many they found, disillusioned and dishonest, playing games with each other and their lovers.

In the midst of his thoughts he caught a snatch of Brianna's conversation as she danced by with Lord Winston, telling him to cease using her toes as footrests.

"Andrew?" Pamela questioned. "You are looking at me with such an odd expression."

"Sorry. I was thinking of something else."

"Beryl, perhaps? I will admit she did mention she could not imagine what had caused such a change in you."

"I have decided I do not like life played as if it were a parlor game."

"I beg your pardon?"

"Beryl is a beautiful woman and she is adept at games. She will find a much better suitor than I."

"Lord, you truly are crying off, aren't you?"

"We would never suit."

"You have the look of a man who has decided in another direction."

"Nonsense."

"Are you quite sure you've not fallen in love with someone else?"

"Love?" Andrew grimaced. "Love is a plaguey nuisance."

". . . Is it?" The music ended and Andrew delivered Pamela back to her husband. "Aren't you going to ask Beryl for a dance, dear Andrew?" Pamela asked sweetly.

Andrew bowed slightly and smiled, offering his arm to Beryl.

"Dear Andrew," Beryl said as Andrew took her in his arms. "I have missed you so very much."

"And I you," he said automatically.

"Have you? I do not think so, you have been so very busy. And I have so very much wanted to make up for all the nonsense and misunderstandings between us. I fear you think me ill-tempered," she said, watching him as his eyes wandered toward the other dancers. "And a bore."

"How nice."

"What?" she demanded, bringing his attention back. "What did you say?"

Her voice was icy. "If you are looking for someone else, I suggest you find her instead of insulting me."

"Sorry."

"Are you? Are you truly? Or is it over between us?"

"Beryl, we have been friends, and friends we shall remain."

She heard the words that dashed her hopes, and did not miss a step in the intricate patterns of the dance. Anger lost to pride as she smiled and told him how grateful she was that he felt the same as she.

While Beryl and Andrew finished their dance, Pamela Hunnicut was paying her respects to Andrew's mother.

"Perhaps you can advise Brianna," the dowager told her. "We have been invited to the Prince of Wales' Masked Ball, and we are trying to select costumes. I have no idea of how things are conducted at Carleton House."

"I should love to help," Pamela replied. "The regent loves the exotic above all else." She smiled at Brianna. "Lady Beryl, for example, has chosen a Turkish costume complete with turban and pantaloons." Pamela watched the girl's eyes cloud over. "Perhaps you could make a costume of a Chinese princess or a figure from Greek mythology."

"Very elaborate, I take it," the dowager said. "Well, I for one am not going to worry about costumes and masks and all, but I know the young enjoy such folderol."

"And the not so young," Pamela added. "If I may be of any service, please let me know. I should enjoy it," she assured Brianna before she left.

"Turban and pantaloons," the dowager scoffed. "Sounds just like something she would think of."

Andrew, relieved she was taking it all in such good stride, was laughing at something Beryl was saying when Brianna looked toward the dancing couple.

"Miss Morris, might I have the next dance?" Lord Skye asked from just behind her.

Brianna turned toward the sad-faced young man. His expression was very much like that of a whipped puppy, and her own softened. "I should like that above anything, Lord Skye. Your grace, would you like something brought to you?"

"I'm fine as I am, go on and enjoy yourself." She watched them move to the dance floor, joining the scores of others.

Lord Skye held Brianna at a proper distance and looked longingly into her eyes. "Are you well, Miss Morris?"

"I am as I appear," she replied.

"You appear to be an angel come down from heaven," he told her, his dark eyes filled with longing.

"And you exaggerate past all common sense."

"It is but the simple truth," he said passionately, but he suffered in silence as Brianna ignored his suit and chatted of friends and coming events until the music ended.

"Skye," the Duke of Ashford said, coming up beside them. "There's no need to accompany Brianna back." He gave Brianna a brief bow. "I believe this is our dance," he said as the waltz began. He did not wait for a reply, his arm already reaching around her waist as his other hand found hers.

They danced without words, staring into each other's eyes. Oblivious to the other dancers, they moved in perfect rhythm to the lush strains of the Viennese waltz, each of them trying to read the other's expression.

Across the floor Beryl moved with Pamela toward a small ladies' parlor. "I tell you, that odious ward of his has caused all this. What did he say when you danced?"

"He said very little, Beryl, we were discussing inconsequentials, nothing of importance."

"He told me we shall always be friends. Can you imagine the gall of the man?"

"My dear, perhaps you should give up the chase."

"I shall give up the chase, and I shall accept the Earl of Greenwich, but I will not let that overgrown young vixen get her hooks into him, mark my words."

"Are you speaking of Brianna?"

"Who else? She engineered that little scene in Sussex, and why else if she had not already set her cap for him?"

"She had help from you, Beryl. Jane confided in me, and I must say I think you underestimated Andrew if you thought he would fall for anyone's schemes, yours or hers included."

"Men are never intelligent when it comes to love."

"Ah, but who is?" Pamela replied as they repaired their hair and powdered their noses.

On the dance floor the waltz was drawing to an end. Andrew held Brianna for a long moment after the music stopped, letting go slowly.

"Thank you," he said in a husky voice.

"Thank you, your grace," she whispered, allowing him to take her back to his mother's side. He went to fetch his mother some refreshment and left Brianna to listen to Annabella's conversation with Lady Rossmore. As they talked, Brianna slipped away. Her heart was beating wildly, hope lodged in her breast and gave her no peace. Andrew had danced with his eyes never leaving hers, and his expression had been so warm it had heated her blood. Each day for weeks he had been more solicitous, each night he had brought her into his arms in a dance that she wished never to end; but never did he speak of what he was feeling. This night he seemed to want to speak, but in the end he had not, and now, released from his arms and alone, she felt bereft and yet strangely elated.

She wandered around the edge of the dance floor and out

into the wide front hall, looking for a quiet alcove and a few moments' peace to calm her confusion. She found a tiny side parlor and slipped inside, closing the door and looking around the small room. It was Lady Rossmore's morning room, and because of the large party, the fire was lit and a lamp burned upon the mantelpiece, bathing the room in shadow-splotched light.

Brianna sank to a chair near the fire and stared into the leaping flames, a bittersweet feeling she could not name rising within her. She wanted to be back in Andrew's arms, she wanted him to feel as she did and was very afraid he never would. But he felt something, of that she was sure. As she tried to imagine what was going through his thoughts, the door opened and Lord Skye came inside, moving swiftly to her side.

"If you send me away, I shall go straight to the devil," he threatened when he saw her frown.

"Alex, you must not say such things."

"Then tell me you do not hate me."

"Of course I do not hate you," Brianna said bracingly. "Whatever could give you that idea?" Alex reached for her hand and saluted it with a gentle kiss that moved her greatly. "Oh, Alex," she said in softer tones. "You simply cannot go on like this."

While Brianna tried to reason with her admirer, the duke stood beside his mother holding the cup he had brought for Brianna. His mother had not noticed whom she left with, he was told, but one quick survey of the crowded room showed him neither she nor Skye was anywhere to be seen.

Andrew handed the punch to his mother and excused himself at the very same time that Lord Skye was looking imploringly into Brianna's sea-green eyes. "If I am to lose you, I do not know what I shall do."

She was fast losing patience with him again. "And how can you lose something you have never had? Alex, at times you say the most foolish things."

"There is no hope for my suit?"

"I'm sorry, Alex, I do not love you."

"If you would but give me a chance . . ."

Brianna looked into the fire. "It is not meant to be."

"If I must give up all hope, will you at least let me kiss you good-bye?" He held Brianna's hands in his grasp and looked so romantic, so forlorn, her heart went out to him.

She thought of Andrew's lips and of the only kisses she had ever known. And in her hesitation, the young Lord Skye saw acquiescence. He pulled her to her feet and pressed his lips against hers.

The duke, after searching the card room, had come down the hallway and looked in upon each parlor in turn. When he opened the door to the small side parlor, he was treated to the sight of Brianna in young Skye's arms.

For one heartbeat Andrew stood transfixed, by the next he had crossed the room in two long strides and grabbed the young man, flinging him around and shooting a wicked jab to the poor earl's jaw.

"Andrew!" Brianna called out, but the blood pounding in his ears was louder than her plea.

His grace of Ashford lifted the younger man back to his feet and very nearly hit him again before Brianna grabbed his arm.

"Don't!" she demanded, and this time he heard her.

Andrew held Lord Skye none too gently with an iron grip on both lapels of the foolish young man's coat, nearly choking the earl.

"If you repeat this mistake, you will wish you had never been born," Andrew said softly.

"I—I can't breathe, your grace."

"And if you have the least notion of having a loose tongue concerning the young lady's allowing you liberties, I must warn you it will be decidedly injurious to your health." And, with that, Andrew released his hold on the boy, dusted off his hands, and walked out of the room without a backward glance.

In the doorway the dowager duchess stopped his progress. "Andrew, I think it is time to call for the coach. Brianna? Go collect the others."

No one argued with the dowager's pronouncement, the ride home being accomplished in such a heavy silence between the duke, the dowager, and Brianna, that the others soon fell quiet themselves.

The dowager decided to have a glass of sherry in the library before retiring, and Brianna accompanied her. Andrew decided to join them, and came in as Brianna was speaking.

"I had no idea men could behave so foolishly."

"To which men are you referring?"

"All of them!"

"Well, I like that," Andrew interjected, coming around to the drinks tray.

"It's a lesson well learned early in life," his mother told the girl placidly. "Makes your later years much more comfortable, my dear. Otherwise you keep expecting them to act sensibly, and they never will."

"Balderdash," Andrew muttered, pouring himself a medicinal portion of brandy.

"Half London has now told me they will either die or go straight to the devil if I do not accept their protestations of undying love and agree to marry them and take them out of their misery."

"Tell them all to go to perdition," Andrew growled.

"Andrew, dear . . ." His mother smiled up at him. "Calm yourself."

"I am perfectly calm," he informed her. "I've never been so calm in my entire blasted life!"

"I can see that . . ."

Andrew ignored his mother's irony and stalked to the fireplace.

"I appreciate your concern for me," Brianna said, coming closer to where he stood. "And your interceding for me this night, although I had no need of help. Lord Skye is a forlorn little puppy and certainly no danger to anyone's reputation."

"All men are a danger," Andrew said grimly.

"I am also obliged to own you have been doing your level

best to be civil throughout what must be trying evenings for you."

"You're dashed right I have." He looked at her suspiciously. "What do you mean, trying?"

"You must be quite bored with my company by now, and by the same round of people and parties night after night."

"And wasting my time dancing attendance at that blasted Almack's—"

"Well, be fair about it, we do allow you to bring us home ever so early so that you can rush off to those horrid gaming hells of yours."

"Of all the ungrateful—and they're not *my* gaming hells. Besides, pray tell how you know about gaming hells, young miss?"

"I'm told they are dens of vice and iniquity and the very best gentlemen avoid them."

"The very best! You are told wrong!"

"It grieves me excessively to have to inform you that all know you are forever in one or another of them doing I blush to think what."

"It would be better if you put your blushes to your own cursed bad manners and your irritating habit of leading these fops on to the point where they fall all over you."

Brianna flushed and stiffened. "I am sorry you find my manners and my habits so appalling."

"Well, they are," he told her irritably. "Letting yourself be taken off alone. Such actions do you no benefit. Along with many other faults I could mention."

"Please, do not bother yourself. I have no wish of causing your delicate sensibilities any further distress. I must apologize for having been such an unwanted trial these past weeks, and I assure you, in future there will be no need of your—as you so *politely* put it—attendance, *dancing* or otherwise! Good night, your grace!" So saying, she marched out of the room, slamming the door behind.

"Miserable child," he muttered. "Dashed glad," he added to the fireplace before draining his glass and going in search of more brandy. As he moved he realized his mother was still sitting quietly across the room. "Let all those young pups that are forever dangling after her take on the cursed stubborn chit."

"Andrew, don't you think it about time you faced up to your real emotions?"

"No!"

Annabella Ormsby stood up and leaned her head to let him kiss her cheek. "Then I'll say good night." At the door she looked back. "It never does one good to deny the truth, Andrew. That is one of the few things my long life has taught me."

He did not answer.

Chapter Twenty-eight

*T*he next day the Duke of Ashford spent an invigorating hour matching fists at Jackson's boxing saloon with the expert himself. After his exertions, he bathed and changed and sallied forth with Lord Effingham to partake of a king-size luncheon at White's Club.

"Heard your speech in the Upper House about the war reparations. Demned good, Andrew, you told them what was what."

"Thank you."

"Nothing to keep you in London now, eh?"

"What?"

"You said you were going down to the country after the session was over."

"Yes, well . . ." He looked down at the veal upon his plate. "I am to attend Prinny's Masked Ball before I leave."

"With Beryl?"

"Lord no. With my mother . . . and Brianna, of course."

"Good Lord, why is your mother going to Carleton House?"

"Because, thanks to you and Rossmore," Andrew said irritably, "Prinny's so curious about my ward he's invited her."

"He shall be shocked at the transformation. You'd best keep a sharp eye on him around her."

"By God, I've had to keep a sharp eye on every male in London these past weeks. Why are you looking at me like that?"

"Oh, nothing, old boy, nothing at all. It was just you sounded almost like a jealous lover."

"That's ridiculous," Andrew said, so sharply that Francis Effingham eyed his friend more closely.

". . . Don't protest too much, my friend."

"I'm late, I must meet my man of business before I dress for dinner," Andrew said, abruptly ending their lingering luncheon.

Brianna was eating dinner that night at the Duttinghams', Andrew and his mother sharing a quiet meal of partridge with French beans and mushrooms. At loose ends afterward, he looked in on a couple of clubs and ended by strolling into the Royal Saloon in Piccadilly, where he was greeted by the sight of Brianna with Lady Hunnicut and two notoriously wild young blades. Andrew ground his teeth together as he walked toward them.

"Good evening, Pamela," the duke said in none too warm accents. "Brianna. I am amazed to see you here."

"Lady Pamela offered to show me some unusual sights."

"She is certainly doing that."

"Oh, Andrew, surely you do not disapprove," Pamela said. "You've always enjoyed coming here."

"I am not just out of the schoolroom," he said stiffly.

"I should say you are not," she agreed, laughing. "Don't be such a stick, this isn't like you at all."

"Isn't it?" Brianna asked, earning a furious glare from Andrew and a speculating look from Lady Pamela.

Andrew's seriousness ended the revelers' carefree evening, and his pointed remarks about how young and innocent his ward was sobered their audacious manners.

As soon as he decently could, he took Brianna's arm and bid the others good night in the frostiest of tones. Leading her to his carriage, he handed her inside and lectured her all the way home about forming unsuitable alliances with the worst sort of people.

"But they are your friends, they told me so themselves."

"That's not the point. I swear, you would try the patience of a saint," he told her.

"I do not mean to."

"That is precisely the problem. You do not seem able to help it, and you are driving me mad."

Brianna looked so thoroughly dejected he reached to see her face better. She leaned her cheek into his hand and closed her eyes, so trusting that a large lump rose in his throat. He fought the urge to sweep her into his arms and kiss her unhappiness away. It cost him great effort to pull away, and when he did, he stared out at the winking streetlamps as they clip-clopped up Baker Street toward Ashford House, unwilling to face her.

"I know now why young girls are not supposed to ride alone with a gentleman in a closed carriage."

". . . Why?"

"You wouldn't understand."

When they arrived at Ashford House, he stepped out and reached inside to help her himself, a footman standing nearby. She stumbled on the top step, his hand catching her and pulling her up, their bodies together for one brief moment. Her stomach did a decidedly uncomfortable flip-flop, her breath catching in her throat.

"Are you all right?" he asked.

"I'm fine," she told him softly as he reluctantly released her. When he let go of her hand, she kept her fingers entwined with his for another moment before she too let go, leaving a very bemused man behind as she lifted her skirts and went up the steps.

* * *

The next morning Brianna opened her eyes to the morning sun, a sense of well-being permeating her spirit. She lay still, listening to the garden thrushes' songs, her blood quickening in her veins. An inexplicable happiness coursed through her, her body light and somehow urgent, as if awake to some coming excitement.

She closed her eyes and remembered his hand against her cheek, shivering at the memory. Her heart told her he cared, he did care, and she rose from the featherbed, going with swift, springing steps to the casement window. Her elbows on the wide stone sill, she drank in the fresh late-spring morning. Her thoughts went back to Andrew, wondering if he too was wakeful. His image behind her eyes brought a glow of warmth gliding down her spine from heart to belly. He made her feel breathless and fragile, unsettling her mind and disturbing her dreams, and she wanted to be his.

She stared down at the gardens, lost in thought, and faced the truth as Nellie came in to bid her good morning and help her dress for the day.

Late that morning the Earl of Pembroke's carriage arrived, his card sent to the terrace where Elaine and Brianna sat drinking lemonade and watching Samuel and Connie pace through the gardens.

"What do you suppose they're saying?" Elaine asked.

"I hope something romantic," Brianna answered. She waved to them, and her brother waved back and then turned his full attention upon Connie.

"I have no right to speak of what is on my mind," Samuel told her.

"You have every right," she replied quietly. Her calm gray eyes looked deeply into his, and he stopped walking.

"I've wanted to offer for your hand since our very first dance, but I have so little to offer as far as worldly possessions go that I—I say, are you all right?"

Connie's head was bent toward her hands, small sniffing sounds emanating from her as she reached in her pocket for a handkerchief. She brought the tiny square of lace and muslin out and dabbed it at the corners of her eyes.

Samuel looked miserable. "Lord, I've made a confusion of it, I know I have. I've just never proposed before—" His words were stopped as she met his gaze with the most alarming sweetness. "I swear I didn't mean to offend," Samuel said desperately.

"Nor did you," Connie said softly. "Nor could you ever."

"But I've made you cry!"

"You have made me the most awfully happy of females."

"Happy? Did you say happy? I mean, do you, could you, possibly consider accepting, do you think?"

"I would be most proud to be your wife."

"I have very little in the way of worldly goods."

"I have no need of worldly goods."

"Oh, Connie!" He let out a prodigious sigh of relief. "May I please kiss you now?"

". . . Yes . . ."

Across the lawn Brianna was smiling happily. "I think they're well and truly smitten."

Elaine looked up to see Samuel clasp Connie to his bosom. "Oh, look," she cried. Elaine glanced at Brianna and saw her lost in thought. "Brianna?"

"I must do something."

"About what?"

"About the duke."

"I don't quite follow," Elaine said. "What has the duke to do with Connie and Samuel?"

"Nothing."

There was a lull in the conversation whilst Brianna was lost in thought and Elaine studied her friend.

"Brianna?" Elaine questioned when the silence grew.

"I have it."

"You have what?"

"It must be at the Masked Ball," Brianna declared.

Elaine leaned across the terrace table. "Are you sure you're feeling quite the thing?"

"I have never felt better, and the ball is the perfect place, with the masks and all. I shall pull it off! But first we must call on Pamela Hunnicut."

"Brianna, what are you talking about?"

"Why, turning the tables on Beryl Cavendish, what else?"

"Beryl Cavendish? What has Beryl Cavendish got to do with anything?"

"We are going to make him think he is with her, so that the realization of whom he really wants to be with will finally be clear."

"You are making no sense."

"Begging your pardon, Miss Brianna." A footman handed her a small silver tray. The card upon it said, "Urgent I speak to you, Bertram," and bore the Pembroke coat of arms.

"Is there a problem?" Elaine asked, seeing Brianna's expression.

"It's Bertram, he's here to see me."

"Oh, I'd best leave . . ." Elaine looked flustered, her cheeks turning pink. "I'm sure he'll want to speak to you alone."

"Elaine Duttingham, you look most flushed. Are you by any chance enamored of Bertram?"

"No, well, that is, I'm sure it does not signify," her friend said.

Brianna told the footman to send Bertram out to them and then scolded her friend. "Of course it signifies, you little ninnyhammer, you two would be perfect for each other. But I thought you were fond of your country neighbor."

"He was the most awfully handsome gentleman I had ever seen. Until I came to London and saw Bertram. But you must not speak of this again," Elaine said swiftly as Bertram headed across the terrace. "Bertram does not know I exist, and I would be mortified."

"Lady Elaine," the young earl acknowledged with a little bow before he turned toward his quarry. "Miss Morris, we must speak," he said in such a grave tone that Elaine's heart sank. She knew what he was about to say. She began to rise, but Brianna sprang to her feet first, forcing Elaine to stay seated by placing her hands on Elaine's shoulders.

"Of *course* we should, Lord Pembroke. Always glad to have a bit of a chat."

"I do not intend a bit of a chat, I—"

"Excuse me, please, but I think my brother is calling me."

Bertram Pembroke looked out toward the pair on the lawn. "Your brother looks to be kissing Miss Powell."

"Yes. I must speak to him about that," she said, and with that Brianna moved swiftly down the steps and across the yard, leaving the Earl of Pembroke at a total loss.

"I say," he said.

"I quite agree," Elaine told him sweetly. "Won't you sit down? I'm sure she'll only be a moment."

Pembroke was watching Brianna cross to the couple beyond the roses and lilacs. "That's deuced behavior, I do say. Excuse me, Lady Elaine, but, well, I've never—"

"I'm sure you haven't," Elaine said soothingly. "You've never . . . ?" she prompted.

"I'm not used to such lack of address and manners. My mother is out of sorts about my offering for Miss Morris, she says no good can come of mixing with commoners, but I've told her Miss Morris is uncommon in every way."

"Brianna is absolutely wonderful," Elaine confirmed.

"But she will have to be a bit more conventional."

"I would not expect Brianna to change, dear Bertram, if I were you. She is herself and I think will always be as you see her now. Nor will I hear a word against her. She is my dearest friend."

"Against her? I'm besotted with her, but by gad, I cannot like the changeability of her nature, nor her alarming propensity for rushing off at every turn. Not like you, Elaine. You are so quiet and comfortable. You are the most understanding and sweetest of ladies, Elaine, you truly are. You never have an unkind word to say about anyone, unlike many others who would have turned cat and clawed at another's reputation."

"There are many sharp tongues," she agreed.

"If only Miss Morris had your breeding and manners."

Elaine gave him a meltingly sweet smile. "Do you like horses, Bertram?"

"Mad for them," he told her, earning another sweet smile.

Across the lawns Brianna chanced a look toward the

terrace after she reached her brother and Connie. "Wouldn't Elaine and Bertram be perfect for each other?"

"Are you trying to match-make?" Connie asked, smiling.

"Of course. Elaine is perfect for Bertram, and I've done a perfectly wonderful job matching the two of you."

"You?" Samuel stared at her. "You've been a social butterfly, never even around these past weeks. But you have the right of it. I've just told Connie she should think twice about my proposal and make very sure, as I'm a rough soldier with a rough soldier's life and a lovely little farm in Kent. That's about the size of it, and not much prospect for fame and fortune."

"And I was telling him I have no wish for fame and fortune," Connie replied softly as Brianna moved away toward the nearby trees and stole back around the house to disappear inside the kitchen doors.

Going up the narrow stairs reminded her of the night of her precipitous flight down them. And being carried back up in Andrew's arms. Something had to be done, and done now. She was managing very nicely with everyone's life but her own.

Chapter Twenty-nine

❧❧❧

The next night was the night of the regent's Masked Ball, and the duke called for their carriage to be ready promptly at nine. He was in the entrance hall when Brianna and his mother came down the stairs, Annabella's hand on the girl's arm, as if to steady herself. She hoped it would have a steadying influence on the girl too. Andrew was staring upward, oblivious of his mother and looking so besotted he might well have been nineteen instead of thirty-six.

What Andrew saw was a Brianna so pale her skin seemed

to glow translucent, her large eyes the color of the deepest part of a forest where green and black commingled into a shadowy mystery and civilization was lost far behind.

She wore a chiffon gown of silver-threaded midnight blue, the material so gauzy it seemed to float over its gold satin underdress. A heavy necklace of gold and silver encrusted over with sapphires and diamonds seemed to have been made for the gown. He recognized his mother's favorite necklace, clasped around her neck and dipping low to rest in the hollow between her softly rounded breasts.

"Good evening, Andrew," his mother said, pulling his eyes away.

"Mother . . . Brianna," he acknowledged with a slight formal bow. He held out his hand first to his mother, helping her up and inside the open chaise. Then he reached back for Brianna. Diamonds winked on gold and silver chains amongst her upswept curls.

"Thank you," she murmured as she took his hand, his other hand going to her back.

He lifted her in and followed, sitting across from the women. "As it is so mild, I thought you might enjoy an open-air ride," he told them as the driver took off around the drive.

Brianna gazed up at the clear night sky. "I can see a hundred stars."

"I can see a thousand," he replied, without looking upward.

"It is a bit warm," the dowager told them both.

The lights of Carleton House blazed their welcome down toward the masses of arriving carriages that were lined up all the way to the top of St. James Street, the pillars outlined with white lamps. Beyond the house the glare and crackle of multicolored fireworks were being set off in the gardens as a brass orchestra and three other bands serenaded the throngs in various parts of the house and grounds.

The party had begun in midafternoon and would go on until dawn, with throngs of Londoners outside the gates and in the street craning to get a glimpse of the royals and their guests.

Brianna tied her mask in place.

"There is no need for your mask yet. Or ever, since you are not about to engage in assignations," the dowager said tartly.

"But it is a masked ball, and my first one. I intend to wear my mask all night."

From the torchlit portico the duke and his guests were ushered into a high-ceilinged entrance hall lined with columns of porphyry marble.

"It's even bigger than yours," Brianna whispered to Andrew, and drew from him a surprised and suspicious sidelong glance.

"You are going to behave yourself," he said, looking at the beauty beside him but remembering the young hoyden that lurked beneath the finery and polite manners.

The rooms were crowded to overflowing with hundreds of people. "Does he come to his own parties?" Brianna asked as they moved through the grandeur of the suite of rooms beyond the entrance hall.

"Upon occasion," came the reply.

The grayish-blue velvet of the room they entered encircled them, from the thick carpet to the settees to the painted ceiling. A three-tiered crystal chandelier hung high above, fringed with gold and reflecting the blue in a thousand prisms.

The throne room was filled with red brocade, and beyond was a circular dining room all mirrors and silver walls. Beyond that glowed a room all rose satin touched with gold. All were framed with gilded cornices, each ceiling a work of art.

French and Dutch and Flemish masterpieces lined the walls, Aubusson carpets lay beneath their feet. Until finally they reached the hot ballroom, overstuffed with people. The regent and the other royals were there, all but Queen Charlotte and his sisters and the unloved Princess of Wales.

The prince regent was dressed in the ceremonial robes of a

Chinese war-mandarin, his ample figure looking even more rotund in the heavy silk. Talking with the regent was the Duke of Wellington himself, looking very military and more patrician than most of those present.

"Ashford," Wellington called out. "And your grace." He bowed to the dowager. "It is a pleasure." The great man turned to Brianna, his eyes widening. "This cannot possibly be our little urchin."

The urchin dropped a deep curtsey and smiled as she rose. "I am afraid it is, your grace."

"Your Highness," Wellington said, and Prinny turned toward the arriving group.

"Ashford, and Lady Ashford, I am pleased you felt well enough to come."

"Thank you, Your Highness," Annabella said with a swift look toward her son.

"This cannot be the scrawny wretch who tore through the castle with all our guards giving chase."

"Your Majesty." Brianna curtsied low.

"Not majesty, yet, my dear. Let me see you."

"But certainly majestic." She smiled and lifted her mask for a moment before replacing it.

"You've done wonders, Ashford, can't imagine how. Now what are you to do with her?"

"I'm not quite sure, Your Highness."

Prinny gave Brianna a very direct head to toe once-over, his gaze a touch familiar when he ended back at her face. "I would know what to do with such a one as this," he said with a bold smile.

"How kind, Your Highness," the dowager said, and drew the girl away from the dais. "Andrew, I think I *would* like to sit for a moment."

When they were safely across the room to a line of velvet chairs, she grimaced. "I would prefer someplace cooler. It's so crowded no one can even dance."

Andrew showed the way through the throngs down a long circular double staircase to the lower floor, on past the library and golden dining rooms to the Gothic conservatory.

"Oh," Brianna breathed, and even the dowager was impressed.

"It is rather nice, isn't it?" Andrew agreed.

"It is a room out of a fairy tale."

Chinese lanterns were hung down the length of the immensely long, narrow room whose doors opened onto lush gardens. A colonnade of carved pillars supported a ceiling of intricate traceries that fanned out in spiderweb patterns. Colored glass lamps were set in the cornices and niches of the stonework; the stained glass around and above filtered the light to give a feeling that was mysterious and fairylike.

Outside in the gardens, refreshments were being served in large tents held up by gilded ropes and festooned with flowers. Glass lusters shone down on silver tureens, dishes and plates filled with hot and cold meats, fruits, and all manner of sauced vegetables and breads, superb wines and iced champagne.

Beryl Cavendish strolled out of the tent, champagne in hand, Francis Effingham by her side.

"It looks like a pleasure garden," the dowager said as she caught sight of them.

"Isn't that Lady Beryl?" Brianna asked innocently, turning her companions' attention toward Beryl. Andrew glanced away as Beryl brought her mask up to her face, holding it by its long golden handle. She was dressed in cloth of gold, from her turban-wrapped hair to the pantalooned harem gown and golden slippers.

"Not a place for well-brought-up young women," Andrew's mother said, watching Beryl. "No wonder he has such a reputation. I should have declined the invitation."

"Oh, no," Brianna said quickly. She looked around as if expecting someone. "At least let me see to some refreshments for you and you will be—"

"I want no refreshments. We have done our duty. We have been seen. The prince will never know whether we were here ten minutes or two hours. Andrew?"

"If you wish."

"My dear Lady Ashford, that is you, is it not?"

Annabella turned to see Lady Hunnicut coming toward them across the lawn not a moment too soon. "Pamela," Annabella acknowledged. "We were just leaving."

"Oh, you can't—not yet. I want you to meet someone. And I am so glad you changed your mind about wearing a costume."

"Brianna convinced me I did not want to appear unmannerly."

"Of course not," Pamela said as she gave Brianna a swift wink and started off with Annabella. "We shall find you two later."

"I don't think—" the dowager was saying as she was led away.

Andrew looked down at Brianna. "I sense your fine hand in this somewhere."

"Oh, look, there's Samuel," Brianna said innocently. "Dear Samuel and *Elaine*, that is you behind your mask, isn't it? How wonderful."

"Brianna, *could* you help me a moment?" Elaine asked.

"May I help?" Samuel asked.

Elaine rewarded him with a huge smile. "I'm afraid this is something that we girls must work out for ourselves. We'll be back directly."

"You're sure you can find your way?" Samuel asked doubtfully. "There are two thousand people here."

"If you stay nearby, we'll be able to find you, we'll only be moments, I promise."

Andrew watched the two young women hurry off. "I don't like this above half."

"Don't like what, your grace?"

"I don't know . . ."

Across the lawns the girls were breathless as they made their way inside to a quiet room. "I had the devil of a time finding one that wasn't being occupied by people doing the most outlandish things."

Brianna laughed. "Elaine, how you do talk."

"Here . . ."

Brianna looked at the gold turban and golden dress Elaine

brought forth from behind a sofa. "It's perfect, I just saw her. How did Lady Pamela manage it?"

"More to the point, I don't know why she is helping, any more than I know how you talked me into doing any of this. I am shaking like a leaf."

Brianna stepped out of her dress and into the golden attire whilst Elaine put on Brianna's costume. "Elaine, before this night is out, you will have your Bertram and I will have my Andrew, if you only remember to keep the mask to your face and say as little as possible."

"I've decided to have a coughing fit. You *are* sure this is going to work?"

"Absolutely. It has to."

Outside the small room the crush of people was almost impossible. Elaine carried a parcel of her former attire as the two girls hugged and went in opposite directions.

Elaine found a footman and gave him the parcel for her carriage and then made her way back to where Samuel and the duke stood with the dowager duchess and Lady Hunnicut.

"I can hardly hear myself think," the dowager was saying. "It is much too—ah, there you are, Brianna, come along."

Elaine fell into place beside the dowager as Samuel looked around. "What happened to Elaine?"

"She told me she was going to see if the ballroom was any less crowded," Lady Pamela answered.

"Andrew, walk us to the carriage, please," his mother called. "Samuel, do you wish to ride with us?"

"Thank you, your grace."

The duke walked beside his mother and the silent Brianna. Annabella assumed Brianna was upset about leaving, and conversed with Samuel on the dangers of an irregular life. "This is not the place for well-brought-up young ladies, the Queen is quite correct."

"Yes, your grace," Samuel said politely.

"Did you see how the regent looked at Brianna, not to mention some of these other rakes he surrounds himself with. Speaking of which, I take it you won't be leaving with us, Andrew?"

"I think I may stay a bit longer, Prinny will expect it."

"I'll send the coach back," she told her son as he helped first his mother and then Brianna into the carriage. She stepped up quickly and nearly fell to her seat.

"Good night, Mother . . . Brianna," he added slowly, trying to make her face him.

His mother's good-night came over the girl's coughing fit as she managed to say good night in a strangled little voice before lapsing into more coughs.

"The night air isn't good for one," the dowager declared, thumping the girl's back, and Elaine nodded, pulling away and stifling her coughs.

Elaine sank back against the squabs, very nearly holding her breath. She wondered if she could make it to Brianna's room without the dowager duchess any the wiser.

Her question was answered a few moments later as the coach clipped along St. James Street.

"I saw young Pembroke with Elaine at the Barnstables." Elaine coughed more.

"Good Lord, you sound worse. Let me feel your forehead. Why on earth are you still wearing your mask?" The dowager reached for the mask strings and Elaine shrank away. "Whatever is the matter with you?" Annabella asked as she pulled the mask off and stared into Elaine Duttingham's frightened eyes.

At Carleton House the Duke of Ashford first procured champagne and then wandered back to the Gothic conservatory, where he stood looking up at the filigreed ceiling for long lonely minutes.

"Your grace." A footman approached. He handed over a small card with Beryl's crest upon it.

Andrew looked down at the note and scribbled a reply, handing it to the footman before he left to make his way through the gardens to the arbors. His mother was right, he thought as he went. It did look like Raneleigh, a den of polite and pretty iniquity.

Couples were scattered about the arbors and the lawns, keeping secret assignations away from the lighted tent and the fireworks that were set off at regular intervals. The band was playing music in honor of Wellington on the lawns, the sounds muffled by the trees and the shrubbery as Andrew found his way through the arbor.

A slim ivory arm stopped him, Beryl's golden turban catching a bit of starlight. She sat on one of the hidden benches, holding her mask in place. He dropped down beside her. "Are you playing games with masks tonight, my dear?"

"Emmmm . . ."

He tilted her face up to his in the darkness and leaned down to her lips, covering them with his own. Her lips responded, alive to his touch. He reached for her, deepening the kiss, finding her tongue and pulling her to him.

She reached to bring him closer, her arms entwined around his neck, her mask forgotten as he sent jolts of unnamed feelings careening down her spine. She was sweet and tentative and eager and needy, and he drank in her sweetness, his arms bringing her closer, his hand reaching for her breast.

She moaned and moaned again, letting him lift her to his lap, letting him remove the golden turban, her hair falling from its pins into errant tousled curls. She kissed him back, kissed his cheek when his lips went to her ear and the hollow of her neck. "Andrew . . ." She called his name softly, her plan forgotten along with everything else but the feelings he engendered as his hand went to her breast.

"Oh . . ." she breathed, unaware of the lights that were coming toward them.

He took her face in both his hands, his lips lingering on hers; slow, compelling kisses that burned through her belly and left her limp and clinging to him, begging for more.

Suddenly they were bathed in lamplight.

"Good Lord, it's the Duke of Ashford," Pamela Hunnicut called out loud enough for all to hear.

"Andrew!" Beryl shouted, pushing past Pamela. "I found out what she was doing and I came to warn you. The little vixen has tried to compromise you!"

"Brianna!" The dowager duchess spoke from behind the

two women in lower and harsher tones as curious people came near, voices blending into a cacophony of questions and laughter.

Elaine drooped beside the dowager duchess. "I'm sorry, Bree, I did my very best."

"She thought to make you think it was me you were with!"

The duke looked toward the vituperative Beryl. "Yes," he said blandly, "I know."

It took Brianna a moment. She pushed away from him, standing with her back to the others, oblivious of all save Andrew. "You knew?"

"Andrew, stand up," the dowager insisted.

"Not quite yet, Mother. I'm not through discussing things with Brianna."

Brianna blinked in the bright lamplight and looked deep into amused blue eyes. "You *knew*," she accused. She backed away from him toward the precisely clipped hedges, and he stood up to follow.

"My dearest Brianna, there is no possible way I could confuse Beryl's kisses with yours. Nor could I fail to recognize the handwriting that so recently sent my household topsy-turvy. How did you manage to steal Beryl's card, I wonder? No, don't answer, it probably will get some poor wretch in trouble."

"You knew all along. Why didn't you say so?"

He grinned. "And spoil your fun? My dear girl, in future, you must remember not to leave one minute and then come back the next, two inches shorter and unable to talk. It does make one wonder."

The dowager glared at her son. "If you knew, you should have stopped her."

"Mother, go away." He turned back to Brianna. "I returned the card to Beryl with a note that someone was impersonating her in the arbor."

"You sent it?" Beryl looked shocked and turned toward Pamela. "You said you had found out."

Brianna was watching only Andrew. "But—you mean, you tried to make them find us too?"

"How else could your plan work?"

"I asked Lady Pamela to help," Brianna said artlessly.

Beryl turned murderous eyes upon Pamela as others began to drift away.

"There's nothing for it," he said with a prodigious sigh and a look toward the others. "I must marry the wench before she ruins some other honorable man."

"Andrew, do be serious!" Brianna stamped her foot and backed away as the duke came toward her. "Andrew, I—" was all Brianna could say before his lips smothered her words.

"Lady Ashford," Beryl cried out, "*do* something!"

The dowager duchess of Ashford turned toward the others. "What do you propose I do? Pamela, stop smiling. Elaine, I am going to have a serious talk with your mother. Well?" she demanded of the others. "What is so surprising? Have you never seen a man and his betrothed kissing in these gardens before?"

"Betrothed?" Elaine smiled as she spoke and Bertram appeared behind her, pulling her away from the others.

"You should not see such shocking things," he told her.

"I agree," Elaine said. She flung her arms around him, smiling up into his surprised face. "I should experience them firsthand!" Bertram found Elaine kissing him before he realized what was happening. And then Bertram kissed Elaine back.

"A den of iniquity, just as I said," the dowager duchess pronounced, looking from Elaine to Brianna. "I wash my hands of all of you."

She walked away, the lights fading away as others followed suit. Behind them Andrew and Brianna did not hear. Wrapped in each other's arms, they were left under the dark star-spangled night sky to find their way home by the light of the moon.

Brianna studied Andrew's eyes in the moonlight. "Are you quite positive you wish to marry me?"

"I had already decided we must marry, you know."

"You had?"

"I had."

"You did not mention such a decision."

"It was the only one I could make. None other would know when to kiss you and when to spank you. And I am infinitely preferable to life as a spinster."

"Spinster! I have my choice of suitors, thank you very much."

"All milksops and dunderheads, not a man amongst them," Andrew pronounced.

"What about you? What sensible female would put up with *your* moods and *your* stubbornness and your complete lack of any romantic sensibilities?"

"I *beg* your pardon! All of London will tell you I am the very soul of Romance!"

"You've not once mentioned the most important thing. You've not once said or shown or even hinted you had the least bit of warm regard for me, let alone that you loved me."

"Of course I love you, you silly goosecap. I've been half mad with it for months, and you well know it."

"I do not. Are you quite sure you love me?"

"Am I sure? Yes, I'm sure. I'm sure you are the most maddening, frustrating, exasperating, willful, beautiful, desirable—" He pulled her toward him, his lips reaching to tell her what his words could not.

"Will you make love to me tonight?" Brianna breathed.

"No," he told her as he drew the low-necked dress down, releasing her breasts. She stiffened as he looked down at the creamy flesh and then bent to kiss each breast, his lips covering her nipples, his tongue teasing her until they hardened, Brianna shuddering against him.

"When?" she whispered in his ear.

"When we are married."

"Oh, but Andrew, I do not think I can wait that long," she moaned.

He groaned and held her closer, night shadows all around them. "You don't know what you are saying."

"I'm saying I love you and I want you to teach me everything."

"Everything?"

"Everything . . ."

"Here?"

"Anywhere . . ." she answered, as far across the lawns Lady Beryl Cavendish was running after the dowager duchess.

"Lady Ashford!" she cried, reaching for the dowager's arm. "You can't let this happen. You must *do* something."

Annabella Ormsby turned and considered Beryl Cavendish for a long moment. "You are absolutely right. I shall have to give Brianna strict etiquette lessons if she is to be Duchess of Ashford. And then I shall order her trousseau."

The Duchess

Jude Deveraux

Claire Willoughby, a beautiful young American heiress, had been trained her whole life for one thing— to be an English duchess. But when she travels to Scotland to visit her fiance, Harry Montgomery, the duke of McArran, she finds out his family is more than she'd bargained for. Fascinated by his peculiar family, Claire is most intrigued by Trevelyan Montgomery, Harry's mysterious brilliant cousin who she finds living secretly in an unused part of the estate. As she spends more and more time with the magnetic Trevelyan, Claire finds herself drawn to him against her will, yearning to know everything about him. But if Trevelyan's secret is discovered life at Bramley will never be the same.

COMING IN HARDCOVER FROM POCKET BOOKS IN FALL 1991

POCKET
B O O K S

BESTSELLING AUTHOR OF
THE BRIDE AND *THE LION'S LADY*

JULIE GARWOOD

Julie Garwood has captivated readers everywhere with her lush breathtaking novels full of passion, intrigue and love.

☐ **HONOR'S SPLENDOUR** .... 73782/$5.50

☐ **THE LION'S LADY** .... 73783/$5.50

☐ **THE BRIDE** .... 73779/$5.50

☐ **GENTLE WARRIOR** .... 73780/$5.50

☐ **REBELLIOUS DESIRE** .... 73784/$5.50

☐ **GUARDIAN ANGEL** .... 67006/$4.95

☐ **THE GIFT** .... 70250/$5.50

Simon & Schuster Mail Order Dept. JJJ
200 Old Tappan Rd., Old Tappan, N.J. 07675

POCKET
B O O K S

Please send me the books I have checked above. I am enclosing $_____ (please add 75¢ to cover postage and handling for each order. Please add appropriate local sales tax). Send check or money order—no cash or C.O.D.'s please. Allow up to six weeks for delivery. For purchases over $10.00 you may use VISA: card number, expiration date and customer signature must be included.

Name _____

Address _____

City _____ State/Zip _____

VISA Card No. _____ Exp. Date _____

Signature _____ 170-12

"THE MOST OUTSTANDING
WRITER OF SENSUAL ROMANCE"
—*Romantic Times*

LINDA LAEL MILLER

Linda Lael Miller has dazzled readers everywhere with her breathtaking sensual novels.

- ☐ **CORBIN'S FANCY** .... 70537/$4.50
- ☐ **ANGELFIRE** .... 70637/$4.50
- ☐ **MOONFIRE** .... 70636/$4.50
- ☐ **WANTON ANGEL** .... 70633/$4.50
- ☐ **FLETCHER'S WOMEN** ..... 70632/$4.50
- ☐ **MY DARLING MELISSA** ... 65264/$4.50
- ☐ **WILLOW** .... 70631/$4.50
- ☐ **DESIRE AND DESTINY**
  70635/$4.50

**POCKET
BOOKS**

**Simon & Schuster Mail Order Dept. LLA
200 Old Tappan Rd., Old Tappan, N.J. 07675**

Please send me the books I have checked above. I am enclosing $_____ (please add 75¢ to cover postage and handling for each order. Please add appropriate local sales tax). Send check or money order—no cash or C.O.D.'s please. Allow up to six weeks for delivery. For purchases over $10.00 you may use VISA: card number, expiration date and customer signature must be included.

Name_____

Address_____

City _____ State/Zip_____

VISA Card No. _____ Exp. Date _____

Signature_____ 172-07